I Right the Wrongs

BY THE SAME AUTHOR

*Misdemeanor Man*
*Dog Stories*

# I Right the Wrongs

A Misdemeanor Man Mystery

## Dylan Schaffer

BLOOMSBURY

Published by Bloomsbury Publishing, New York and London
Distributed to the trade by Holtzbrinck Publishers

All papers used by Bloomsbury Publishing are natural, recyclable
products made from wood grown in well-managed forests.
The manufacturing processes conform to the environmental
regulations of the country of origin.

The Library of Congress has cataloged the hardcover edition as follows:

Schaffer, Dylan.
I right the wrongs : a novel / Dylan Schaffer.—1st U.S. ed.
p. cm.
ISBN 1-58234-506-6 (hardcover)
ISBN-13 978-1-58234-506-2
1. Attorney and client—Fiction. 2. Manilow, Barry—Appreciation—Fiction.
3. Public defenders—Fiction. 4. Football players—Fiction. 5. Trials
(Murder)—Fiction. 6. School sports—Fiction. 7. Singers—Fiction. I. Title.

PS3619.C315I17 2005
813'.54—dc22
2004023842


First published in the United States by Bloomsbury Publishing in 2005
This paperback edition published in 2006

Paperback ISBN-10: 1-58234-570-8
ISBN-13: 978-1-58234-570-3

1 3 5 7 9 10 8 6 4 2

Typeset by Hewer Text Ltd, Edinburgh
Printed in the United States of America
by Quebecor World Fairfield

For Dennis Riordan and Harold Rosenthal, who,
for reasons that remain fuzzy, gave me a start

*With all memory and fate driven deep beneath the waves*
*Let me forget about today until tomorrow*

—*Bob Dylan*

# Prologue

"**G**ORDON SEEGERMAN?" A nurse, dressed in scrubs crawling with the sniggering faces of a hundred cartoon cats, pokes her head into the waiting room. "Would you come this way?"

She weighs me and takes my blood pressure.

"Are you all right?"

"I'm fine, thanks," I say.

She gives me a sideways glance. The cats on her uniform gawk at me. I follow her into an examination room.

She looks at her clipboard. "Just the blood draw today?"

I nod too enthusiastically. She stretches a length of rubber around my arm. My veins bulge. I make a fist, she sticks me, and sucks out two vials of blood. And it's done. So simple. Years spent worrying about this moment and it's over in ten seconds.

In two weeks, I'll return. I'll sit in the waiting room and flip through a *People* magazine while my heart tries to pummel its way out of my chest. A nurse will call my name. I'll walk into a doctor's office. And the doctor, having spliced and diced my genes and taken a close look at my fourteenth chromosome, will tell me whether, like my father, I am destined, in the not-too-distant future, to lose my mind to early-onset familial Alzheimer's disease.

That, or I'll let the appointment pass and go on not knowing.

"You have the follow-up visit all set, right?"

I nod. She looks at me for a moment longer and then says, "Try not to drive yourself too crazy, Mr. Seegerman. You haven't quite made it through the rain, but, somehow, you'll survive." The woman knows her Manilow.

I smile. She arches her eyebrows and, before I can thank her, spins out of the room.

# 1

**F**ORTY-ONE DAYS EARLIER, April 28, 2004.

"Vegas," I say, raising my beer.

"Vegas." My bandmates Preet Singh and Terry Fretwater, join me.

"Vegas can bite me," our fourth, the exceedingly pregnant Maeve O'Connell, grumbles from across the room. She is splayed out on a threadbare, sagging couch, confined upon medical advice to horizontality. "*I* ain't drinking to Vegas."

"*You're* not drinking period," I add.

For her soon-to-be son's sake, Maeve has taken leave of her essential pleasures: alcohol, caffeine, tobacco, young women, and, most agonizingly, the Mandys, our Manilow tribute band. We're gearing up to play a gig at a bar in the Mandalay Bay hotel in Las Vegas, the day before Barry appears in concert there, his first show in two years. It is our shared dream to perform for the man, to receive his blessing, and to take our Manilow mission to unbelievers nationwide.

We're in the wretched, windowless garage, behind one of Preet's father's convenience stores, that serves as our studio and clubhouse. It's nine-thirty P.M. and, though May is two days away, the temperature outside is around ninety degrees. Inside, with our amps cranked and Preet's colossal computer rig whirring furiously, it must be a hundred. I'd like to pour the beer on my head, but we're auditioning girl singers, so I don't dare. It's been some time since I had a proper date.

"Who's next?" I say. Preet glances at his notes.

"Joe."

Maeve, who describes her place of birth as a town where the necks are red, the men are named Ned, and the children are inbred, chuckles and drawls, "This ought to be interesting."

I wipe a line of sweat off my forehead. "If you don't pipe down, Preet's going to snitch you off to Aineen." Maeve's home-confinement-enforcing twenty-five-year-old daughter.

Our ad in the local alternative paper makes clear we're looking for a woman, to temporarily replace Maeve, to get us through Vegas. Joe better be wearing lipstick. Terry kicks open the door.

Joe is not wearing lipstick. Joe has a goatee.

"I sing in falsetto," he says, and shrugs.

Terry looks to me for approval, but it's too hot to have an opinion. We pop a beer for our guest and take him through the introductory drill.

*Listen carefully, Joe. We're not impersonators, got it? We don't do dress-up or camp. We don't do irony. And we don't do covers. We do homage. We're a tribute band. We're translators, envoys, mission-aries. Probably you're a wonderful person. You may even be able to sing. But if you don't get what we're doing, if you're not truly and unapologetically on the bus, you're wasting our time.*

Joe looks bewildered. He does not appear to have the slightest idea what we're talking about. He glances around the rehearsal space, blank-faced, looking for a bus, I suppose.

"Everybody ready?" Terry asks. We toss the newbie a softball: "Weekend in New England." He has a terrific voice, evocative of Aaron Neville. But there's nothing about the performance that convinces me he's here for Manilow, that he shares our vision.

My cell phone, parked on Preet's keyboard, shrilly cuts into the middle of the song, which sputters and then expires. Preet answers.

"Ferdy," he says, holding out the phone. Ferdy is my grandfather. He turns a spry and cantankerous ninety in a week.

4

I wave away the call.

Preet tries, but fails to cut off the old lunatic, who shrieks his way through some sort of narrative that ends with a series of demands. The content is a mystery to me, but the tone is unmistakable.

Preet folds up the phone and tosses it at me. "The cops just arrested Marcus Manners."

"No shit," Terry and Maeve say.

"Now *there's* a stunner," I say. "Who's Marcus Manners?"

"The leading high school quarterback in the state," Preet reports. "Apparently he's also Bea's godson."

Beatrice Johnson married my grandfather a year ago. She is a charming and accomplished woman of some eighty-three years and two hundred and eighty pounds.

"He's about to graduate from Hills," Terry explains. Hills High School, the most upscale of the city's public schools.

"And why do *I* care?"

"Ferdy says you're the kid's lawyer. They're all downtown waiting for you."

"All *whom?*"

"Not clear."

"Did he say what the deal is?" I ask.

"He mentioned a dog. And O. J. Simpson. It was a bit hard to make out," Preet says. By now Joe seems genuinely alarmed.

I grab my keys. "The name again?"

"Marcus Manners."

I walk to the door. Joe has his back to me. I point at him and then slash my index finger across my throat.

My name is Gordon Seegerman. I'm an assistant public defender for the city of Santa Rita, California. I'm assigned, as I have been for nearly a decade, to the misdemeanor division. Each morning I wake up, drive sixteen minutes to my dank office in the basement of the

Santa Rita municipal building, and settle into my job as a cog in the creaky wheels of the criminal justice system.

A file appears on my desk. A man has been arrested for a petty crime—stealing a slice of pizza, or being drunk in public, or showing his genitals to someone who isn't interested. I meet the man. I pretend to commiserate when he explains: *they got the wrong guy; they planted the evidence; the witness is lying; I was holding the stuff for my cousin.*

I nod a lot. I tell him everything is going to be fine. Later I discuss the case with a deputy district attorney. He or she makes the standard offer: seven months county jail or one hundred hours community service or a stay at a drug rehab outfit. In turn, I make a halfhearted, short-lived, and uniformly ineffectual attempt to improve the deal. I take the plea offer to the client, who yells at me, says he wants a real lawyer, tells me I'm an idiot or worse. And then, in a few days, he pleads guilty.

I take as few cases to trial as humanly possible. I avoid promotion—to the felony division, to the serious cases—as I might the Ebola virus. What ambition I have I save for my music, for my commitment to Manilow. What energy I have I exhaust, mostly, handling my dad, who, perhaps simply to irritate me, ten years ago developed a rare form of Alzheimer's. Imagine a toddler after a few shots of Jack Daniel's—that about describes my father.

My job is my job. I lay low. I try not to attract too much attention. Every two weeks I'm pleasantly surprised to find that the city has deposited a sum of money in my bank account. I can't say I believe this money is earned, but I'm not inclined to return it.

Two blocks short of the Hall of Justice complex—courts, district attorney and public defender offices, Santa Rita Police Department headquarters—I stop my frail, front-bumperless, white Toyota station wagon at a light. The windows are closed, and the air-conditioning is

6

turned up so high it's strafing my forehead. I therefore can see, but not hear, a woman on the corner talking into a cellular phone. She's in her mid-thirties, dressed for work at a place where dress matters. I have seen her before, but I can't think where. She's stick-thin, with a perky but not large bust, heavily made up, blond. Her nose curves abruptly at its end. Her shoulder-length hair hangs straight, at attention, paralyzed by product.

She pulls the phone away from her ear, fixates on the sidewalk for a moment, and then fires her mobile at the pavement. I'm rooting for her to stomp it. But she drops to her knees, returns the phone to her bag, and buries her face in her hands. Meanwhile the driver behind me lays into his horn, and I'm off.


I park across from the Hall. A crowd is gathered out front. TV microwave vans line the curb. A group of people who must be attached to the vans—reporters, camera people, techs—moves toward me as I cross the street. They do not look for oncoming traffic. A reporter—dark suit, microphone in hand, brown helmet-hair, more than his fair share of teeth—reaches me first.

"Are you someone?" He's frantic.

"I don't think so."

The reporter pokes the microphone in my face. The others circle around.

"Ted Garnett, FOX 4. You here on the Manners kid?"

"I'm with the public defender," I say, reaching to shake the reporter's hand to buy a few seconds. The handshake is unexpectedly clammy and limp.

The camera people shove to the front. The lights blind me.

*What are the charges?*

*Are there drugs involved?*

*Has he lost his scholarship?*

*Is the family going to make a statement?*

7

*Where is Marcus?*

*Can we talk to Marcus?*

A more experienced person would ignore the questions and irritatedly push away. But the spotlight stuns me, as does the notion that someone, somewhere, might care what I have to say. So I stare into the camera and confess my total ignorance.

## 2

THE HALL, normally dead this time of night, buzzes with activity. I walk over to a window where during the day an SRPD officer points people in the right direction. A sheet of plywood blocks the window, but I can hear goings-on inside. I knock and the barrier slides open a few inches.

"I'm Gordon Seegerman, with the PD. Can you tell me where you're holding a recent arrestee named Marcus Manners?" The deputy, his eyes locked with mine, slides the window shut.

I turn around. A mob, as voracious as the media horde outside, heads for me across the worn, gray linoleum floor. At the front of the assembly are my grandfather and his plus-size spouse.

"Gordon. Where the hell you been?"

I duck around the corner, rap at the door to the SRPD office, and push my way inside to relative safety. After a bit of finagling I convince the bored-looking desk officer to get me some information on the Manners arrest. She makes a call and a minute later the cover sheet of a police report coughs out of the fax machine.

Manners, Marcus. Eighteen last month. The charges don't look terribly exciting. Some dope in a car. And there's a Penal Code 487(f) charge, one I've never seen before: theft of a dog with a value less than four hundred dollars.

"This kid's some sort of sports hero, I guess?" I say.

"I see you're a big football fan."

"That's the one with the clubs and the little hard ball, right? Are you going to cite and release him?"

"New policy on these drugs-in-cars cases. No OR before arraignment."

In other words, the kid goes to jail until he makes bail or a judge says he can go home. And judges don't work nights.

I take a deep breath, dip my nose into my left armpit to check the stench, which is considerable, and return to the lobby. The crowd's plumped to about thirty. Beyond my grandfather and Bea, I recognize only one person, city councilman and mayoral candidate Jeremiah Pluck. Pluck, early sixties, is a man whose day begins happily only when his photograph appears in the paper. He is extremely tall, with the sort of loose, fleshy face infants like to grab at. When he smiles, his small eyes nearly disappear into his head, which is clean-shaven. He has a small diamond stud in his left ear. Although it is sweltering, Pluck is dressed in a finely tailored three-piece suit. The pants bulge at his midsection. Beads of sweat prepare to leap from his upper lip like skydivers.

Pluck introduces himself, indicating, without expressly stating, that I ought to be damn glad to meet him. He identifies several people in the almost uniformly African American crowd. I meet the defendant's father, Speed, and Marcus's girlfriend, Lucy, who is Pluck's daughter. And some others, too, who make clear they aren't too happy about Marcus Manners's circumstances. And even if it's not my fault directly, or indirectly, or really by any rational analysis at all, they appear ready to blame me for the whole episode.

After the introductions I suggest we gather so I can answer any questions. Pluck points the group toward a corner of the lobby. By now several of the reporters have joined the crowd. The camera people set up and fire their spots. I hold my hands out in the glow. The profound contrast between my pale skin and scant curlicues of black knuckle hair is sickening. Pluck quickly takes over.

He speaks at half volume and half speed. For the first couple of lines, with the group still congregating, it's almost impossible to hear him. But shortly the lobby hushes. When a siren flies by outside or a pair of officers, talking animatedly, pass the crowd, Pluck drops his head slightly, and waits.

"I remember the day they took O.J. away. I remember the day I saw the Rodney King video. I remember the day they shot Amadou. Do we let these ugly episodes get in our way, slow us down? No. We put them out of our minds. We focus on the important work of improving this city for *all* its citizens. And then a thing like this happens. They take this young man from his home. They put him in a cage. It reminds me. It makes me wonder. I don't know what all it means just yet, but I got to tell you I don't like the way it looks. Let me just say to the Santa Rita Police Department, and the district attorney, and the mayor: we are here, we are not going anywhere, and we will be watching. We *will* be watching."

The short homily is interrupted repeatedly with *that's right*s and *mmm hmm*s. Finally, the crowd picks up Pluck's closing refrain and chants it. He wades in to press the flesh. Then he rejoins me. I can't believe I have to follow this guy. I would very much like to go home.

"Hello." I smile. No one smiles back. "I'm Gordon Seegerman with the Public Defender's Office. I don't know much about the situation yet, but I can tell you our office will do whatever we can to help Mark."

The group grumbles, "It's Marcus, Marcus."

Shit. "I'm sorry. Marcus. Of course. I'm not much of a football fan," I add, grinning sheepishly.

No response. Tough crowd.

"We ought to be able to get him bailed out tonight."

"Can you tell us what the charges are, Mr. Seegerman?" It's the cell phone–hurling lady, who turns out to be one of the TV reporters. Which, I now see, is why she seemed familiar.

"I really don't know enough to comment. I should go upstairs and speak with the arresting officer and with Marcus before I say anything else."

"Will you be making a statement later?" She smiles at me. I smile back. Which I suppose isn't the right thing to do because several others catch this interchange and they don't seem to approve.

"I'll come back out this way and try to give you some information."

"Can we talk to Marcus?"

"That's up to him."

Not an altogether shabby performance, I think. I assume it goes unnoticed that, while making my remarks, I've poked my left index finger through the pocket of my khakis.

When the group begins to break up, I pull my grandfather aside.

"Who's with S.?" I say.

S. is my dad, ex-SRPD detective, Alan "S." Seegerman. Left alone, S. can be counted on to attempt to operate dangerous machinery—blender, lawnmower, that sort of thing—or to break into the liquor cabinet in a semiconscious attempt to relive his days as a lush.

"King's there," Ferdy says, sternly. King is my older brother. "You take care of business. I'll worry about your father."

A deep paranoid streak tends to make Ferdy sound a bit disputatious. Otherwise he's an angel, having served as mother, father, and grandparent for me and my brother since my mom died.

I retreat, with Pluck, his daughter, and Speed Manners into an elevator.

Speed is a few inches taller than me, but his shoulders are collapsed and his back bowed, so our eyes are level—his are red and watery. His face is blotchy. His chin and neck are covered with mottled stubble. He shakes my hand again, thanks me for coming down so late. His heavily hooded eyes dart momentarily to Pluck's while he is speaking.

The girlfriend, Lucy Pluck, says nothing. Like her father, she's tall, nearly six feet, I think. She's wearing shorts and I can see she has the muscular legs of a serious athlete, a basketball player or sprinter or something. Her hair is cut close to her head. She has extraordinarily long eyelashes, large, clear eyes, the sharply structured cheekbones of a runway model, the build of a—

Anyway, Pluck's caught me sizing up his daughter and the look on his face doesn't say, *Be my guest*. I shift quickly into lawyer mode.

"Has Marcus been in any prior trouble?"

"No," Pluck and Lucy answer together.

"Where was he arrested?"

"At our apartment, on Grant Street," Speed says. In West Santa Rita, the section of the city in which, say, a rich white person is least likely to be found. Unless, of course, the rich white person happens to be in the market for a little crack.

"Did the arresting officer tell you the charges?"

"No. He pulled Marcus out and told me to stay inside."

"They found some marijuana in a car, a Honda Civic," I say. "Is the car Marcus's?"

"We both drive the Civic," Speed says. "I don't know about any drugs."

"No. Of course not," I say. I mean it, too. This guy doesn't smoke dope or do crossword puzzles or volunteer at the Humane Society. This guy drinks. You spend enough time dealing drunk-driving cases and drunk and disorderlies, you start to have a knack for picking the lushes out of a crowd. Plus Speed's breath reeks.

"It wasn't his," Lucy blurts out. Pluck gives her an admonishing glance.

"There's also a charge involving a dog, theft of a dog," I say. "Does that make any sense?"

"There was a dog barking outside our house late last night and early this morning," Speed reports.

"Can someone make a thousand dollars bail?"

13

Speed nods, though he seems less than certain.

"We ought to be able to get him out tonight. I wouldn't let Marcus make any kind of statement before we get things sorted out."

Suddenly I sound like a lawyer. I have no idea where this comes from. I may well be parroting something I saw on television.

"I'll handle the media, Mr. Seegerman," Pluck jumps in. His volume and cadence pick up away from the crowd. He sounds like he's giving orders to a slacker staff member. "You get Marcus out. Then we'll sit down and decide what next."

Pluck grew up poor on the west side, worked his way up through the city's democratic machine to a spot on the city council. Along the way he made a killing in real estate. Now he's in the midst of a contentious mayoral campaign against the present district attorney. Pluck is the self-anointed, but also widely supported, voice of Santa Rita's black community.

The elevator dings and settles at the top floor of the Hall, where new arrestees are booked, interviewed, and housed until they get bused over to the county jail.

"Let me be clear, Mr. Seegerman," Pluck says before the elevator door opens. "I don't know what the boy did, and I really don't care," He curves his *r*s like a Ferrari around a hairpin. "I've been tending Marcus Manners like an orchid since he was a child. And I don't intend to let anything get in his way."

# 3

A S A RULE, I'm fond of dogs. My middle-aged dachshund, LeoSayer, urinates on me with some frequency. Nevertheless, I adore him.

But the beast that lunges at me when I step off the elevator, into the sixth-floor booking facility, is another matter altogether. It's the size of an upright piano, with what appears to be a dyed, neon red stripe down its back. The dog rears up on its hind legs and looks set to disembowel me. I back up a step, trip over Pluck's glossy wingtip, and topple. I've never been on the floor of an elevator. It's disgusting. I'd like someone to press "L," to send me on my way. But I, frighteningly enough, am supposed to be the one among us who knows what he's doing.

The cop holding the dog by a flimsy leash thinks my panic and pratfall hilarious and permits the animal to nearly smother me before withdrawing it from the elevator. I ask to see the arresting officer.

Moments later I'm in a small interview room with Officer Karl Dent. He's forty pounds overweight, feckless, and bitter. Dent, late fifties, a few strands of sickly gray hair slicked along the sides of his swollen skull, beer belly falling over his belt, hands me two crumpled pages, the beginnings of the Manners police report, and plops down in a chair.

I say, "You've seen the mess outside, I presume."

He makes fleeting eye contact and then tilts his head back to stare at the yellowed, pockmarked ceiling. His manner is that of a stage actor—Karl Malden or Orson Welles. He may well be insane.

"Ah yes, the fourth estate come to whip the dark masses into a froth," he says, still gazing upward.

"I was hoping you'd be okay with letting him bail out here instead of the jail so we could move things along a bit."

Dent laughs. His belly jiggles diagonally.

"Mr. Seegerman seeks an act of munificence. Isn't that rich."

"Seems to me it's in everyone's interest to tie up things here without a fuss. You want to move him, it's fine by me. You guys ought to have some fun after Pluck tells the crowd and the press you've got his future son-in-law in with the gangbangers and redshirts." In other words, the really bad guys, who reside, some semipermanently, at the county jail. "He's likely to remember your name when he's mayor."

He stares at me but says nothing for a whole, tense minute.

"I quite looked up to your father, you know. We were in the academy together."

"I'll send him your regards," I say.

"He was a brilliant detective, perhaps the finest this county has ever seen. Too bad how things turned out. Really. A gen-u-ine tragedy."

Dent doesn't seem sorry about my father's downfall. He seems, rather, to relish the opportunity to replay the events. I don't give him a chance to go on. I push back my chair, stand, and take a step toward the door.

"Very well, junior," he relents, snidely. "Inform the councilman if he comes up with the cash, we'll release the boy from here. And do tell your dad we miss him. We haven't had a decent scandal around here in too long."

If I kick the table hard enough, I could shatter his ribs.

"Very nice to meet you," I say, slamming the door behind me.

My indignant exit is utterly blockheaded because, per my earlier request, Marcus Manners has been delivered to the hallway just outside the interview room. Not only do I look like a red-faced, tantrum-throwing four-year-old in front of my client, but also there's nowhere else for us to meet, so I'm forced to return to the room where Dent is still savoring our brief conference.

The officer takes his time to stand. Rather than exiting, he waits for us to sit. Then he places his puffy, but finely manicured, hands on the edge of the table, leans halfway across, to within inches of Manners's face, and barks, "Hike."

Manners sits stone-faced. Dent snarls and walks out.

I've survived hundreds of initial client conferences. I've met all sorts of defendants—loonies, losers, deviants, druggies, hysterics. After a while it becomes routine. No matter how bizarre the person or the alleged crime, after nearly ten years, it rarely registers.

Typically I stride into the interview room with a look on my face that says, *Please listen carefully. I'm a lawyer, not a shrink and not a priest. I get paid to keep you out of jail, if I can, but don't expect me to be too genial, or to act like I care.* I brief him on the charges, the process, and get out of there before he realizes he's the client, that *I* work for *him.*

But despite my usual nonchalance, meeting Marcus Manners makes me nervous as hell.

There's a way in which Manners, who slouches low in his seat and puts his hands behind his neck and leans his chair back against the concrete wall, seems above it all. I've no reason to believe he's a dunce, but by the look on his face he doesn't appear even to know he's in trouble, let alone that he ought to appreciate my showing up to assist. All of which renders useless my usual, we-both-know-you're-guilty-and-we-both-know-you're-lucky-I'm-here attitude.

After introducing myself I say, "What was that about?" Dent's weird vocalization is still ringing in my ears. Manners shrugs but says nothing. I pretend to study the police report. Actually, I'm trying to catch my breath. "So, Bea's your godmother."

"Yup."

"That's great. That's great. You know I'm Ferdy's grandson." No reaction. "He and Bea asked me to come down tonight to see you, help get you bailed out. Your dad's ready to pay up so we should have you out pretty soon."

Manners says nothing. He doesn't move his head. His lips don't part. His eyes are slivers. He has thick black lashes that curl precipitously at their ends. And the same heavy lids as his father. I think you'd say he has bedroom eyes. His hair is closely cropped. There isn't a single blemish on his face. He has a small nose, and when he takes slow, deep breaths, I can see the nostrils collapse slightly. Despite his arrest and the ruckus downstairs on his behalf, the kid looks ready to set sail for dreamland.

"Most likely I won't be representing you. Either your family will retain a lawyer or some other public defender will be assigned to the case tomorrow." Nothing. "Questions? Comments?"

Manners moves his head from left to right, and right to left, once, almost imperceptibly. And we're done.

He precedes me out of the small room and now I can see that the kid looks like a quarterback. He has a leggy, sinewy, but not muscle-bound frame. And his hands are enormous. They look pancaked, like they've been run over by a steamroller.

I set up Speed Manners to make Marcus's bail. And we agree to meet the next day, though it's a meeting I have no intention of attending. By then I'll have handed them off to another assistant public defender. I'm happy to have helped out tonight, to make good with Ferdy and Bea. But with the Vegas show less than six weeks away, I need a new case—particularly one that looks likely to get media attention and may require some actual work—like a persistent canker sore.

I take the back stairs, to avoid the press and Ferdy, and exit into the parking lot at the rear of the Hall. I burst out a metal door, but the heat hits me, and I gear down to an amble. I look up at a cloud of moths

18

flickering around a floodlight. I do not care for moths or any other sort of unpredictable, fluttery, flying insects or whatever they are.

"Gordon Seegerman." Behind me, alone, her face half in a shadow, is the cell phone-tossing reporter lady. "I'm Cindi Paris. From Channel 2." Though I'm fifteen feet away, she sticks out her hand.

"Hello, Cindi Paris from Channel 2."

She walks up. We shake. It's been a while since I've touched a female hand. Cindi Paris's feels pretty good.

"I didn't mean to scare you," she says.

"You didn't scare me."

Awkward silence. Like, are we standing here for a reason? Was there something you wanted, Cindi, or shall we dance?

She finally says, "You want to get a drink?"

"A drink."

"You probably have someplace to go."

It's past eleven. Terry and Preet have by now given up on me. Actually, I could use a drink.

"I can't help you on the Manners case, Cindi. I'm not his lawyer. I don't know anything you can't easily get from the cops."

"You can help me with background. I've done mostly soft features before. This is my first criminal case. It'd be nice to have someone to come to with dumb questions."

"And I look like the guy for dumb questions?"

"You look like a nice man who might be willing to help out a struggling reporter."

Rarely does anyone refer to me as a "man," let alone a "nice man." It's unsettling.

"How about I ask *you* a question?" I say.

"Name it."

"What do you think of Barry Manilow?"

"Barry Manilow?" She laughs and then stops abruptly. "You mean, like, 'I Write the Songs' and all that?"

19

"That's right. 'I Write the Songs' and all that. Love him? Hate him?"

"I guess I'd have to say more hate than love. But it's not something I've thought about a lot."

We're below the spotlight. I wonder if people like this, TV people, who look so Barbie-good, actually get it on the same way us ugly folk do. I suppose their sex must be cleaner.

"Well, then, Cindi Paris from Channel 2, consider yourself extremely fortunate. You are about to be enlightened."

# 4

I'M AWAKENED AT six-thirty the next morning by cacophonous and patriotic clapping, stomping, and singing in the hallway outside my bedroom door. It's my dad. I hear King stumble across his room and crack his door at the end of the long hallway.

"Shut the hell up and go back to bed," King growls. "It's the middle of the night." He may as well be reasoning with a couch.

"You want to make the coffee or dress the lunatic?" I yell from my bed.

King starts down the stairs. "You couldn't make a decent cup of coffee if your life depended on it."

S. was the un-father. He spent my childhood becoming a famous police detective, drinking himself numb and, finally, steering clear of our house while my mother died. Then, he was nothing if not full of life—quarrelsome, swaggering, bubbling over with ardor for all things criminological. He could be counted on to have something critical to say about almost everyone and everything. Especially me.

For years after his diagnosis he was disconsolate and all but mute. With his memories fled his bad-tempered relish for living. But the silence, the gloomy hush, has since given way to a sort of cheerful inanity. Now he performs "The Star-Spangled Banner," "My Country 'Tis of Thee," and "America the Beautiful," often in mangled combination. Before his brain was muddled, S. might have whistled a little now and again, but he wasn't the sort who sang. Cops don't sing. Homos, public defenders—they sing.

21

This morning it's "Yankee Doodle Dandy" mixed with "The Battle Hymn of the Republic." And S. is high-stepping up and down the hall with the zeal of a majorette at the head of the Rose Parade.

I push my father into his room.

"Ferdy's coming soon, so we better get you dressed. So tell me, Pop, who's Ferdy?" Doctor's orders: keep him cogitating.

"Ferdy?"

"Exactly. Who in the world is Ferdy?"

"Ferdy," he says, looking at me like I'm the one with the memory problem, but still unable to find the answer.

He attempts to pull on his boxer shorts but has both legs in one hole. The effort is nevertheless ardent. He is like a three-year-old, as determined as he is clueless. Once attired, S., an attractive man, who's still muscular and has thick, wavy black hair with streaks of white at the temples, likes to admire himself in his bathroom mirror.

"And where is Ferdy, who happens to be your father, taking you this morning?" I say. He stares at his reflection the way an animal might, not at all clear what to make of his likeness. "I'll make it easy. Multiple choice: Iceland, Pluto, or the Stonehenge Senior Center in Santa Rita, California?"

My father's slow decline is, for me, uniquely unpleasant. When I was a kid, he ignored, humiliated, and occasionally kicked the shit out of me. Now I have to mind him. Plus, unlike most Alzheimer's, Pop's illness was caused by a gene. And it's an autosomal dominant gene, meaning there is a 50 percent chance I'll end up in his befuddled shoes. So far I've chosen not to get tested, but it's a decision I revisit hourly.

He stares at himself some more, smiles from ear to ear, and sets into a loud rendition of "America the Beautiful."

King, who's short, fat, balding, bearded, thirty-one, and far more likely to plod or to lumber than to erupt, erupts through the door to my dad's room.

"Have you seen the television?" He says, appalled for some reason.

He herds S. and me downstairs into the kitchen and aims a remote like a pistol at a TV on the cracked and grime-laden tile counter. He flips through a few channels. Then I see myself on the screen, microphones in my face. My lips are moving. But, I am relieved to report, someone else is providing the commentary.

I know I'm not attractive. I'm short, stocky. My nose bulges, my ears jut, my curly hair is unruly and commonly lopsided. From the rear I appear to be wearing a miniature yarmulke, which in fact is an incorrigible bald spot. But still, one rarely is forced to come so directly to terms with one's ugliness. Mirrors are two-dimensional. They are static. And after nearly three and a half decades, I know what to expect, I know how to hold myself to best effect.

Without warning, the television shows the animated, three-dimensional me. It is not amusing.

King, equally wound up and incredulous, says, "*You're* Marcus Manners's lawyer?"

"No," I answer.

The text at the bottom of the screen reads, "Gordon Seegerman, lawyer for Marcus Manners."

"Do you have any idea who this guy is, Gordon? He could win the Heisman."

"That's a trophy, right?"

My father gazes at the television. For a moment the nine-year-old in me hopes he'll be proud. But it's too late. No way he knows it's me.

"He stole SI's dog?"

Saint Illuminatus is the city's biggest Catholic boys school.

"I must have met the dog last night. He had a red stripe on his back."

"That's Red." King is hysterical. "Those guys are gonna go apeshit, Gordy. Seriously, they don't mess around. You don't just kidnap Red. That's their *dog*. You understand what I'm saying?"

23

King stuffs his face with breakfast cereal that hasn't had the benefit of soaking for a time in milk. And he doesn't bother to close his lips while he chomps. The sight of him, therefore, is equally sickening and deafening.

"I think I get the drift."

"We should get Manners to sign some stuff," he says, shifting gears to his eternal and hopeless effort to make a buck. "There's money in autographs, you know, even for college players."

"Is that a fact?"

"Absolutely."

"He's Bea's godson, King. Ferdy asked me to come down to the Hall last night. I have no intention of representing him, let alone exploiting him for your benefit."

"What the hell do you mean you're not going to represent him?" Ferdy says, joining the Seegerman men in the kitchen for the morning cabinet meeting. "You're damn well going to represent him."

King and I live with our father in the falling-apart-at-the-seams mansion where we grew up. We both have day jobs. King's changes frequently, although it usually involves his selling something no one has any use for. Lately it's some sort of miraculous mop. Ferdy and Bea, and a rotating team of Bea's children and grandchildren, manage day care when S. isn't at Stonehenge.

"Good morning to you, too, Grampa. And even if I wanted to handle the case, and I don't, it's not up to me. There are a lot of other lawyers in my office. I'm sure Marcus would prefer someone who knows something about football. Plus, wouldn't you expect Pluck to bring in private counsel?"

"Pluck doesn't give a damn about anyone other than Pluck. Don't count on him to come through with a dime."

"What about the father?" I ask.

"Where's he going to come up with that kind of money?"

"How long has he been on the bottle?"

"He has good reason," Ferdy says, gnawing at a chunk of two-day-old bread.

"Don't these big athletes get money from Nike and Gatorade or whatever?" I say.

"Of course," King answers. "From alumni, agents, sponsors. They hide it in offshore accounts."

"Amazing." I return to my grandfather, who is infinitesimally more likely to be a source of reliable information.

"And the mother?"

"The mother?" Ferdy gives me a half-worried, half-incredulous look. Discussions of past events between me, and someone who knows I am at risk for early-onset Alzheimer's, are often tinged with fretting. *Gordy, you really don't remember?*

"Where's she?" I say.

"The name Grace Manners means nothing to you," Ferdy says.

"Other than my sense that she's probably Marcus Manners's mother, no."

"How about Zora Neal's Bookstore?"

My father shifts impatiently in his seat. He requires feeding. I pour some cereal into a bowl, saturate it with milk, and carefully guide it into S.'s mouth. His hands shake relentlessly. He has no problem getting around, but his small motor skills are shot.

"I had a friend in high school named Nora Beale," King adds, a proud grin on his face.

Ferdy's turns a pale shade of blue. "I suppose I shouldn't be surprised neither of you is familiar with a bookstore. For your information, Grace Manners and some others, including Pluck, opened the store in West Santa Rita in the eighties. Put books in the hands of a lot of kids."

"Which they used to beat the hell out of each other," King adds, chuckling.

I say, "I do vaguely remember. Some drug thing went bad there."

Ferdy gestures dangerously, a knife in his right hand and a mass of cheese in his left. "For once will you get your facts straight? Grace Manners was entrapped, sent to jail, and murdered, probably by the police. *Those* are the facts."

"Which ought to bear significantly on the dog-napping case," I say.

"Don't be so smart, Gordy. The SRPD set up the mother, and they sure as hell wouldn't think twice before setting up the son. A lot of white people don't like it when a black man looks like he might get somewhere in the world. Look at O.J."

He does not appear to be kidding.

"You must be kidding."

Ferdy says, "Your father had something to do with it."

"With O.J.," I say.

"Didn't Grace Manners shoot some cop?" King adds.

I have only the slimmest recollection of the events. I was nineteen at the time, already off at college in L.A. I must have seen something on television.

"No. She didn't shoot some cop." Ferdy is disgusted. "You both ought to read a newspaper once in a while." Making his point, Ferdy snatches the unfurled *Santa Rita Journal* from the kitchen table and stomps into the living room to wait while we ready S. for his departure.

# 5

**M** OST DAYS I SLIP into work, through a broken emergency door at the back of the Santa Rita municipal building, down a little-used stairwell, and into my ten-by-eleven-foot basement office, without attracting the slightest notice. If I'm not required in court, at the Hall of Justice, I luxuriate over a cup of coffee and the paper. By ten-thirty, Terrence Fretwater, my fellow Barry-loving, dreadlocked Adonis, guitar-wizard, crooner best friend, who is also a much-sought-after investigator in the Public Defender's Office, usually joins me for a chat, good for an hour or more. By eleven forty-five it's time for an early lunch. Work is accomplished, when work is accomplished, in brief interstices between leisure activities.

Today, sadly, is not a normal day. Duke Abramowitz—misdemeanor supervisor, boss-in-theory—stands in my office doorway. He has to duck to avoid conking his head on the door frame. His bowlegs, lean figure, dark suit, bolo tie, and cowboy boots make him look like the undertaker in a western.

"Did you think about consulting me before going on television, Seegerman?"

I squeeze past him, toss my briefcase on my desk, settle into my squeaky swivel chair, and put my feet up.

"Would you mind the poster please?" Duke jerks his hand off the wall where he'd come into momentary contact with my nearly life-size Manilow poster. It was my mom's, so it has special significance to me. I'd prefer not to find Duke's oily prints on Barry's black tux.

27

"How about you brief me on the Manners thing?"

"There's no *thing*, Duke. My grandfather is married to Manners's godmother. They called me. *After* work, I should add. I talked to the arresting officer and I talked to Manners. I got him bailed out. End of story." I start into the day's legal newspaper and my cinnamon roll. "Was there something else? I'm actually kind of busy right now."

"Don't assume you're getting the Manners assignment. That's up to the chief." The chief public defender. "I got to be honest with you, Seegerman. Even after all these years, sometimes I wonder if you've got what it takes."

"Duke, let me put your mind at ease," I say, not glancing up from the paper. "I have nowhere near what it takes. Which is why I couldn't in good conscience accept the Manners assignment." I look up and smile, my cheeks puffy with mushy sweets.

He tosses a manila envelope onto my desk. Manners reports.

"Chief wants us in his office in thirty. You better look those over," he says and is gone. I spring out of my chair and into the hallway.

"Duke," I screech. "Duke."

I return to my office, to my newspaper. The reports mock me from the edge of my cluttered desk. I say, out loud, "Marcus Manners is not my problem. I don't have the time." I lift my head and yell into the hallway, at no one, "Las Vegas, Nevada. Barry Manilow. One Night Only. Can you people understand that?"

The envelope containing the Manners reports does not take the hint. It remains. All right, fine.

Dent took the initial report from one Jackson Bulley, who lives at 1000 Francis Lewis Lane. It's the Swell estate, not far from my house.

Stanton Swell was among the largest landowners in California. In the early part of the twentieth century he donated most of his holdings in the Santa Rita hills to the county, which used the land to form a string of parks. Thanks to Swell, you can drive five minutes from my house, walk a hundred yards, and find redwood trees the height of a ten-story building. The Swell estate was the family's local compound. I had no idea they'd unloaded it.

Bulley, a professor at Santa Rita State University, owns Red, the mutt that attacked me at the Hall last night. As my brother reported, the dog is the mascot for Saint Illuminatus. Bulley is an alum. Two days earlier, on Tuesday, April 27, he woke in the early A.M., walked out to the dog's kennel, and found Red missing. He called the police when a search party had no luck locating the animal.

Bulley claimed Red is of little value to anyone other than the Bulley family and the SI faithful. And he was confident the dog did not simply go wandering—it's kept in a fenced run with a latched gate, which was closed when he reached it Tuesday morning. Red, according to Bulley, can't operate the latch. He deposited the dog into the corral Monday night at around ten P.M. Bulley's son, Brice, said he was inside the house all Monday night and heard nothing unusual.

The next morning, April 28, someone waved down an SRPD patrol car on Grant Street in the heart of West Santa Rita. A dog, tied to a fence at the back of a fourplex, had been barking incessantly since late the prior night. The animal lacked identifying tags. The officer subdued the mutt, walked it into the building, and checked at each apartment to see whether the dog belonged to anyone. At the last apartment, Marcus Manners answered.

Manners quickly identified Red. The rivalry between Hills High and SI is long-standing and nasty; he'd seen the dog at SI games for years. But he denied knowing anything about how the dog ended up in his backyard.

News of Red's rescue reached Jackson Bulley before it reached Officer Dent. Upon learning that the mutt was found languishing behind the home of Hills High's star quarterback, Bulley demanded Manners's arrest. Now concerned that Bulley's wealth might suggest access to police higher-ups, Dent trudged off to investigate.

After knocking on a few doors in the Bulleys' neighborhood, Dent found a witness. At around ten o'clock on Monday night, Layne Maddox, seventy-one, was out walking his dogs. He saw a tall black man standing by a small, dark-colored car parked off Lewis Lane at the edge of the Swell land. He was sure the man was black, despite the hour, because his dogs growled ferociously and pulled toward the vehicle. The dogs, apparently, are racist. The man leaned against his car, his back to the street, turning only slightly when the dogs went berserk. Maddox reported that the license number began with "2K." He identified the vehicle as a Honda. When he returned from his walk half an hour later, the car was gone.

Dent determined that a 1989 black Honda Civic, license number 2KDP419, is registered to one Marcus Manners, resident of 445 Grant Street. He concluded that Manners, alone, or perhaps in league with other members of the Hills team, kidnapped his rival school's mascot.

So, on Wednesday evening Dent obtained a warrant and headed off to West Santa Rita to arrest Marcus. In the small lot behind the apartment building he located the Civic. He peered into the vehicle and observed, on the floor in front of the passenger seat, a bag of marijuana.

Two hours later Manners is busted and disgusted. The police work is dazzling.

Terry joins Duke Abramowitz and me in our cramped conference room.

As a rule, I don't meet. I find gatherings in the workplace to be uniformly unproductive. But the person set to chair this particular meeting is my employer, the chief public defender. He is from a place in Scotland so rugged and so manly that the women there have chest hair and drink seawater. Anyway, that's what the chief claims—and without a hint of a smile. I need my job and the chief scares the wits out of me, so today, I meet.

When the chief arrives, I run down what I know about the evidence so far and my interactions with the press and Councilman Pluck.

"Can someone give me a good goddamn notion what any of this has to do with O. J. Simpson?" The chief seems perpetually on the verge of stripping off his jacket, climbing into the ring, and beating the beard off someone. "Pluck's gone out of his mind this time."

"I couldn't agree more, sir. I only brought it up to give you an idea of how it's playing."

"I'm not a moron, Seegerman. I know why you brought it up." I lower my head to indicate our agreement—*I* am the moron. "A stolen dog and a bag of dope. What an idiotic waste of resources."

"My impression is the case is being driven by the dog's owner."

The chief flips through copies of the relevant documents.

"Oh crap." He slams his thick frame back into his chair and puts his hands behind his neck. "The goddamn Swells."

"Sir?"

"The dog's owner, Mr. Bulley, married Stanton Swell's granddaughter, Ella Swell. Which makes the dog a Swell." Which must also be why Jackson Bulley is living on the Swell estate. "What about the drugs? Whose car is it?"

"The defendant's," I say.

"Actually, not the defendant's," Terry counters, sliding a document across the table.

Officer Dent's report says the vehicle is registered to "Marcus Manners." But it turns out there are two such people, the young football hero and his father, whom everyone calls Speed. The car is registered to the senior.

"Am I to understand the boy is elsewhere when the drugs are discovered?" the chief says.

"He's upstairs in the apartment," I say.

"Is there a warrant for the car?" the chief says.

I flip through the file. "Doesn't look like it."

31

"There's your 1538." In other words, a motion to suppress the drugs. "Assuming the case stays in the office, I want a motion this thick, Mr. Seegerman." An inch. The chief looks around, with a "nice meeting, what's for lunch" look on his face. "Fretwater will join you."

"Sir," Terry objects. "Usually the misdos go—"

"Not *this* misdo, Mr. Fretwater. Not with the Swells involved. Also Pluck is bound to turn it into a campaign issue. The matter'll want an experienced team. Keep me apprised." The chief rises. We rise. He walks to the door and kicks it open while scanning the front page of a newspaper. "Will you do us all a favor then, Mr. Seegerman? Stay away from the press. They slaughtered your father. You ought to know they're scum."

"Yes, sir," I call out. "The family and Pluck mentioned wanting to meet today. Might you be available?"

"Time?"

"Around one-thirty. Before the arraignment."

"You and Fretwater handle it. I'll drop in if I can."

The chief leaves.

"What just happened?" I say.

Boss-in-theory, baffled by the ease with which we nabbed the hot new case and unable to decide between disgust and panic, gathers his papers and flees.

"Somehow you got us both assigned to Manners," Terry says.

I stare at the reports scattered on the conference table. "It's a total nightmare."

Vegas. Barry. We don't have time for work.

"It'll be fine," Terry says.

"You know, sometimes optimism is just delusion with a smile."

# 6

IT'S TWO P.M., time for the Manners arraignment, the initial appearance.

The afternoon calendar, in Department 10 of the Santa Rita Superior Court, is the starting point for all criminal prosecutions in this county, and the ending point for many. The gallery is filled far beyond capacity with families of those recently arrested, or about to plead guilty, or soon to be sentenced. The defendants, who in most cases are in custody, sit in the jury box, shackled together. The private lawyers mill around, contemplating their billable hours. The court staff shuffle papers, whack at keyboards in front of enormous and antiquated monitors, talk on the phone in whispers, and keep the peace. The judge arraigns recent arrestees, imposes bail, takes pleas, sets trial dates, and pronounces sentences.

Judge Garnett Reasoner, who presides in Department 10, looks something like the horizontal guy at a wake. The skin on his face, the color of tracing paper, is lined with thin gray-blue veins. His dentures are too big for his head, so his sealed lips bulge. And atop his head, about a dozen white strands hang on for dear life. At one point he had a reputation for toughness and intelligence. Now he has a reputation for being incredibly old, spiteful, and unfamiliar with legal developments post-L.B.J.

Reasoner does not like me. He treats me like I'm a defendant. I never appear before him without my checkbook, because he frequently holds me in contempt.

The gallery is more densely packed than usual today. The crowd is better dressed, less fidgety. It's Manners. Nothing of significance is likely to happen at this hearing, though. Reasoner will arraign the defendant and he'll set trial dates. Perhaps he'll thrill us with his canned lecture on the dangers of intoxicating substances.

But while the court appearance won't be momentous, Pluck wouldn't miss the opportunity to turn it into a campaign appearance. And he means to make a point by packing the room: *We're watching.*

Before the hearing I sit with Speed and Marcus Manners, Bea Johnson, Pluck and his daughter, and two of Pluck's staff in an unventilated conference room next to Department 10. I run through my "Misdemeanors 101" spiel. Marcus says nothing and, as in our first meeting, looks alternately bored and on the verge of nodding off. When there seems nothing left to say, I gather my things and stand.

"Shall we pray?" Pluck says.

I don't pray.

I look at Bea. She points at my chair. I drop back down. We join hands.

"Heavenly Father," Pluck begins, smiling, looking directly at me, as if to suggest that it's mostly for my benefit.

Trials and tribulations. Counsel and guidance. Blessings and love. Pluck goes on for a couple of minutes. None of it registers. I'm stuck on his first few lines. They hit me hard.

"God, please hear us. We ask you to take Gordon Seegerman by the hand, take his hand, Lord, and please"—Pluck squeezes his eyes together and scrunches up his face—"hold it tight and don't let it go."

Call me an unbeliever, call me a sissy even, but I really do not want to hold God's hand.

I stand against a wall of the courtroom while Judge Reasoner calls various cases, moistening his thin, pale lips with his thin, pale, and disgustingly pitted tongue every time he weakly bangs the gavel down upon his bench, sending another poor bastard off to prison. Finally, half an hour later, the clerk calls *People v. Marcus Manners*. The gallery comes to attention.

We wait. Nothing. Usually at this point someone from the DA's Office, whoever is going to prosecute the case, stands up and introduces him- or herself to the court. Other deputies crowd the prosecutors' table, but none, apparently, has the Manners assignment. They look at each other, and around the room. Finally, one stands.

"Your Honor, this is Mr. Velikovic's case. I just saw him in Department 9. Could we pass—"

*God, if you're listening, thank you. Also, if you want to hold my hand, I'm okay with that now.*

"No, Miss Whoever You Are, we cannot pass," Reasoner growls. "Many of the people in this courtroom are here for this matter. I myself am a Saint Illuminatus alumnus, class of 1940"—the judge at this point executes some kind of strenuous arm gesture, which, I assume, demonstrates his lifelong loyalty to SI—"and therefore I have an interest in seeing this matter resolved expeditiously."

The crowd grumbles, unhappy with Judge Reasoner's unabashed bias in favor of the mostly white, affluent Catholic school. The judge's voice is feeble, too low to carry to the back of the courtroom. So he uses a microphone. Imagine Don Knotts as the Wizard of Oz. Through the speakers, Reasoner sounds something like that.

"Good afternoon, Your Honor. Gordon Seegerman, assistant public defender, for the defendant who is present and out of custody."

Marcus, dressed in a fine, cream-colored linen suit, a pale green tie, and two-tone shoes, slowly makes his way to the front of the room. Two hundred brows furrow with concern for young Marcus.

"Who asked you, Seegerman?" Reasoner whines back at me.

Now the crowd is downright unruly, halfway out of their seats, preparing to leap to my aid at a moment's notice.

"Sorry, Judge."

Moments before a pitched battle erupts, deputy district attorney Milo Velikovic, a six-foot-four, three-hundred-pound behemoth, enters the courtroom.

Velikovic and I were in school together. He was the sort of law student who parks in the first row of the classroom, who raises his hand to answer every question, and who never, ever, comes close. He's the guy whose answers are not simply wrong; they are snort- and wince-inducing.

I have no idea what combination of résumé fraud and bribery landed him in the DA's Office, and I have no idea how he ends up filing a high-profile case like Manners's. But, if I have to litigate, I can't think of anyone I'd rather litigate against.

Milo, a badly dressed, chain-smoking, frozen-dinner-eating, Serbian immigrant, feels genuinely bad putting people away. The minute you put an ounce of pressure on the guy, he's ready to give away the farm.

Judge Reasoner insults Milo and fines him a hundred bucks. The Manners crowd loves it. Then the judge arraigns Marcus. When the kid says "not guilty," the gallery cheers. The judge orders the bailiff to clear the room. Ten minutes later we—Milo, Marcus, me, and the court staff—are alone.

Then Reasoner drops a bomb. "Counsel, my sense is this case is going to require special oversight. It is my intent to preside. Any objection?"

Reasoner is not a trial judge. He is not a motions judge. At best he is a traffic cop—he sets dates, sends cases to other judges for trial, imposes sentences that have been worked out in advance. No one tries cases in front of Reasoner. He's a disaster.

"Well, Your Honor, I don't have an immediate objection, but I'd reserve the right to exercise my 170.6 challenge."

"Are you suggesting I cannot be impartial in this matter, Mr. Seegerman?"

The law gives me the right to say so, whether I'm justified in doing so or not. Essentially, I can challenge the first judge assigned to try the case, with or without grounds to say he's biased.

"No, Judge, but the statute—"

"The statute what?" Judge Reasoner screeches.

"I'm sorry, Your Honor. But with all due respect, I reserve the right to exercise my 170.6 challenge."

"Overruled." He slams down the gavel on the bench, coming precariously close to his own fingers. The ruling makes no sense. There's nothing to overrule, no pending motion. "How long to try it?"

I've been in the case less than a day. I have no idea. But I'd like to get out of here before Reasoner jails me.

"No more than three days," Milo responds, a cheerful, cigarette-stained yellow toothy smile on his face.

"Probably more like a week, Your Honor."

Reasoner sets the first day of trial for June 2, the Tuesday before the Manilow concert in Vegas on the fifth. We're set to play the evening before.

"Could we have the following week, Judge," I say. "I have a previous commitment to be out of town on Friday the fourth."

"And I have a vacation set for the seventh," Reasoner says. "What's your excuse? Your client's not willing to waive time?"

Obviously I'd much prefer to kick the whole thing down the road for a couple of months. And I'd suggested in the meeting with the Manners crew that it might make sense to let things cool down for a while, see if Jackson Bulley might lighten up. But Pluck wasn't buying. He must figure the trial will give him a boost in the August election.

"Not at this time. How about the week before?"

"Madam Clerk?" The clerk and judge confer for a moment. "Sorry counsel, all tied up through Monday the first." Reasoner is gleeful.

I turn to Terry and give him an eyebrows-raised, *I told you so* look.

As I emerge from the Manners arraignment, I'm accosted by a gang of media types. Cindi Paris's head appears for a moment in the middle of the pack and then vanishes.

*Let me just say this, ladies and gentlemen of the press. Years ago my father, a widely respected police detective, was involved in a tragic incident in which a young girl was killed. As many of you now know, he was suffering at that time from the early effects of Alzheimer's disease. His conduct was not exemplary, but then, neither were the circumstances usual. I do not stand here today to rehash those events, nor to defend my father. He made serious mistakes. He was an alcoholic. His conduct resulted in the death of a child. His professional life was cut short. His career ended ingloriously.*

*But I have in mind, ladies and gentlemen, that your treatment of him was appalling. It showed no regard for his enormous contributions to this community, or for the complex truth of the situation. Frankly, I don't trust you. I look forward, therefore, throughout these proceedings, to having nothing to do with any of you. Thank you very much.*

Which is certainly the statement I should have given. Instead, the whole thing comes to me later that night, lying in my bed, unable to sleep because the heat wave that gripped the city a few days ago is determined to wring the last ounce of moisture from my body before it relents.

As it occurs, to the reporters' shouts of "Were the drugs his?" and "Mr. Seegerman, Mr. Seegerman" and "Will there be a trial?" and "Is Marcus going to make a statement?" I respond, with a silly, guilty-looking grin on my face, "No comment."

That line works for a lot of people. In my case the press isn't buying it and for a few moments they become furious. I have the sense they might assault me. Pluck steps forward. He says nothing of substance. He gives them no more information than I did, but they seem temporarily placated. I hide behind the councilman and when things begin to break up I sneak out the rear of the Hall.

# 7

"**T**HAT ONE WAS CUTE," Maeve says. "Too bad she can't sing worth shit."

Maeve, when not on pregnant bed rest, is the tyrannical office manager at the Public Defender's Office. She is also, as she would say, a *lez-bean*, and one particularly fond of young straight girls, just the sort who've been wandering into Preet's studio all night to sing for us. It's nine P.M. and still more than ninety degrees inside the garage. My soggy socks slip around inside my shoes. We've auditioned another gang of wannabes. All fine. None the woman we need.

"I hope you're enjoying yourself," I say. "Don't you think you should go home?"

"Actually, I'm trying to kill the little parasite in time for Vegas." She winces and braces her hands behind her back.

"The parasite heard you," I say.

"I still find it impossible to envision you rearing a boy," Preet says.

Maeve sits up on the couch and says, "Believe me. I wouldn't be in this situation if I'd thought I was gonna have a male child."

For the first several months Maeve swore the conception was immaculate. Now she admits it was not, although she has not volunteered additional details.

"I'm starting to think we should just do it with the three of us," Terry says, from the slightly cooler cement floor of the garage where he is reclining. "We're blowing a lot of prep time."

The Mandys play regularly around the Bay Area, and we've developed a solid following. Manilow was set to attend one of our local shows years ago, but he never made it. So when we found out about Vegas, we jumped at it. Maeve figured she'd be fine, still weeks away from delivery. She didn't count on the bed rest issue.

"If one of you wants to pull it out of me right now—"

"Maeve, give it a rest already," I say.

Preet's cherry-candy-colored upper lip, set off by his silky, glossy, black beard and mustache, and similarly-hued unibrow, begins to twitch slightly. He walks over to his stack of keyboards, adjusts his teal turban, and picks out the first few chords of the Manilow tune "Friends"—not one of the megahits, but a damn respectable song. Plus, he has a point to make. It's the wrong time to start bickering. I jam around on our ratty upright. Terry slowly rises and picks up his guitar.

Then we sing. Terry and I each take verses, then together, harmonizing on the choruses. It's good, but not good enough for Barry. We need the girl.

When we shut down the tune I can hear Maeve sniveling over on the couch.

"We weren't *that* bad," I say.

"Yes you were. You were *gawd* awful. I'm sorry, Gordy. I know it's my fault. I didn't—"

At this point snot and tears and choking prevent even minimal comprehension. But I get the gist.

"How could you have known?"

"I'm just so stupid. What the fuck was I thinking? What am I going to do with a boy? I haven't touched a dick on purpose in thirty years."

"You'll be fine. I promise," I say, not believing a word. "Everything is bound to be fine."

"It's not the same when it's a baby," Terry adds. "The baby doesn't know he has a dick. It's only when he figures out what he can do with it—then you're in deep shit."

A few minutes later Aineen, who is also her mother's assistant at the Public Defender's Office, shows up. She is heavily pierced and tattooed, muscle-bound, with sharply cut, dyed-blond hair, army shorts, and a tank top that looks like it may have been sprayed on. Maeve is supposed to be home, in bed. Aineen is not pleased. Over Maeve's loud and profane protest, daughter removes mother.

We're shutting down the equipment and packing up for the evening. My head is close to an amp when Terry hits a few power chords.

"Do you mind?" I say.

"What's the story with Manners?" Preet says.

"The story is it would likely spin out of control unless carefully handled by a brilliant legal tactician such as myself."

"I understand he stole a dog from some estate in the hills," Preet says.

"Allegedly," I say. "He's innocent until I plead him out, which I intend to do as soon as humanly possible."

"The dog is SI's mascot," Terry reports. "More important, the judge set the trial for June 2."

Preet is speechless.

"I'm dealing with it," I say.

"Is he good for it?" Terry asks.

"I don't know and I could care less."

"How?" Preet says.

"What do mean, *how*?" I say.

"*How* could you care *less*? You said, 'I don't know and I could care less.' I'm wondering under what circumstances you could care less?"

"I remain confused."

"What's your gut?" Terry says. "Manners took the dog?"

"From the reports, I'd say he's as good for it as anyone else. I mean, he's on the rival team. The dog's in his yard."

42

"Anyone could have put it there," Terry counters.

"They have a witness with no obvious ax to grind who puts him in the right area at the right time to grab the mutt."

"Black guy. Small car. It's pretty thin."

"License plate beginning with '2K'?"

"Maybe."

"What about the pot?" I say.

"All right. He's good for the pot," Terry agrees. "Unless it's the father's."

"I don't think so. He's married to the bottle and he's not the sort who cheats. You know anything about the cop who took the report? Karl Dent?" I ask Terry.

He shakes his head. "I'll ask around."

"Don't waste your time. This one is going down in record time. I'm sure I can get them to agree to probation and a little community service."

"Where was the dog?" Preet asks.

"It's owned by a guy named Jackson Bulley, who married one of the Swells. Ella Swell?" Terry looks at me for confirmation. I nod. "They live up at the Swell estate on Francis Lewis."

"Professor Jackson Bulley," Preet says. "A total asshole. I was in a couple of his classes at State."

"What's his deal?" I say.

"He teaches some of the upper-division computer science classes. His son is a bit of a cyber celebrity. I assume neither of you has heard of Total High."

Our friend Preet. Mostly, he spends his days computing. If there is such a thing as brown pallor, that is Preet's color after years staring at strings of incomprehensible code, day and night. He drinks a lot of sugary soda, is dateless, and probably virginal. But he breaks the computer-geek mold in some respects—he's carefully coifed and well spoken. He is rotund and bashful, but not at all insecure.

43

Total High turns out to be a crude, Web-based, interactive computer game created by Brice Bulley, Jackson Bulley's son, an SI senior, and some of his friends.

Preet demonstrates, clicking around on the screen. "It's never been of much interest to me, but it is very popular among the alienated-programmer set."

It's a virtual high school. Players join cliques or gangs, and battle other players, earning points for various acts of violence, vandalism, and depravity. The art and animation is rudimentary—the characters look like they've been hastily cut from magazines.

But the game itself is as complex as it is disturbing. A lacrosse player earns 100 points for his group, for example, by taking the virginity of a cheerleader. There are gang wars set for various times of the day in which players employ weapons of all kinds, from switchblades to grenade launchers.

Principal Zux, who threatens students and teachers alike, can be pacified only through the sacrifice of freshmen, upon whom he feasts. Battles often occur in the virtual school's graffiti-filled and vilely unsanitary lunchroom and bathrooms. Adolescent boys unquestionably crafted the game. There is considerable stuffing of heads in toilets.

Many of the cliques that appear in the game are unfamiliar to me— the Francines, the Yos, the Dirts. But there are others that were around when I went to Hills—the Goths and Geeks and Punks and Skaters. I was a floater, bouncing among groups and never squarely fitting in anywhere. I hid my passion for Manilow. I played in the band. I made it through without making much of a mark. But I avoided becoming a target, which was no small accomplishment.

Preet says, "It's actually quite an achievement if you consider that it was created by a bunch of kids with chores and homework."

On the screen Preet moves into Total High's virtual library and immediately faces a monstrous figure—half woman, with enormous, mostly exposed breasts, and half monster, bloody and mutilated. Its eyeglasses are horn-rimmed and slipping down its nose. It is unquestionably a librarian, and hardly the scariest I've come across.

"RIF," Preet says, quickly backing his character out of the library.

"Reading is fundamental," I say.

"Repulsive, imposing fiend," Preet says.

"Really interesting female," Terry adds.

# 8

SPEAKING OF WHICH, the next morning I'm sitting on a bench outside the Santa Rita District Attorney's Office. My great love, my one and only, the dark-haired, blue-eyed beauty called Silvie Hernandez, most definitely an RIF, exits the DA's Office.

"Hey, Gordy."

"Ms. Hernandez."

"What are you waiting for?"

"You."

Which is not true, because actually I'm waiting to meet with Milo Velikovic to discuss settling the Manners case. But also is true, because I'm in an essentially permanent state of waiting for Silvie.

"Good luck with that," she says.

"Thanks."

"Manners?"

"Mmm."

She sits. Her long, thin, olive-skinned neck is less than a foot from my nostrils. The aroma makes me want to become a better, less cynical, less sardonic person. *I can change*, I'm inclined to promise the aroma. *I swear I can.*

"How's it going?" she says.

"Other than I miss you desperately, superbly," I say.

"How's Manners?"

"That I couldn't say. As for *People v. Manners*, I expect it will be resolved in a matter of hours."

"Reasoner's really presiding?"

"You heard?"

"I not only heard, I guffawed."

"Anyway, it's just another reason to hope that your man Velikovic will have the good sense to make me a reasonable offer before I run him over at trial."

Silvie and I met in law school, fell in love, and performed together as a Manilow duet. Our relationship officially ended years ago. She abandoned Barry, got married, and then committed the ultimate offense: she left her big-firm job and became a DA. Her husband ended up with his own criminal problems a year ago and went off to a federal prison camp. They've been legally separated since. Not divorced, just separated. Perpetually separated. Which is enough to drive a torch-carrier insane. The husband is due to get out in a couple of months.

"Actually I've been meaning to call you," I say. "I have a small favor to ask."

"No."

"I assume you've heard about Maeve."

"No."

"She's having a kid."

For several moments the news is too much for her.

"Maeve in your band?"

I nod.

"That's horrifying. Doesn't she already have a daughter? I thought she was a lesb—"

"The relevant thing is, Manilow's in Vegas in June. We're playing the night before and we're hoping Barry will show. Unfortunately Maeve's on bed rest until she pops."

"And?"

"And we're looking for a singer." I fake a smile.

She gets up, nervously shuffling her stack of files.

47

"Gordy. Give me a break, all right?"

"Jesus, Sil, relax. I'm not asking you to marry me. It's one set. A few rehearsals. You know the material."

"I used to know the material."

"It's in there. You don't forget how to swim."

"The timing is very bad."

"I understand that." In short order she's going to have to confront her marriage, her future. "And this might be exactly what you need right now. Come to a practice. See how it feels. Deep down you know you miss Barry."

"I just can't," she says, backing up.

I start singing "The Two of Us," the Manilow number we used to open with, years ago, at tiny venues around town.

She forces a frown, turns on her spiked heels, and escapes.


"Gordon Seegerman, my man, what's happening?" Velikovic says, squeezing through the door to the DA's Office. We shake. He does his best to sound at ease with the language, but he doesn't quite make it. The syllables are crammed together awkwardly. He pronounces my name "Gore-Done."

"How'd you end up drawing Manners, anyway?"

"I'm the dog department," he answers, proudly.

Now I get it. Someone figured Milo would do the least damage away from any real cases. So he handles anything relating to dogs: bites, barking, abductions. Velikovic got the file before anyone realized who the defendant was.

"You got an offer for me?" I say.

"For you I have a great offer. One you will not be able to refuse." He gruffs up his voice a bit and it occurs to me that he may be making a *Godfather* reference. I ignore it because he may not be making any kind of reference, and I don't want to confuse the poor bastard.

"Reasoner scared the crap out of you, huh?"

"You kidding me? I got no problem with Reasoner. Only Fischer"—Garland Fischer, the elected DA of Santa Rita County and Pluck's opponent in the August election—"wants to make it go away."

"He's a smart man, Mr. Fischer. What's the offer?"

"Your guy pleads to the dog charge. We will dismiss the 11357." The marijuana offense. "One-year unsupervised probation and fifty hours of community service."

Not the whole farm, but the barn and the tractor.

"I'll take it to the family. How about he makes the year, you and me file a joint 1203.4." This is done all the time. If a defendant successfully completes probation, and doesn't look likely to be heading for a life of crime, the court can wipe the slate clean. But Reasoner is unlikely to go for it unless Milo is on board.

"No problem. Maybe I could get him to sign a football or something."

We shake. "Maybe."

The Manners posse—Bea, Pluck, Marcus, and Speed—descends on my office two hours later. I insist on a few minutes with my client, alone, before we meet as a group. I want to pitch the deal without Pluck's interference.

I shoo the gang into the hall and close the door. When I turn back to Marcus, he's already sitting in a chair across from my desk, flipping through my newspaper. He does not look up when I walk toward him. The kid scares me. And after my brief introduction to Total High, I know exactly why. Around Manners, I can't help feeling like I'm sixteen again, back at Hills, watching the beautiful people—the football players and cheerleaders—strut around like the rest of us are illegal aliens.

"Here's how I see it, Marcus. It's early, and things can change. But most times this"—I hold up Officer Dent's report—"more or less tells the story. I'm happy to hear whatever you have to say. But right now, with the offer I have from the DA, I'd have to recommend that you plead guilty and get on with your life."

I figure he'll lash out at this. Most defendants, even those with no chance of prevailing at trial, initially are quite resistant to the idea of admitting their guilt. Manners says nothing.

"The DA's willing to dismiss the marijuana charge, which is a good thing. They want you to plead to the dog count and do some community service. I'm sure Councilman Pluck can arrange something that won't be too taxing. You'd have to avoid any other legal problems for a year. Then you come back here and we get the whole thing erased from your record. Like it never happened."

He does not hesitate. "All right."

"That's it?"

He shrugs.

Suddenly I love him. I love this guy. The exceptional defendant, willing to take his lumps. No whining. "You want to tell me what happened?"

"We took the dog."

"*We* took the dog."

He shrugs.

"And *we* had the bright idea to tie up the dog behind your house?"

"We took him over to my friend's and left him there. I don't know how he ended up at my house. I guess my friends put him there. I'd rather not bring them into it."

"That's noble of you. Your friends delivered the dog into your backyard without telling you."

"It got there somehow."

"I guess so. And *why* did you take the dog?"

"It wasn't a big thing, you know? Some SI players messed with our goalposts a few weeks ago. We were just playing."

"And the drugs?"

50

"I don't smoke weed."

"Any idea how it got into your car? Your friends, maybe?"

"No."

"How did you know the dog wouldn't be inside the house? I mean, how'd you even know you'd be able to get onto the property?"

"You the police or my lawyer?"

His quietness isn't shyness or reticence or fear. He's a watcher, this kid. When finally he does show a bit of himself, it's clear he's no dummy.

I chuckle. "I don't know. I suppose I'm just curious. The houses in that area aren't exactly right on the street. It's pretty impressive that you got in there without setting off any alarms. You found the dog. He didn't bark."

"We brought some dog treats. One of my friends had been up there before. He saw the dog was staying outside. We just walked in from the road."

"Very nice."

"Thanks."

"You're welcome." We look at each other for a few moments. He does not blink. "So we're together on the plea? You think Pluck or your dad are going to give us a problem?"

"My dad won't say anything. Jerry maybe."

"And what do you recommend we do if *Jerry* objects?" He does not respond. "How about we tell him to fuck off." Finally, a scarcely perceptible grin. "Good. Then that's what we'll do."

Pluck does not resist, though. When I explain the offer and the benefits of pleading out, he seems to grasp the advantages of putting the case to sleep. The dog came to no harm. The drug thing disappears. The local news will feature the story for a night, and then it will go away.

They thank me. Bea winks. Marcus and Speed and Pluck line up to shake my hand. It's my pleasure. I'm just doing my job. I feel

51

authoritative. Like a real lawyer. These good people placed their confidence in me. They relied on me to be in charge, to take the lead in a crisis. I stepped up. I feel damn good.

It does not last.

# 9

MONDAY MORNING MILO and I go to see Judge Reasoner, to pitch the Manners plea deal.

Most defendants plead out. That's because most defendants are guilty and have no rational basis for believing they can win at trial. Prosecutors like pleas because they get convictions without doing any work. Same goes for defense lawyers: pleas mean cases go away painlessly. And most judges will approve most plea agreements because judges, like nearly everyone else in the criminal justice system, are happy to do as little as possible as long as they keep getting a paycheck.

Milo and I therefore have no reason to suspect Reasoner will reject our plan. But Milo and I are not, you might conclude, the swiftest kayaks on the river.

We stand in the doorway to Reasoner's chambers, hoping he'll notice us, invite us in to chat. He's reading a casebook. I can see from the number on its spine it's a very old reporter, from the forties. Perhaps he's remembering his life through the cases that punctuated it. I think of my dad, how his past has been stripped away, how he'll never have the pleasure of remembering the big wins. Milo and I stand there for several moments, eyeing each other, waiting for somebody to make a move.

"I'm listening," Reasoner calls out.

"Afternoon, Judge," I say. "We were hoping to have a word with you about the Manners case." He says nothing. He does not look up from his book. He taps the pointy nail of his right index finger, slowly, rhythmically, on the page. "Can we come in?"

Reasoner looks up. "That's fine."

"We've been talking about trying to deal the case," Milo says. His jovial manner does not change in Reasoner's presence. The guy's impressive. After the disaster in court a few days ago, I'd be mumbling and have my head down.

"I was under the impression Seegerman intended to bump me."

"Judge, what I said was I wanted to reserve my rights under 170.6. I was just taken aback when you said you intended to sit on the case. I was trying to protect my client."

"Protect your client from what?" I say nothing. "You believe I am capable of judging the appropriateness of a plea arrangement?"

"Yes," I say.

"But not to rule on motions or preside at a trial."

"I didn't say that."

"You implied it. You impugned my impartiality. Even my competence. Coming from you that is particularly irksome."

I ought to just get up and leave. But I'm a second son. I'm the kid who can't stand the thought of someone not liking him. I survived on charm. If my father was drunk and my mother was dying and my brother was sulking and sullen, shut into his room, I was across the street entertaining the neighbors, working the crowd, mining for affection.

"Your Honor, I meant no offense. The statute gives me the right—"

"I am aware of the statute."

"I was trying to apologize."

"Ineffectively."

"We've been talking about settling the case," Milo says, as if he has just walked in, missed the tense interchange.

"What's the offer?" Judge Reasoner croaks. I should be so lucky. Milo explains the deal.

"You've discussed this proposal with your client, Mr. Seegerman?"

"Yes," I say, moping.

"Yes what, Mr. Seegerman?"

"Yes, Your Honor, I have discussed the offer with my client and he is fine with it."

"Well, I am not," Reasoner says. "Boys and girls around the county look up to this young man, and I don't intend to send the message that you can use narcotics and get away with it. He pleads to the drug charge and does forty-five days in the county jail. Anything else, gentlemen?"

"I don't think Marcus or his family will accept it. He'll admit taking the dog. It was a prank. The SI team wrapped the Hills High goalposts in toilet paper a few weeks ago. He swears the marijuana isn't his."

"He pleads to the drug charge and he does the forty-five days," the judge insists. "Or he goes to trial. Let's be clear, though, Mr. Seegerman. If your client is convicted on the theft charges, I would be inclined to impose the maximum sentence." A year in the county jail. Reasoner goes back to his volume of cases. He's through with us.

"Your Honor, I think there's something else to consider here." He does not look up. His finger is back to tapping. "As you saw in court the other day, this case has already received a lot of community attention. Marcus's mother—"

Reasoner snickers. "Mr. Seegerman, I presided over Ms. Manners's case."

"I didn't know that."

"Well now you know. She was a drug dealer, too, as I recall."

I let the remark pass.

"Marcus has a lot of support in this city. The reaction to his being forced to do jail time is going to be extraordinarily negative. We're just trying to settle the thing before it blows up into something ugly."

"Mr. Volicurik, does it sound to you as if I am being threatened?" Reasoner seems to go out of his way to ruin Milo's name.

"All I'm saying is there's more at stake here than simply making an example of a kid who made a mistake," I say. "Don't send him to jail."

"For the last time, Counselor, he pleads to the drug charge and he does forty-five days. I recommend you tell your client to take the offer, because from my review of the file, he has no defense."

Outside the chambers. Milo is almost in tears.

"He's totally out of line, Gordon. I'll try to get Fischer to go to him directly."

"He knows I'm screwed. I can bump him, but he's the one who decides where we go. There are plenty of judges in this building who won't budge off his position. And he's right about the lack of a defense."

"I'll talk to Fischer."

I shrug. Won't do any good. Reasoner's suited up, he's on his horse, and he's riding into battle.

# 10

I'S MONDAY NIGHT. We're rehearsing at Preet's. The heat is unrelenting. Maeve is not in attendance. We jam for a while and then shut down the equipment and share some beers and a spicy veggie and rice thing Preet's mother delivers from the store out front. I fill them in on the disaster with Reasoner.

"Extremely bad," Terry says.

"Maybe we should cancel the gig," Preet says. "It's beginning to be difficult to ignore the signs. First Maeve, now this."

"No, no, no," I say. "There are no signs. I'll figure a way to deal Manners before the show. Moving right along, did I mention the death threat?" I pull a crumpled sheet of paper out of my briefcase and hand it to Terry. "Ten years as a PD and I have to wait for a freaking dog-napping case to get my first death threat. It hardly seems fair."

He reads the scribbled note, which says, "The friend of our enemy is our enemy. Be careful." I got it in the office mail.

"I'm sorry to tell you," Terry says. "I don't think this qualifies as a death threat."

"Excuse me. Of course it's a death threat."

Preet reads the note and says, "It doesn't name you."

"So. It was—"

"Also, I don't see a reference to death."

"This is unbelievable. The threat is implicit, Terry. Be careful of what? They're going to rearrange my CD collection? You don't say *be careful* unless you intend violence."

"Who?" Preet says.

"Some SI loony, I assume. Shows what going on television gets you."

"You don't seem too concerned."

"Keep the note. If I go missing, you'll turn that over to the authorities. It's pretty hard to believe someone's going to off me because of a freaking dog."

"I asked around about the cop, Karl Dent," Terry reports. "The name raised a few eyebrows. Nothing concrete yet. But he seems like he's sort of on his own at the SRPD."

"Meaning?"

"He's had the hills patrol for a couple of years, but he rides alone." Terry shifts his weight from one foot to the other while he's speaking. He looks like a recently sprung jack-in-the-box. "Seems like he may have had some internal affairs trouble. He had to take a leave of absence a while back. If I had to guess, I'd bet it was a substance problem."

"Get what you can," I say. "If there's a decent Pitchess maybe Reasoner will relent." A Pitchess motion asks the court to reveal the contents of a police officer's personnel file. If he's ever lied or cheated on the job, it's in there.

"The timing is unbelievable," Terry says. "Don't you feel like we've been here before?"

"Not really, no."

"Dunn?" Terry says.

A year and a half back we were preparing for a local gig at which we thought Manilow might show. A few weeks before, Duke stuck me with an exposure case—People v. Harold Dunn—that turned into a bit of a nightmare. I could barely keep my head screwed on, scrambling to work up the case and prepare for our appearance at the same time.

"This isn't Dunn. It's not even close. It's a dog-napping and a bag of dope. I'll deal with it."

"This whole thing is killing Maeve, you know," Preet adds.

"I admit it sucks," I say. "But none of us told her to get pregnant. And in my opinion we can't let this chance go by without giving it a shot. The minute she's able, she's back in. In the meantime, let's find a singer. All right. Let's quit debating and solve the problem."

My cell phone rings. It's the reporter, Cindi Paris. She wants to meet. She says she has something for me on Manners. We had an uneventful drink the night of Manners's arrest. She asked some questions about the process. I gave her my introduction-to-Manilow lecture. The last thing I want is for Preet and Terry, both notorious gossips, to get the idea I'm having a thing with this woman, so I walk outside with the phone. I agree to meet her and return to the studio.

"I'm going. Ferdy needs some relief." It's convenient, having a father with the needs of a toddler.

"Where's King?" Terry says.

My face flushes. Seat-of-my-pants fabrication has never been my strong suit.

"Some work thing," I say.

"Silvie?" Preet says, sensing my prevarication.

"No, not Silvie," I say. "What are you talking about?"

"That thing you're doing with your teeth." He mimics the sound of me forcing air through my teeth to clear unsightly debris. "You only do that when you're about to speak to an age-appropriate female."

Having nursed me through years of Silvie-related misery, the Mandys are strongly opposed to my having even cordial relations with my ex.

I look at the now amused Terry. "Did you have something to add or am I released?"

59

# 11

I STAND IN THE parking lot of the Singhs' convenience store and look at the city lights. Where is the fog, the thick mist that usually hangs over the city like an ice pack, sucking the warmth from the sidewalks? Where is the permanent fall?

I drive from Preet's at the edge of the hills, downtown, to Department 13, a dimly lit, crusty bar and steak house across from the Hall of Justice where many of the Hall's habitués—DAs and PDs and cops and judges and clerks and even some defendants—can be found after hours.

Cindi is parked in a booth, in the back of the bar, about as far from the action as possible. She's a local personality of sorts. Perhaps she can't just slip onto a stool at the bar, order a gin and tonic, and be left alone.

"Hey there."

"Hi," I say back, waving from several steps away. She stands. She sits. I sit.

"Thanks for coming down."

"No problem. What's up?"

"You want a drink?"

She's attractive, if you like the pointy-cheekbones, long-nails, skinny-legs, orange-painted-lips, silky-black-blouse, bleached-teeth look. It's not my thing, but lots of men go crazy for it and Cindi gets plenty of attention from guys cruising to and from the restroom.

"Assuming you're buying, sure."

She fetches me a whiskey from the bar and returns. My father drank gin and Scotch, neat and neat. On principle, therefore, I drink only bourbon on the rocks.

"So, is it now safe to say you're Marcus Manners's lawyer?"

"Sadly."

"I thought we might help each other out. I come across relevant stuff now and then. People talk to me."

"And what am I supposed to do in return? No one talks to *me*."

"If you're going to give anything to the press, give it to me first."

"People do this, right? Make special arrangements, exclusives, that sort of thing."

"People do."

"You're the first and only person to ask. So I guess it's fine."

She reaches in her purse, removes a crisp envelope, pulls out two xeroxes, and places them between us on the table. Then, with a dramatic flourish, she attempts to slide them across to me, but the sheets get hung up on table-gunk. Finally she flips the documents around. They are copies of pages from the directory of an organization called Saint Illuminatus Forever—a fraternity of men who attended Saint Illuminatus High School, peaked in their senior years, and now spend their evenings reminiscing in a cigar-choked club downtown. One page contains the photograph and bio for Professor Jackson Bulley. The other is for Santa Rita Police Officer Karl Dent.

"Very interesting. Could be like a local *Da Vinci Code* thing. Catholic school football fanatics conspire to ruin the life of the public school quarterback."

"These SIF guys take their sports pretty seriously."

For a second I think about telling her about the wacko letter I got at the office, but quickly decide against it. It'll end up on the evening news.

"I may be able to use it."

"So we have a deal?"

"What can I tell *you*?"

"Is there going to be a trial or is Manners going to plead?"

"For the record, my client is not guilty and looks forward to his day in court."

"And off the record?"

I see my brother King walk in and up to the bar. This isn't particularly a surprise nor a problem. My brother, like my father before him, is a drinker. I don't know what makes someone an alcoholic, so I don't know if King is one. He drinks. He drinks regularly. He drinks to excess, I suppose. My dad consumed Great Lake quantities of liquor before the AD fried his brain, but he was very rarely observably intoxicated. King is a less-practiced drunk—he can be belligerent; he is often maudlin.

So, not a surprise—King works nearby and can often be found at Department 13. And not a problem—because the bar is crowded, I'm well hidden, and given my brother's beeline for the booze, I doubt he'll want to chat anyway.

I'm back to Cindi momentarily, and then we are both startled by shouting at the bar. One of the shouters is King. The other shouter is a head taller and looks like the sort of person who spends his time lifting things: crates or weights or concrete or something. I can see by the flush on King's face that he's already inebriated, and therefore cannot be relied upon to approach this conflict in the manner most likely to result in his continued existence.

Without explaining to Cindi, I head for the ruckus. Before I arrive, the shouting turns to shoving. King is not easily shoved, because of his girth. But neither is his opponent. Both hold their ground. Patrons nearby shrink from the action. When I reach the bar, I begin to make

62

out bits of the argument. King has accused the large man of swiping his tip money. The large man is threatening my brother with an untimely demise. Which would be particularly unfortunate in King's case. Unlike me, when the doctors concluded that my dad's illness was genetic, King got tested. He is negative. To escape the AD, and go down in a bar fight—tragic.

"King," I say, trying to distract him, to defuse the situation. He acknowledges me but does not move.

Now, facing he-who-lifts-things, I apologize profusely. I blame the liquor. I tell the man King's just out of an institution. But my presence only increases the man's rage.

"I know *you*. You're the lawyer for that punk Manners." I'm stunned. And then worried. Suddenly I'm in the fight. The man jabs at my chest and I collapse backward a few steps, barely remaining upright. "You better watch your back. That boy's going down." Despite his thick head and violence disposition, the man doesn't seem particularly drunk. And the warning doesn't seem to be offhand.

Then Cindi walks up and it's as if someone has lifted the stylus off the turntable. The din vanishes. The tension evaporates.

"You're the lady from Channel 7," the large man says, looking directly at her breasts.

"Channel 2 actually," she says, her pearly whites on display. "Would you mind going back to your drink? We were just leaving." The man insists on an autograph, on the back of his T-shirt. I feel rather bad for Cindi. The shirt is sweat-stained. But she placates him and he disappears into the crowd, a triumphant smile on his face.

King is speechless. And despite his bulk, with Cindi's hand on his waist, he glides toward the exit like a ninety-pound figure skater. Outside he tries to take off for his car. I block his escape and tell him to stay put. Then I return to Cindi.

"That was impressive," I say.

"So is he going to plead?"

"Off the record, yes."

She heads across the street, in the direction of a shiny BMW SUV. When she reaches the double yellow line, she pirouettes and points at me.

"Don't forget our deal."

I dump King at home and then call Silvie from my car.

"What are you doing?" I say.

"I was working. Now I'm talking to you."

"Let's have a drink. I'm at Department 13."

"Gordon."

I've made this call a hundred times since the feds carted off her husband. On a few occasions the response has been something other than an exasperated "Gordon" or "go away" or "quit stalking me." We have lunch sometimes. And dinner rarely. She has not given me the slightest hope of reconciliation. I remain, nevertheless, cautiously optimistic.

"Silvie."

"I'm not hanging out with you at eleven o'clock at night, especially not at Department 13."

"How about a walk? When I saw you at the Hall you seemed like you could use someone to talk to."

"Thank you for the offer. I don't need anyone to talk to. I especially don't need you to talk to."

"That's not nice."

"Too bad. It has nothing to do with you, you must know that."

"I know that. Did you give my proposal any more thought?" She says nothing for a few moments. "Silvie?"

"Actually, yes."

"Really?" Suddenly I'm not simply hopeful, I'm expectant.

"What do Terry and Preet think?"

"They're thrilled."

"You haven't asked them, have you?"

"Of course I have." A total lie. "They're psyched."

Life, despite the bar fight, and the recent accumulation of threats relating to the Manners case, momentarily is sweet.

I dream of Manilow. We're walking side by side on the Las Vegas Strip. It's a stifling summer night. The streets are packed with bachelorette parties, and diminutive men and women from Central America handing out cards for hookers and phone sex lines, and, among the throngs of tourists, an extraordinary density of fake breasts. Manilow is dressed in full concert regalia: red tuxedo, leather shoes shined to within an inch of their lives. We stop to watch the fountain show in front of the Bellagio.

He's just finished playing for twelve thousand adoring fans, and has one of the most recognizable faces on the planet, so the fact that no one stops or even ogles him strikes me as extremely odd. I keep looking around, checking for gawkers, but the crowd is focused on the thousands of undulating streams that shoot out of the pools and leave behind a far-off, mocking mist that makes the night seem even hotter than it is.

We chat aimlessly. I ask him about a key change in "Can't Smile Without You." He compliments me on our performance the previous evening, says it's obvious we understand the music. We discuss a possible collaboration. I'm unexpectedly calm. He's just a human being. A great man, a great artist, but also a decent guy. There is no reason in the world I should not be able to have a normal, relaxed conversation with Barry Manilow. None.

Then I hear the strident bleeping of my cell phone, which cuts through the Vivaldi being piped out of speakers surrounding the fountains, and rapidly attracts annoyed stares from the crowd. I slap my pockets and search inside my sport coat, but I can't find it. To my horror, attracted by the incessant ringing of the mobile, the crowd sees that it's Barry, and swarms us. I try to protect him, and to find and extinguish the damn phone, but it's no use. They are on him like yellow jackets on a half-melted Snickers bar.

"What the f—" I stab at the buttons on my cell phone. The thing refuses to stop ringing.

I look at the screen. Terry.

"What?"

"Good morning, Gordon."

"What?"

"You remember Chief mentioning Ella Swell?"

"What time is it?"

"It's time for you to get up and face the mess your life is about to become."

"What time is it?"

"Ella Swell."

"I remember, I remember," I grumble. "Married to the guy with the dog."

"*Used* to be married. They found her body on the Swell estate this morning."

"Oh Jesus. Who called?"

"Duke. He didn't have any details. Apparently the cops are already out at Manners's place running a search."

"You must be kidding me. Why?"

"Got me. He said to find you and tell you to get the *hell* out there."

"Fine, I'm getting."

To the tune of the ominous opening notes of Beethoven's Fifth, Terry sings, "Dunn, Dunn, Dunn, Dunn."

66

The Dunn case, as I mentioned earlier, began as a simple exposure prosecution. Then one of the witnesses got herself whacked, which complicated matters somewhat.

"It's not Dunn," I shriek into the phone and click off.

# 12

**M**ANILOW MATTERS.

Say it to yourself. Say it out loud. Tell your friends. Write your high school sweetheart. Call your therapist. It's time to settle this thing. It's time to put it to rest. One more time, all together now, *Manilow matters*.

Barry Manilow is among the most successful recording artists in history. He's sold more than fifty million albums. He had twenty-five Top 40 hits in ten years. He had five number-one albums in a row. He has a Grammy and an Emmy and a Tony and an Academy Award nomination. Thirty years after "Mandy," he sells a vast volume of records. Barry is indisputably, irrefutably, huge.

Manilow has an unbeatable story too. He was a poor, shy, Brooklyn kid, a mail clerk at CBS Records who dreamed of being a musician, an arranger, but never a celebrity. And though Barry went on to become one of the biggest stars on the planet, he never lost his sense of humor, his unassuming, retiring style. He stayed close to his family, he remains true to his roots. He may live in California, but he still *sounds* like he's from Brooklyn. He is as real as real gets.

Barry also has the best-organized, closely knit, loyal, and long-standing fans in the world. There's no group of music enthusiasts that has taken a worse beating over the years. But despite the ridicule, Barry's fans know their man and they stick with him.

But these are not why Manilow matters; these, rather, are the *matters-Manilow*. They are what we see when we see him. They are what we talk about when we talk about him. Barry is big. Barry is loved. And Barry is lovable.

So why does Manilow matter?

It's the music. And it's that simple. Do yourself a favor. Put aside your judgments, close your eyes, and listen. Listen to "Even Now." Listen to "Somewhere in the Night." Listen, to the hits, to the lesser-known tunes. Whistle along with the introduction to "Can't Smile Without You." Sing along to "Mandy." Even if you think you absolutely can't stand Barry Manilow, take some time and listen.

If you have a heart and a soul and are not so emotionally stunted that you can't be reached, what you'll find is that the songs are not simply inspiring and passionate and thrilling. They aren't simply a nearly perfect amalgam of words about love and life, on the one hand, and music that is as deceptively simple as it is emotionally affecting, on the other.

What you will find is that Barry's songs are timeless. And they are timeless because they mirror, unabashedly, candidly, who we are. Manilow matters because his music is a looking glass to which we'll always be able to turn to get a glimpse of ourselves.

# 13

I WOKE UP WITH a headache, and now my skull throbs to the beat of Terry's baritone—Dunn, Dunn, Dunn, Dunn.

I stop for a giant coffee on my way over to Marcus's place in West Santa Rita. I sit out on the curb. In ten minutes I see seven SRPD patrol cars fly by, their sirens bent on negating the effect of the caffeine on my agonizing head.

When I arrive, I see Marcus in the rear of one cruiser and Speed in another. Several nervous-looking patrolmen herd Pluck and a crowd of perhaps fifty rubberneckers—residents of the building, neighbors—across the street.

Pluck launches into a briefing without the slightest ramp-up. Before ten, it's already sweltering, and he's suited up as if it's a brisk fall day. He does not appear to be annoyed that I'm late, or pleased to see me.

A couple of hours earlier the SRPD served a search warrant at the fourplex. Speed calls Pluck, Pluck calls my office, but I'm busy dreaming Manilow dreams. Despite his official status, Pluck hasn't been able to get much out of the officers involved, but he's watched them move stuff from the house—clothing, shoes, books. He points, wildly, all around the property.

There are already two television satellite vans on the street. A third pulls up and out pops Cindi Paris. She and her crew survey the scene and then walk to within ten feet of us. I notice that the fly on her slacks is down. Now here's an interesting situation. We've had a few drinks.

We may even be friends. Does that give me the right, or perhaps even the responsibility, to point out the downed fly? Before I can resolve the question, Cindi walks up and sticks a microphone between Pluck and me. Some other reporters see her and dash over.

"Has Marcus or his father been arrested?"

"Does this have something to do with the Ella Swell killing?"

Pluck loses it when he hears about Swell. I pull him aside and tell him what I know, which is next to nothing. I'd heard a short report on the radio. Swell's body was found on the estate late last night.

"She stopped by my office last week." He's shaken, incredulous even. "I hadn't seen her in years. Is that what this"—the search—"is about? They think Marcus—"

The press inch closer to our conversation. Pluck deals with Cindi and the lot, and I'm off to see what's happening with my client.

Officer Dent leans against the patrol car in which Marcus sits, staring straight ahead. I knock on the window. He turns his head to nod hello. He's cuffed.

"Morning, Seegerman. Lovely day for a homicide, don't you think?"

"Is my client under arrest?"

"Detained for the time being."

"I assume there's a warrant floating around."

He points to the side of the building where a gaggle of cops in street clothing stand around smoking. A head shorter than the rest is Detective Mick Bacon. I walk over.

"Well, shit, if it ain't little Gordy Seegerman."

"Mick."

In a fair world Mick Bacon, and not Robin Williams, would have been cast to play Popeye in the feature film. He looks just like the cartoon character and he has the same tough shell and decent nature. And he smokes a pipe, although not of the corncob variety. He was my dad's closest friend on the force. Mick was a regular at our home

71

when my mom was alive, when we had a home and not a nursing facility.

"How's the old man?"

"Lost, but otherwise fine, thanks. You should come by some time."

"You bet. I've been meaning to do that."

"You want to fill me in?" I say.

"You're the designated loser?"

I bow. Mick hands me a search warrant and accompanying affidavit. The warrant says nothing about Swell. Not a surprise given how recently they found her. It authorizes the cops to search the Manners place for evidence of narcotics distribution. We walk a few yards away from his colleagues.

"You know, I don't actually give a shit about any of this," I say. "But I'm beginning to look like a bit of an idiot in front of my client."

"You worried about Manners or Councilman Puke?"

"I gather you'll be supporting Fischer in November?"

Mick and Garland Fischer and my dad went to high school and entered the force together. Fischer eventually went to law school and rose through the ranks of the DA's Office. He and Mick remain best buddies.

"If Puke wins, I'm moving to Frisco."

The special mayoral election in August—following the untimely death of the man elected a year ago—looks to be too close to call. The cops have clashed with Pluck repeatedly over the years, and have come out strongly in favor of the DA.

"Can you just tell me what the plan is so I can do some damage control?"

"We'll be out of here soon."

"My client's not being arrested?"

"We'll arrest him if you want us to. Usually you guys are trying to get your clients *out* of jail."

"At least that way I'd have a clue as to what the hell's happening."

Mick lowers his voice and takes a step toward me. He sucks hard on his pipe, realizes it is unlit, removes it from his mouth, and stuffs his thumb in the bowl. "I assume you've heard there's a rich lady up in the hills who isn't feeling so good today."

"And there's some reason to think Manners is good for *that*?"

"I'm not the primary, so I don't think. They tell me get a warrant and take a look, so I'm taking a look."

"Who's the primary?"

"Nick Baptiste. He's up at the estate."

"What's his story?"

"He's an asshole."

"Wonderful. What's the deal with Swell?"

"She's been cooking. Not clear how long. We have your guy on the property last week. To snatch the dog. Maybe to deliver a package. We found some coke near Swell's body."

"That's ridiculous. How do you go from personal use amounts of dope to coke dealing? And even if he is dealing, that automatically makes him a suspect in the homicide?"

"That, and the fact that he had a motive, puts him on the short list." He takes a step back and smiles. "Quit worrying. We'll release him in a few."

"What motive?"

"How about she killed his mother?"

Before I can follow up, an officer calls for Mick and he returns to his SRPD klatch.

An hour later I'm inside Marcus and Speed's cluttered, ratty, two-bedroom apartment. The place looks like a candidate for demolition. With the exception of some family photos, there's little worth salvaging. Stained carpets swathe the floors. The furniture is chewed up. A fire-retardant substance that resembles petrified cottage cheese flakes off the ceiling in spots, so, apart from the stifling heat, I feel I'm caught in a light snowstorm. There's one unexpected note to the place: it's crammed with books, piles of them. Serious stuff too: math and philosophy and classics. A six-volume collection of Bernard Shaw's plays litters the living room floor.

Speed's made an effort to tidy up some of the booze, but he's missed a few dusty bottles next to the couch and sandwiched between stacks of books. Marcus is slung across a couch in the living room. Speed, next to him, rubs his hands back and forth across his stubbly cheeks. Pluck, in an adjacent dining area, has a phone to his ear. He listens while he stares at a picture of the young Manners family—Grace and Speed and Marcus as an infant.

Marcus slowly makes his way through the warrant. I stand and pace a few steps in each direction until he finishes. Various questions occur to me, beginning with whether he happens to have had occasion to kill Ella Swell, but I decide to deal with the narrow issues that directly impact my life.

"Our big problem at the moment is Judge Reasoner doesn't want to go along with the plea deal. For some reason the judge seems to have it in for Marcus."

Pluck interrupts his call and bellows from the dining area, "Speed, will you please enlighten the man." The councilman continues to eye the Manners family portrait.

"Judge Reasoner said he presided in Ms. Manners's case," I say. "You think that's it?"

Speed is silent. He looks down at his knees.

"Of course that's it," Pluck says, covering the mouthpiece of his mobile phone with his palm, finally turning his head away from the photograph. "He's got no business sitting on Marcus's case."

"Unfortunately, there's not very much we can do about that. Even if we bump him, it's very unlikely another judge is going to come off his position on the plea. Anyway, my sense is Reasoner will eventually cave. He's just sweating us. That's his style."

"That's fine. We'll do our own sweating in the meantime." Pluck, off the telephone, now stands too close to me in the small living room. "A few hundred people outside the Hall calling him names all day, every day. Deaf as he is, that oughta do."

I ask my client to walk me out.

"I'd like to have the names of your friends," I say. He shakes his head. "Look, Marcus, it pains me to say this, but if one or more of them is white, and maybe from someplace other than the west side, and we convince the DA and the judge we're going to drag them into it, we might make the whole thing go away. Otherwise, we may well have to take the case to trial and I don't see much hope there." No response. Walking away, I say, "Do me a favor and at least think about it."

"I already did," he says.

Back at the Hall, news of Ella Swell's demise has spread. It's already been a murderous year, forty-nine homicides to date. And after this high-profile killing, along with the possible Manners connection, a spooky hush creeps over the place. People rush through their days, eyes aimed at the floor.

I'm in my office. I can feel the veins in my temples pulsating. It's not even one P.M. and I've already soaked through the dress shirt I intended to last a week. I try to remember what it felt like to be me several days ago. I was mildly depressed, nervous about the Vegas gig, and at risk for cognitive collapse, sure. But now I'm all of those things *and* everyone wants a piece of me. PD staff who days ago could not have positively identified me as a coworker hover outside my office. When I emerge to pee or refill my coffee mug they bombard me with questions and advice.

*My* case, the Manners misdemeanors, could not be less interesting.

Even the client, for all his local celebrity, wasn't enough to send my star shooting. And though no one in his right mind is going to let me get near a homicide case should Marcus end up getting charged, just the smell of Swell blood wafting over Santa Rita has turned me, to my considerable annoyance, into the momentary go-to guy.

# 14

I ESCAPE EARLY AND head home. In front of our creaky Craftsman at 4200 Candlewood Lane is a large courtyard, surrounded by a stone wall, behind a nine-foot-tall hedge. Walking past, it's impossible to see in. Which is good because my father has taken to sunbathing in the nude. He was no sort of naturist in the old days. But now, for reasons we have given no doctor the opportunity to explain, clothes are a bother. The weather has permitted, recently, and so long as the gate is locked, and he can't go wandering in the buff, there's no harm.

I take off my jacket, pull an old, rusted chaise next to him, and stretch out. The sun soaks up some of my overflowing unease. LeoSayer runs circles around us. He gnaws, with the side of his mouth, on a half-disintegrated and rotted tennis ball that is nearly the size of his head. I swipe it from him and toss it across the yard. He looks despondent, having no clue it's a game, believing he is being punished.

I notice my father is wearing a gaudy woman's bracelet around his left wrist. My mother's. Otherwise he is stark naked.

"Nice bracelet," I say. "I could never get away with such a bold move. I've just never had your fashion guts."

He smiles and nods.

"You know, Dad, in France they call tennis *baz-ket-bol.*"

He smiles and nods.

When I see my father, in the half moment before I remember that his brain is fried, I alternately want to throw my arms around his waist and bury my head in his broad chest, or kick him in the balls. Then I remember and I'm just glad it's him and not me. Not yet, anyway.

"Pluck's calling all over town to get folks down to the Hall tomorrow. You aware of that?" Ferdy asks, an admonishing look on his face.

Monday is family-dinner night. We grill or call out for Chinese or pizza. We're not particular. We like our steaks rare, our beers cold, and our vegetables in limited quantities and smothered with cheese. We eat on blue plastic plates. We use splintery chopsticks or disposable utensils.

"Yes," I say.

"So now they're gonna try to pin the Swell murder on the kid?"

"I certainly hope so."

"Nice attitude."

"I'm just saying, no one will care about the dog case anymore and I can get my life back."

"What Swell murder?" King looks up from his noodles.

"Where have you been all day?" I say.

"Some people have jobs."

"I suppose you think the kid's guilty," Ferdy says, and then sucks a noodle noisily into his mouth.

"*What* Swell murder?" King demands. We fill him in.

"How should I know? You're the one who knows him."

"Who says I know him? I've seen him up at Bea's a few times. I can't say I have a real feeling for the boy. He sticks close to Pluck."

"Manners killed Ella Swell?"

Ferdy and I answer simultaneously, respectively, "No" and "Probably."

Throughout dinner I keep wondering whether King intends to acknowledge me for saving his rotund ass last evening. And whether he'll give me crap about the TV reporter. He says nothing.

\* \* \*

78

Monday, late. Terry and Preet and I sit on the stairs outside Preet's garage drinking beer, watching the goings on in the convenience store parking lot. A tall man slams the door of his vehicle, turns, and quickly approaches us across the lot. Marcus Manners.

For a moment I have the feeling he does not recognize us, that he's going to ask us to buy him some beer.

When I was Marcus's age we'd loiter in the parking lots of convenience stores, our radios blasting adolescent contempt, looking for someone to buy our booze. The best prospects were the dedicated drunks, middle-aged men or women, coming for their vodka fifths or forty-ounce brews, glad to have a few minutes of companionship.

Anyway, as I ought to remember, Marcus does not drink. Or smoke. Or do much else wrong except steal dogs from rich people. And maybe kill them.

"Hello, Marcus?"

"Hey," he says.

"You here for the nachos?" He shakes his head. "You want to talk?" He nods. The swagger isn't gone. But for the first time I can see a crack or two in the façade. "How'd you find this place?"

"Bea."

"Ah."

Preet is a big sports fan, and he perks up when I introduce Manners.

"The police are parked outside my house," Marcus says.

"Not a huge surprise, really. They have a big problem on their hands with the Swell killing. They have to look like they're doing something. Just try to ignore them."

"I wasn't dealing any drugs," Marcus says.

"They found some cocaine in the house of the woman who was killed. They figure you were up at the property and you have the pot charge, so they figure maybe the coke came from you. I'm not saying it did, but that's what's going on."

Marcus points at our lair. "Is there a computer in there?"

Preet chuckles. "You might say that."

We walk into the sweltering studio and over to Preet's workstation, a mountain of computers, monitors, and other unidentifiable hardware stretching three quarters of the way up an eleven-foot wall. Marcus pecks at a keyboard for a minute and a familiar image comes up. It's the home page of Total High, Brice Bulley's interactive high school game. Preet's unibrow arches precipitously.

Then Marcus clicks repeatedly on the Total High banner. A password screen pops up, and he types something in it. A squat animated character pops out of the bottom corner of the monitor and walks, left to right, peeling back the screen as if it were a curtain. At the top, again, is the name "Total High," but beneath it is a column of phone numbers and accompanying passwords. Call the number, provide the password, get your drugs delivered.

"The Internet is a miracle," I say. "It seems unfair that we didn't have this when we were in high school."

"This is Brice Bulley's thing?" Terry asks.

"Supposedly," Marcus answers. "I don't know him."

"Then how do you know about this?"

"If you go to school in this city, you know about it."

"You think this is where the coke in Swell's house came from?"

"I couldn't say. All I know is I didn't have anything to do with any drugs."

"You have the password."

"It's my friend's."

"But you *were* up at the house to take the dog," Terry says.

Marcus nods.

"With your friends, whose names are—" I say. Marcus smiles. "Go home. If the cops follow you, wave. The coke thing is irrelevant. Once they arrest someone for the homicide, they'll find someplace else to park. I promise."

Marcus shakes hands all around and takes off. He seems genuinely grateful. I sit against a wall, beer in hand, enjoying the moment. The kid finally realizes I'm his best friend in the world right now. He finally opened up. I *am* the man.

# 15

THE NATIONAL PRESS descends upon the Santa Rita justice system by midday Wednesday. They can be found skittering around the Hall like expensively dressed rodents.

At an afternoon press conference Detective Baptiste reports that Ella Swell was found, shot to death, at an undisclosed location on the Swell estate at about eleven the preceding Monday night. Asked whether the killing might be related to Swell's role in the 1988 slaying of an officer outside Zora Neal's, a bookstore in West Santa Rita, Baptiste declines to answer. Which, of course, means yes. Asked if Marcus Manners is a suspect in the case, Baptiste says all relevant witnesses will be questioned in short order. Which, too, means yes.

The rodents eventually figure out that I represent Manners and track me down between appearances. I blow them off for most of the day, but with the rumor mill in heavy operation, by the afternoon the chief suggests I try to defuse some of the speculation about my client's role in the homicide. Shortly before close of business on Wednesday, I walk out onto the front steps of the Hall. All I have to do is clear my throat and they come running.

"Good afternoon. My name is Gordon Seegerman. I'm with the Santa Rita Public Defender's office. I represent Marcus Manners regarding charges that he removed a dog from the Swell estate."

I try to take a busy, no-nonsense, annoyed-to-have-to-deal-with-the-media tone. But my sentences swing upward at their ends, making my assertions sound faintly like questions.

"I understand from questions put to Detective Baptiste earlier today that some of you may have the impression my client was involved in the tragic death of Ms. Swell. That is wrong. He was not. And the police have given us no reason to think Marcus is a suspect. He'll assist the investigating officers in whatever way he can. Thank you."

They want to know if he was at the estate and when, if he took the dog and why, if he was dealing drugs and to whom, if Marcus had been acquainted with Ella Swell at Hills High.

"How would he know Swell?" I ask.

Another reporter shouts out that Swell worked at the Hills High School library. I didn't know that. I try not to look stunned, ineffectively, no doubt.

Next morning I'm bouncing around departments in the Hall. This is my life, appearing in one court, setting dates, running over to another, asking for a continuance. I keep my eggs in the air. Once in a while one smacks into my head and I have no choice but to actually accomplish something—file a motion, pick a jury, examine a witness. But mostly it's a question of popping my head into each of my cases to say hello and good-bye, and hightailing it before I get roped into productivity.

At lunch I roam the halls looking for Silvie. I find her holding court in the cafeteria with a slew of buttoned-up, clean-shaven, buzz-cut prosecutors. It's a pathetic scene, really, these boys, fawning, swooning over their gorgeous colleague. None of them has a prayer.

She sees me and raises her voice.

"Hold the phone, Stone. Here's the famous criminal defense lawyer Gordon Seegerman approaching the grill station." I ignore her.

I eat alone, and when the crowd around Silvie thins out, I walk over. When I do, the last of the fawners scampers off.

Silence. I let the tension build for a moment.

"So?" She acts, but cannot actually be, clueless. I sing the first few couple of lines of "I Made It Through the Rain."

"I *said* I'd think about it."

"That's great, Sil. I guess maybe I didn't explain about the time frame. The gig is on June 4, like, this year. We have an extra ticket for Manilow's show the next night, if you want to go." And after the concert, who the hell knows? I mean, it is Vegas.

"I'm not sure. It's still complicated between us, right?"

"What's complicated?"

"There are still feelings."

Because I remain desperately in love with Silvie, I cannot help but scour every sentence that comes out of her mouth for signs that she might one day return. In this case, "there are still feelings" sounds, to me, like "I still have feelings" and not the more logical, "*You* still have feelings."

"Feelings, schmeelings." She raises her eyebrows. "Sil, the whole thing will be over in a month. A few rehearsals. We go to Vegas for the gig. We see Barry. And that's it. What's the big deal? You obviously want to do it."

I desperately, painfully, want not simply to kiss her, but to suck her entire body into my lungs. I want to stand on the table and howl, *ALL OF THIS IS TOTAL BULLSHIT. COME BACK. YOU ARE THE ONLY WOMAN I WILL EVER LOVE.* But I do not, which I consider to be a real achievement.

"I sort of do," she admits. "There's a part of me that misses it. But I really don't want there to be any misunderstanding between us."

"Totally, completely separate from the fact that I may, on very rare occasions, miss being your boyfriend, please do this. If you don't, we're screwed. We've auditioned several thousand people. None of them is you. The hole is round and all we've seen are squares. You are the circle."

"I am the circle," she says, a bit robotically. She has a resigned look on her face.

"You are definitely the circle."

"I thought Maeve was the circle."

"Maeve may some day, again, become the circle. These days she's more an irregular heptagon." I know nothing of geometry. This is Preet's crack. "Please say yes."

She says nothing. Which is not "no," so I'm immediately elated and start contemplating ways I can expand her implicit "yes" to a wedding and babies.

"I think you should know I've been seeing someone, Gordy."

This is not "no," either, but my delusions of grandeur are now not simply deflated, they are punctured and flying around the room haphazardly, making farting noises.

"You're kidding me?" She does not budge or react or say a word. "Who?" I'm furious.

"That's not the point."

"Who?"

"You're going to challenge him to a duel or something?"

"Yes."

I believe in only two things in life with absolute, unshakable conviction. One is that Barry Manilow is a musical genius. The second is that if Silvie Hernandez is *seeing* someone who is not her presently imprisoned husband, that someone should be me.

"I'm not telling you who. This is exactly what I was just talking about. You're still too involved."

"I'm not too involved. I'm just—what about Bart? You said you—"

"I'm not getting into this with you, okay?"

"Who?"

"Gordy."

"Just tell me."

"No. Anyway, I understand you've been occupied yourself lately."

"What the hell's that supposed to mean?"

For a moment I am legitimately confused. Then she puts on her TV

85

announcer voice: "You give us thirty minutes, we'll bring you the county, and the world."

I don't believe it. "Silvie—"

She pops out of her seat. "You need to start living your life."

"I'm living my life just fine."

"Good. Then we don't have a problem."

"What about the band?" I say.

"I'll think about it." Her tone softens and she says, "You sure you haven't changed your mind?"

I don't know. Maybe.

"Of course not."


There's a knock on my office door. Please let it be Duke. I'll quit. I'll tell him to take his endless list of misdemeanors and shove it. Or I'll just sock him in the stomach for no reason whatsoever. It's Detective Mick Bacon. I whistle the Popeye theme song.

"You got a minute?"

"No."

"It's about Mr. Manners."

Mick sits and crosses his feet on my desk. He has remarkably small feet. He wears off-brand black sneakers.

"You must have paid a fortune for those," I say.

"Nine eighty-nine at Cullens."

"Does Baptiste know you're here?"

"Listen, Nick says, 'Pick up the kid and bring him in for a talk.' I say, 'Let me go talk to his hotshot PD, see what we can work out.' I don't want to hurt Manners if we don't have to. The kid's got a big future."

"Mayor Pluck's freaking you out, huh?"

"Listen wise guy, you and Baptiste were busy sucking on your mama's boobies in '65." The riots. "I've seen this city go to shit. If it's possible, I'd like to avoid a big old west-side mess."

86

"Actually I was born in '69." I push my chair back and put my feet on the desk. I have relatively small feet and they are nearly twice the size of Mick's. I have no idea how the man remains upright. "So?" I say.

"I got to talk to the kid."

"About?"

He gives me a look like, come on, sonny, we both know who's the real hard-ass here.

"Swell was living in the guesthouse. Things haven't been so hot on the home front. The husband assumed she was out of town last week. All we know is she's in the house for days, probably several, before he finds her. We're working the obvious angles, but so far, when it comes to Ella Swell, we don't know a whole hell of a lot."

"And my guy is supposed to help you with that?"

"The bad news for Manners is we have his prints in the house."

"Really?"

"There's the coke at the guesthouse and your guy with the dope in his car."

"Which, if you think about it, hasn't become any more significant than it was two days ago."

"People at Hills saw them together in the past few months. She worked in the library at the school."

"Someone *saw* them together at the school?"

"Several people, actually. He's in the house, he's into the drugs. He's got the frigging dog, Gordy? We gotta talk to him. Probably it's not him. But Baptiste has his heart set on Manners. Your guy better start filling in some blanks."

"Forget it. There's nothing in it for us."

"Baptiste will go to the press, you know. He'll kill the kid with this. Manners still has to graduate. He's betting on the scholarship."

"And Pluck will answer back with more noise. And more heat down at the Hall. He'll have your boss on the phone all day with the press.

And he'll use it against Fischer all the way to the mayor's office. It's not happening, Mick. My guy has nothing to gain and everything to lose."

If the police believe you committed a crime, no matter how ardently you deny it, after questioning you, they will still believe you committed the crime. *And*, no matter what you say in the interview, they will believe that your statements prove it. Rule number one in dealing with police officers, therefore: keep quiet.

"So? What do *you* think? Is he the bad guy?" Mick says.

We both watch him twist two paperclips into a figure that looks vaguely like a dog.

"You know what?" I say. "I don't care. All they pay me to worry about is the misdos. You want to do me a favor, charge him with the homicide. I'll dump the case upstairs faster than you can suck a can of spinach through your pipe."

He stands. "We gotta problem here?"

"There's no problem. My client's not talking to you."

"Gordy, come on."

"Sorry. Just a depressing day all around."

"Girl trouble?"

"Life trouble."

"Hey," he says, smiling his crooked, teeth-apart, tongue-perched-on-his-lower-lip, I-may-be-short-and-alone-and-an-aging-detective-being-muscled-aside-by-the-new-blood-but-I-still-have-the-world-on-a-string smile. "At least you got Manilow."

# 16

**M**ANILOW. I WONDER. Sometimes I think it's had to do with Silvie all along. I mean, sure, I've been Barry X since I was a kid. The music was there for me when my mom was dying. My loyalty to Barry was born out of that horror. But I won't pretend it didn't fade a bit in my teens. I never let it go completely, but the Manilow I played in college I played on my headphones. It wasn't something I shared.

Silvie changed that. We confessed our passion for the music to one another, and then to the world. We started getting serious, about the relationship, and about performing. Then the Alzheimer's nightmare hit. I freaked, dumped her, and have been trying to find a way back into her life ever since.

Some big part of my dedication to Barry has been to impress her, to try to get her back. So if Silvie is gone for good, what's the use?

The next morning, I'm in my office, clinging with both hands to a flimsy Styrofoam cup filled with black dishwater that is endeavoring, without success, to pass for coffee. I have the cup braced against my face, the hot liquid resting against my lips, burning them slightly. I smoked half a pack of cigarettes, drank most of a six-pack, and slept three hours last night.

On my desk is a page with a crudely drawn picture of a man hanging by his neck from a gallows. By the X's in the man's eyes, I believe him to be deceased. Had the artist included spaces for letters at the bottom of the page, I might have assumed I was being invited to play the word game hangman. As it happens, the page contains the same admonishment that appeared in the prior missive. *Be careful.* Also, taped to it is a rather attractive picture of me sitting in my car in the parking lot at work. And I found the missive pinned to the gate outside my house.

The door is shut. Office etiquette says don't knock unless absolutely necessary. There is a knock. I ignore it. Another. I say nothing. It cracks open.

"Hello, Gordon." Milo Velikovic, seeming uncharacteristically dejected.

"Milo."

"I'm sorry to tell you I have to take away my offer, unfortunately."

"You're sorry to tell me you have to take away your offer, unfortunately."

"Yes."

"Okay."

"Don't blame me. I didn't want to do it."

"I don't blame you. Reasoner wasn't biting anyway."

"It's Swell."

"What does Swell have to do with anything?" I bark at him, and then instantly feel like a jerk and try to smooth over the moment. "What's the word in your office? You guys really think Manners is the shooter?"

"Fischer"—the DA—"anyway. He doesn't want to do Manners any favors, probably because of the election and everything."

Fischer narrowly lost the last mayoral contest. The guy who beat him had the courtesy to die a year later. I suppose now he's not anxious to appear too friendly to a potential homicide suspect.

"Tell me something, Milo. What do you know about Silvie Hernandez?"

"I know she's hot," he says, and gives me a wink.

"No, like who she hangs out with, who she shows up with at office dinners."

"And what's in it for me?"

"How about I'll tell you when you have food on your face, like now for instance."

He swipes at his chin and exits into the hallway. "I'll ask around."

I was the kind of lunchtime school yard kickball captain who always chose the worst kid first. I wasn't trying to make a point or be a hero. I really loved that kid. I feel kind of the same about Milo.

Two hours later, Terry's in my office with a tuna sandwich from the Hall cafeteria that smells like it was assembled around the time of Sputnik. I'm on my fifth cup of coffee. Exhaustion has been vanquished by the jitters. Maybe it's the threatening note. Maybe it's the caffeine. I'm working my way through the paper, much of which is given over to every imaginable angle on the Swell killing—no modest feat in light of the lack of actual news.

Terry launches into his canned, "Geez Gordy, don't you think it's time to get over her and move on with your life" lecture.

"How many years *has* it been?" I say, so proud of my dedication to Ms. Hernandez.

"Ten plus, right?"

"Twelve."

"Twelve years. Maybe it's time. It's not like you haven't taken an interest elsewhere along the way."

"I have?"

"Myla?"

I fell for a federal agent involved in the Harold Dunn case. We spent some time together after the trial wrapped, but she ended up with a transfer east. I quickly returned to my Silvie obsession.

"And you see how well that turned out."

"And I hear you went out with Cindi Paris from Channel 2," he says.

"Who told you that?"

"She's perfect. She has that whole—" His hands take over.

91

"Exactly. 'The whole,'" I say. "She's nice and smart and cute and not Silvie. She has never been and will never be the woman I love."

"Keep seeing Cindi."

"Will you quit that? I've never *been* seeing Cindi. I'd like to figure out who Silvie's seeing, though. And you, my friend, are the man for the job."

"What difference could it make?"

"I was thinking about this a lot last night, and it seems to me the whole *new guy* thing is just a final hurdle she's thrown up. She basically admitted she still loves me. It's a test of my commitment. It's the last leg. You know what I'm saying? You don't run a marathon and walk away in the last fifty yards. You crawl. You claw the ground with your fingernails and pull yourself to the finish line if necessary."

"Gordy, the marathon has been over for a week, and you're still in the hospital suffering from dehydration-induced delusions."

"You're not going to help me."

"No."

"Fine. You have anything useful for me?"

Terry has been off doing what Terry does—scrounging for information, working the phones, keeping his ear to the grindstone or wherever ears are best placed to hear the very latest about the very latest. He has what every masterful investigator has: the rare ability to fit into nearly any milieu, and to act like he already knows the answers to the questions he's asking, like he's just looking for confirmation.

"You want homicide or dog-napping?"

"Dog."

"Dent went to SI."

"Half of the SRPD went to SI, Terry." The school, like the force, is heavily populated with Irish and Italian Catholics.

"He played football. *And*," he pauses, "he's SIF."

"As is Jackson Bulley," I say. "Hence the red dog named Red."

"How'd you know that?"

"You think I spend my days writing poetry to Silvie? I have my sources."

"As for Dent, he got dinged by internal affairs at least once for bullshitting his way into a warrant. I've heard some other noises too, so definitely run the Pitchess."

"Reasoner will be dying to grant that, I'm sure."

"I'm still working on the kid, Brice Bulley. I can't get anything on the drug thing from my usual people, which is kind of surprising. It may be limited to the high schools, which means it wouldn't necessarily show up on their radars. Preet said he'd check around online. I still have to see the witness on the dog thing, Layne Maddox, but I'm thinking I'll wait until the Swell thing shakes out a little. The SRPD seems particularly sensitive about this one. *Now* you want to hear about the murder?"

"No."

"I should have more by Monday, but there's a tox report that says there was coke in her system when she got hit."

"We knew there was coke in the house."

"Maybe it did come from Bulley."

"Did I mention that I don't want to know any of this?"

"Swell gets eleven years on the manslaughter in '88. Her father, Stanton Swell Jr., dies in '90. Apparently most of the money goes into a charitable trust. She gets the estate and enough each year to keep her in good drugs. She gets out in '94, meets Jackson Bulley at State, and marries him in '97."

"Thrilling."

"You want to hear the best part?" His eyes light up. "She's the librarian."

"At Hills High. *That* was in the *Journal*." The local daily.

"In the game, Gordy. The librarian in Total High." It takes a minute, but then I remember. The grotesque, half-naked figure in Brice

Bulley's computer game. "If that's how he felt about his stepmother, maybe *he's* the bad guy."

"Terry. The misdos. Please. Focus on the misdos."

"What do you make of Manners?"

"It's not my job to make anything of Manners."

"Something's up there." Terry taps his head, hard, which sends his dreads bouncing. "I was watching him the other night. He's working something out. I don't know if he did Swell. But something's going on up there."

"Keep me posted on that. By the way, I may have solved our girl-singer problem."

"How?"

"Surprise."

"Give me a break—"

Speed Manners wanders into my office.

"I'm sorry to bother you." His lips are pursed, his brow furrowed, his frame is bent over—it's an indelibly sorrowful, blameworthy look, as if all the bad stuff has been somehow deserved. "If another time would be better."

"Your timing is ideal, actually." To Terry, I say, "Read this on your way out." I pull the most recent threatening note out of my desk and hand it over. "I hope the fact that I found this at my *house* will convince you of its seriousness." Staring at the page, he closes the door behind him.

"I wanted to thank you for all you've done for Marcus. I'll bet you didn't expect it to turn into such a mess."

"I haven't done anything and so far it's not that much of a mess. We'll have it cleaned up soon enough."

"I did have something about the case I wanted to say." He waits. I nod. "I understand there's a witness who claims he saw Marcus in our car near the property where the dog was taken."

"The description isn't particularly convincing, but there is a witness."

"I had the car that night, the 26th."

"The whole night?"

"I didn't get home until past twelve."

Probably he's lying. Probably he's doing what he thinks a father should do. The kid says he took the dog. I really don't have a reason to doubt him.

"I'm still hopeful we won't have to go to trial, but if we do, that will help. He's quite impressive, your son. You must be very proud."

"Since Grace died, I haven't been much use to him. I've had my own problems. Marcus lived with the Plucks for years. It wasn't until a couple of years ago that he moved back in with me."

"The athletic ability must have come from somewhere."

He chuckles. "Yeah, well, I was a sprinter. There wasn't a whole lot of money in running fast in those days. Truth is, for a long time the coaches and Jerry, they've been the real parents. I tried to stay out of the way."

"You have a pretty good relationship with the councilman?"

"I was a total loss back then. Stuck on the pipe. Marcus was headed for the foster system and then, man, who knows. Jerry was there. I gotta give him that." Speed is silent for a moment. "They think Marcus killed Ella Swell?"

"I don't think they have a coherent theory, or any concrete evidence, but he may well be on what I expect is a very long list."

"You know Swell worked at Hills?"

I nod. "Did you know her?"

"Years ago. She and Grace were friends."

My cell rings.

# 17

IT'S CINDI PARIS.

"It's a client call," I tell Speed. "Could I have a minute?"

He closes the door behind him.

"You sound like hell," she says. "Are you sick?"

"I had a rough night."

"Getting jiggy with your brother."

"Something like that."

"I thought you'd want to know, the police just picked up Marcus Manners."

Shit.

"Where?"

"At his house."

"Do you know what the story is?" I say.

"No. I'm on my way downtown."

I toss my coffee into the trash, fly out of my office, and nearly smack into Speed. He follows, up a flight of stairs, across the courtyard, through the Hall, down the front steps, north half a block, to SRPD headquarters. Pluck is already outside, as is a camera crew; a second when Cindi shows. They are on top of us.

"Give us a moment, please," Pluck says, holding off the press. He is unruffled.

"What's happening?" I say.

"One of the neighbors called. She said a couple of police cars were over at the house. While we were on the phone, they left with Marcus."

We walk inside and inquire. A cop disappears for a couple of minutes and says he's having trouble tracking down the detectives. He asks us to wait.

We're being played, no doubt. The more time they have with Marcus alone, the more likely he is to say something, to answer a loaded question or make an incriminating statement, out of anger or frustration. They shouldn't be questioning him. I was clear with Mick. But they have more to gain by trying to elicit the information than the misconduct will cost them in court. The most I can do is get the statements excluded. They can use the information to develop other leads.

What was I just saying? If you have even the slightest reason to believe the cops think you did something illegal, whether or not you actually did, don't talk to them. They are not your friends.

After another several minutes we learn that Manners was taken to a satellite station fifteen minutes away. That station is further from his residence than the SRPD's main office, but Baptiste would have guessed we'd hear about the detention, or arrest, or whatever it is, and descend on headquarters. Pluck and Speed and I rush over to Pluck's car—a brand-spanking black Mercedes, I can hardly help noticing—and take off.

The press vehicles follow. It's kind of exciting, actually, like a motorcade—the Benz followed closely by the satellite vans. When we reach the station in north Santa Rita, Pluck dumps me before parking. I run inside, my heart pounding, and demand to see my guy. They are prepared for us. "Take a seat," the desk officer tells me. "I'll tell the detectives the cavalry has arrived."

A few minutes later Detective Nick Baptiste strolls into the lobby. My first thought is, *Holy shit, it's the guy from United Airlines.*

A while ago, United started doing its preflight introduction and safety thing on video. A skinny white dude with an intensely annoying, shit-eating grin comes on and says, "Welcome. By now you've stowed your bags," and so on. Anyway, Baptiste is that guy. Not a look-alike. He is the actual person on that video. I'm sure of it. I'm so blown away that for a minute I forget why I'm there at all.

"I don't think we've met," he says.

Oh, believe me, pal, we've met.

"Gordon Seegerman. I have the impression you're hiding my client somewhere around here."

"Mr. Manners mentioned you."

United guy hands me some papers. Court orders: for blood, hair samples, a cheek swab. And for photos of the kid's body.

"We would have produced him," I say.

"Listen, Mr. See—"

"He's represented, Detective. If you want my client, you call *me*."

Mick Bacon steps in.

"Gordy, what are you making a fuss about?"

The room is filling up. Speed and Pluck stand a few steps away. Others, reporters, rubberneckers, gather around. We step back into the police offices beyond the lobby.

I turn to Mick. "I was pretty clear Marcus wasn't interested in talking."

Baptiste says, "He's been cooperative without being the slightest bit helpful. I'm sure we have you to thank for that."

"I told him the guys with the badges aren't as nice as they seem to be on TV."

"You know, you might do your client a favor and check the attitude," Baptiste says. "We don't know who did Swell. Personally I hope it wasn't Manners. But I don't see what he has to gain by saying nothing. There's no way around he's in the guesthouse, and he's there recently. We have them together repeatedly at the school. There's more, too, Seegerman. A lot more. But I'm not in the mood to share. You want to play lawyer, that's fine. We have enough to file yesterday. But we don't want to look like assholes and ruin this kid's life if there's something we're missing."

"*And* you don't want to spend the summer in riot gear over in West Santa Rita."

Baptiste aims an incredulous look at Bacon. Then he returns to me. "You oughta see the pictures, Counselor. Someone blew this woman apart. If Marcus Manners is the guy, let 'em burn the fucking city. He's going down." Baptiste strolls off.

"Straight as an arrow, that guy," Mick says. "And Manners has a nice big bull's-eye painted on his ass."

"I'll keep that in mind," I say. "Am I missing something?"

"Like the man said, Gordy, if you want inside, you gotta have a ticket."

"I'm trying to do my job."

"So am I. If he's the guy, fine, we bust him. But, please, don't come in a week after we finish putting out the fires and tell us he was in Florida when Swell got hit."

"I hear you."

Mick lowers his voice. "I don't need him on tape. Just get what you can get and get it to me before this thing gets out of hand."

"So what else is there?" He gives me a dirty look. "Mick, I'm going to have to be very nervous before I beat up my client to get him to start working for you."

He looks past me and lowers his voice. "We got a witness who sees them go into the house. Together. He hears Manners yell her name. And he hears shots."

"That's all?"

"We got blood, Gordy. On the kid's shoes. Her blood."

Okay, fine, now I'm very nervous.

"I'll talk to him."

"Talk to him."

"Did I not just say I'd talk to him? Jesus."

My client finally emerges. He does not look particularly shaken by the detention and hair plucking and blood taking. At least not compared to how I must appear after hearing that the SRPD has more than enough evidence to bust Marcus Manners for the Swell killing, and send my fair city into paroxysms.

We gather in a tight circle on the sidewalk outside the station. Marcus reports that the police took close-up photographs of his bare torso. I have no idea what this is about, but the pictures aren't likely intended for *Sports Illustrated*. The press hovers around us waiting for a statement. A shiny green Honda del Sol wings past the building, screeches through a U-turn, and parks. It's Lucy Pluck. She jogs over to us and wraps herself around Marcus. She diverts our attention for a few moments while she covers Marcus's face with kisses.

The teen-romance moment concluded, I whisper, "This is what we call fishing with all of your poles. They can't arrest Marcus, but they can fairly easily convince one of their friends on the bench to sign a warrant for samples."

"They must have some reason to believe he was involved," Speed says.

"They think he was up on the property to take the dog sometime around when Swell was shot," I say. "That's enough to get the court order. You want me to make a statement?"

Pluck doesn't bother to turn me down. He steps out of our circle and addresses the cameras. I stand alongside, with a grave look on my face. I lock eyes with Cindi Paris and raise my eyebrows. She wiggles hers up and down while Pluck goes on.

Afterward, I peel Marcus away from Lucy as we head for our cars and tell him to come up to the house Sunday afternoon. It's Ferdy's birthday barbecue. Pluck and Bea will be there. I don't leave him room to say no.

# 18

"**Y**OU DOG." Terry grins like a stoned man and sways like a disoriented rabbi from side to side in the doorway to my office. The man is like a shark, in constant motion.

"Yeah, well, you know how it is." I have no idea *what* it is, let alone *how* it is.

"My guess is Silvie's going with us to Vegas."

I screw up my face. "Are you insane? Absolutely not."

He sticks his right index finger in midair. "She knows the tunes. And I know the way you think. You bring her in to sing, you get close, so forth, so on."

"Believe me, that's the last thing I need to deal with."

"Then who?"

"You'll find out when I firm it up. Believe me, it's not Silvie. Speaking of which, any movement on the boyfriend ID?"

"I told you I'm not getting into that."

"That's not what you told me. What you told me is you thought I should let it go, that it's been long enough, that she's a ghost, that I'm telling myself stories. I remember this crap, you know."

"I'm still not putting a tail on a deputy DA."

"Why not?"

"You worried about the letter?"

"You're the man with the street cred. You think I need to go out and buy a Hummer?"

"Probably some SIF crazy with too much time on his hands. If it escalates let me know."

"Meaning?"

"I don't know, car bomb, that sort of thing. Where were you before?"

I'm stunned, but only slightly. "Working."

I fill him in on developments.

"They're close, but they must be missing something big," he opines. "I haven't heard anything about a motive."

"Mick said something about Swell killing Manners's mother. That make any sense?" I say.

"No, but I wasn't really paying attention when that whole thing went down."

"Speed said Ella Swell and Grace Manners were friends. All Ferdy told me was Grace Manners had a bookstore. Apparently Pluck was involved, too."

"What was I, fifteen?"

"Seems like just yesterday, huh?"

"Actually, yes," Terry says.

"Ferdy also said my dad had something to do with it."

"You could give it a try."

"No, actually, I couldn't."

The problem isn't that I'd get nothing. I might get a lot. But I'd have no idea whether I could rely on it.

"I'll get Preet to pull up whatever the *Journal* has."

"What's the point? Mick gave up a lot, and I doubt he gave up everything. Which means they already have Manners boxed. Even without a strong motive theory, he's busted unless he can come up with a mighty good reason Ella Swell's blood is on his Nikes."

"So she had a nose bleed."

"On his shoes."

"What's the connection to the dog thing?"

"None as far as I know."

"Maybe Manners is good for both? Shoots the lady, grabs the dog," Terry says, acting out the scene. "Do they have the killing pinned to the night with the dog?"

"I'm sure this will surprise you, but I haven't seen the murder book. The thing I can't figure out is why they don't just arrest him."

"I'm sure they're just worried about the troops out west. Things are already pretty active outside the Hall these days."

"That seems to be Mick's concern. I suppose Fischer may be trying to push it past the election."

"Swell was coked up, right?"

"So you've told me."

"So maybe she's got a habit and she hears around Hills Manners is dealing. He hooks her up and then for some reason she threatens to snitch him off, so he shoots her, and he figures he'll take the dog too."

"A misdemeanor of opportunity?"

"Why make an extra trip?"

"Exactly."

I sit in the last row of the gallery in Department 9 at the Hall. Silvie is arguing a motion in a robbery case. I can see only her luminous, black-coffee-colored tresses and her lean hands, clutching the edges of the podium. And I can hear her raspy voice while she makes mincemeat of a crumpled old defense lawyer who appeals to the judge's frat boy mentality by calling her *Miss* Hernandez and suggesting by his tone that no one this beautiful ought to be trusted. I hate them all—the judge who leers at her from the bench, the defendant who keeps checking out Silvie's perfect rear, a deputy sheriff who looks about to nod off, but must anyway be harboring indecent thoughts about my ex.

If I'm straight with myself for ten seconds, it's obvious Terry's right, that I hang on to Silvie to fulfill some unidentified neurotic need, and not because there's any realistic chance of a reunion. She—at least the she who once was my girlfriend—*is* a ghost. I suppose if I found the right person, Silvie's hold on me might fade. I suppose I hold on to her to avoid finding the right person, or something equally twisted.

Playing with her again, using Barry to try to rekindle the romance in her, seemed like a good idea a week ago. Now I don't know. I don't relish the reminder that she's off with yet another person who isn't me. But she seems to need it now, and the last thing I want to do is stand between a woman and her Manilow.

When I arrive at Preet's for rehearsal at eight that night, Maeve O'Connell is in attendance, sort of. Aineen now has her mother under twenty-four-hour watch, so our fourth won't be joining us bodily until sometime after the parasite emerges. But Maeve does not intend to be left out, and so has pressed Preet into setting up a remote communications system. Two small video rigs descend from the ceiling and, through some minor miracle of bandwidth, transmit our doings across town.

"Are we live?" I whisper to Preet, pointing at the camera. He nods. "She sees and hears all. Like God."

It's a nightmare. I expect Silvie in an hour. And Maeve can't stand my ex. It's partly to do with Silvie's easy beauty and her professional success and her sophistication. But I think Maeve mostly dislikes Silvie because she loves me. She has watched me run into the same wall over and over and over again and, finally, has come to blame the wall.

"I heard that, Gordy," Maeve's voice booms across the studio like the announcer at a rock concert. Preet, being Preet, isn't satisfied with a simple speakerphone. He has Maeve routed through our amps "Y'all trying to hide something?"

"It's just weird not to be able to see you, too," I say, not sure whether to answer to the camera or at the drawl emitting from the speakers.

"Get used to it. Anyway I look like day-old dog shit."

"Ah, yes, but you're all caught up on your daytime television."

"People are fucking idiots. Now you're caught up, too."

"So, I understand you have a solution for Vegas?" Preet says.

"What solution?" Maeve squawks.

"Are we going to practice?" I say. Terry and Preet stare at me. And so does Maeve; I can feel her eyes on me. "Maybe. That's all I'm saying."

All at once they say, "Bullshit."

I sit down at the piano and pound out the first chords to "Could It Be Magic," which is based on a Chopin prelude. They head for their instruments. And, finally, we play. Most Manilow songs we unravel one way or another—often they end up nearly unrecognizable. But not "Magic." It insists on unerring fidelity. Who are we to mess with perfection?

An hour later Maeve seems to have fallen asleep. Between songs we can hear soft, rhythmic breathing and an occasional snort. I walk over to Preet and indicate, without daring to express aloud, that I'd like him to pull the plug on the remote hookup. He walks to his desk and, gingerly, flips a few switches.

"Good?" I whisper. He nods. "My friend is coming in a few minutes and it might be better if she didn't immediately have to deal with O'Connell."

"And you're sure your friend isn't Silvie?" Terry says.

"You propose to have Silvie fill in for Vegas?" The usually imperturbable Preet is now, momentarily, perturbed.

"It's not Silvie. I don't know how much clearer I can be. Not Silvie. Not Silvie. Not Silvie."

Silvie Hernandez walks through the open door two minutes later.

Tense handshakes all around. I'm ready for the stunned silence and the out-of-the-corner-of-their-eyes glances.

We chat for a while, describe the plan for the gig, let her take a look at the arrangements. Then, we jam. Preet fills in on the drums for "It's

106

a Miracle," our blockbuster opening number, Silvie stands next to me at the piano. When she opens her mouth, I fall in love all over again.

She is brilliant. Her body arches, her eyes roll halfway back into their sockets, and for the length of the tune she's inside it. My loyalty to Maeve is absolute; she is the fourth Mandy. But it's impossible not to wonder whether Silvie Hernandez might be the best natural Manilow tribute singer on the planet.

In the middle of "Through the Rain" my cell phone rings. "Maeve," I report to the others. Terry and Preet go pale. Thrilled by Silvie's performance, the ease with which she slipped into the mix, we'd forgotten the pregnant one.

Silvie is briefly confused, and then quickly briefed.

"You want me to hook her in again?" Preet says. I shake my head and let my mobile ring out. But she's onto us, and calls every line in the room before we relent and return her to her exalted, all-seeing place.

When we're finally live, I say, "We were just trying to get you hooked back up."

"Bullshit. What's going on?"

"You fell asleep. We were trying not to disturb you."

"I did not fall asleep, neither." She is becoming increasingly agitated and now, fearing Aineen's wrath even more than Maeve's, I cut in.

"You know Silvie Hernandez, right?"

Silvie ducks into the line of one of the cameras, smiles, and waves.

"What the fuck is she doing over there?" There is silence for several seconds. I see Terry back into a wall, bracing himself. "Gordon."

"Yes, Maeve."

"I believe y'all are trying to kill my unborn child?"

For some reason this strikes me as funny and I begin to laugh. No one else follows.

"I should go," Silvie says. Before I can utter a word, she is out the door. I chase after her into the parking lot.

"You were fantastic, seriously. It has nothing to do with you. She's just unhappy about her situation. We'll deal with it."

"Either way is fine. I had fun," she steps in and hugs me, which is the first time our bodies have been in close contact in years. The effect is part agony and ecstasy, with the latter prevailing by a nose.

Before I reenter the studio, I can hear Maeve's harangue. I take a deep breath and walk in.

"Maeve," I yell, cutting her off. "Listen and don't interrupt. She knows the material, she sounds good, and she's the right fit. I'm not asking you to be happy about it. And I admit it's going to be tough for me. You know how I feel about her. That hasn't changed. But I'm doing my best to put that aside for a few weeks. Manilow. That's the goal. Putting on the best show we can in Vegas, and reaching Barry."

"Now *you* listen, you piece of shit. I've been hearing you whine for—what? Hold on a second." Maeve is now conversing with someone else, Aineen probably, who has heard her yelling and insists that she end the conversation. A struggle for the headset and microphone ensues, which, mercifully, Maeve loses. She is gone.

We stand, staring at one another.

"That was fun," Terry says.

"I'm not wrong, though. Silvie's the one."

They sneak glances at the video cameras, and then nod.

108

# 19

BELIEVE ME. If I make it to ninety—hell, if I make it to sixty with my brain even halfway intact—you'll find me sitting under a palm tree somewhere sipping a frozen rum drink, watching the waves, telling my life story to anyone who'll listen or no one at all.

Ferdy has a different view of things. We—he and I and King and S., the Seegerman men, such as they are—stand around the cluttered back patio at 4200 Candlewood with Bea and some of her family and a few of Ferdy's pals. Marcus Manners and his posse, the Plucks and Speed, are here. Some folks from the neighborhood have wandered over to make sure the plumes of black smoke rising from the yard are not the start of the Great Santa Rita Fire. It's Ferdy's birthday barbecue.

"You kill a rich woman, watch out." Ferdy swings around the word "watch" like a whip he's deciding where to crack.

With the exception of the neighbors, who generally keep their distance, this is a crowd that knows not to get in my grandfather's way when he's on a tear. They know he's had a trying nine decades: a wife and child lost in the forties, grandsons without a mother, a son with Alzheimer's. So they give him room to rant. And they don't contradict him when his lecture wanders off into the land of the totally made up. On his gravestone you will find the following inscription: *Howard "Ferdy" Seegerman. Beloved father and grandfather, often wrong, but never in doubt.*

Ferdy's preaching to the choir, but he seems not to notice the absence of an opposing view. He addresses his remarks to Pluck, but he intends them for the crowd.

"This isn't about Swell. And this isn't about Marcus. I'll tell you exactly what this is about. It's about payback. This is about the Santa Rita police not being satisfied with their pound of flesh. They want ten pounds."

"That's right," Bea and several others mumble.

"I'm old, people, and *I* remember '88 like it was the day before last. You better believe the SRPD remembers. Those boys have been waiting fourteen years for this chance."

Actually, it's sixteen years, but there's no way I'm going to be the one to point that out. I try to ask around about drinks and food orders, but Ferdy jumps right back in.

"You won't hear me say Swell had it coming. I'll tell you this, though. Where I'm from, a rat is a rat. Rich, poor, black, white, green, you don't rat out your friends. You don't even rat out your enemies. You keep your mouth shut, and if that means you take a beating, then you take a beating. If you rat, you got what's coming," he says, thus contradicting his very recent promise to avoid suggesting that Ella Swell deserved to be shot.

Marcus does not appear to be moved by Ferdy's speech. He loiters by the grill watching King cook. They talk sports. Lucy sticks by her father for most of the evening. Pluck keeps his arm draped over her and whispers to her on occasion. With his head to her ear, she nods or breaks into a big grin. She has excruciatingly white teeth.

We eat steaks, and salads and corn and fresh bread supplied by Bea and her progeny. There is a cake and the singing of "Happy Birthday," which my fundamentally shy grandfather attempts to cut short at several points. Then, past nine o'clock, with the sun finally down and the faces of the revelers half aglow in columns of light emanating from cobweb-encrusted spotlights attached to the house, I decide enough is enough. Someone better say something nice about Ferdy or the old bugger is going to spend the next ninety years in a really bad mood.

"I've only known Ferdy Seegerman for about thirty-five years." The chatter ceases. All eyes come my way. "A lot less than some of you. But as he's my grandfather, I think I'm in a good position to say a few words about him."

I glance at Ferdy. He's damn pleased. He stares down at the patio, two hands braced on a metal cane he doesn't really need but likes to use for effect. A couple of times he shakes his head in disbelief when I bring up a forgotten episode. When I'm through, the crowd claps and waits for him to speak. But he does not, cannot. He says, "Thank you, thank you all for coming." And that is it. He hugs me and thanks me, whispering in my ear, "You're a good boy, Gordy."

Later, I go inside to fetch some beer and find the statuesque Lucy Pluck washing dishes in our sink. I insist that she desist. She refuses, so I sit at our badly chipped, round, white Formica table. She says nothing, but she turns around and smiles at me a couple of times.

"I hear you're off with Marcus to Colorado in the fall."

"Mmm hmm," she says. "I'm not looking forward to the cold."

"You ski?"

She laughs. "*Water* ski maybe."

"You should have gone to L.A."

She stares at her reflection in a large yellow dinner plate and says, "I told him, 'M., please, someplace warm.'" She turns to me. "You ever try to convince Marcus Manners of anything?"

"How long have you two been together?"

"We've always been together." She's eighteen, and she speaks with the conviction of an old woman. "You know we grew up in the same house?"

"I heard that."

"His father was on crack. He got off the drugs and now he's an alcoholic. Some people are just like that."

"I suppose that's right."

"It all worked out for the best, though. Marcus learned a lot from my father. I doubt he would have achieved so much as a quarterback if he hadn't lived with us."

"I'll have to take your word for that. I've never been much of a football fan. All those hairy, sweaty men piling on top of each other— never really appealed to me."

She does not react. Perhaps the sound of the water drowns me out. She vigorously scrubs a plate, looking out at the partyers on the patio.

"I don't have anything against Speed." She turns and smiles only half-apologetically. "Like my father says, God has his plan."

# 20

**W**HEN THE CROWD starts to thin out I grab Marcus for a walk around the neighborhood.

"I heard you used to live around here?" I say. He's in a nodding mood tonight. "I've been up here my whole life. The thing about the hills that always amazes me is how rich people still mess up their lives. Seems like they ought to be able to manage better than other people."

My homily does nothing for Marcus. He breathes deeply though his nose, apparently enjoying the warm night air and the smell of the towering maple trees that line the streets.

"Take Ella Swell, for example. Lots of money. All the privileges. Ends up in prison and getting herself shot before the age of forty."

I wait for some kind of reaction. There is none.

"Here's the thing, Marcus. As much as I enjoy listening to my grandfather going on about the cops, you and I both know the shit is about to hit the fan." I stop. He takes a couple of additional steps, but does not turn to face me. "One of the detectives on the Swell case is an old friend of my dad's. He's given me enough to convince me you're at least a highly relevant witness. If half the stuff he's telling me is true, and I think it probably is, you're not just *a* suspect, you're *the* suspect. And the only reason you're not face down on a bunk in lockup right now is because you're Marcus Manners, and the cops and the DA know this is one they'd better not screw up."

Still nothing. He's in front of me and turns, looking over my head at

113

the shimmering Santa Rita skyline, maybe thinking this view, from the hills, shortly won't be within his reach.

"People saw you with Swell at school. Your prints are in the guesthouse where she was staying. And someone who was up at the estate says he saw you and Swell go into the house together last week. The same someone says he heard you yelling Swell's name and then heard shots. My friend says they found some of Swell's blood on your shoes.

"If there's something I should know about any of this, it's time to speak up."

He says nothing. I figure that's it. He's the guy. That's his answer.

We walk in silence for another few minutes. I think of the repercussions, the trial, the sentencing hearing at which a judge sends high school All-American Marcus Manners off to spend the rest of his life in prison. I'm not sure Santa Rita can handle it.

A late-model BMW sedan turns the corner and drives by us. Half a block later it screeches to a stop. It backs up and parks, in the middle of the street. A few moments later four men surround us. My attention shifts between them. One is short and thin. One is short and fat. One looks fit, with a close buzz cut. The fourth, who looks like he might once have been a lineman, is wearing a hat, a red, terry, floppy job. Otherwise they share a sort of uniform: khaki shorts, belt, sneakers, polo shirt. They seem grown up to me, like they might be dentists or investment bankers or something. The short, thin one is missing a pinky, or maybe it's just curled into his palm.

The one with the hat quickly emerges as the leader. He puts his nose against Manners's nose and looks like he's either going to kiss or head-butt the kid. Instead he insults him, calls him a punk, spews racial epithets not worth repeating. He doesn't seem to have a particular agenda, though his tone is menacing enough.

Marcus hardly reacts. He doesn't say a word.

The leader orders another to hold Marcus's arms. Manners, seemingly resigned to the beating, does not struggle. I try to grab the leader's shoulder. He backhands me and sends me to the ground. "Be careful, *Seegerman*." I decide to stay there for the time being. The hatted one pummels Manners in the midsection. They release him and he drops to the street.

They walk unhurriedly to their car and drive off. There isn't enough ambient light for me to catch the license plate.

I get up and help Marcus to his feet. I'm perspiring heavily. I may be on the verge of a coronary.

"You okay?" I say.

"Yeah."

I dig in my pants for my phone.

"What are you doing?" Marcus asks.

"I'm calling the fucking cops."

He says, "Don't," but gently. It's an appeal, not an order.

"I was just held hostage." He shrugs. "Jesus, Marcus. People can't go around beating the crap out of other people. Is this about the dog?"

"Ella told me all this was going to happen."

"That you would be assaulted during a stroll with your lawyer?"

"No."

"What then? She knew someone was going to shoot her?"

He nods. "That and she said the cops would come after me. Because of my mom."

"When did she say all that?"

"I had some problems in one class and my guidance counselor hooked me up with her. I knew who she was, that she knew my parents. I went over to the library and we talked about whatever book we were reading in the class. She helped me with my papers. It wasn't a big thing. That was in the fall, during the season. After I didn't see her much. Then, like around March, she caught me after school one day and asked me did I want to go talk."

"She had something on her mind?"

"She wanted to tell me all about Grace and everything. I guess they were pretty close. Ella told me a lot."

"Like?"

"Just about the store. How it started and all my mother did over on the west side."

It doesn't appear to be a relief to him, finally letting some of it out. But the discussion doesn't upset him either. His bearing is the same as when he was standing with King, discussing the upcoming college football season, steak-smoke wafting into his face. He is unruffled.

"We hung out a few times. I didn't see her for a while. Then, like a couple of weeks ago, she called. She said she wanted to talk. She sounded kind of upset. She told me, like I was telling you, she was afraid. She said she wanted me to know the truth about what happened with my mom. She called me from her car. She wanted me to go with her to the house so she could give me something she wrote. She was planning on giving it to the newspaper. But she wanted me to see it first. So I went up there with her."

"When was that?"

"Tuesday before I got arrested."

"Tuesday. Night?"

"Yeah. Like ten, probably."

"The witness in the dog case has you parked on the side of the road near the Swell estate on *Monday* night."

"That wasn't me."

"You're sure?"

"Yeah."

"But you *were* at the house, for the dog."

"I'm telling you it wasn't me. My car wasn't up there. My dad had the Honda that night."

"He told me that."

"You talked to Speed?" There is a tinge of anxiety in the question.

"Is that a problem? He just wanted to tell me about the car."

"Whatever."

"So she picked you up at your house?"

"We drove up to her place. We went inside. I was there, like, five minutes. She asked me to walk over to the pool house where they have a refrigerator. She wanted me to get some beer. When I was up there I heard shots. I ran down and I saw her. Then I walked home."

"Didn't occur to you to call the police."

He shrugs. Black kid, fancy neighborhood, rich lady with holes in her. Not an entirely irrational response.

We stroll for a minute more.

"I know we've been through this before, but what about the coke?"

"That's bullshit." He is momentarily agitated. "I never gave her any drugs."

"Did she seem like she might have been using drugs?"

"I can't really say."

"Was that night the first time you were up there?"

"I was over once before. I helped her move some stuff from the main house."

"You think anyone saw you then?"

He shakes his head. "I doubt it."

"Tuesday night. She picks you up. You drive up to the estate together. You don't see anyone." No. "You're there a short time. She says get beer. You go to get beer. How far is the pool house?"

"Pretty far. A few hundred yards at least." If nothing else, the kid knows his yardage.

"You get the beer and hear the shots on your way back?"

He thinks for a moment. "I think I had the beer when I ran down, but I'm really not sure."

The hallmark of someone telling the truth about past traumatic events: some of the particulars are lost. Too much detail and you know the person's lying, or at least filling in the blanks.

"How many shots?"

"At least a couple. I can't say exactly."

"Was the front door open?"

"You mean when I got back?"

"Yeah."

"No." His brows tighten; he's picturing it. "There are sliding glass doors in the back of the house. They were open."

"Before you left for beer?"

"I think so. I know they were open when I got back."

"She's lying on the ground?"

"On a couch in the living room."

"How'd you know she was dead? Did you touch her?"

"No. She wasn't moving."

"Did you walk around where she was?"

"I don't remember. I wasn't there too long."

"Did you move her?" No. "Did you say her name, to see if she was alive?"

"I don't know."

"That's important, Marcus. Think about it." He still can't say.

I like this guy. I don't want him to go to jail for the rest of his life. I half believe what he is telling me. I half know there's more to it, and that some of it may not reflect well on him.

"She said she had something to give you. Something she was writing. Where's that?"

"I don't know."

"So who did it, Marcus? Who was she scared of? The husband?"

"I guess he was pretty upset when she moved out. But she didn't seem scared of him."

"She talked to you about him?"

"Yeah."

"What about the kid? Could it have had to do with the drug thing?"

"I doubt it. She liked him more than the husband. He was helping her with her computer."

"So who? She must have given you some clue."

We reach my driveway. Or I do. He stops fifteen feet back. I turn around. We stand there, silent, for thirty seconds before I realize he's waiting for something. He can't say it, maybe isn't even quite sure what it is. I do, though.

"Have you talked to Pluck or your father about any of this?" He shakes his head. "That's good. Don't. Don't talk to anyone." A long pause. "I'm not a cop, Marcus. The truth? Who done it? All that? That's not what I get paid to worry about. That's the cops' problem. My job is to poke holes in things.

"Like you and your friends took the dog. And let's just say it *was* your dope. Personally, I don't give a rat's ass. My job is to get you the best deal I can. This situation with Swell, though, it's something different. Anyway, I'll talk to my friend, see if I can get them to put the brakes on. Maybe he'll have an idea of what do with all of this."

He wants my help. For reasons that are totally beyond me, it isn't Pluck or Speed or the police or his teammates he trusts. It's me. God, or someone, better help this kid, and soon, because if I'm his best hope, he's in deep trouble.

"You sure you don't want to call the cops?" I say. "Those guys might have fun in lockup for a few hours?"

"I'm sure."

# 21

"**H**ARD TO BELIEVE, HUH?" King slurs. "Ninety years old and still the biggest mouth in the room."

An hour later the crowd's departed. I'm out back tossing trash into an enormous plastic bin. King, well into his second six-pack, watches me and offers just this sort of dazzling commentary. Under other circumstances I'd insist that he pitch in, but the risk of him crashing to the ground and me spending the next fifteen hours in the emergency room waiting for some medical student to stitch him up seems sufficiently great that I don't bother.

"He seemed like he was having fun," I say.

"He should be. With all his admirers"—the word trips around his mouth several times before finally emerging—"around. I've never heard so much bullshit in my life."

King's allegiance was always to my dad, to the cops. He assumed he'd end up on the force and went in another direction only after Pop got forced out of the SRPD under less-than-honorable circumstances. King holds his tongue while our granddad spouts his left-leaning conspiracy theories. Rather than letting out the frustration and bitterness—at the way life has disappointed him, at his hero's cognitive demise—he drowns it in booze and buries it in calories. But now, alone with me, he can't help himself.

"What do you think? You think the police go around framing people and making up evidence for fun?"

Sotto voce I say, "Not *just* for fun."

"Huh?"

"You looked to be getting along well with Marcus."

"He seems all right to me. But if he killed that woman, he should go to jail."

"Fair enough."

I clean in merciful silence for several minutes. He continues to drink.

"So, what, you're poking that TV reporter?"

"Absolutely."

"That's a relief. It's about time you stopped chasing Silvie." Apparently uncertain that he'd actually uttered the last sentence, he repeats it.

"You don't think she's worth chasing?"

"That's not what I'm saying. You gotta know when to give up, though." He makes two fists and swipes them across his body, one after the other, seeming to intend a boxing move. Instead, he looks, and, by the way, smells, like a wino swatting flies. Then he sings, "You gotta know when to hold 'em, know when to fold 'em—"

"I think I've got the idea, King."

"Now all you gotta do is get tested and you'll be all grown up."

I've had it and head for the house. From the steps I say, "Just like you, you fat, alcoholic, worthless piece of shit."

"What?" he mumbles.

I turn to face him. "I *said*, I've been thinking about it."

Later Ferdy and I are inside cleaning. Terry walks into the kitchen from the back patio.

"Only five hours late," I say.

"Your brother is sleeping on the ground outside."

"I'll get him." Ferdy leaves.

"So?" I say.

"So, let's go for a ride."

I toss a grease-laden dishrag into the sink and grab a hunk of cold steak.

"Any place but here."

"Where to?" I say.

"To see a guy who might have something for us on Manners. Might be nothing. Might be something. Either way it's going to cost."

"Who?"

"Why else would I bring *you* along?"

I fill him in on my conversation with Marcus, which, now that I think about it, was very weird.

The kid has to be full of it. Why not go to the cops? Explain what happened. It's not that complicated. If I really thought Manners had told me everything, I'd probably let Mick have at him. But something else is going on. Something to do with the drugs no doubt.

"And why me? Pluck's practically the kid's father for crying out loud. He's the reason Marcus isn't down already. What can *I* do?"

We drive in silence for a few minutes. I say nothing of the assault. A couple of threatening notes and a bar fight are one thing. Now it occurs to me the earlier warnings and this attack may have something to do with the Swell killing. I'd like to figure out how before Terry pops his top over it.

"You did a pretty good job on Maeve on Friday," he says.

"Excuse me? *I*, as opposed to *we*?"

"I didn't ask Silvie to be in the band."

"She's not in the band, Terry. She's filling in for Vegas. You seemed pretty pleased with her until Maeve showed up." I frame the last two words in finger quotes. "I'm getting tired of her trying to control everything from her sickbed. I'm not the one who got her pregnant."

"No?"

"No," I say, disgusted.

"That was a joke."

122

"I'm aware of that."

"She feels left out, that's all," Terry says. "She'll get over it. You could be a little nicer to her."

"No I couldn't. Anyway, how am I not nice?"

We pull up a block short of a bar in West Santa Rita called Shortz. Three things should be said about this establishment. First, it is a bar that attracts a uniformly African American crowd. White people do not go to Shortz.

Second, it was the site of one of the most notorious crimes in this county in the last twenty years. Long story short, drug dealers mad at other drug dealers shoot up the place and kill a bunch of people. Shortz has not shed its reputation as the place to be if you're in the mood to be gunned down by angry gangsters.

Finally, the bar is owned and operated by a very old, very short man called, appropriately, Shortz, who is a bit of a legend in our city for no reason other than that he has owned this bar for more than fifty years, and has managed to stay alive.

I give Terry a confused look.

"Come on. All you have to do is act black," he says, a half-smile on his face. "On second thought, wait here. I'll go get him."

Which is no less terrifying: alone on a hot summer night, in Terry's gleaming, mint green, 1968 Mercedes convertible, the top down. The word *target* might as well be flashing in neon on my forehead.

In several minutes Terry emerges and says the guy, Eugene, won't leave the bar. My options are to give Terry all my money and wait in the car for God knows how long, or to brave Shortz.

I follow Terry inside. Because he is a gorgeous man—a beefy, nattily attired stunner with long dreadlocks and a lissome gait, the sort of guy women whistle at from limousines—he sucks up most of the attention as we make our way through the long room to the end of the bar. When we reach Terry's pal, we park on stools to his right. I'm at the end. I don't dare look around, but I'm surprised, disappointed almost,

123

to notice, in the mirror behind the bar, that no one is looking at me. No one cares enough to glower. At Shortz, I'm not white. At Shortz, I'm invisible.

Eugene stinks, mostly of cigarettes, but also of booze and body odor. He's fifty or so. He has a ponytail. Dense pockmarks crumple his cheeks. He wears a paper-thin red silk dress shirt, black slacks, and leather sandals. His extraordinarily long toenails are painted glittery gold.

Terry sticks out his hand and I slap down a twenty, and then another twenty, and then another. The man takes the cash, folds it into a tight wad, drops it in his shirt pocket, lights a cigarette, and explains as follows.

Eugene's cousin's husband, named Roy, a Mexican dude, whom he knows from around, is fucking—Eugene's word—one of the house-keepers at the Swell estate. Eugene sees Roy at another bar. Roy, apparently a high school football enthusiast, tells Eugene he was up at the estate and saw Marcus Manners with some white lady. Roy says Marcus and the lady looked like they were more than friends. A week later, different bar, Eugene and Roy are hanging out and the cops come in and grab Roy.

"Did he say anything else?"

"Nope."

"Anything about hearing shots?" I say.

"Nope."

"You're sure about that?"

He gives Terry a look like, *Is this guy for real?*

"What about hearing Manners yell something from inside the house? Someone's name. Anything like that?" I say.

"Alls Roy said is he seen Manners with the white lady and the boy look like he was gonna get hisself some."

"Have you seen him since?" Terry says.

"I heard he in PC," Eugene says, meaning Roy is in protective

124

custody in the county jail. It also means Eugene has some acquaintance with the workings of the criminal justice system, which does not come as a shock.

"Do you remember which night you had the conversation with Roy?" I say.

He does not hesitate for an instant. "April 28. Same day I got married, nine years now." Eugene sways his head mournfully. "Biggest mistake of my life."

We do not stay to explore his marital woes. Rather, we bid a fond farewell to Eugene and to Shortz and make our way out of West Santa Rita.

"We having fun yet?" Terry says.

Not fun, exactly. But I'd be lying if I said the kid hasn't hooked me. Maybe the reason Marcus opened up to me—instead of Pluck or the cops—is because, as hard as I've tried to hide it, he senses my concern.

"I can't believe I just paid sixty dollars for that. Mick told me the same thing for nothing."

"Mick said the witness heard shots. Roy didn't say anything about shots to Eugene."

"You think this Eugene person has a memory worth betting on?" I say.

"I don't know," Terry answers. "You think Mick might have added a detail or two to get you to sit on Manners?"

"Mick Bacon? Behaving like a cop?"

# 22

**M**ONDAY, MAY 10.

Terry and I arrive at the residence of one Timmy Peretz slightly after three P.M. The house looks like a California ranch house on steroids. It must be a half mile from one end to the other. Plexiglas bubbles pop out from the roof at irregular intervals. There is an enormous red maple in the front yard, its branches filled with plastic birds. When we walk up to the house, we trip some kind of invisible switch and the birds emit a canned tweet that sets a pack of dogs in the house to barking hysterically.

Given that Judge Reasoner hasn't granted a suppression motion in recorded history, I have to assume the drugs are coming into the case, and so it seems almost a waste of time to try to formulate a defense to the dog-napping. Even if I were to get acquittals on that charge, Reasoner needs only a single misdemeanor to stick Marcus in jail.

My shot at getting my life back is to get the case dumped pretrial, and the way to do that, barring a plea deal, is to convince Milo's boss that if my guy goes down on the misdos, then so too will some white kids whose well-connected parents and fancy defense lawyers will not only drive him insane in the process, but also may well dash his mayoral hopes.

Marcus hasn't wanted to play fink, but between calls to coaches and teachers and some documents—letters, a yearbook—the SRPD took from the Marcuses' apartment, Terry and I pin Marcus's likely dog-napping cohorts down to three guys, all members of the Hills High offensive line. Peretz is our first victim.

I ring the doorbell. The dogs continue their howling, but there is no answer. A radio blasts from behind the house. We walk up a side yard and behold Tim and a young woman, limbs entwined, mashing their faces together on a chaise lounge by a large inground pool. Timmy is wearing swim trunks. The woman has on a skimpy bikini that is askew, thus revealing much of her not-insignificant bosom. At that age I would not have been comfortable wearing a bathing suit while making out with a minimally clad female. Let's just say the lack of support would have been embarrassing.

We watch for a while. I clear my throat loudly, three times, before Tim ceases groping, glances my way, and pops off the girl, who may well be grateful, able to breathe for the first time in God knows how long.

Tim jogs over to us and shakes our hands. He's only an inch or two taller than me, but two of me thick and two of me wide. He wears wraparound sunglasses and has no neck at all.

I hand him a subpoena.

"It's just a formality," I say. "No big deal."

"Several people have left us with the impression you might be able to help us help Marcus," Terry says.

"Whatever," Timmy says. He turns back repeatedly to check on his scantily clad companion and then attempts to return the paper to me.

"You helped relieve the Bulleys of their dog, right?"

"I'm not even supposed to be talking to you."

"Why's that?"

"Just hold on."

On his way into the house he points to and mumbles at the girl, who does not respond. He returns with a business card for a private defense lawyer with whom I'm acquainted. The proper thing to do in this circumstance is to go away. The proper thing to do is to call the lawyer. But the business card simply provokes Terry.

"You don't get a lawyer unless you're guilty. So now that you've confessed, maybe you could help out your friend and talk to us for a minute?"

"What difference does it make, anyway, if they're going to charge him with murder?"

He's a big boy, but he can't hide his frustration about having his hands tied by his parents, who are no doubt responsible for the lawyer, or his guilt about leaving Marcus holding the bag for Red, or his anger at us for stepping in just as he was about to get laid.

"Is that what the police told you?" Terry says.

"It's in the paper."

"I suppose you're right, Timmy," I say, emphasizing the first syllable of his name, as I might have had he pushed me off the jungle gym in first grade. I let a couple of moments pass.

"Did you see them together?" Terry says. Peretz nods. "Did he ever talk to you about her?"

"I told the police everything. Why don't you ask them?"

"Wake up, man," Terry says. "You think they're on Marcus's side?"

"Manners told me they were friends," Peretz says.

"That's it?" Terry pushes.

"That's pretty much it."

"But you knew they were sleeping together, right?" Terry says.

Timmy now has his eyes glued to the ground. He taps his big toes simultaneously on the plush, heavily irrigated lawn.

"Come on, Timmy, give us a break here," Terry says. "You're screwing over your friend, letting him go down for something we all know you did together. With DiFilippo and Ma, right? Those guys were with you and Manners?" He refuses to face us. "And what about the dope? That was yours, right? Marcus was hanging on to your weed?" Nothing. "Fuck, man, the least you can do is give us a little guidance. What about Swell?"

128

"He never said they were together. But he didn't deny it, either."

"And what do you think?"

"I think my beer's getting cold," he says, half smirking, half horrified by his own conduct. He turns quickly and quickly walks off.

We start to back away. I stop. "Here's something to think about, Timothy." He faces us. "I'm gonna call you as a witness. I'm gonna put you on the stand so your friends can see you on television. And I'm gonna make you look like the putz you really are. And you know what? It isn't going to help Marcus one bit. But I'm going to do it anyway, because I don't like you." We walk away, slowly, chuckling quietly.

My heart races. I'm a terrible, mean person. I have no intention of calling him as a witness. He won't do Manners any good. I feel like racing back and hugging the big lug, telling him I'm sorry.

We knock at Dante DiFilippo's house. His mother answers. She does not open the door. She yells, "What is it?" We ask her to open up. She yells again, "What do you want?" We try, although the sound barrier makes communication arduous. After a bit of a struggle, she tells us Dante is not at home and then slides a business card under the door. It is the same card Timmy Peretz handed us minutes earlier. She says if we have any questions, we should call the lawyer.

Back in Terry's car, we consider forgoing the last visit. It seems clear the guys are represented, that they've been advised not to talk to us, and that they intend not to come forward to take some of the heat off Marcus. But the third house is on the way back to Preet's, where we're rehearsing in a couple of hours, so it seems silly not to give it a try.

We find Daniel Ma, apparently alone, in a modest house at the foot of the hills. Ma is obese. It's hard to imagine him chasing down defensive linemen intent on bashing in Manners's head. He sits in his living room playing video basketball. His shake is limp, clammy. His

129

head is enormous, and shaved straight across the top. He does not immediately tell us to get lost.

The moment we park on a plastic-encrusted couch, I hear muttering from another room. It sounds like Chinese. There is a pause, and then it continues, louder this time. Daniel unhurriedly picks his large frame up off the floor and walks out. We hear an exchange, which becomes heated for a minute, and then abruptly ends. He returns.

"Everything okay?" I say. He grunts. Then the vocalizations restart and Daniel again disappears. A few minutes later he rejoins us.

"Are you sure?" I say.

"My grandfather thinks you're the police."

"Is he okay?" Terry says.

"He thinks you're here to take me away."

"There's probably been a lot of police around here lately."

"They came around."

I hand him a subpoena. Like Peretz, he fishes out the lawyer's card.

"We're just trying to help your friend here. We think if it wasn't just Marcus involved, the district attorney would be less likely to push it."

He won't give up anything on the dog.

"They said he's going to prison for killing Ms. Swell."

"And what do you think?"

"I don't know." He is silent for a minute. The video game on the television, in standby mode, chirps at regular intervals. "I knew her. She tutored a lot of the guys on the team."

"She seems to have been a very decent person. She helped Marcus too, right?"

"Marcus?" He chuckles once, and then his face is again blank.

"She didn't tutor Marcus?"

"I don't know. I guess so."

# 23

"**WE MISS YOU**," I say. Maeve snorts and looks away. "Desperately."

It's early evening, Tuesday, May 11. I'm in Maeve's flower-jammed boudoir. Manilow's smiling visage peers down upon us from the wall. Aineen sits on the opposite side of the bed, monitoring her mother's anxiety level. If I upset the pregnant one, I'm toast.

"I'm out the door not five minutes and the wench is in there with y'all, smiling and wiggling her ass around." Maeve flashes a fake grin and squirms around in the bed.

"I didn't see any wiggling," I say.

"Mom."

Annoyed, Maeve says, "Aineen, why don't you run out for some cigarettes? I'm running low."

Aineen says, "I'm not going anywhere until the boy is breathing on his own."

I cut in. "I didn't think it would upset you this much. Silvie and I used to gig together, as I'm sure you remember. I know what she can do. She just told me she's dating someone else, so I assure you it's not about trying to get her back."

"You expect me to believe that?"

"No. But it happens to be the truth."

"I thought she was married to that Setz guy."

"She is. He's otherwise occupied these days." In prison, that is.

"Faithless bitch."

131

"Never one to judge. That's what I love about you."

"Whatever."

"It just makes sense, Maeve. She knows the material, she has the voice. Not as great as yours, but a reasonable, short-term substitute. We tried it with just the three of us and it's no good. You agree we have to take a shot at Vegas, right?"

"And what about you? You like playing the martyr?"

"A martyr for Manilow. Sure, why not?"

"You know, Gordy, I was nineteen when I had Aineen. Got so drunk I forgot I was a lesbian and let some cretin impregnate me. That was hard." She stretches out the last word, almost singing it. "I didn't have nothing but Barry back then. Then the girl went and got herself on drugs. That was really hard. Barry got me through that one too. I owe him and I feel like I've let him down. You understand?"

I do.

"Don't expect me to pretend to like it," she goes on. "But I'll try to be civil if that's what you want. You damn well better keep me plugged in the whole time."

"No problem."

"No more trying to cut me out."

"Who tried to cut—"

"Gordon."

"All right. Fine."

"You don't talk about band business with Silvie over beers or dinner or a blowjob," she warns. "In fact, I don't care if the wench is there or not. You don't so much as think about Manilow unless I'm online."

At Preet's, four hours later, post rehearsal. Silvie leaves. I'm pleased with our progress.

"Maeve?" I say, looking up at the camera.

132

"You're asking me to *judge*?" Her voice fills the sweltering garage.

"I think so."

"I just want to be careful not to *judge*, Gordy, because I know you think I'm *judg*mental."

"Mom." We hear Aineen, in the distance, try to calm her mother.

"I was just kidding," I say. "You're not judgmental. We value your opinions. We need your guidance."

"You suck, that's what I think," she drawls.

"Seriously?"

"Listen to me Gordy. You gotta get over her, at least until Vegas. You're too reserved around her, too fucking controlled. She's just a woman. She shits. She bleeds on her underwear like the rest of us. Her husband's in prison for fuck's sake. Get the hell *over* it."

"Mom."

"Aineen, will you *please* give me a fucking break. You guys, am I right or what?" I look at Preet, and then Terry. They scatter. "Manilow's gonna see through that shit in five seconds. You go to Vegas like this and Barry shows up? Then we're fucked permanently."

The chatter ceases for several minutes. I slide slowly down a painted cement wall, onto the floor of the studio. Terry fiddles around on the keyboards. Preet sits in his enormous leather chair at his computer station. He is the first to break the silence.

"I thought you might be interested that Jackson Bulley was previously married to one Margaret Bulley. He also happens to have a domestic violence conviction."

"No shit," Terry says, pointing his right index finger at me, meaning, I suppose, to suggest, *Ah ha*! He races over to Preet's computer.

"Shit," Preet says.

"Run the ex-wife," Terry says.

Preet picks at the keys for a minute. Then he smiles. "I am so good I terrify myself."

133

"She's up on Raleigh," Terry says. A few blocks up the hill from the Singhs' store. "Let's walk over."

"I'll go," Maeve says. "I need the exercise. Someone keep me on the cell."

"Fine," I say. Anything to ward off the truth—implicit in Maeve's critique, in the boys' averted eyes—that I'm destined to spend the rest of my life yearning. It may be even worse than that. I'm beginning to wonder if it's the yearning I'm after, and not the girl at all.

We walk six blocks to the former Mrs. Bulley's residence. There is a moving truck parked out front. A small, middle-aged woman with short, bleached-blond hair sits on the stairs leading up to the house. She is smoking a long, thin, brown cigarette and holding a glass from which she sucks a clear beverage through a straw. When we walk up to the house, the spicy smell of undiluted gin wafts toward us. She has the flushed and flaccid cheeks of a boozer. She offers us a drink. Preet and I decline.

Terry says, "Sure, why not?"

He grabs Mrs. Bulley by the hand, yanks her up, and steadies her while we walk through the bare house to the kitchen. All that remains is a carton of Tanqueray quarts.

"The police were by here a few days ago. I *told* them he killed her." Jackson Bulley, that is.

"What makes you say that?" Terry presses.

"He's a mean little shit, that's why. The ridiculous thing is, *he's* the one who left *me*. Fifteen years down the drain. He laid eyes on Ella Swell and that was it."

She tries to say the name with contempt, but her drunkenness dilutes the venom, so it comes out almost wistfully, as if she can see why he might have left her for Ella.

Terry slips into investigator mode. His voice is soothing. "I understand Mr. Bulley has a domestic violence conviction."

"I never meant for that to happen. I just needed a breather, so I called 911. I tried to tell them it was a big mistake, but they wouldn't let it go. He had to go to some counselor, but nothing changed."

Now she is near tears. We wait for her to blow her nose.

"Does your son live here?"

"Used to. Half the week. The other half with his father. Now he's off to college, so I figured, why stay around."

"Did you know anything about the relationship between Mr. Bulley and Ms. Swell?" I say. "We understand they'd been separated for a time when she was killed."

"Brice gave me the whole story. She dumped him and moved out. She was going to let him stay on the property until Brice graduated."

"You really think he killed her?"

"Oh sure. He liked living in that house. He probably loved her too, in his way. I always thought he loved me. He wouldn't have been able to stand the idea of her leaving him. Also Brice said he thought she had a boyfriend. That would have driven him crazy."

"Did Brice know who Swell was seeing?"

"It's that football player. The one who took the dog."


"Now I *know* the two crimes are connected." Terry's pumped, jogging, backward, down the hill toward Preet's place. Every few steps he completes a couple of deep squats while we catch up. "Bulley set up the dog thing to cover up the murder. He'd probably seen Manners up at the house, or maybe heard about it from one of the staff. So he kills her and sets up the kid with the dog."

"Just so we're clear, you're aware that Marcus confessed to taking the dog. Anyway, what about Roy?"

"Bulley could have paid him to go to the cops."

"He didn't go to the cops, Terry. He went to a bar and blabbed to Eugene. The police found *him*."

"Bulley could have paid Roy to shoot Swell."

"What about the blood?" I say.

Ignoring me, Terry says, "Manners admits he's in the house. Bulley or Roy sees them drive up together. Bulley or Roy watches them go in. And Bulley or Roy waits until Manners leaves to shoot her. Then later one of them delivers the dog to Manners's place. Plus," he says proudly, "you have to admit it's weird that the cop assigned to the dog case and Bulley are both in SIF?"

"I think it's a coincidence. And forgive me for repeating myself, but Marcus admits he took the freaking dog."

For the past hour Preet has carted Maeve around inside a live cell phone. Her chatter has kept him occupied and mostly silent. Now he joins in.

"Don't forget about Brice. The whole thing may be his doing. Perhaps he resents Ms. Swell for breaking up his parents' marriage. Or it may relate to the drug operation."

"Marcus said they got along fine," I say.

"Bulley or Brice or Roy," Terry says. "They could have done it separately. They could have done it together."

No one is listening to me anyway, so I keep my mouth shut and hope the conversation burns itself out before I am driven insane. I desperately need to forget about homicides and death threats and focus on the misdos. My future is in Manilow, but for the time being, I need my day job.

Preet reports Maeve's take: "She says she doesn't know how it happened but she's quite certain Bulley did it. She says she hates to burst our bubbles but Ella Swell preferred girls."

I grab the phone. "Swell was gay?"

"I personally never had the pleasure of her company, but that's what I heard," Maeve says. "I saw her around too, and I know a fuzz-bumper when I see one. I'm not saying she was never with a man. All I know is she *preferred* girls, as any sane woman would."

A variety of sardonic responses come to mind. But I hold my tongue. She's back on board. No reason to risk another meltdown.

# 24

THURSDAY, MAY 13, in my office. Terry barges in holding a box of *Santa Rita Journal* and *San Francisco Chronicle* articles, pleadings, transcripts, photographs. Over the past several days Preet and Terry and their friends in useful places have scraped together materials on the Zora Neal's prosecution and the subsequent killing of Grace Manners—from the court file, the Internet, the newspaper archives.

"Please don't bring that in here," I say.

He holds the box above my desk and drops it.

"The truth will set you free my friend," he says.

"Who says—"

Duke Abramowitz materializes outside my office in the dimly lit hallway and says, "Chief wants to meet on Manners. Conference room at noon." Then he is gone.

"Who says I want to be free?"

Terry's already into the first folder. I grab a hunk of documents from the box. The truth is, I care. About Marcus. Despite myself, about the truth. Anyway, before I get in bed with Mick Bacon in an almost certainly futile attempt to avoid my client's arrest for murder, I ought to be on top of the history, maybe take an educated guess at what Ella Swell had in mind to tell Marcus the night she was killed.

So, '88.

Santa Rita has always had a secret fondness for its bad boys and their contraband. If you plan to be in bed before the wee hours, don't get Ferdy started on the subject of the mob and the drugs and guns and booze they smuggled into the harbor and ran through the juke joints of West Santa Rita during World War II. The sixties and seventies brought hippy acid factories and enormous patches of dope deep in the parkland Ella Swell's family donated to the city.

But nothing ever hit this town as fast or hard as crack cocaine in the eighties. Before the party was over, hundreds of young men and women, some involved and many not, had been gunned down in turf battles between gangs. Thousands of people had poisoned themselves or saddled their unborn children with their addictions. And thousands had been shipped off to state and federal prisons to serve decades for their roles in the collective madness.

In Santa Rita the big dealers knew how to protect their interests. They drove around the west side in limos handing out hundred-dollar bills. They showed up like sports heroes at the bedsides of sick kids with toys and cash for medical expenses. And they invested in local businesses, including Grace Manners's bookstore.

Grace was a schoolteacher. Frustrated by the shortcomings of a profoundly underfunded public school system, Manners quit her job and started Zora Neal's Bookstore in the heart of the west side. The store became a community center of sorts. Among her investors was future Santa Rita councilman Jeremiah Pluck.

From the outset the store was a losing proposition, requiring infusions of cash to keep the lights on and the kids who came for a reading circle on weekends in milk and cookies. Just as the drive-by shootings and addicted babies were becoming a regular feature of the evening news, some of the brighter narcotics entrepreneurs began to burnish their images by supporting black-owned businesses.

By early 1988 it was an open secret that A. C. Colder, the original, and most adored, of the local crack kingpins, had taken it upon himself to keep Zora Neal's afloat. The *Journal* ran a picture of

Colder, dressed demurely, reading *Green Eggs and Ham* to a gang of mesmerized five-year-olds.

Colder was a soft-spoken autodidact who dropped out of school at thirteen and by his mid-twenties handled most of the cocaine distribution in the northern half of the state. For years he operated with near impunity and his gang, the Jefferson-Posse, or J-Posse, named for the street in West Santa Rita where Colder grew up—effectively controlled the west side.

In February of 1988 the J-Posse mistakenly gunned down a couple of kids in an affluent neighborhood, and quickly the folks pretending to run the city got busy. Weeks later the feds busted Colder for tax offenses. He pled out and headed off to prison camp in Arizona for eighteen months of R&R.

In July the SRPD got wind of a significant delivery to Colder's operation. According to the warrant, a confidential informant told police that Colder and his gang were using Zora Neal's as a warehouse. Kilos of cocaine would be delivered to the store and then distributed to various crack cook operations around northern California. The police raided the building on Sunday morning, August 31, 1988. A gun battle ensued. When it was over, a twenty-four-year-old police officer, Robert Howe, and two J-Posse members had been killed.

Grace Manners was at Zora Neal's when the police stormed the building. She was arrested, along with other staff members, and charged with Howe's murder and conspiracy to distribute cocaine. Also included in the roundup was twenty-three-year-old Ella Swell, a volunteer reading teacher.

The government charged the Zora Neal people—Manners, Swell, and others—with aiding and abetting the Colder narcotics operation. Allegedly they allowed Colder to use the premises—an unlikely target of police scrutiny—to store drugs. And, at least according to the criminal complaint, members of the bookstore staff fired weapons at police on the morning of August 21st.

The DA's office knew it would have a tough time proving who fired the shot that killed Howe, and it knew Santa Rita juries are notoriously hostile to the police. But it also had Ella Swell to squeeze. Facing life in prison for aiding in the cop killing, she flipped and agreed to testify against Grace Manners and two J-Posse members who were in the store with her on the 19th. As part of the deal, charges against some other bookstore employees were dismissed. The gang defendants pleaded guilty to the conspiracy charges and went off to prison. In the end, only Grace Manners remained in the case.

Black versus white. Rich versus poor. Old Santa Rita versus new. As the black community sank beneath the weight of the crack scourge and as Colder's gang grew increasingly rich, powerful, and untouchable, the city braced for the trial. But it never happened. A few weeks before jury selection someone sliced Grace Manners's throat in the cafeteria of the Santa Rita County Jail. No one was ever charged with the killing. Ella Swell pleaded guilty to manslaughter and went off to prison to do her five and a half years. Six months later, still doing time in Arizona, Colder got hit.

I remember being home from college and watching coverage of Colder's funeral on television. The procession—mourners dressed in white tuxedos and a horse-drawn carriage to carry the casket—wove its way through the downtown on a chilly, fog-drenched January morning, thumbing its collective nose at the SRPD and the city government, and arriving finally at a church in West Santa Rita where a crowd of several thousand people gathered to pay their final respects. Colder was royalty in those parts, and he went out with commensurate pomp.

Without Colder, the J-Posse eventually imploded. Rival gangs absorbed Colder's drug business. By the early nineties the epidemic had burned itself out and the price of coke had plummeted. With profits evaporating, the drug dealers sold their houses in the hills and their Porsches and went back to their small-time operations in West Santa Rita where the cops don't bother them too much.

"Any reason to think Grace Manners was contemplating flipping on Colder?" Terry asks.

"Not that I know of."

"He would have had the reach in the jail to take her out," Terry says.

"Seems like it would have come up long before trial. If Colder was really worried, why would he have waited so long? She was a threat to someone, though. Did you see those pictures?" Grace Manners, with her neck sliced open.

"It's weird they never charged anyone with it, though, with as much profile as the case got," Terry says. "I'm curious if Dent had his hands anywhere on this thing. The SRPD could have ordered the hit, to retaliate for the cop."

"Ferdy said my dad was involved. Maybe he had her killed. That would have been just like him."

"What about Pluck?" Terry asks. "You see his name anywhere after '88? He's all over the stuff about the bookstore, before the raid. Then he disappears."

"They busted the people in the building. He wasn't there."

"I guess. He could have been the informant, though."

"A hundred people could have snitched off that delivery or any other one. I'm sure lots of people tried. The SRPD just didn't give a shit until the J-Posse started killing white people."

# 25

**D**UKE AND I SIT at a conference table. The chief paces, looking out the floor-to-ceiling windows into the reception area. Aineen, who, when she isn't babysitting Maeve, has taken over not only her mother's duties at the Public Defender's Office, but also her abiding sense that she is the only trustworthy person in the operation, sits at the reception station painting her toenails.

"Can you explain to me why every other call these days is about Manners?" The question, I conclude, is rhetorical. "I'm beginning to tire of it." The chief is troubled. "What's happening with the misdos?"

"The deputy is anxious to deal it but Reasoner seems bent on teaching Marcus a lesson. He's looking for a plea to the drug charge and forty-five days. Normally I'd have to recommend Manners take it. He could do ninety days actual time on the marijuana alone. But he's got graduation coming up and then football camp in Colorado in a few weeks."

"Priors?"

"Nothing."

"Is it triable?"

"They have the dog and they have a so-so witness who sees the car and someone who could be Manners. The client's father will say he had the vehicle that night. On the drug thing, the officer who found the marijuana has had some problems and he's a big SI fan. So we may have a rather far-out frame-up theory there."

"What about a 1538?" The motion to suppress the drugs.

143

"I've got it mostly done." An utter fabrication. "I'll file this week."

"Good. Give the officer a spanking at the hearing and then take Reasoner's temperature again. See whether you can get him to back off a bit. Seems like a community-service case to me." I nod and gather my papers, but he's not through with me. "Am I to understand that Mr. Manners is a suspect in the Swell homicide?"

"Nothing official, sir. But I've had some off-the-record conversations with one of the detectives on the case. My sense is the SRPD is nervous about a potential meltdown on the west side. So they are moving gingerly. But they are definitely moving in Manners's direction."

"What's the picture—briefly."

"There's a witness who puts Manners in the house the night she was killed, or the night they think she was killed, anyway. The witness says he hears shots and Manners, or someone who sounds like him, yell Swell's name from inside the house shortly before the shots."

I can't tell you how professional and cool I feel sitting at the fifteen-foot mahogany conference table with the chief, briefing him on a murder case. Misdemeanor Man, my ass. If it weren't for Barry, I'd be more than ready for the big time.

"I should add that Terry and I interviewed someone who appears to have spoken with the same man, the witness, and I think it's an open question what the witness actually saw and heard."

"It's an open question?" the chief says, although by his tone, this query may well be rhetorical. Rapidly I feel much less cool.

"Apparently the cops also have Manners's prints in the house and Swell's blood on a pair of his shoes."

The chief chuckles with his lips sealed, which fills his mouth with air. His cheeks pop out, Dizzy Gillespie–style. "You're joking."

"No, sir."

"And who disclosed this mountain of evidence to you, the suspect's lawyer?"

"Mick Bacon. He's—"

The chief looks at me like I've just asked to marry his nine-year-old daughter.

"I damn well know Michael Bacon, Seegerman. He's a cop and it sounds to me like he's handed you a bucket of bulls bollocks."

The alliteration, said with the chief's grindy Scottish accent, is amusing. I don't dare laugh, though, because apparently I've screwed up. Duke, however, is unable to contain himself. When he stops chortling, we resume.

"Sir?"

"Christ almighty, man. Have you seen a report on the prints?" Definitely rhetorical. "Or the blood? You're supremely confident they have Ella Swell's blood on Marcus Manners's shoes because you've not only seen the report, and interviewed the crime lab technician who took the sample, you've seen the damn shoes."

"No, sir."

Duke is enjoying my dressing down far too much. I would very much like to disembowel him with my teeth.

"What the SRPD has, if memory serves, is a *crap* allegation that Manners is involved in some coke dealing, based entirely on a bag of dope in his car, right?"

Without warning, I'm under cross-examination.

"That's right."

"And, according to Michael Bacon, the most reliable of sources, of course, they have a *crap* witness, most probably a pro"—in other words, a person who provides information to the police as a vocation—"who has given a *crap* statement that Manners was in the right place, although not necessarily at the right time. There's nothing more to it?"

"That's it."

"And no doubt Bacon told you all this because he's a Hills loyalist and he can't stomach the thought of Manners going off to Pelican Bay." One of California's nastiest prisons.

"He was hoping I'd let them talk to Manners."

"Ah, now *that* comes as a shock. Surely—"

"No."

"Outstanding, Seegerman. You've managed to behave like a public defender, if only fleetingly."

"I did have a conversation with my client about the events."

The chief walks to the door and opens it.

"Christ, I can't take any more. Next you'll be telling me he confess—"

"He didn't confess."

"Well, that's a relief. I suppose if he had, you'd have brought it to the attention of the authorities forthwith. Do us all a favor, Seegerman. Try to keep in mind where you're employed. Leave the police work to Michael Bacon and his pals. They have a hard enough time as it is without your help."

He leaves.

"Well?" Duke says.

I stare at him, unblinking, until he gathers his things and leaves.

An hour later, in my office, Terry reports that Roy, the key witness against Manners, is actually Rogelio Contreras, heroin addict, violent felon, and, as Chief had guessed, a professional snitch. He's as much on the police payroll as the guys who maintain the patrol cars.

"Please listen to me, Terry. I'm serious now. I'm doing everything I can to keep my shit together."

"You're fine."

"Yes, right now, fine. Ten minutes from now, who knows? In any case, I've been instructed to do my job and stay out of the murder investigation. That's precisely what I intend to do."

He has a sheaf of court documents in his hands.

"You won't believe this."

"Do I have to beg?"

"Contreras is on probation in six different felony cases. He gets popped, they plead him and give him probation. He gets popped again, and again, and still, no prison time. In one case the *DA* was the one arguing for him to get OR." In other words, released on his own recognizance, which normally would not be an option for a lifelong criminal like Roy, or Rogelio, or whoever he is. "He couldn't have done as well if he were the judge's little brother."

"Perhaps I've been insufficiently clear. I'm under double-secret probation."

"Why?"

"Chief is of the opinion I let Mick get the best of me. He thinks they're way short of enough to bust Manners, and they're trying to get me to deliver him."

"Could be. Seems like it still makes sense to get what we can from them, assuming we don't have to give them anything on the record."

"Perhaps, and perhaps not. Right now I have to write an unwinnable suppression motion."

"Good luck with that. I'll spend some time looking into the '88 thing."

"What '88 thing?" I say, the scowl on my face, I hope, adequately conveying the degree to which I'm not interested.

# 26

SEARCH AND SEIZURE 101, the condensed and unabashedly biased version.

The Fourth Amendment says that the "right of the people to be secure in their persons, house, papers and effects, against unreasonable searches and seizures, shall not be violated."

There are two major misconceptions about this provision.

First, people believe it somehow prevents objectionable police conduct—for instance, breaking down a door and searching a house for no reason whatsoever. In fact, because the cops are the ones with the guns, they can do pretty much what they please. It's only when, in the course of a criminal prosecution, they try to use evidence found during such a search, that they face legal obstacles. Tell an officer who comes to your door that he or she is barred by the federal constitution from entering, or searching, or seizing, and you are likely to experience firsthand the inability of the law to protect your privacy. You are also likely to see an amused cop.

The second misconception follows from the first. It's true, of course, that there are rules about the circumstances that must exist to justify a search. An officer who wants to root through your underwear drawer and hopes to present, in court, what he or she finds, must either have a warrant or special grounds—called exigent circumstances—to justify a warrantless search. For example, if a cop has good reason to believe you have drugs in your pocket, and sees you flee from your kitchen to your bathroom, he or she does not have to phone up a judge and obtain a warrant to follow you and look for the drugs. The high probability that you are about to flush your dope down the toilet justifies the search even absent a warrant.

The thing is, though, the rules that preclude the admission in court of evidence obtained during searches that are both warrantless and otherwise unjustified are, for the most part, meaningless. That's because the people who enforce these rules are judges. And judges are almost always former prosecutors.

Which is not to say that judges never exclude evidence due to Fourth Amendment violations. They do. It happens. But it happens so infrequently these days that cops don't pay much attention. Most of the time they figure if they get the guy with the drugs, everyone's better off. And a judge, who may have to face election, is rarely, very rarely, going to let the bad guy go because of an illegal search.

Search and Seizure 101, condensed and unabashedly biased, as applied to the Manners case.

Officer Dent had reason—with the dog behind the apartment building and the witness who saw someone who looks like Marcus, driving a car that looks like Marcus's, near the Swell estate—to make the arrest on the dog-napping charge. Based on this evidence, he got a warrant to make the bust.

He might well have convinced a judge that he should, too, be able to search the car—for dog hair or other evidence that Marcus was involved—but he didn't. It's possible that he simply overlooked the issue. But it seems far more likely that the lazy cop, unhappy about leaving his cushy post in the hills and venturing into the west side, wouldn't have wanted to waste his time applying for the appropriate documents. If the car needed searching, he'd search it. And if he found something he could use, with the assistance of one of his pals on the bench, he'd figure a way around the Fourth Amendment problem.

So, with a rookie officer riding shotgun, Dent drove over to West

Santa Rita. Once they arrived at Marcus's building, the rookie stood watch in front while Dent took a look around. According to Dent, he wanted to see if the vehicle with the license plate beginning with "2K" was parked in the covered carport behind the building. He found the Civic and matched the license plate to Speed Manners's registration. That ought to have been it. Without a search warrant for the car, he was not there to explore. He was not there to see what else he could find. But Dent, the dedicated public servant, decided to look in the windows of the vehicle.

What he'll say, of course, is that the drugs were in "plain view." This is one of the circumstances the courts have held justifies a warrantless search. If an officer is otherwise operating within the bounds of the Fourth Amendment and sees evidence of a crime in plain view, even if he has no warrant, he's entitled to search and seize.

There are three problems with plain view in this case, each of which will be the subject of an argument in my motion to suppress.

First, from discussions with my client and his father, I've learned that the car is always backed into the carport and that the space is very tight. For that reason, they park the car along the passenger-side wall, making it slightly easier for the driver to get in. So, Dent had to be looking either through the windshield of the car—from where he couldn't possibly have seen a bag of marijuana on the floor—or in the driver's side window, from where such an observation would have been very difficult. Even if he saw the dope, then, it's not logical to say that it was in *plain* view. It took quite an effort.

Second, I've seen the bag, and it's about as innocuous looking as you can imagine—a wrinkled brown paper sack with its top twisted closed. Any normal person would have assumed it was stuffed with trash, not drugs. So, again, it's silly to say the *drugs* were in plain view, because all that was in plain view, really, was a small brown garbage bag.

Finally, Dent is lying his ass off. He's too fat to squeeze into the space to see into the driver's side window. And, anyway, no self-respecting pot smoker would leave his or her stash on the carpet in front of the passenger seat because such carpets are notoriously hard to get pot *out of* when the pot smoker inevitably, while stoned out of his or her gourd, steps on or kicks the stash. Also Dent, according to Terry's research, has lied before. And he's got a decent motive to lie in this case, which is that there's a longstanding, racially charged rivalry between Hills and SI, and any member of Saint Illuminatus Forever, given the opportunity to ruin the life of the finest quarterback in Hills's history, is honor and duty bound to take it.

I'll file my motion and put Dent on the stand and pull his pants down for the world to see. And Judge Reasoner, having failed to read, let alone consider my motion, will deny it. Which, as I was saying, is why you shouldn't put too much faith in the Fourth Amendment.

Moments before I leave for the day, my intercom buzzes and Aineen's bored-sounding voice pipes into my office.

"Gordy, call on 62."

I lean into the speakerphone. "Any idea who it is?" No answer. I dial the front desk.

"Aineen."

"Yeah, Gordy."

"The call on 62, did you get a name?" An unapologetic *no*. "Would you do me a favor and see who it is? I'm on my way out." No response. "Aineen?" Nothing. I hang up and buzz the reception desk again. "Hello, Aineen."

Now a voice that is not Aineen's says, "I think she's gone for the day."

I tap the button on the phone, putting whoever's on 62 on the speaker.

"This is Gordon Seegerman. Can I help you?" Nothing. "Hello."

"I have something important to tell you."

It's a man's voice, flat, probably a solicitation of some sort.

I pick up the phone.

"Whatever it is, I'm really not interested."

"Are you interested in staying alive?"

"Yes." I know I'll kick myself later for not coming with a wittier retort, but the man's tone is so uninflected, almost robotic, that it's profoundly unnerving.

"We know everything about you, Seegerman."

"Okay. Is there something in particular you want?"

"Your father must be ashamed."

"What the f—"

The line goes dead. Not five seconds later my cell rings.

I say to myself, "You must be kidding me." The screen reads, "Private Number Calling." I cancel the call. The phone rings again.

"Hello." It's Cindi Paris.

"You have anything for me?" she says.

"Actually, I do."

# 27

N EXT MORNING, FRIDAY, May 14. I'm in my office putting the finishing touches on my suppression motion. Terry bounds in with Ricardo Lara, one of the senior lawyers in my office. Lara, nearing retirement, is a tall, thickset man. He has a bedraggled appearance: his shirttails fall out of his baggy pants, his tie is stained, his full head of gray hair is tousled. His office is legendary for its disarray. But his total lack of poise has served him well in court. Juries love the guy. They trust him. He wins cases that can't be won.

"Terry tells me you're dredging up ancient history," Lara says.

"Terry is dredging up ancient history. I'm writing a loser 1538."

"Ricardo represented Ervin Nichols," Terry says, holding up a yellow folder I assume is Nichols's case file.

"Is that a fact?"

Nichols was one of the J-Posse gang members arrested at Zora Neal's Bookstore following the '88 raid.

"Stupid case," Lara says. "Ervin wasn't more than sixteen or seventeen. He was one of A. C. Colder's crew, but very low-level. Just happened to be at the wrong place at the wrong time. With the dead cop—what was his name—"

"Robert Howe."

"Howe, right. It got ugly. They were ready to charge Nichols with specials." Making him eligible for a sentence of life without the possibility of parole. "I had the kid's family up there for weeks crying and begging. The cops thought they might get him to flip on Colder, but that would have been suicide. They knew Nichols wasn't a real player, and they couldn't make him as the shooter, so eventually they let him plead to a second." Second-degree murder, which means he does fifteen years and then has a shot at parole.

"You ever figure out how the cops knew Colder was using the store as a warehouse?"

"No. Everyone assumed they had someone inside the store. Before that the SRPD never came close to a big shipment, and they had wires all over the place. They'd picked off Posse guys here and there, but never with any significant quantities. And the guys were so scared of Colder—or loyal, I suppose—that no one inside J-Posse flipped, even after Colder went down on the tax beef. So it really *had* to be someone at the store. Does this have some bearing on the Swell thing?"

"No," I say.

"Probably," Terry retorts. "Marcus Manners and Swell recently became friends. Apparently she was going to tell him some kind of big secret about '88 when she got hit. Manners claims she knew someone was coming after her."

"There also happens to be a bunch of incriminating evidence against Manners, so we're not banking on his story," I add.

"Could Nichols know something about it?" Terry says.

"He probably knows lots of interesting stuff. I haven't talked to him in years. I suppose with Colder dead he'd be less concerned. But unless he's found Jesus, I'd bring along an incentive," Lara says, grinning.

Lara leaves. I go back to editing my motion. Terry reads the Nichols file. He flips through the papers loudly. He shakes his head and grunts knowingly several times.

"I have an hour if you want to go up to talk to Bulley," he says.

Jackson Bulley is a witness in the dog-napping case, and if I'm going to try it, due diligence requires me at least to knock on his door.

"I need to get out of the office anyway," I say.

154

I stand. He does not. He stares at a multipage document from the Nichols file.

"Guess what this is," he says.

"No."

"Warrant affidavit for the bookstore bust."

A warrant application, for an arrest or search or wiretap, typically contains an affidavit from a law enforcement officer setting forth facts known to that officer that justify issuance of the warrant by a judge.

"Are you driving?" I say.

"I think I'd better," he says, holding up the affidavit. It's signed by Alan S. Seegerman.

"Ferdy said my dad was involved. I don't see how it matters."

Actually, I'm beginning to wonder. The anonymous caller mentioned S. Ashamed of *what*, exactly? He was never happy about my work, but I have no reason to believe he'd be more embarrassed by my representation of Marcus Manners than any other defendant.

I'm slunk down on the front seat of Terry's Mercedes. He's heading toward the hills, for the Swell estate. The midday sun hits the top of my head. After a few minutes my curls are warm to touch.

"Let's assume for a minute Manners is totally straight up," Terry says. "She picks him up. She sends him for beer. He hears the shots, runs back, and she's history. So far everything the cops have fits with that."

"Except for Roy."

"Come on. We both know Roy gets paid to say what he's told to say. Maybe they got lucky and he's really on the property that night. Maybe he even sees them together. But as for the details, forget it."

"Consider it forgotten."

"So Swell says she wants to tell Manners the truth about the bookstore thing. She wants him to know the truth. She tells him someone is going to kill her. And just when she's about to spill the beans, she gets hit?"

"And?"

"And, it's got to be that she knows who the snitch was. Whoever it is, that's your shooter. And your dad knows."

"And you expect my father to remember, let alone reveal this information to us?"

"Other people at the SRPD must have known. Ask Mick. He and your dad were partners, no?"

"No. Before that."

"We could ask him."

"*I* could ask him, that's true. If *I* were inclined, which *I* am not."

"You know, sometimes you really sound like a lawyer."

"Really."

"Yeah. You should watch that."

"I'll try." Instead of heading for the hills, Terry drives to Preet's. "Why is Preet coming?"

Terry turns to me, cocks his head to one side, raises his eyebrows, and says nothing.

The turbaned one stretches out across the back seat for the climb up to the Swell estate.

At the compound, a retractable iron gate is open. We continue up a long driveway, which splits. The left fork heads off to three buildings. One must be the house in which the SRPD found Swell's body. We take the right fork several hundred yards farther to a cobblestone parking area with a large eagle fountain at its center. The main house is a slate-encrusted monster of a building.

We ring. A young Latina—Rogelio's love interest?—answers. Before Terry can charm the woman and launch an interrogation, I ask for Professor Bulley. In a minute he arrives, dressed in a white tennis outfit and brown loafers without socks.

"Mr. Velikovic warned me you might pay a visit."

He's a little man, thin, fit, energetic, bald, well tanned. His words are carefully clipped at their ends.

I extend our condolences and he thanks me, but says nothing more about his wife's death. When I introduce Preet as a consultant to our office, Bulley remembers him immediately.

"One of the few As I've ever given. Glad to know you're putting your skills to good use."

Preet is beyond pleased. I believe he would, now, gladly mow Bulley's lawn. Preet is also horrified. He would like to explain that no, actually, he's just along to gawk. He is a computer security expert, a well-known programmer.

"I don't want to take up too much of your time. I'd just like to firm up some of the details about the dog," I say, hoping, against hope, as it happens, that the animal is not immediately summoned for viewing. Red runs toward me and flings his station-wagon-sized frame against my midsection. His tongue slaps against my bare arms.

"Down. Down, Red," Bulley shouts at him. I would very much like to mace the beast.

"Nice dog," I say, when Red has finally been restrained.

"Let's go out back so Red can get some air."

Let's.

"Out back" is the size of Nebraska. We sit around a glass table on a patio large enough to be the foundation for a good-size house. Bulley happily recounts the events relevant to the dog-napping. He pets and glances adoringly at Red while he describes his upset during the dog's absence.

I say, "I'd hoped to give you some idea of what Marcus has been through and, even accepting that he may have made a stupid mistake and taken your dog, perhaps—"

"I read the papers, Mr. Seegerman. I'm also in close touch with Detective Baptiste regarding the investigation into my wife's death. I know enough to know your client probably killed her."

"If that's the case, he'll be charged and spend the rest of his life in prison. Which makes the dog-stealing thing sort of meaningless, if you think about it."

"Not to me."

"The dog wasn't harmed."

"True, but irrelevant."

"We understand the dog may have been taken in response to a prank by some SI players," Terry adds.

"And if those young men were caught, they should be prosecuted as well. I don't condone criminal activity on either side. I understand Manners was also caught with drugs."

He's a perfect asshole, just as Preet described him.

"Do you know the officer who arrested Marcus, Karl Dent?"

"I don't think we'd ever met before the recent events." Probably a lie. Hard to imagine they haven't run into one another at SIF.

"Would you mind answering a few questions about your wife?" Terry jumps in.

"I suppose that depends, Mr.—"

"Fretwater."

"Mr. Fretwater. Sorry. Good with numbers, bad with names."

There's no stopping him. I could clear my throat. I could kick him under the table. But Terry is something like a bulldog with its jaws on a beloved, deflated football. Any effort to pry him from the topic will be futile. Besides, he's enjoying himself so much it seems a shame to interfere.

"Is it fair to say you were separated at the time of her death?"

"As far as it goes, that's fair. Ella moved down to the guesthouse weeks before she was killed. We had our difficulties, as all couples do. We were still married when she died."

"Was it your impression that she had begun a new relationship?" Terry asks.

Now I cannot help but kick him. As predicted, it has little effect.

"It's my *impression*, to use your word, that she was spending time with Manners, though I can't tell you the nature of the relationship. We never discussed it. She knew his parents before she went to prison."

Terry is trying to get under his skin, but it's not working. Bulley's calm. He pets the dog. He says nothing remotely incriminating.

"And what about your son's relationship with Ms. Swell?"

"They were quite close, actually."

"Could we ask him some questions? About the dog."

"He gave a statement to the police, Mr. Fretwater. You'll have to be content with that."

Bulley declines, on police orders, to let us tour the guesthouse. He shows us out, and watches—dwarfed by the colossal, arched entryway to the manse—as we climb into Terry's car. I wave as we pull away.

"Nice guy," Terry says.

"It actually gives me some hope in the misdemeanor case," I add. "The jury's going to hate him."

# 28

THE NEXT MORNING, Saturday, May 15, I sleep until nearly ten and get up in an unusually good mood. It's unlikely to last, so I try to revel in it for a time. By noon I'm out on the patio with the paper. S. is back to jumbled patriotic crooning. While I'm taking care of some yard work, I join in.

The boys and Silvie arrive around four for a bit of laid-back rehearsing and burgers. Away from the studio I feel less bad about excluding Maeve. I want to have a chance to work without her intimidating presence. Silvie ought to have a chance to get comfortable. Plus, I want the ex to come back to the house, to see my dad, to see that I'm a grown-up now.

Silvie arrives first. Through grimy curtains in the living room I sneak a look at her, standing on the front porch. She repeatedly bends her knees and bows her legs, and then straightens them. She did the same thing, before, standing naked on our bed, making some point or other. And she swings her head around, first to the left, then to the right, to clear her face of stray hair.

My father was well enough, when Silvie and I were together, to have an opinion of her. His opinion was that I'd won the lottery, that I was totally undeserving, and that I'd most likely screw it up. Right on all accounts.

When the boys arrive, with S. our only audience, we run through a few tunes in my cavernous living room. S. tends to leer, and Silvie, who thought my father charming and sad in the old days, seems resigned to the role of leeree. Her tank top keeps my father occupied and docile.

Later, in the kitchen, scraping carrots for a salad. Through a window I watch Terry and Silvie debate charcoal-lighting technique. Preet joins me.

"Terry says you're seeing the reporter from Channel 2."

"Jesus." The last thing I need is for Silvie to hear that. "I'm not doing anything with her, let alone *seeing* her. She's nice, though. Perhaps you'd like to date her. I could set it up."

"I'm a Channel 4 man, myself. You'll be seeing her again?"

"What is this? No. I doubt it."

"Was she a print reporter at one time?"

"Why?"

He hands me a reprint of a *San Francisco Chronicle* article from 1994. The headline reads, DEBUTANT-CONVICT: THE STRANGE DAYS AND LONG NIGHTS OF ELLA SWELL. The byline says, "Cindi Paris."

I read the article. It was printed shortly after Swell's parole. It's a lifestyle piece: Swell goes to prison, Swell manages to keep her hair and nails looking good, Swell gets out and tries to figure out what next. It says almost nothing about the circumstances surrounding Swell's arrest and plea. In fact, the only thing of interest in the article is the byline.

"So?" I say.

Actually, not so. Until now Cindi had left me with the distinct impression she's new to the world of criminal justice. She certainly never mentioned any familiarity with Swell. But I have no intention of getting Preet or, God help me, Terry worked up over it.

"I thought it might interest you."

"Not particularly. Has Terry seen this?" I say. Preet shakes his head. "How about we keep it that way. Okay?"

"Got it."

"Preet. I'm serious. Let me try to figure out if it means anything before you set him off."

"On my honor."

After dinner, Silvie says her good-byes, and the boys and S. and I pile into Terry's car and park by Lake Lanier, the shallow, saltwater pond in the middle of downtown Santa Rita that is more commonly known as Bird Shit Lake because it's a rest stop for thousands of migratory birds. Each year Santa Rita throws itself a party to celebrate the city's founding, 152 years ago. The festivities culminate in a pyrotechnics display.

I'm a total sucker for fireworks. I immediately revert to age five, standing with my hand in my mother's, thrilling and wincing to every whoosh and ka-boom. And as hard as I try, I can't avoid tearing up when the reds and greens and yellows splash and sparkle and boogie around the black and blue sky.

We spread out a blanket on the grass, park my dad, and sit around him. It's best to keep him penned. He has a penchant for wandering. And God knows what old friend or enemy or girl-friend or boss will want to come over to say hello. It's good to have him out, to be out with him. But there's no reason to risk riling him.

Before the light of day makes its final exit and the fireworks get under way, I hear a bullhorn and muffled chanting. We're sitting fifty yards from a raised platform where a couple of state legisla-tors, the acting mayor, police chief, DA, and other dignitaries sit. The ruckus is heading toward us. I can hear the ruckus, but I cannot see the ruckus, mainly because everyone around us is standing to try to see the damn ruckus. Finally, I stand. So does S., though I doubt he has any idea what's going on. It's a demonstration, an angry parade.

Pluck is at the head of the line, which extends as far as I can see. The councilman yells through the bullhorn, "*What do we want?*" And the demonstrators respond, "*Justice for Marcus.*"

The group draws closer and gets louder. There are a few boos from the fireworks crowd, but mostly they support the marchers. There are shouts of "Marcus, Marcus" and others I cannot make out. I feel surprisingly proud. I should join them. He's my client. I'm the one fighting for him behind the scenes. These people should know who I am.

Then I feel a sharp pain in my left shoulder. I yell, "What the fu—". Heads yank around.

Before I know what's happening, my band-mates wrestle S. and me to the ground. I'm bleeding steadily. But that's not the biggest problem, because now S. is howling, having twisted his ankle during the operation to separate his incisors from my arm. My father is furious, writhing, screeching incoherently. The others stand. I remain on the ground, hugging and pinning S., which is no easy feat because he has six inches and forty pounds on me. I sing, "Oh say can you see" in his right ear and beg him to sing while he wrestles with me. After a minute his rage subsides.

We limp back to Terry's car and wing our way to the closest emergency room. It's Founders' Day so the incidence of picnic-induced food poisoning and drunken violence is at its zenith. The waiting room is crammed and malodorous. We will no doubt be here for most of the night waiting for a doctor to examine S.'s foot, which has swollen to the size of a cantaloupe and is the color of a blueberry. So I send Preet and Terry to my place to fetch my car.

I feel weirdly good having sort of beat up my dad. I fantasized about it when I was a kid, when he regularly humiliated me and occasionally knocked me around to prove he was the boss. I should leave him here to fend for himself. That's what he would have done—called my mom and headed to a bar.

163

We sit for a couple of hours in silence. Then he begins to hum "America the Beautiful." I hum along with him.

"Hey, Pop, you know how you're always talking about being a police detective."

"I *am* a police detective."

"For the Santa Rita Police Department, right?"

"They call me S."

"Okay, 'S.' it is. You must have worked on some pretty big cases."

"I had dinner with the governor." Probably a fantasy, but who the hell knows. I should remember to ask Ferdy about that one.

"That must have been interesting."

"Oh yes," he says. "Are you in law enforcement?"

"Something like that."

He begins to hum again, loudly. Normally this is embarrassing, because my father doesn't *look* like someone who hums at an irritating volume in public places. But in this context, with people puking and ranting and hacking and fainting around us, I'm hardly concerned about appearances.

"So what was your most famous case?" I say.

"I taught at the academy."

"What about the J-Posse case? You remember that one? There was a shooting at a bookstore."

"Yes, of course," he says smiling.

"Tell me about it. I noticed that you signed the warrant for the bust at the bookstore."

"Oh yes." Still smiling.

"There was an informant mentioned in the warrant. Who was that?"

"They told me I would be chief."

"Who told you that, Pop?"

"Are you in law enforcement?"

"What about the J-Posse case? You had to have been running the

164

snitch all along. He was your guy. Someone who knew Colder was taking drug deliveries at the bookstore."

"I taught at the academy."

"I want to know about the J-Posse thing. That was one of the big ones."

"Oh yes."

"So? What happened? Who was the inside guy? Who was your snitch?"

"I once had dinner with the governor."

Dr. Jennifer Lediger, approximately age twelve, walks up to us to get a sense of the urgency of my father's injury. She has a small diamond stud in her nose. Her jet-black hair is streaked with magenta. My father shoots out of his seat, always quick to come to attention in the presence of an attractive female. But he's forgotten about the injury, puts his weight to the bad ankle and nearly crumples. But Dr. Tween, in a surprising show of strength, catches S. under the arm in mid-crumple.

I explain that he has Alzheimer's and that he twisted his ankle. The doctor examines S.'s foot and says it's probably a sprain. She informs us that the wait for an X-ray is three hours. Then she notices the blood on my arm.

"You get stabbed?"

I turn to show her the injury. "Bitten."

"That's ugly. Your dad do that?"

"My dog."

"Is your father on antipsychotic medication?"

"Antidepressants."

"Human bites cause nasty infections. Have whoever sees you later clean it up and give you some antibiotics. And get your dad to his primary doctor soon. These things tend to escalate."

Dr. Know-It-All moves on. We sit. S. sings and hums and wiggles around in his chair.

165

"How's the foot, Pop?"

"Mick knows," S. says.

"Mick knows what?"

"*My country 'tis of thee—*"

# 29

"**A** HIKE?"

"Yes, a hike," I say. "You know, birds and trees. The absence of concrete and garbage. If you want what I have, you gotta hike. My dog needs a walk."

"I don't remember hiking being part of our deal," Cindi says.

"Do you know how to walk?"

"Yes."

"Do you own a pair of sneakers?"

"Yes, although they've never experienced anything other than a treadmill."

"I'm sure they'll be fine. I didn't have an Everest ascent in mind."

"A stroll."

"Precisely."

"Couldn't we just have lunch?"

"We'll get something on the way and eat there."

"On the ground?"

Given that Cindi and I have had a total of two in-person meetings, and as a result nearly everyone thinks we're dating, I decide to meet her someplace secluded. I want to know why she approached me and what she's after.

She lives in the hills, in a large, ultramodern, steel and cement and glass house, with massive windows and views to San Francisco and beyond. When I arrive, she's still deciding on a hiking outfit. I wait in the living room. There is almost nothing in the house: a few pieces of spare furniture, some enormous abstract paintings,—originals, I think, by artists with names I vaguely recognize. There are a few books. There is no clutter. The kitchen counters are empty. There are no dishes, no newspapers.

"Go out on the terrace," she bellows from somewhere in the bowels of the structure. "I think there might be some birds out there. That's nature, right? Maybe we could just stay here and drink."

"Do you actually live here?" I shout. "Where's all your stuff?"

"I'm neat."

"Apparently."

She comes out in fairly, but not absurdly, tight jeans, a T-shirt, and the whitest sneakers I have seen in my life. They must be right out of the box.

"Will this work?" she says.

"Your shoes might get a little dirty, but if that's okay, you're fine."

"Oh, I don't care. These are old."

She's sort of adorable in her obsessive-compulsiveness. I *should* fix her up with Preet.

"You'd be better off in shorts."

"I don't do shorts. I thought a skirt wouldn't work."

"You thought correctly. The house is incredible. Is that a real Diebenkorn?"

"You're not one of those people who has a problem with money, I hope."

She says this in the strangest way, half kidding, half serious, half unsure whether she is serious or kidding.

"I don't think so. I mean—"

"My father's in real estate. He's retired now, but he did well. He also collected art. He was actually friends with Diebenkorn."

"Very nice."

"My parents own the house, but they let me stay here."

"You grew up here?"

"Up the hill."

"So you went to Hills?"

She chuckles. "Public school?" She wags her finger. "Boarding school. First Massachusetts, then Switzerland. My father wasn't too interested in children. He shipped us out of here as soon as he could."

"How *was* Switzerland?"

"Very nice. Good skiing."

"You ski, but you don't hike."

"That's true. I never thought of that. Skiing is basically hiking."

"Except for the gondola to take you up the mountain and the fashionable attire."

Cindi proves herself a perfectly capable hiker. In fact, she's in much better shape than I am and she keeps getting ahead. I tell her it's not supposed to be exercise.

We walk along a ridge a quarter mile above the creek from which the redwoods drink. It feels like I could almost jump and land safely in the canopy. We climb up over a small hill and down to a clearing, away from the trail, for lunch.

"You seem like a very nice guy," she says.

"I'm a phenomenally nice guy."

She laughs slightly too hard, and then pauses for too long.

"I don't know exactly how to put this. I really appreciate your helping me out on Manners."

"But."

"Well, I just don't want there to be any misunderstanding—" she points back and forth between us—"about, you know."

"Ah, yes." I ape her finger-pointing maneuver.

"You know what I mean, right?"

"I do. I think we're fine. I've got enough problems in that department already."

"I've heard."

169

"What have you heard?"

"That you're totally obsessed with your ex-girlfriend."

I'm stunned. "I'm sure whatever you heard is vastly exaggerated. Anyway, it's complicated. What about you?"

"Complicated."

"Complicated good or bad?"

"Just complicated," she says. "My complication is in New York and I'm here, so—"

"You couldn't get a job in New York?"

"Maybe. It's complicated. Did you actually have something on Manners for me?"

I take her article about Swell out of my back pocket and hand it over.

"Wow. You're quite a sleuth."

"How'd you end up in television?" I say.

"Did you actually read this article? I'd never have survived as a writer. My dad got me that job."

"So," I say.

"So—"

"I'm just wondering whether you approached me at the Hall that night with something in mind."

She does not pause for even a moment. She looks me directly in the eye.

"My older sister and Ella knew each other. They went to Kettlewell Academy." The preppiest of the small, private prep schools in town. "You know, when I called you the other day I was going to tell you this."

"And?"

"When you mentioned the threats you were getting, I guess I forgot. It wasn't a big deal, really. I was looking for something interesting to cover when I was interning at the *Chronicle*. My sister suggested I write to Ella, and one thing led to another. I wrote the article, we

170

became friendly. Not friends exactly. We saw each other a few times over the years. I went to her wedding. Even when I was interviewing her when she was getting out of prison, I didn't ask her about her case, and she didn't talk about it.

"About three months ago she asked me to have lunch. She'd lost a lot of weight. She looked very pale. I thought she might be ill, but she denied it. She'd separated from Jack and I thought that might be the problem. But she didn't seem to want to talk about that. She wanted to know if I'd be willing to make public some information she had about the police raid on Zora Neal's Bookstore in 1988. I assume you're famil—"

"Intimately."

"She was incredibly vague. Obviously, now I wish I'd tried to get more from her, but she seemed so unwell. Part of me thought she might be having emotional problems too. She seemed kind of paranoid."

"Did she give you any idea of what she was talking about?"

"Just enough to get me interested, and nowhere near enough to report, or even really to pursue. She said one of the Zora Neal's people was working for the police back before the raid. I guess the informant told them A. C. Colder was using Zora Neal's to store drugs. The same person gave them the information about the shipment of cocaine on the morning of the raid in '88."

"But she didn't give you a name?"

"She said it was a prominent member of the community; someone whose career would be ruined if anyone found out he'd been working for the police. Pluck's the obvious candidate. He was involved in the store. He's the one running for mayor. Maybe he was unhappy about what was going on with Colder. He would have had some justification, I think. Ella wanted to know whether I was interested. She said she'd write the whole thing down and give it to me, dates, names of corroborating witnesses, cops involved, the whole thing."

"Did she say how she knew so much?"

"No. She *did* say she thought the person would try to kill her. Which is really the only corroboration I have for her story. I really didn't take it seriously. She never got me the details. She never called me again. But she did end up dead."

"Have you gone to the police with any of this?"

"I told Ella she ought to. But now that she's gone, I don't know. I mean, she seemed a bit off her rocker. What am I supposed to say? She knew who the informant was in the J-Posse case? She thought that person was going to kill her? I assume the police know who their own informant was, and they've probably given some thought to possible motives. If they had evidence Pluck shot her, he'd be in jail, no?"

"Did you have the sense Swell had gotten involved with Manners romantically?"

"Really?"

"I'm asking."

"She didn't mention a relationship. She did say she was going to tell him the story. She felt he deserved to know the truth about his mother."

"And what's the truth about his mother?" She shrugs. "I assumed the threats, and the assault on Marcus, were about the dog. Coming from SIF. Now I'm thinking I should probably be freaking out?"

"I don't know. I'll report it if you think it will help."

Terry will combust. Maeve—Jesus. "That's a bad idea. I'll talk to Mick Bacon."

"You think the dog case will go to trial?"

"Bulley's not about to let it die. I suspect he thinks Ella left him for Marcus. Probably, if they charge Manners with the Swell killing, the misdemeanors will disappear. But for reasons I can't explain, the cops don't seem to be in a rush. Sometimes I think it has nothing to do with the crowds outside the Hall every day and everything to do with ruining my musical career."

"How's that?"

I give her the scoop on Vegas. We eat and drink for a while. The sun is warm. The sky is blue. We stretch out on the blanket. Her hair is mostly product-free today. And the makeup is at a minimum too. I like her. In a world without Silvie I might even date her.

I get home in the early evening. Ferdy is on the couch napping. I tiptoe up two creaky stairs before he wakes.

"What the hell happened to your father's foot?"

"How's he doing?"

"He's sleeping. But he was a royal pain in my ass all day."

"He tripped before the fireworks. I took him to the emergency room. They said it's just a sprain. It looks worse than it is."

"It looks bad."

# 30

IT'S TUESDAY, MAY 18, around 5:30 P.M. Terry's Benz is in the shop, where it has a second home, so he's hitching a ride. In a far corner of the Hall parking lot, with waves of heat wafting up from the pavement, Mick Bacon is waiting for us. He's left several messages over the past week.

"Evening, Gordon. Terrence. Another toasty one, huh?"

I look around to make sure Duke and the chief are not in sight.

"Hey, Mick."

He blocks my way with his cinder block of a body.

"Manilow waits for no man, I guess," Mick says.

"Could you, please?"

Letting me pass, he waves a folder in my face. "DNA report. Guess whose skin is under Ella Swell's fingernails?"

"Manners—" Terry leaps in.

"There's nothing to discuss," I cut him off.

Terry gets in the car and rolls down the passenger window. Mick bends down and now the window frames his heavily wrinkled forehead and his square jaw.

"We got a big fat hook into your snitch," Terry says, unable to restrain himself.

"Oh yeah, what do you got?"

"We got Rogelio Contreras."

I know exactly what goes through Mick's mind when he hears the name of the witness the cops have had in lockup for days, who no one outside of the SRPD is supposed to know exists. He thinks, *this kid is wasting his life; he ought to be working for me.*

"This has been fun. Are we done?" I say.

"I thought we had a deal," Mick says.

"What I said, if you remember, is I'd talk to Manners."

"And?"

"And I talked to Manners."

"And?"

"*And*," Terry yaps from inside the car, "Contreras is a pro—"

"Terry, could you please shut the hell up."

"Obviously *you've* been doing some poking around," Mick says.

"No, *Terry* has been poking around. *I* have not poked. Nor do I intend to begin poking any time soon."

Before I can pull away, Mick opens the rear door and climbs in. He dons a pair of reading glasses that make him look like someone's grandfather and then opens a small notebook. He speaks while he traces across his notes with his calloused, crooked right index finger.

As I'm not nearly strong enough to pull Mick out of my vehicle, I screech out of the lot. My immediate intent is to drive to the Bay Bridge, park, and jump.

Mick reports, "Swell's in a hotel in Palm Springs from Wednesday, April 21, to Tuesday, the 27th. She rarely leaves her room. She's on an Alaska Airlines flight into Santa Rita that arrives around four P.M. on the 27th. She calls Marcus from her cell phone at nine-fifteen. Contreras sees them go into the house about an hour later. He says they have their hands all over each other. He hears Manners yell her name. Then he hears shots. We got prints, we got her blood on his shoes, now we got his skin under her nails."

"Then what the hell, Mick?" I'm out of my mind. Weaving all over the road, cutting cars off pell-mell. Terry has a wide-eyed, where-the-hell-is-this-coming-from? look on his face. "What do you want from me? You *know* who killed Swell, so go arrest him and leave me alone."

Yelling at Mick is something like walking into a telephone pole and then punching it out for getting in your way.

"I'd love to, but the kid didn't do it."

I look at him in the rearview. He's serious.

"What makes you so sure?" Terry asks him.

"What did Manners say?" Mick leans forward and rests his chin on my seat.

I don't respond. Terry and Mick both stare at me. It's true, as the chief said, that Mick Bacon is a cop, and cops sometimes lie—to cover up mistakes, to make sure someone they believe is guilty gets his due. And sometimes to trick gullible people like me into revealing secret, privileged information.

"I want you to know I'm violating my most solemn obligation to my client by telling you this," I say.

The truth is, I trust Mick. I believe him to be a decent, honest person. I don't think he's trying to set me up. And if I'm wrong, if my client ends up in prison for the rest of his life because of me, I'll never believe anything he says again. That, and I'll be unemployed. And probably homeless.

They continue to stare at me.

"Fine," I say. "Let's make a deal. I'll tell you what Manners said. You get Fischer to dump the misdemeanors. If Manners goes down on the murder, my case is going to disappear anyway. And if I help you find Swell's killer, there ought to be something in it for me."

"I'll see what I can do," Mick says. "I personally don't give a damn about that SI mutt."

"And we want the report of the Contreras interview," Terry adds.

Mick laughs. "Okay, you got it. So what do I get for all this?"

"You get nothing. Everything I'm about to tell you I have personally made up. None of it comes from my client. Understood?"

"Yes, sir, Counselor, sir."

I let Mick in on Manners's version of events. The basics, anyway,

176

the facts that might help get Marcus out of hot water. Unless I have a better idea who's the bad guy in the whole mess, I don't intend to give him the weirder stuff: that Swell knew she was about to be killed, that she was about to reveal some kind of dangerous truth to Marcus, or that the whole thing may relate to the J-Posse case. Or about the letters and assault, at least not in front of Terry.

"It's total bullshit," Mick says. "We know Manners was with Swell a lot during the last couple of months. He's lying if he says different. Bulley says they're poking each other. Same for Contreras. He said they were all over each other walking into the house. Also, Swell's blood is on the *top* of the kid's shoe, not the bottom. So he's there when the shots are fired. He's lying, but he's still not the shooter."

"How do you know?" I whine. "What makes you so sure? You're positive he's there, you've got all this evidence. Why are we having this conversation?"

Mick waits a couple of beats, drops his eyes and the corners of his mouth, and says, "I'm the kid's real father."

"What?"

"Jesus, kid, relax." Terry thinks Mick is hilarious. I do not. "You ever seen Manners throw a football? It's an incredible thing. He's an artist. There's no fear in him." Mick, whose shoulders are arthritic, tentatively, painfully, lifts his right arm to imitate my client. "It's like he's out back playing catch with his dad. He doesn't see the defense. He doesn't even see his own line. All he sees are receivers and holes to run through. He's gonna be a great one. You take my word for it."

"Which is relevant to the Swell killing how?"

"Who said anything about Swell?"

"What about the husband?" I say. "Why isn't he the obvious candidate? I doubt he was happy about Manners doing his wife. I assume you know he has a DV prior. You guys should be all over him."

"Believe me, I squoze that one dry." *Squeezed*, Mick. The past tense of *squeeze* is *squeezed*, not *squoze*. I smile and say nothing. "They'd been apart for a while when she got hit. Bulley had a new lady before the shooting. And the lawyers say he doesn't do any better with her out of the way. All the money stuff was handled before they got married. It's a dead end. The house, all of it, goes to State." California State University, Santa Rita.

"What about the fact that Brice Bulley is dealing coke out of the house?" I say. "What's his alibi?"

I expect to get the same respectful, admiring look Mick gave Terry when he mentioned Rogelio. But I do not.

"We heard about that right away. Those SI shits were lined up five deep waiting to snitch off the Bulley kid. The thing looks like it was pretty small-time. We had three guys on Brice for two hours, weeping, pissing his pants. He's not the guy. Everyone we talked to—the kid's mom, his friends, the father—everyone says Swell and the kid were tight."

"She's in the house for days, at least, right? Before anyone notices?" Terry asks. "I don't get that."

"The guesthouse is up a separate road from the main house," Mick reports. "Bulley says they haven't seen much of each other for a while. Coming and going is all. We confirmed that with the staff."

"What about Rogelio? He hears the shooting and does nothing?" I say.

"He figures he's suspect numero uno if he says anything. Only reason we got to Rogelio is he spilled to his lady friend up at the estate."

"Forget Contreras for a second," Terry says. "How sure are you the shooting goes down the day Swell gets back from Palm Springs?"

"Pretty sure. She's got a post office box down the hill. She picks up the mail after she flies back into town the 27th, and that's it. No more pickups. Bulley doesn't see her, but he sees the car by the house around the same time. Says he thinks the car wasn't moved after Tuesday.

Only reason he found her later on is he had something for her to sign, the following Tuesday."

"Anything useful in the autopsy?" Terry presses.

"She takes three shots: right arm, shoulder, and chest. The chest shot is the killer, went through her heart. There's residue all over her clothing, but we can't tie it to one of the shots in particular. All three are at fairly close range. From where we found the bullets, it seems like she's either standing or moving backwards toward the couch when she takes the arm shot. The others have to have her on the couch because we recovered both bullets there. Probably a revolver, but it's hard to say. The slugs are all mangled. We didn't find any casings. She also snorted cocaine not too long before she died, within a few hours."

It occurs to me that Terry and Mick have become some kind of team. It's a scary thought. I'll lose my job. My client will sue me for ethics violations. I attempt to wrest control of the situation, momentarily.

"Did the autopsy indicate that she was ill, maybe very ill?"

"Not that I know of. Was she?"

"Maybe."

"Where'd you get that? Manners?"

"No."

Even Terry is perplexed. "Who?"

"Someone."

"Bulley didn't mention it." Mick's definitely interested. He starts scribbling in his notepad. I'm the son again, and I like it. "So were they poking each other?"

"How should I know?" I answer.

"What's she doing calling him and taking him up to her house at night?"

"Poking him I guess." I smile. Terry is desperate to expand on my story, to explain Swell's motivation. I don't give him the chance. "What about the computer in her house?"

179

"Our guys couldn't find anything useful on it."

Terry and I turn to each other. *Preet.*

"Just get us the computer," I say. "If there's something on it, we'll find it."

"What am I gonna do, lug the thing home with me? You think Baptiste isn't watching me?"

"Tell us about '88," Terry says.

"There's not that much to it. We got information a coke dealer named A. C. Colder was using Grace Manners's bookstore for drop off and distribution to his cookers. We raided the place and took some fire from inside. I was riding with a rookie named Howe who got hit. Twenty-four years old. We took out a couple of Colder's people and arrested some others in the building, including Grace and Swell. We were against cutting Swell any slack, because of Howe, but Stanton Swell worked a deal for her. Then Grace got hit in jail and that was it."

"So who killed her?" Terry says.

"We never could make any of the girls in the jail. Everyone got real quiet. I assume Colder ordered the hit. He was doing a federal bit at the time. I'm sure he was worried we might flip her."

"And what about your informant? Who gave up Colder on the bookstore thing?"

He laughs. "You know who can answer that question, right?"

"He's not being too cooperative these days," I say. "He said *you'd* know."

"Sorry kid, the old man's flipped his switch on that one. He ran the guy, alone as far as I know. I wasn't involved until we took down the store. You think the Swell killing has something to do with all that?"

I quickly deflect the question. "What's this about skin under her nails?"

"The report came out today," Mick says. "Don't ask me to explain it, but I'm told it's his. We took pictures of Manners the day you were up at North station, but we didn't see any big scratches on him."

"Rogelio told you they looked like they were more than friends?" Terry says.

"Yeah, he figured the kid was about to get lucky. He said they had their arms wrapped around each other when they were going in the house. But the ME says there's no evidence she had sex, with Manners or anyone else."

"If she's sick, he could have been holding her," Terry says. "Maybe she scratched one of his arms on the way into the house."

"Or maybe she scratched him while he was shooting her," I say. "Right? He's two feet away, she grabs his arms, he fires. You still haven't explained how you're so sure the mountain of evidence against Manners doesn't prove exactly what it appears to prove."

"You gotta see the kid throw, Gordy," Mick says. "If you saw him throw, you wouldn't be talking like that."

# 3 1

NEXT DAY, TERRY, back behind the wheel of his precious Benz, pulls up to my house to drive me to work. Ferdy has my car for the morning. My grandfather is a notoriously aggressive and absent-minded driver. I have no realistic expectation of seeing my vehicle again.

Terry looks set to wing off to the coast after dropping me at work. He is shirtless, in swim trunks and flip-flops. Leather aviator goggles make him look like a prehistoric bird of some sort.

"Very nice," I say.

"Thanks." He pulls away with a screech. The top is down. While driving he reaches his right arm over the seat and retrieves a pair of goggles for me.

"No, not for me," I say. He shrugs and tosses them in the back.

"So, the reporter knew Swell," Terry says. I give him a dirty look. "Preet told me."

"I'd never have guessed."

"She bed you to get to Manners?"

"No, she did not bed me to get to Manners. She did not bed me at all. And if she had bedded me, it would have been because I'm brilliant and handsome."

"You couldn't question her judgment there."

I smile. The charmer.

"Apparently their families were acquainted. She was interning at the

*Chronicle.* She did the piece when Swell got out. They saw each other a few times over the years."

I tell him the rest.

"So Pluck's the bad guy?"

"I have no idea."

"It's got to be Pluck."

"Probably. I mean, probably that's who Swell had in mind. And probably that's what she was planning to unload on Manners. I haven't heard anything from Mick about any *evidence* Pluck was the shooter."

"Except an eyewitness."

"Who? Rogelio?"

"Not Rogelio, Gordy. Manners. It makes perfect sense. Why do you think Mick is so hot to question the kid? Manners sees Pluck whack Swell, or he hears the shots and sees Pluck take off. Either way, he knows who the shooter is. And that fits with all the other evidence—the blood on his shoe, for instance. But Pluck's like a father to the kid. No way Manners is going to snitch him off. Especially because Marcus has no way of knowing Pluck touched Colder on the bookstore thing, which eventually got his mother's throat cut." He stares ahead silently for a couple of minutes. "I bet it's all on the computer."

"Sad we won't be able to get to it. You didn't tell Preet about that, did you?"

He ignores the question. He tears around a corner and, the Mercedes's shocks not being what they used to be, bounces into the parking lot at the rear of the Hall. But he does not stow the car. Instead, he pulls up to the sidewalk. Preet and Aineen O'Connell, also dressed for a summer outing, hop in. Before I can protest or escape, we're off. Preet and Aineen strap on their goggles. I have the urge to sing "O you pretty Chitty Bang Bang." I'm in trouble.

"I have a court appearance in fifteen minutes," I say.

"Bullshit. I checked your calendar," Aineen says, handing me the remaining pair of goggles.

"Why are *you* here?" She shrugs. I look at Terry. He pays no attention to me and pulls the car out of the lot.

I have no idea what's happening. My birthday is still two weeks away. I'm not sufficiently addicted to drugs or alcohol to require an intervention. There's the Silvie thing, but that's been going on forever.

"Where are we going?"

"Relax," Terry says. "I don't want to hear you whine for three hours."

I strap on the goggles.

Preet leans forward and sticks his cell phone between Terry and me. Simultaneously, we say, "Hi, Maeve."

"Dear Mr. Manilow," Preet shouts above the wind and traffic and growling engine, reading from a legal pad. Terry snorts. "What's wrong with that?"

"*Mr. Manilow*," Terry says. "You must be kidding me."

"What, *Dear Barry*? The man is not our friend, Terry. Just because we are fond of him does not suggest he is fond of us."

"He'll be fond of us soon."

"Thus proving my point. In any case, there's no reason to take license." Preet's cell phone is now on his lap. It's tied by a wire to a headset, so he's in constant communication with Maeve. He points to his ear. "She is in complete agreement with me. *Mr. Manilow*."

"Let's just hear it," I say.

The letter to Manilow about the June fourth gig at the Mandalay ought to have been in the mail a week ago, but we haven't been able to nail it down. Preet agreed to take a first stab at it.

He continues, "We are among your greatest admirers—Maeve, will you please. Just listen to the whole thing and then—right. She says she agrees we should listen to the whole thing. Okay. Dear Mr.

Manilow." Terry snorts again, but Preet ignores him. "We are the members of a band dedicated to your work. We are among your greatest admirers. Barry X and the Mandys will be playing a show at the House of Blues in the Mandalay Bay hotel on June fourth at ten P.M. Should you be in Las Vegas by that time, we would be extremely honored if you would attend the show in whole or in part, and give us the benefit of your honest appraisal. Best regards, so forth and so on."

Preet looks up, expectantly. Then his face collapses. "Maeve says it's worse than shit."

"Maeve," I lean over the seat and get within six inches of Preet's mouthpiece. "Just because you're having a miserable life doesn't give you permission to be a total asshole."

Preet says, "She's sorry. But she still thinks it's worse than shit."

Terry says, rapidly, "Dear Barry. What's up? Barry X and the Mandys here. We thought you might be able to be at our Valentine's Day gig in Santa Rita, but something came up, I guess. No problemo. You *are* one hard-to-pin-down superstar. Anyway, we just wanted you to know that we'll be in Vegas, at the House of Blues, the night before your gig, warming up the fans. We'd be totally psyched if you could come by and check us out. Out for now, the Mandys."

As he glances around for reactions, the car weaves dangerously across the four-lane freeway. He doesn't seem to notice.

"I will not be a part of that," Preet says. "It's inane. Maeve agrees."

We drive in bad-tempered silence for a while.

"Dear Mr. Manilow," I say, staring ahead. "We write to tell you about our show, June fourth, at the House of Blues in the Mandalay."

"Maeve says 'louder.' "

"Fine," I shout. I start from the beginning and then continue: "If for some reason you've forgotten us, we're a California band dedicated to your music. Like all of your fans, we're extremely excited about your concert. If you have a chance, we'd be honored to see you at our show."

"Maeve says it's bad, but it's the least bad of the three."

"It sounds like it's written by a lawyer," Terry smirks.

# 32

**W**E TRAVERSE THE blistering, prehistoric lakebed that forms California's farm-rich Central Valley, debating the Manilow missive, and make our way into the slightly cooler foothills of the Sierra Nevada. At noon we pull into the visitors parking lot of Mule Creek State Prison in Ione, California. Mule Creek is like most of the newer prisons in the state—massive concrete pods abut large cement "yards," which in turn are surrounded by row upon row of fencing, some electrified, some not. All of it is topped with razor wire. We peel ourselves off the sticky leather seats. The others change into clothes more suitable for an inmate visit. My suit is nearly soaked through.

I don't like prisons. I know there are people who can't be trusted to live civilly. They should be sent to Club Med. Put fences around Club Med and let them tan themselves to death. It's depressing that we can't do anything more imaginative with criminals than cage them and feed them bad food and let them kill and rape each other.

"You coming?" Terry says.

"Nichols?" I ask. Ervin Nichols. The J-Posse gang member jailed in '88 following the Zora Neal's shootout.

"Let's go," Terry says. "We're already late."

"And Aineen?"

"Incentive."

"Ah."

"Maeve says she heard that," Preet reports.

I unplug the phone from Preet's headset and talk to her directly.

"Sadly, no cell phones allowed." Before she can deafen me, I click off.

If you want to get into prison, commit a crime. Otherwise, it's a chore. Just to get into the parking lot we had to wait in a long line of cars to pass through a checkpoint at which a guard picked through the Benz. Then, at the prison entrance, we spent twenty minutes filling out forms and submitting our identification for exhaustive review. Next followed the searches, which stopped just short of full body-cavity exploration. I had to pull my pants legs up past my shins and dance around like a puppet. Terry's dreadlocks posed an additional obstacle. He had to drop his head over, and to the side, to reveal any hidden shanks. Then we got on a bus, which arrives irregularly, that delivered us to the visitors center, where there were more forms and more searches. Then there was a long walk, through various security gates, metal detectors, and the sneering looks of guards and inmates alike, to a visiting room.

Because we're here on a legal visit, we get a private meeting room. Actually it's more a pen than a room. It has chain-link walls and a chain-link ceiling. The fencing is covered by translucent Plexiglas sheeting, which provides a degree of privacy. There's a round table and orange plastic chairs; one of us will have to stand, because there are only four. There are two doors. We enter through one. We wait for Nichols to arrive through the other.

Twenty minutes later a guard leads the prisoner into the room. Nichols has no idea what to make of us, but also, perhaps, he has not had a visitor of any kind in a long while. He knows enough not to start talking until the guard is out of earshot. The officer shuts Nichols in the room. The prisoner, shackled at the ankles, sticks his cuffed hands through a slot in the door. When he pulls his hands back to the room they are free to write or punch us out or whatever.

Terry makes the introductions. We shake. It's unclear at this point whether he's found Jesus. But he quickly finds Aineen, although her presence seems to confound him. She's removed her facial hardware for the day, but still he doesn't know quite what to make of her.

"You want to buy me a soda?" he asks her, grinning.

One quickly learns the dance of the prison visit—come with pockets brimming with quarters. There are vending machines with junk foods of all stripes. "You want to buy me a soda?" means *Start pumping in those coins and don't stop until I explode.*

It takes us twenty minutes to get Ervin settled with his popcorn and his chocolate bars and his noodle soup. He is a small, very light-skinned black man who must be in his early thirties but looks younger. He has long hair in thin braids fixed into a single thick bunch. His jaw muscles tense and release visibly with each mouthful of popcorn. The veins on the tops of his hairless, bulky arms remind me of a transit map. His eyes are too far apart. His ears are very small and set into his head like a dolphin's. His lips are flaky and cracked. His face is hairless.

"You might be one of the few people left who can remember what happened back in '88," Terry says.

He says nothing. He is still. It reminds me a bit of my first meeting with Marcus Manners, but Nichols, while just as nonresponsive, seems more anxious. His eyes flit from side to side.

"I understand you may be getting out sometime soon," I say.

"Who told you that?"

"Your public defender, Mr. Lara. He thought you'd be coming up for parole soon."

"Lara don't know shit. Parole *hearing* ain't mean nothing," he says, disgusted by my ignorance. "They *supposed* to give us a date, but they just say come back next year. Same shit every time."

"I'm sorry. I didn't know that."

Okay, I'm done. Can we leave now? I'm intensely uncomfortable in Nichols's presence. His circumstances are so miserable as to be absurd—a seventeen-year-old boy swept up in the crack craziness, sent to prison, forever.

The smile returns to Nichols's face and he scoots his chair a few inches closer to Aineen's. He gazes at her, smiling. It seems menacing to me. She looks back, unfazed, as in *Puh-leez, even if I was interested, what are you going to do for me here?*

"Can you tell us what happened in your case?"

He shrugs. "We was dealing drugs. That's what happened. Shootin' people and makin' money. Havin' us some fun too. Too much fun." He is trying to impress Aineen, keeps looking over at her. But she has a bored expression, and Nichols's tone becomes increasingly hostile.

"You remember a woman named Ella Swell?"

"Grace Manners's girl. She used to hang at the store. She got herself shot, huh?"

"You remember Grace Manners?"

"You ever see her picture, man? Can't nobody forget that girl. That's the only woman I ever saw A. C. respect."

"Colder and Grace were friends?" I say.

"Yeah, they was *real* good friends." He laughs. "I wish I had me a friend like that over here." He looks wistfully at Aineen. "How 'bout you be my friend?"

No doubt she would like to grab Ervin by his balls, hoist him above her head, and hurl him across the room. But she knows she's here as bait, and she plays her part without complaint.

"Wasn't she married?" I say.

"Maybe. Like I said, her and A. C. was together, least until he went down. He act like that boy was his own son."

"Marcus. Grace's son?"

"Mmm hmm."

"So, who snitched off Colder on the bookstore thing?" Terry says.

Nichols keeps sneaking glances at Preet's turban. "You a Muslim?"

"Sikh, actually. Although my primary spiritual focus is Theosophy."

"You ever figure out who put the cops onto the store?" Terry presses.

"Nope."

"Colder and Grace Manners, huh," Terry says. Nichols tenses and leans back in his seat. "So he wouldn't have ordered her killing?"

"I heard one of them Posse girls done her."

"On Colder's say so, right?"

Nichols has been balancing on the two back legs of his chair. He slams the chair to the floor and reaches across the table for Terry's dreadlocks. Hair in both hands, he pulls Terry out of his chair, across the table, and starts twisting his head like he intends to remove it. The move paralyzes Aineen and Preet and me for a moment. Then Aineen starts hollering for a guard. Beneath her shrieks I can hear Nichols asking Terry, "Why you come up here asking me this shit? I shouldn't *even* be talking to you."

Terry, apparently not bothered by the assault, responds, "What are you so worried about?"

"I ain't worried 'bout *nothing*. You the one got to be worried now."

A guard blows into the room seconds later, peels Nichols's hands off my bass player's locks, and removes him from the cage.

# 33

THE FINAL GATE closes behind us. We walk into the visitors parking lot and settle into the Benz. I always feel faintly guilty walking away from a prison, like I'm actually an escapee. I have the urge to make a run for it.

"You guys ready for this?" Terry says.

"Maeve says she's ready," Preet reports.

"How's your head?" I say.

Preet says, "Maeve wants to know what's wrong with Terry's head?"

The attack doesn't slow him down in the least. "A. C. Colder was Manners's father. Swell decides to tell Marcus the truth. Speed doesn't want Marcus to know. So *he* shoots Swell before she can spill."

"Just so I'm absolutely clear, the working theory now is Speed was the shooter?" I ask.

"You heard what Nichols said."

"He said Colder *acted* like Marcus was his child. I also saw him in the midst of what looked like a psychotic break. Forgive me if I'm not hanging on his every word."

"That was my fault. I got in his face."

"I assume you still believe Manners was an eyewitness? Same setup, different bad guy."

"It's the same problem for Marcus, right?" Terry says. "He doesn't want to snitch off the man he believes is his dad."

"Speed?"

"Right. And he believes that because Swell didn't have a chance to tell him the truth."

"Does this mean you no longer think it was Pluck? Or do we now have two shooters?"

Terry reflects on that question for a moment.

"Maeve says she still thinks it was Bulley."

"I doubt they'd do it together," Terry finally says. "Could be, but it seems like the motives are too different."

In Davis, a college town outside of Sacramento, Terry pulls into my favorite out-of-town burger joint, called Murder Burger.

"How appropriate," Preet, a strict vegetarian, says.

We load up on grease and carbs while we sit in traffic on our way into Santa Rita.

With his mouth almost completely filled with food, Terry says— actually, I have no idea what Terry says. He tries again, disgustingly, several times. Finally he approaches intelligibility.

"We have to get that computer to Preet. Once we figure out what Swell had in mind to tell Marcus, then we'll know for sure."

"You don't need to get the computer to me," Preet says. "You only need to get me to the computer."

"Maybe Mick can get us in," Terry says, looking at me expectantly.

"And maybe it will snow tomorrow."


Twenty minutes short of the city I remember that I'd turned off my cell phone at the prison. When I turn it on, it rings almost immediately. It's Speed.

"I tried your office. They said you haven't been in all day," he says. "What's up?"

"Could you come by the apartment?"

"Now?"

"If you can."

"Is everything all right?" He sounds shaken.

"Just come over."

I click off. I have no intention of involving the crew in this mess, whatever it is. I turn to Terry. "Ferdy. Pop's foot is driving everyone crazy."

"How's your shoulder?" Terry says.

"All right. I'm on antibiotics. I don't recommend having a demented parent."

"My father once put a golf club through the windshield of our car," Terry says.

"What was that about?"

"I don't know. It was a long time ago. Something with my mom, I guess."

"No biting, though?"

"No."

"Maeve says she has a cousin who bit off one of her husband's balls," Preet says.

"Seriously?" Terry says, wincing.

Aineen says, "Darleen O'Connell. They're still married. He was screwing around and gave her some kind of venereal disease."

Preet chimes in, "Maeve says you just don't fuck with O'Connell women."

Sensing my urgent need to tend to my father, Terry dumps me at home before delivering Preet and Aineen to their cars at the Hall. King is reading in the living room.

"Where have you been? Ferdy and everyone else on the planet has been trying to find you."

"Did someone die?" I say.

"How should I know?"

"Where's S.?"

"Upstairs. What'd you do to his damn foot?"

"Grandpa didn't say what's going on?"

194

"He said the *damn* city's probably going to burn down tonight and make sure to keep the *damn* doors locked. Other than that, no."

I change and rush over to Marcus's place. Speed opens the door. The atmosphere in the apartment is funereal. Lucy Pluck sits on the living room couch sobbing uncontrollably. Bea is trying to console her. Ferdy is in the kitchen unpacking take-out Chinese food. They send me into Marcus's bedroom.

I crack the door a few inches. Marcus is on the bed. Pluck sits in a chair next to him. He stands and shakes my hand when I walk in. Marcus sits up and nods at me. His left arm is in a sling. His face is swollen.

"What happened to you?"

Pluck answers, "Retaliation, that's what happened."

Some men followed Marcus into a parking lot, dragged him out of his car, and socked him up.

"I hope you're a righty?"

"We had him looked over at the hospital," Pluck answers. "They didn't do any permanent damage. But they hit him in the head a few times, so the doctor said to keep him in bed tonight and watch for signs of a concussion."

"Did you talk to the police?" I ask.

Pluck walks to the door. "That's a bone of contention. Perhaps you can talk some sense into him." He leaves.

"Could you identify them?"

"Maybe."

"The same guys as before."

"One of them, I think. The big one. Not the others."

"They say what they wanted?"

"Not really."

"Was it racial?"

"It doesn't bother me."

"Your call. Doesn't seem quite even, you take their dog, they get to

195

beat up on you every chance they get. Too bad I wasn't there to defend you."

He smiles slightly. "I just want to graduate and get out of here."

Keeping my voice down, I say, "I did some poking around after our conversation the other night. And I talked to my friend the cop. Anything you want to change about your story?"

"I told you the truth."

"But you spent more time with Ms. Swell than you said."

We can hear Pluck and Ferdy muttering threateningly in the living room.

"I told you I was up there."

"You did, that's true. But you also did your best to minimize it. Was there something between you and Ella? Maybe you were more than just friends?"

He laughs, but I do not. He stops, and then looks at me like I am insane. "No."

"Jackson Bulley had the impression you were sleeping with his wife."

"Maybe *he* killed her."

"Maybe. The police don't think so. But anyway, he must have had some reason to believe you were having an affair with his wife. And the witness who says he saw you walk into the house with her on the 27th also says you looked like more than friends."

"Well we weren't. We weren't even friends really."

"But you did see her several times in the six weeks before she died?"

"I told you. I helped her move some stuff."

"And the other times?"

"We just hung out. She talked about my mother, about the book-store and all that."

"Did she tell you what happened at the store the day your mom was arrested?"

"Not really. She told me some people at the store got into drugs. She said my mom wasn't responsible."

"Did she mention A. C. Colder?"

"No. But I know who he was. Ella gave me some newspaper articles."

"You understood Swell was a witness against your mother, that she was going to testify?"

"She explained all that."

"But you didn't blame her for your mother's situation?" He shrugs. "Did she tell you who killed your mom?"

"They never caught anyone."

"But she didn't have a theory?"

"She didn't talk about it."

"Did she seem ill to you?"

"Not really. Like how?"

"Weak. Losing weight. Something like that." He shakes his head. "You know you don't have to lie to me, Marcus. I'm not the enemy."

"I know." He seems to. It's hard to reconcile all the pieces, but he appears to be telling the truth.

"My cop friend told me they have a DNA test showing your skin under Ella Swell's fingernails."

"Seriously?" I raise my eyebrows. He does not look away. "I don't know anything about that."

"It doesn't necessarily mean anything. They can test very small amounts of skin. It could have been from anything. But it gives them another pin to stick you with. Did Swell ever mention a television reporter named Cindi Paris?"

"No. She said she was going to talk to the newspaper. She didn't say anything about TV."

Ferdy jumps on me when I emerge. "You talk sense into him."

"He's got plenty of sense."

"You don't think we should call the police?" Pluck says.

"He's the client. I just follow orders."

"This is crazy," Bea says. "This city has gone crazy. Over a damn dog. I'd like to know what you plan to do about this, Gordon? The boy is your responsibility now."

There's a part of me that wants to tell my elderly sort-of-grandmother the truth, which is that I intend to do nothing about it, that I have far less power to affect Manners's future than she imagines. And that I'm fairly certain, innocent or guilty, he's going away for the Swell killing. Seems like the best thing to do is to keep my mouth shut.

"What about his case?" Speed says.

I give them the schedule—the upcoming suppression hearing, the trial dates.

"We may be able to convince Reasoner to back off his position on the plea deal, but I wouldn't count on that."

Lucy has regained her composure. She listens quietly while Pluck and Ferdy vent. When they are through, she speaks softly.

"I wish I could tell them all to just leave us be. They're just trying to drag us down before we can get out of this stupid city."

Pluck pets his daughter's head and says, "I wouldn't let that happen, Luce. You *know* I'm not going to let that happen."

# 34

I'S MONDAY MORNING, May 24. Milo Velikovic and I sit in Reasoner's court waiting for the clerk to call our case. We're on for my suppression motion. The room is packed with Manners loyalists. Marcus's latest thumping doesn't seem to have reached the press, but I doubt Pluck has kept it from the posse. They look jazzed.

I'm nervous, but not overly so. The crowd is with me. If I perform just north of miserably, I'll be a hero. There's no question of actually prevailing on the 1538. Reasoner denied my Pitchess motion—to reveal Dent's probable history of on-the-job misconduct and lying—and he's made it clear he believes the suppression hearing is a waste of time. He'll do everything he can to protect Dent.

But the crowd will get what it came for. We'll spill some blood—mine, Dent's. We'll give Reasoner an opportunity to humiliate the lawyers. And we'll stoke the fires burning in Marcus Manners's name around town.

The judge is later than usual. Perhaps he's finally expired.

"You still want to know about Silvie?" Milo says, with a faint smile.

"Sure." My heart does a couple of somersaults.

"Are you sure?"

"Milo, believe me. It's not a big deal. I'm just sort of curious."

"This is between us, right? You didn't get it from me."

"Will you get on with it?"

I want to know everything. I want to know nothing. Suddenly my confidence about the hearing evaporates. Milo's timing is suspect. He knows just what he's doing. He's set me up, the bastard.

"Fischer's going to put the Swell case to a grand jury," Milo reports. That's not good.

"Which has what to do with Silvie?"

"I'm going to tell you."

"When's the grand jury set?"

"Soon. I don't know exactly."

In state court, when the district attorney believes he has probable cause to charge someone with a felony, typically he files a criminal complaint. Some time later there's a preliminary hearing at which a judge decides whether the DA was right about the state of the proof. If there's sufficient evidence against the defendant, the case goes to trial. If not, the case is dismissed. Although because the judge who makes that decision is almost always a former DA, the case is never dismissed.

There is another, less common route to trial. The prosecution can present the evidence against the defendant—witnesses, documentary evidence, and so on—to a group of sixteen citizens, a *grand* jury, that meets privately. Unlike at a preliminary hearing, the target of the grand jury—in other words, the person who will eventually become the defendant—does not have a right to be present during the proceedings. The target can't offer evidence. He can't cross-examine witnesses presented by the government. And if the DA calls the target to testify, his lawyer can't be with him to defend his rights.

The grand jury hears the DA's version of events, and the DA's argument in favor of the charges against the target, and then decides whether there's sufficient evidence to indict the person for whatever crimes are alleged. If the grand jury finds probable cause to indict, the case goes to trial.

I've never understood why state prosecutors don't use grand juries more frequently. The DA doesn't have to give the defendant an early shot at his or her witnesses, or expose the details of his or her theory.

The prosecutor can spin the evidence to favor his or her view of the case. The DA even gets to call the future defendant to the stand and rip him to shreds, or make him look like a criminal if he takes the Fifth.

It makes perfect sense that Fischer would want to avoid a preliminary hearing in the Swell case. No gallery filled with Manners supporters. No defense lawyers playing the race card on television every night. No character witnesses saying Manners wouldn't hurt a fly. By presenting the case to a grand jury, the cops can avoid the potentially riot-inducing act of arresting Marcus Manners for murder until they are certain there will be a trial. And, most important, candidate Fischer can point to the grand jury and say, *Hey, don't blame me. Sixteen citizens of this county heard the evidence and they say Manners killed Swell.*

Milo continues, "Silvie's working with Sid Bateman to prepare the case."

"You must be kidding me." Here she is showing up for rehearsals, strumming my pain with her fingers, singing my life with her words, and in the meantime she's preparing to push my client over a cliff. "Who's the boyfriend?"

"Are you sure you want to know this?" I give him a blank stare. "Bateman."

"Sid Bateman." Milo shrugs. "Not Sid Bateman's grandson?" Bateman must be twenty years older than me. "Isn't he married?"

"Separated."

"Dipping her pen in the company ink. I don't like it one bit."

Bateman's the best trial lawyer in the DA's Office. The thought of them together is infuriating. The man has a comb-over, a potbelly, and the pastiest complexion since Ping-Pong balls. And he's old. It's like she's designed her boyfriend selection solely to infuriate me.

Now I'm not nervous about the crowd or freaked out about Silvie working the Swell grand jury or anxious about Reasoner abusing me. I'm pissed and ready to rip Dent a couple of new orifices.

The clerk calls the case. Marcus sits at counsel table with me. He seems uncharacteristically uneasy. His leg springs up and down and he keeps turning around to check on Lucy and Pluck. He's recovered from his recent beating quickly. There's still a little swelling around his eye, and his arm isn't much use, but he's cleaned up well for the appearance.

"Where'd you go to high school, officer?"

Dent is on the stand.

"Relevance, Counselor?" Reasoner immediately jumps on me.

"As Your Honor is aware, there is a long-standing rivalry between my client's high school and Saint Illuminatus. Officer Dent attended SI. I'm informed he is a member of the leading SI booster group. It goes to credibility."

"No, it doesn't. Move on."

The crowd grumbles. Reasoner whacks his gavel on the bench.

"Perhaps some of those in the gallery have never attended a court proceeding before. This is not a sporting event. One does not cheer for one's team. One listens in silence. Moreover, this is not a democracy. I am the king here. I will close this proceeding to the public if there is further comment. Have I made myself clear?"

The gallery is a child. Reasoner is a father with a belt behind his back.

"At some point you obtained an arrest warrant for Mr. Manners."

"Yes, sir. That is correct."

"So you went to his apartment house in West Santa Rita with the intent of taking him into custody."

"Correct, sir."

I look at him for a moment. He's enjoying himself too much. Most cops don't like the witness box. It's the rare setting in which the badge and the gun lose their clout. And usually I enjoy their uneasiness, because atop the body of every officer I've cross-examined, sits the head of my father.

Dent, though, probably has a hard time getting taken seriously on the street. Here he has a captive audience, a chance to perform.

"And when you arrived at the house, you immediately executed that warrant."

"Mr. Seegerman," the judge cuts in before Dent can answer. "Look over there." Reasoner points his decrepit forefinger at the jury box. "Tell me what you see?" I drop my head. He snarls, "Tell me."

"I see the jury box."

"And who do you see in the jury box?"

"No one."

"Keep that in mind."

Back to Dent. "What did you do after you arrived?"

"I posted Officer Botka near the entrance and walked around the building to a rear parking area in an attempt to locate the suspect's vehicle."

"And why did you do that instead of simply executing the warrant?"

"Well, there's no doubt we had a sufficient quantum of evidence to make the arrest. But the investigation was ongoing. I was considering an additional charge of vehicular trespassing. I wanted to see whether the car was parked at that location. Also, the area near the Swell estate where a witness observed the vehicle was covered with gravel. I hoped to check the tire treads for gravel."

"And you found the vehicle registered to my client's father in the carport."

"That is correct."

"And you checked the tires."

"Yes, sir."

"At that point your investigation of the vehicle was complete, was it not?"

"Well, that would depend, sir. Complete as to the matter of the dog, yes, sir. Complete as to other matters, no, sir. As I noted, the investigation was ongoing."

Dent lies. I know it's hard to believe. A man in blue. Sworn to uphold the law. But trust me. I can see him sweating and twiddling his thumbs and shifting around in his seat.

He lies. He claims the car was parked with its nose in. Despite his girth, and the small space between the car and the concrete walls of the carport, he testifies he walked up the length of the car, crouched down, and checked the right front tire. He says he stood up and he saw the pot on the floor in front of the front passenger seat, in plain view. He says the marijuana was packaged in a manner that is common practice among drug dealers. It's all nonsense.

"Have you ever known a marijuana user to store his drugs on the floor of his car, Officer?"

"I've seen it. This isn't a population known for its mental acuity, Counselor."

To his credit, Reasoner spreads his abuse around. He lays into Dent for wasting the court's time with his inappropriate and overlong comments.

"You planted the marijuana in the car, didn't you, Officer Dent?"

That one's for the crowd. It's not as if I really expect Dent to break down and admit what seems nearly certain—that he simply took it upon himself to "find" the pot in the car to make the charges against Marcus a bit sexier. Reasoner is off the bench faster than I'd imagined possible.

"Counselor," he shrieks. "Approach."

When I arrive, he whispers, "You'd better have an offer of proof for me." In other words, some kind of evidence to back up my suggestion of wrongdoing by Dent.

"I am informed and believe Officer Dent has fabricated evidence in the past to obtain a search warrant." Terry mentioned something like this. I have no real basis to make the claim, but that's not my fault. If Reasoner had given me Dent's personnel file, I wouldn't have to be shooting in the dark. "I also believe he's an SI alumni, a rabid SI football fan, and—"

"That describes me, Seegerman."

"Your Honor, this officer has a reputation for misconduct in the department. I have the right to present that in the context of this hearing. I ask you to reconsider your Pitchess ruling."

"That's enough. I'll throw you in jail, Counsel. Watch it."

After Dent skulks out of the courtroom, I put on Marcus and Speed, to describe how they share the car, how they always park it nose-out, and the features of the carport that make Dent's story totally unbelievable. I introduce pictures of the car and the parking area that bear out their testimony.

"Anything else, Counsel?" Reasoner says.

Milo passes on cross. He hardly needs it.

"Should we address the points and authorities now, Your Honor?"

"You think something you will say in argument will significantly assist me in making my ruling?" No response is required. "I didn't think so. The motion is denied. Court is adjourned."

He whaps his gavel on the bench. The clerk scrambles to get the gallery on its feet before Reasoner, impressively spry today, scampers down from the bench and out the back of the courtroom.

# 35

**M**ICK BACON STOPS by my office as I'm packing up for the day. I pull him into my office and close the door. "Would you please call ahead next time? I'd rather not be seen with you."

"What?" He looks slightly hurt.

"My boss believes you are manipulating me and undermining my client's interests."

"*I'm* trying to save Manners's touchdown-throwing ass. I have feelings, you know."

"Can we move this along?"

He pops open his briefcase and starts thumbing through some papers. "Fischer's about to hit the grand jury for an indictment against Manners."

"I heard that," I say.

"I'm losing control, Gordy."

"I don't know what you expect me to do. He's *your* friend."

He sits, looking downright depressed.

"Yeah, well, for some reason on this one he's not listening. Maybe it's me. Maybe I'm losing it. But I just don't think the kid did it. I can't prove it, though. If there's a way out, Manners has it in his head." He tosses a folder on my desk. The Rogelio Contreras interview report. "That's for your pal."

"I don't know what else to say. I told you what Marcus said about what happened."

"That's true," he says, skeptically.

Actually, it's not true. The guy looks at me with his big blues, the saggy lids, the big schnozzle, practically calling me a liar.

"There *are* a couple of other details. Frankly, I figured it was bullshit until recently. But now, I don't know."

"I'm listening."

"Please tell me you're not screwing with me."

"You think I'm not out on a limb on this thing, coming over here?"

"When Swell called Manners on the 27th, she apparently had some big news to tell him. Some secret relating to '88. He told me she'd talked to him about his mother and about the bookstore before, but she never got into details about the J-Posse case. That night she wanted to spill something."

"Like?"

"Just listen. She picks him up and says she's got something to give him, something she wrote. Maybe from the computer. Maybe not. They go up to the house, and it's like I told you, she sends him out for beer, she gets hit. That's his story. Manners says she never had a chance to talk to him. She did tell him she was going to get killed."

He looks at me while he rolls the new facts around in his head.

"She *said* that?"

"According to Manners." *And* Cindi, but God knows I'm not going down that road. "We also talked with a guy named Ervin Nichols last week."

He smiles. "That piece of shit. Where's he at?"

"Mule Creek. Except for when he tried to rip Terry's head off, he was perfectly friendly. Seems ridiculous the guy's doing life because Colder was paying better than McDonald's in those days."

Mick's mood sharpens abruptly. "Bobby Howe was twenty-four years old with a new kid when they hit him. Thirty years I got in and he's the only partner I lost."

"I read the reports. I didn't see any evidence Nichols had a gun."

"I don't care who hit Howe. We weren't there for a party."

207

"Anyway, Terry figures the Swell killing is related to the bookstore thing, so he dragged me up there. He asked Nichols if he knows who told the cops Colder was using the store as a warehouse and he went nuts."

"He's worried about getting a snitch jacket."

"Probably. He did say that Grace and Colder were an item."

"Wouldn't surprise me. I heard the husband was on the pipe in those days. And that was one gorgeous lady."

"Doesn't that make it unlikely he had her killed?"

"You kidding me? Colder was a snake. He was already down then." In other words, in prison. "Got a good taste of incarceration. She probably had stuff that could put him away for good. It had to be coming from Colder."

"So what happened to him?"

"Three-three hit him." J-Posse's rival gang.

"What a life."

He stands. "By the way, whoever your source is on Swell, he was right. She was on her way out." He removes a sheet from his briefcase. "Hepatocellular carcinoma."

"Which is?"

"Some bad liver thing."

"The coroner missed it?"

"Hard to imagine," Mick chuckles. The local coroner's office has been the target of state investigations, court inquiries, and damning newspaper series over the past few years. "Probably he just wasn't looking. The shot to the chest was the killer. Swell's doctor's been out of town since before the shooting. I talked to him this morning. He said she'd have been dead in a month or two."

I walk across town and reach City Hall around five-thirty. In the cavernous, marble-encased lobby I run into Cindi Paris.

"How's your client?" She has on her TV voice, and in this echo chamber it seems too loud.

"Considering the increasing likelihood of life in prison, he's excellent."

"I heard he had a little run-in, maybe with some SI people."

"That's strange. I didn't hear that."

"Gor-dy."

"Cin-di."

"Is he all right?"

"He seems fine. I can't say I have much insight into the kid."

"Was it the same group as before?"

"Off the record?" She nods. "Marcus said it was the same idiots. But he was anxious not to press it. Seems to me if it was really SI guys, he'd be inclined to fight back. There's something else to it."

"You think it's connected to the threats?"

"I don't know. None of it makes much sense. I'm actually heading to meet with Pluck right now. You think I should ask him if he shot Swell?"

"I just left there. You heard about the grand jury?" I nod. "I went up to get a comment."

"And?"

"His secretary said he was tied up. Is Marcus going to testify?"

"For the record, my client won't be spilling his guts without complete immunity. Off the record, I have no idea."

"I really didn't think it would come to this. What about your case?"

"Unfortunately, still on."

"Anything I can do?"

"Unless you're willing to testify that you're a dope-fiend dognapper, no."

She grabs my arm with her hand. "I had a really nice time with you the other day."

"Hiking?"

She thinks for a moment, looks surprised, and says, "I guess so."

"You seem to be in an awfully chipper mood," I say.

She laughs and looks down at her shoes, which happen to be the pointiest I've ever seen. They look downright homicidal.

"Just happy to see a friendly face," she says, and hugs me.

I watch her walk away, scanning for possible witnesses. Sometimes I wish Silvie didn't have such a hold over me. This constant vigilance is exhausting.

I'm in the waiting room outside Pluck's office. The receptionist wants to know if I have an appointment. I hand her a business card and say, proudly, *I sure do.* She asks me to wait. The reception area is elegantly appointed. Oriental rugs line the dark, burnished wood floor. No doubt the furniture would prefer that I stand, but luckily, it cannot speak.

Over the next half hour three people enter the waiting room and stroll into Pluck's office, closing the door behind. After each one walks in, the receptionist smiles at me and says, "He should be right with you." Clearly this is a lie. She has had no communication with the councilman since my arrival. She has not picked up the phone. She has not left her desk. I hear Pluck raise his voice a few times. Finally all three visitors leave, looking chastised. She picks up the phone, whispers for a moment, hangs up, smiles, and says, "He should be right with you."

Pluck asked me to come by, I assume, to discuss the grand jury, and keeps me waiting for forty-five minutes. So when I'm finally admitted, I'm not pleased, but immediately I can see it's the wrong time to be snippy. He does not spring out of his chair and apologize for keeping me waiting. Instead he sits, looking bewildered, much like he appeared when I told him Swell had been killed. Finally he shakes himself out of it. But he has none of his usual fervor.

"I understand there's going to be a grand jury." His tone is doleful.

"I just heard that myself."

"What does it mean?"

210

"Hard to say, really. Fischer has some evidence. And it's safe to say Marcus is the target. But this case has been pretty weird from the beginning. To be perfectly honest, I have no idea what's really going on."

"As you can imagine, Mr. Fischer's door has been closed to me on this one. Will Marcus be called to testify?"

"I assume I'll get a subpoena for him sometime soon."

"Then what?"

"That's up to Marcus."

"He can refuse to testify?"

"Sure. He can plead the Fifth. Or he can tell them what he knows."

"Which is?"

"That's up to Marcus to tell you."

"I'm just worried for the boy."

He invites me to sit down and offers a drink. I decline, but he pours himself a tall one.

"Did you ever meet Ella?"

"No. I've seen pictures." Postmortem pictures, which weren't particularly flattering.

"She was a funny woman. Sharp. And with a mouth on her. She was one of the few white people who hung around the bookstore."

"And what about you? Where did you fit into the deal?"

"By that time I had some property in the area. I leased Grace one of my buildings at a discount and made a small investment. I wasn't part of the day-to-day operation."

"And what about '88?"

His tone sharpens. "I told her to stay away from Colder. No one could tell Grace Manners a damn thing. When she was killed, my late wife and I felt we should take in Marcus. Speed was in no condition to raise the boy."

"Could Marcus have believed Swell was responsible for Grace's death?"

"If Marcus decided the moon was made of Swiss cheese, you couldn't talk him out of it. He's got his mother's stubbornness. It was Ella who was supposed to testify against Grace, so I guess he could have blamed her. It's ridiculous, though. Grace had her eyes open. She knew exactly what she was getting herself into with Colder. I told her again and again." Pluck's frustration is palpable. "He was bad business that guy, deep down bad."

I have no idea who killed Swell, but it's now clear to me Pluck was the snitch. It was his building. He would have known Colder stored drugs there. He knew Grace was cheating on her husband with the kingpin. And he obviously had no great affection for Colder. A man like Pluck wouldn't have sat idly by. He would have done something.

# 36

I'S NINE P.M. Wednesday night. I was supposed to be at Preet's half an hour ago. S. and I ate a lovely dinner of frozen pizza and canned peas. The peas remind me of my mother. She had a thing for fancy English sweet peas. Not one to needlessly dirty a bowl, she'd open a can, cut in a few fat chunks of butter, and put it in a saucepan with an inch of water. Ten minutes later she'd wrap the can in a potholder and shovel the peas into her mouth. And mine, once the can cooled a bit.

King is occupied. Ferdy is late. S. is still recovering from his collapse at the lake, so I can't very well lug him to rehearsal. Cindi is on the television news reporting on the continuing Manners-related protests at the Hall. My father reclines on the couch with his feet on our fraying wicker coffee table. I bring him Fig Newtons and milk. He watches the tube. I watch him.

The further S. is from his history, the less he seems meaningfully human. He's sailing blissfully toward the life of a banana slug. I assume I'll follow him into oblivion. It seems too much to suppose both King and I could have dodged the AD bullet. It's terrifying, though, the thought of one day, perhaps not so far off, morphing into a memoryless mollusk.

Ferdy finally wanders in at nine-thirty. I quickly gather my things.

"Did you forget I have rehearsal?"

He ignores me. "Pluck said you stopped by. He seems real impressed with you."

"That's weird. I haven't done anything yet."

"I wouldn't trust him if I were you."

"Fortunately for us both, you are not me. He seems to have generated a lot of support for Manners."

"Like I told you—Pluck worries about Pluck."

"Are we through here?"

"No." He points at a chair in the living room. "Sit."

"I was supposed to be out of here an hour ago."

"Sit." I sit. He parks, next to S., who smiles at us both and hums, tunelessly, to himself while staring at the TV. The sound is off. The windows are open. I can hear crickets or something. "A very nice doctor named Jennifer Lediger called to ask about your father. From Santa Rita General."

Gulp. "That's nice. Can I go now?"

"We're hiding things from each other?"

"What?"

"Why didn't you tell me?"

"It wasn't a big deal. He got freaked out because of the crowd and the demonstration. I should never have dragged him out to the lake."

"*And* he bit you?"

"I'm really not sure what happened. It's more like he fell and hit me with his teeth."

"The doctor said he was psychotic."

"The doctor said—that's horseshit, Grandpa. The doctor was about nine years old, and by the time we got to the hospital, dad was fine. He was just freaked out by the crowd and the noise. Does he look psychotic to you?"

We both look at S. He looks like a happy, harmless idiot.

"She sounded cute," Ferdy says, smiling.

"Who?"

"Doctor Lediger."

214

"She wasn't cute." Actually she was sort of cute. "Anyway, the relevance of that would be?"

"Just trying to grease the wheel a little."

"That's very nice. I'm greasing my own wheels these days."

"How's your arm?"

I make my way to the door. "It's fine. Everything's fine. I know what you're thinking and I don't want to talk about it."

For years we've talked about moving my dad to a nursing home. There may well come a time when we can't manage. But if he goes, we'll need to sell 4200 Candlewood to finance his care. I'm not ready to let go of my mother's house.

"Don't get yourself in a knot. I don't want you to feel like you have to hide things from me."

"Fine. Good-bye."

Silvie and the boys are jamming when I arrive. I ask the ex to step outside. Maeve, overseeing the affair from her sickbed, does not object. I suppose she senses a meltdown in the offing.

"I hear you're about to ruin my client's life." My tone is spiteful. "You expect me to just go in there and rehearse like nothing's happening?"

Who knew Manners's predicament would move me to risk pissing-off the ex? I'm suddenly at risk for becoming the sort of lawyer who stays late at work and feels bad if his clients go down. The thought stuns me momentarily.

"This was your idea, Gordy. Remember? *You* said it would be fine."

"Ah, yes. But *you* believed me."

"I like it too. I had no idea how much I missed Barry."

"I'd like to know where all this is going. You don't seriously think Manners is good for the homicide?" She refuses to respond. "And *you're* going to try it?" Nothing. "Well?"

"I'm not getting into it with you." She points inside the studio. "Me being here has nothing to do with work."

215

"How about Sid Bateman?"

"What about Sid Bateman?"

"Sid—fucking—Bateman," I say, with an exaggerated shake of my head.

She flies into the studio and returns with her bag. Speeding past me she says, "*You* need to get a life."

I yell across the parking lot, "Sid fucking Bateman," and regret it immediately.

The boys gawk at me as I enter the garage.

Maeve booms from the speakers above. "Elvis has left the building, ladies and gentlemen."

"What just happened?" Preet says.

"She wasn't feeling well. It's no big deal." Several moments of awkward silence. I walk to the mini-fridge and pop a beer. "It's fine. I'll talk to her. We'll work it out."

"You okay?" Terry says, as calmly as Terry can manage.

"Yes. I'm o-kay. *O-kay?*"

Maeve and Terry and Preet respond, "*O-kay.*"

We play a couple of tunes. Then, after, Terry says, "You read that report?"

"What report?" I answer, and tip most of what is either my third or fifth beer down my throat.

"Rogelio Contreras."

"What gives you the right to go into my office and rummage through my shit?"

"I didn't have to rummage." He walks over to his backpack and fishes out the document. "There's not much in it we don't already know. Contreras takes a little walk, which puts him in the area of the guesthouse. He sees a car pull up. He recognizes Manners, who gets out of the passenger side. The trunk pops open. Manners lifts out a box, walks to the door, opens it with a key, disappears inside. He

216

comes back to the car, opens Swell's door, and pulls her out. Contreras thought she looked drunk. They walk together into the house. A few minutes later he hears a male voice—Manners's, he assumes—yell, 'No, Ella, no.'"

"That's in quotes?" I say. "What Contreras heard?" Terry holds up the report.

"He says he cruises out of there a few seconds later, after he hears three shots, close together."

"And it's clear the statement from the house is followed by the shots?"

"Yeah."

"By the way," I add. "Mick confirmed the bit about Swell being sick."

"When?" Terry is appalled to be slightly behind the curve.

"The same time as he gave *me* the report on Contreras. You're supposed to be my support staff, you know. Not the other way around."

"How sick?"

"A-few-months-to-live sick."

"If he yelled no, maybe she committed suicide," Maeve posits, nonchalantly.

Suicide. Maybe. No.

Terry's eyes light up. He points at the amp. "Right."

"Three shots, Terry. Arm, shoulder, and a killer to the chest. She's standing when she gets hit in the arm, and the others are on the couch, remember?" I'm pleased with myself, recalling the details of our conversation with Mick. Alzheimer's, schmalzheimers. "A suicide is a single shot to the head or in the mouth."

Maeve says, "All I know is I've seen enough TV to know you don't say 'No, Ella, no' when you're about to shoot Ella."

Terry, dangerously jazzed, gets off the floor and speed-walks a lap around the room.

"Maybe it's a mercy killing. Let's say they were really in love. She tells him she's dying. She doesn't want to end up in the hospital with a tube down her throat. She shoots herself in the arm while she's standing. He says, 'No, Ella, no.' Then he shoots her on the couch." He punches the air in my direction. "That works."

"Except Contreras says the shots are all *after* he hears Manners or whoever it was."

"Come on. You have to admit it's close."

"No, actually, I don't. And anyway, it hardly helps my client, right? He's guilty of manslaughter at least, and maybe murder. If he's very lucky, he'll do ten years."

After a few moments contemplating the ugly consequences of this truth—the guilty plea, the family torn apart, the burning of Santa Rita—my cell phone rings. It's past eleven. It must be an S. disaster.

"Where are you?" It's Mick Bacon.

"Don't old people sleep?"

"Can you get down to the Hall with your computer friend?"

For several seconds I stare at the little red button on my mobile that would cut off the call. Then I lower the phone. "Can I get down to the Hall with my computer friend?"

Preet jogs to his workstation, straps on a massive battery pack, and stuffs a bunch of other gear into a backpack. He's been waiting for this moment.

The Manilow cover band goes on a dodgy reconnaissance mission. If we're lucky, they'll let us play a reunion gig at the prison Christmas party.

# 37

**F**IFTEEN MINUTES LATER we are parked at a curb, twenty feet from a side entrance to police headquarters. Mick and Preet disappear inside the building. *Our* mission: we have no mission. Do nothing. Wait.

Minutes later I see a car pull into the nearly empty parking lot across the street. A man parks, steps out of his gleaming SUV, aims his alarm remote at the vehicle, and heads in our direction.

"Drive. Now," I yell at Terry, who is slouched down in the driver's seat, half asleep.

"What?"

"Now."

It's Baptiste. Terry guns the engine and rips down the street. I turn back to look. Baptiste stands in the middle of the block looking our way. There's little light, so I doubt he can make out the car, let alone the plates.

"Where are you?" I bark into my cell phone.

"What do you mean 'where am I?'" Mick says. "I'm inside with your pal. Where the hell do you think I am?"

"Baptiste—"

"Shit—"

At this point Mick must hear Baptiste. He stashes the phone but does not turn it off.

"Maeve wants to know what's going on?" Terry says. The pregnant one follows the action through his cell.

"Shut up." I crank the volume on my phone and jam it into my ear. It's just possible to make out the conversation.

"Mick."

"Hey Nick. How you doing?"

"Same old song."

"Your wife kick you out again?"

"Something like that," Baptiste says. "I think I left my phone inside."

"Oh yeah? I didn't see it."

"Well, if the batteries are still good, I'll know soon enough." A door opens. I hear footsteps. Baptiste must have another cell phone in his hand, because shortly I hear a mobile in the distance. "There she is." Sound of steps. "You coming?"

"Yeah," Mick answers.

A door shuts. Preet is now permanently trapped in some basement evidence room where he'll be forced to feed on tissue samples and Marcus's clothing until he's discovered, perhaps weeks from now, and thrown in jail for tampering with evidence.

"Any developments?" Mick says.

"Nah. You see that piece of ass Sid Batemen has carrying his bag?"

"Oh yeah."

"What's her story?"

"Silvie Hernandez. She's a climber."

"I'd like to climb her."

Fuckers.

"I bet you would."

Terry says, "Maeve still wants to know what's happening."

I raise my fist and he shrinks back against the driver's side window.

"There's something about a woman DA," I hear Baptiste say. "Makes me want to be a bad, bad boy."

"Your wife'll be happy to hear that."

I see them emerge from the side door.

"Wife?"

That's good for a hoot. They wave good-bye and walk to their cars in the parking lot. They both pull out in our direction. I order Terry to take off. We circle the block a couple of times before Mick shows. He doesn't bother to stop and say hello. He parks and reenters the building. My cell rings a couple of minutes later.

"I heard that bit about Silvie," I say.

"He's a piece of work," Mick says.

"I really didn't appreciate that."

"I'll be sure to register your complaint. Your pal's still working. We'll be out in a few."

Fifteen minutes later Preet and Mick emerge. Preet climbs in.

"So," Terry says, anxiously.

"I didn't see anything relevant," Preet reports.

Mick says, "That's what our computer guys said."

"I'm surprised," I say.

"Some financial data," Preet says. "Documents related to her work. No data files of any size, and nothing relating to Grace Manners."

Mick pulls his head out of the window, says, "Tick tock, Gordy," and strolls off.

I lean out the window. "Hey Bacon," I yell. He stops but does not turn around. "Tell Baptiste that if he ever disrespects Silvie Hernandez in my presence I'm going to rip his fucking lungs out."

Mick waves and moves on.


"Librarians do it between the covers," Preet says nonchalantly, as Terry pulls the Benz away from the curb.

Terry, who has his cell phone pasted to his ear while he drives, laughs. "Maeve says computer programmers do it with mice."

Preet, unimpressed, turns to me. "You mentioned Brice Bulley was helping Swell with her computer?"

"Yeah. Manners said Swell and the kid were tight."

"Someone, Bulley probably, had his hands on Swell's PC before the police took it. There's a data file of significant size that has been corrupted," Preet says. "It may have contained what you're looking for. Now it's garbage. When I opened the file, it's mostly junk. But that line appears several times: *Librarians do it between the covers*."

"So—"

"Where else have we seen a librarian recently?"

"Oh shit," I say. Total High. "The files are in the game?"

"Or we'll find some other kind of clue. Just depends on how much fun Brice intended to have with us. I assume someone is meant to find the data files eventually. There's little use having a treasure hunt if there's no treasure."

"Why don't we go talk to the kid?" Terry says.

"The dad nixed that," I say.

"So?" Terry says, indignant.

"Anyway, that may not be necessary," Preet says. "Let's see what I can do tonight."

An hour later we're lolling around Preet's garage while the turbaned one works his magic. It appears to soothe him. Every so often I wander by Preet's workstation. Total High screens are up on three monitors. I have no idea what he's up to. I'm exhausted and expected in court at eight-thirty A.M. for a pretrial in the Manners case.

"Look at this," Preet calls out. We jog over. On one shelf of the Total High library is a row of volumes marked "Bulleytins." "Anyone want to bet?"

Maeve yelps from the speakers, "What, what?"

I describe the scene for her. Preet clicks. A password screen pops up. At the top, it says, "What took you so long?"

"Any guesses on a password?" Preet says.

No takers.

Preet turns to another keyboard, clicks around for several seconds, and then returns to us. He types in a string of numbers and letters, and a new screen appears.

"It's the same password Manners used to get into Total High. I recorded it when he was in here. And there's your document." Preet could not be prouder.

"What the hell?" I say, genuinely freaked out by his acuity.

# 38

S O, THEN, AT NEARLY TWO A.M., the truth. The answer. In a nice, neat package, ready for delivery to Mick Bacon or the DA or the grand jury or the press. Ella Swell, a couple of months away from dying, decides to put things in order, to make amends. She writes it all down because she figures, correctly as it turns out, that the person she's about to take down will try to stop her. And, with the exception of her stepson, whom she apparently trusted, she hides the document from everyone other than the person she wrote it for: Marcus Manners. Then she gets shot before she can show him where to find it.

Preet prints out the journal and Terry reads it out loud for Maeve's benefit. It's a weird scene, the four of us up in the middle of the night, listening to a dead woman's diary. Call it Mani-noir.

I understand why people like reading mysteries and legal thrillers and private eye books. The clues, neatly dispersed over a few hundred pages, lead inexorably to an answer. The reader follows the cop or the prosecutor or the private investigator down a series of dead ends. And then, with reader in tow, the protagonist realizes she or he has been looking at things all wrong, backward, inside-out. I suppose there's a profound satisfaction knowing if you stay up late enough you'll find your way out of the maze.

Personally, I can't handle mysteries. If you live in my world, you know fiction is absurdly neat and orderly and improbable. In reality, mostly, one is truly clueless. It's not that one *could* have figured it out, if only one had been smart enough. In reality, mostly, one never figures out anything and the bad guys get off. Or, in rare cases, the bad guy almost gets off, but a turban-topped computer geek hopped up on root beer and Manilow pronounces his binary abracadabra, waves his digital wand, and the answer pops up in boldface and large type on his monitor. You couldn't put that in a mystery because the reader, who knows better, would say, *yeah, right.*

And the answer is? Drumroll please . . . Jeremiah Pluck.

"It's pretty unbelievable," Terry says, when Preet reaches the end of the narrative.

"It's slightly *too* unbelievable," I say. "If Swell was so blameless, how come she pleaded to manslaughter? And if Pluck was really the one feeding the cops, wouldn't he have told them Swell wasn't involved?"

In the journal Swell says Pluck was the one who fingered the August '88 coke delivery to the bookstore. Just as Cindi suspected.

"Probably with the dead officer they weren't in the mood to cut anyone any slack," Terry says.

"Mick said that. But with Stanton Swell behind her? Come on."

"Anyway," Terry goes on. "Even if Swell was more involved than she wanted to admit, that doesn't mean the rest of it isn't right."

"Pluck's problem is he was *fucking* her." The word parades off Maeve's tongue with a sort of infant-eating-sweet-potatoes, messy, guiltless glee.

In the journal Swell claims she and Pluck had an affair in the year before the Zora Neal's raid.

"And?" I say.

"And, if he sticks up for Swell with the police, maybe his wife gets wise," Maeve says.

"But *you* still think Bulley killed her," I say.

225

"I told you what I think. I don't think Swell was fucking Pluck, Bulley, or anyone else without tits."

"So she's making the whole thing up," I say. "Do you have the slightest evidence that Ella Swell was a lesbian?"

"I know what I know. Anyway, all you got on Pluck is motive. Bulley had that too, even if she was straight, which she wasn't. Either way, she left him. And you guys said Bulley thought she was screwing Manners. I'm sticking with the wife-beater until I hear something concrete."

I turn to Terry. "And not a particularly strong motive. It's almost fifteen years ago. And it's not like Pluck was a full-time snitch. I mean, you can hardly blame the guy? He sees this dirtbag dealer moving in on a legit business he's helped finance and he's pissed. You don't think the black community would understand that today? They remember how bad it was."

"A snitch is a snitch," Terry retorts. "Nobody's going to elect the guy mayor if he was working for the SRPD, even fifteen years ago. *And* he was doing the white girl. He's dead if it comes out."

Maeve booms from the amp, "Lez-bean, lez-bean, lez-bean."

In the journal Swell says that on the morning of August 21, 1988, a Sunday, she received a call from Pluck. He told her to stay away from the bookstore all day. Ella tried to reach Grace, but had no luck. She sped into West Santa Rita and found Marcus's mother at the store. A short time later the SRPD surrounded and raided the facility.

"Pluck mentioned he saw Swell before she died," I say.

"Why don't you tell anybody this stuff?" Terry says.

"It just occurred to me, actually. It was just after they found Swell. The cops had a warrant for Manners's place. Pluck was there. I told him about Swell getting shot. He said she stopped by a few days before."

"So, that confirms her story," Terry says.

Swell's journal says that upon her arrival in Santa Rita on April 27 she drove to Pluck's office. She thought he should know that she was dying, that she intended to enlighten Marcus, to reveal Pluck's role in the J-Posse case. He listened to her and seemed to understand. He was not angry. There remained powerful feelings between them. She said she was sorry too. And then she left.

"I really doubt he shot her," I say. "He seemed shocked when I told him she'd been killed."

"That's bullshit," Terry says.

"Maybe."

"We got to get to the Bulley kid." Terry says. "He had access to the documents. The kid could be the key to the whole deal."

I collect my things and stand at the door.

"Sleeeeeep," I say.

"What about Silvie?" Terry says.

"Sleeeeeep," I repeat, and walk out.

It's nearly two, now. The hills are deserted. There's no breeze. Columns of light from every-so-often streetlights swarm with bugs and flecks of dust rising with the day's heat. Barry's on my tape deck, singing "Lay Me Down," perhaps the best ballad ever. I drift up to a stoplight.

From half a block behind, a vehicle races at my car and squeals to a halt inches from my rear bumper. I twist my head around to check it out. A man leaps out of the car and jogs toward my open window. It's the pinkyless dude.

Moments later two other men, neither recognizable, lumber over, place their hands on the sides of the hood of the Corolla and rock my poor old wagon violently back and forth between them like two vexed gorillas.

The rockers step away and the car behind me inches forward, eventually pushing my car a few feet. The driver backs up about ten yards, guns the engine, and then shoots toward me, stopping inches short of a collision.

"What the fuck do you people want?" I yell.

The gorillas and four-finger Fred stroll to their ride, which pulls out in the opposite direction.

I arrive home a few minutes later. After two hours in bed staring at the ceiling, trying to figure out what's happening to me and what I ought to do about it, I pop a little blue pill and sleep.

# 39

HALF OF SANTA RITA is in Judge Reasoner's court the next morning for the Manners pretrial hearing. The mood is festive. Marcus's posse sports attractive red ribbons. Mine is in my pocket for the time being. The crowd believes victory is within reach. It's like the ballroom of a downtown hotel, hours before the last ballots have been cast. But exit polls show the candidate winning by a large margin.

And for the first time since I've been involved in the case, it occurs to me I am really, deeply, profoundly in trouble. And it's not because of my slight, blue-pill-induced fuzziness.

The people smiling and winking and flipping me greetings from around the room, while I bullshit with Milo Velikovic, get their criminal justice from television. On TV the defendant always has *some* sort of defense. He may be guilty and he may be on his way to the hoosegow or the chair. But it's hard to imagine an episode of *Law and Order* in which defense counsel stands up to argue the case, throws up his hands, and says, "So, how about that Saddam Hussein?"

Come next Wednesday, the people in this room, the ones with the ribbons at least, will expect me to have something to say—about the drugs, about the dog, about the grave injustice that has been perpetrated against Santa Rita's favorite son.

And unlike most of my cases, this *feels* like a trial I ought to be able to win. Even if he took the dog, the evidence doesn't seem overwhelming. There ought to be some way I can use the fact that the DA has unfairly targeted Marcus. He wasn't alone that night. And if you ignore for a moment an unexplained bag of dope on the floor of his car, there's no reason to believe Manners is fibbing when he says he doesn't use drugs.

Sadly, none of my doubts about Milo's case have led to a real, live, ladies-and-gentlemen-of-the-jury, reasonable-doubt-inducing defense.

The answer in a normal case would be to deal it. Take the DA's best offer. Enter a plea of guilty, do the forty-five days, and move the hell on. But even if Manners took the dog, even if the dope was his, I don't see telling the kid to take the six weeks in jail. The crimes just don't warrant that sort of time.

I'm not particularly worried about Milo. And while Reasoner is guaranteed to beat the hell out of me at trial, I'll wear his every nasty word like a badge of honor.

It's the crowd that scares me. They're counting on me. And they've been with me so far because I've been with Marcus. I'm his protector. The minute they see I have no idea what I am doing, that I have no plan, they'll take away my ribbon, or worse.

Typically we conduct the pretrial hearing in chambers. The judge takes a last shot at pushing the parties to settle. The lawyers haggle over scheduling and jury instructions. When all the particulars are resolved, we put the matters on the record, in open court, in a summary fashion.

But with Reasoner the Capricious at the helm, the chance of dealing the case apparently nil, and the gallery teeming with Manners supporters, I figure I might as well let it all hang out. The more they hate the judge, the less likely they are to run me out of town when the case goes down the toilet.

"Time estimates, Counsel."

"How long does the court intend to set aside for voir dire?" In other words, to pick a jury.

"Wednesday afternoon for jury selection."

"Your Honor, it may make sense to plan for a full day. The problem

I see is that both the *Journal* and the *Chronicle* have repeatedly suggested my client is a suspect in the Swell homicide investigation." The gallery grumbles. "It wouldn't surprise me—"

"I understand the point. Wednesday afternoon for jury selection."

Terry is with me at counsel table. He leans over and whispers in my ear, "I think he has his transfusions Wednesday mornings."

"Did you want to add something, Counsel?"

"No, Your Honor. That's fine."

"Really, Mr. Seegerman. If you and your associate would like to put your comments on the record—"

"Thank you, Your—"

"Don't you *dare* cut me off, Seegerman."

I stand. "I apologize, Your Honor. I have no further comments on the jury selection issue."

"What's the proposed trial schedule?"

"I have five witnesses, Judge," Milo says. "I can easily get through them Thursday. I don't know how much cross there will be."

"We haven't decided whether the defendant will take the stand, Your Honor, and we'll reserve regarding our own witnesses. It will depend on how Mr. Velikovic's case comes in."

"A range, Mr. Seegerman. Fewer than five? More than five hundred."

"Around five."

"Then I see no reason we can't conclude and argue by week's end."

"That's fine."

"I have your jury instruction submissions. I'll have a final copy to you by next week. Any in limines?" Motions governing the conduct of the trial itself.

"No, Your Honor."

"Anything else?"

"I would ask the court to reconsider its ruling vis-à-vis Officer Dent. I—"

"Denied."

More grousing from the crowd.

"Will the court allow to me to make my record?"

"The record is more than sufficient, Mr. Seegerman. I won't have you grandstanding for the media. Feel free to file a writ."

"Just for clarification, is the court excluding all references to misconduct by the officer?"

"My ruling is my ruling, Counsel. You filed your motion. I denied it. Clear?" He starts packing up. "Would Counsel please approach." I have no idea what's happening. We're off the record now, at the bench. Reasoner goes on. "I've had a request from Channel 2 for permission to broadcast the proceedings."

Cindi. Nice of her to warn me.

The blood rushes out of Milo's face. He looks like he might pass out. "Television?"

"I oppose it, Judge. I think it will distract the jury. With the Swell investigation and the rest of it, I think it's going to be hard enough as it is to get fair jurors."

"I'm inclined to permit it," Reasoner says.

"I'd like to have a chance to file a brief," I say.

Reasoner guffaws. "Seems to me anything jointly opposed by both the district attorney and the public defender is probably in the public's interest. Better go out and get a new tie, Seegerman."


Silvie Hernandez is standing at the back of the room when I walk out. I wonder whether I'll always feel this way, if I'll always suffer so much the moment I lay eyes on her. It's almost enough to hope I get Alzheimer's, and soon.

"Nice job winning over the court, Seegerman," she says. "Trial should be fun."

"You don't have anything better to do with your time?"

"Just curious."

"Doing reconnaissance for your grand jury."

She lowers her voice. "It's not my grand jury."

"My client's not testifying, Silvie, if that's what you're here to find out." They can call him to the grand jury, but he doesn't have to talk unless they immunize him. Given that he's the target, that seems unlikely.

"I've been through the book, Gordy." The murder book. "He better say something because the next step is a 187." A murder charge.

"What, now that you have your lawyer hat on you're suddenly willing to talk?"

"I don't see why we can't try to figure all this out like two people who care about each other." Care. Yeah. That about sums it up. I'm on the verge of saying *Sid fucking Bateman* when she stops me. She lowers her voice. "Don't. Whatever it is, be an adult and don't. I'd like to play with you guys in Vegas. I've been having a tough few months and it's helping."

"I'm so thrilled."

"I'm sorry about things. You know." She cocks her head to one side slightly and smiles apologetically. "Are you all right?"

"My client's not testifying, Silvie. Feel free to tell Fischer exactly that. I know what you have, and you don't have shit. Even if you get an indictment, (a) you'll get crushed at trial, (b), Fischer will get crushed in August. Not to mention the fun the SRPD ought to have on the west side this summer."

I walk away. It feels good to bounce her around a bit. Take that, my love.

# 40

**F**RIDAY, MAY 28, with Terry, in my office. We're reading the paper, which contains a full report of the Manners status hearing and an unexpectedly flattering description of my suit. Mick Bacon walks in, closes the door, and parks next to Terry.

"I got something good to trade," Mick says.

"For what?" Terry says.

"For whatever you guys got last night."

"We didn't get anything last night."

"Bullshit. Your friend with the headgear was lying his ass off." Preet does happen to be a preternaturally poor prevaricator. He moves his head about involuntarily when he strays from the truth. "Plus, I dropped a wire in your car."

"Swell was sleeping with Pluck back in '88." Terry cannot help himself.

"That was on the computer?" Mick says, seeming genuinely surprised.

"You did not drop a wire in the car," I say, continuing to read the article about myself. Finally, with Terry on the verge of blurting out the whole thing, I hand Mick a copy of Swell's journal. Truth is, I'd decided to turn it over to him anyway. After the episode in the hills last night, I'm beginning to wonder whether the Mandys and I haven't gotten in a little over our heads. And if I end up face down in Lake Lanier any time soon—whether it's because I represent the dog-napper or because the truth about '88 threatens Pluck's political future—I'd like the bad guys to get theirs.

I sit back in my chair, feigning indifference, while Terry spends the next ten minutes recounting Swell's story.

"Believe me, Swell was way more involved than she cops to," Mick says. "She didn't take the manslaughter deal for no reason. We had information *all* the people at the bookstore, including Swell, were actively involved in Colder's operation."

"And the stuff about Pluck?"

"Your dad was running the informant, Gordy, not me. It was understood there was someone inside. But I don't think three people in the SRPD knew who he was."

"That's not what S. said."

"What?" Mick says.

"I told you. He said you knew."

"Knew what exactly?"

"I'll get back to you on that."

"It had to be Pluck," Terry says.

Mick points to the journal. "Could be. But she doesn't actually say in there Pluck admitted it to her, either in '88 or now."

"Anyway, all that matters is that Swell *believed* it was Pluck," Terry says. "She went to Pluck with the story and a few hours later she gets shot. What else do you need?"

Mick gets up and gives me a stern look. "The same thing we needed last week, Gordy. We need Manners."

"Fine, we're all clear," I say. "Now what do we get for solving your case for you?"

He walks up to my desk, sticks out his fist and opens it. A scrap of paper floats onto my desk.

"I can't get rid of the misdemeanors. But that's the next best thing."

He leaves. I unfurl the scrap and see the following in Mick's shaky scribble: *Phan v. Dent, Federal District Court, Northern District of California, Case No. CIV 92-21397.* I hold it up for Terry to see. He springs out of his chair and races into the doorway.

"I can't believe I missed this. It'll take me a couple of days to run down the file. Get Preet on the phone. Tell him to find what he can."

I have no idea what ever gave me the idea that I am driving the bus. I am clinging for dear, sweet life to the spare tire at the back of the bus. And the bus has no brakes.


And it just turned down a really steep hill.

Five hours have passed. I've written the beginning of a jury argument for the Manners trial. It's not until I sit down and decide how I'd like to argue a case that I really absorb the relevant materials: reports, witness statements, my client's version of events. Until I know where I'm going, the route is a blur.

For example, it occurs to me, admittedly a bit late in the game, that the Swell estate has a retracting iron gate at its entrance. It must be closed at night. So far I haven't heard anyone suggest how Manners or anyone else got past the gate. I suppose he, or they, might have scaled the wall going in, but how did he or they get out with a hundred pounds of Red?

Terry rushes in. The file in the federal civil case of *Phan v. Dent* has been archived, as he suspected. But Preet came up with a name and an address.

We zip across town to Santa Rita's predominantly Asian section. Some people call it Chinatown, but that hardly makes sense anymore. These days there are as many Laotians and Mien and Vietnamese and Bengalis as there are Chinese inhabiting the low-rise apartment buildings and hundred-year-old Victorians that crowd the area. Smoke and steam from roasting duck and pots of boiling noodles and baking pork buns pipe out of rickety ventilation units and cover the area with a mouth-watering haze.

"Brice Bulley's on some kind of trip."

"Physical or spiritual?" I say. "The father made it clear he was off-limits. No?"

236

"I'd really like to have a whack at him. Other than Manners, he may be the only one who had access to Swell."

"I'm sure you have plenty of things to whack in the meantime. Just try not to whack near me."

"How's Silvie?"

"She's perfect. Thanks for asking."

The address is for a small restaurant, Pho Phan, which serves, we soon learn, tasty rare-beef soup and green papaya salad. It's past the lunch rush, so the place is empty. Our waitress, a twentysomething Vietnamese woman, zeros in on Terry immediately. She is gorgeous, clipped black hair with streaks of blue dye, eyes with the shady shine of a full moon.

We ask if she knows how we can get in touch with An Phan. She is Ly Phan. An Phan is her grandfather. He's in back. But he speaks no English. She'll have to translate. She smiles at Terry. He smiles back. I will surely be ill.

She disappears for several minutes.

"What," Terry says, nonchalantly.

"What is it with you? We're supposed to be working."

"I am working."

"Working *it* and *working* are not the same thing."

An elderly man in professional kitchen attire meanders out from the kitchen. A cigarette is stuck between his lips, but he does not suck on it. The ash is half an inch long. When it seems certain to fall, he flicks his head to the left and catches the ash in his hand. He has a closed-mouth grin that does not leave his face. He points to his chest and says his name. We say ours. The conversation stalls.

Ly Phan returns with a box of court documents.

"I was at UCLA when it happened," she says.

"I went to UCLA," I say. The comment falls flat. She continues, her eyes glued to Terry.

"The police were looking for some people involved in drugs. They

237

came to my grandparents' apartment, but it was the wrong address. They had no translator. My grandfather didn't know they were police, so he refused to open the door. He thought they were trying to rob him."

An Phan nods constantly during her narration. When the cigarette burns out, he replaces it. Otherwise, I don't see him open his mouth a single time. The man must have powerful nostrils.

"They broke down the door. They said they found drugs in the apartment and arrested my grandfather."

I flip through some of the court documents in the box. Dent was the lead on the bust, which occurred in 1991.

"They reversed the charges when they realized it was a mistake." *Dismissed*, not "reversed." I keep quiet. "My grandfather was a famous poet in Vietnam. He never had anything to do with drugs. He got a lawyer and the police had to pay him money."

Actually, a lot of money. Mr. and Mrs. Phan filed a civil rights action against Dent and the SRPD in June of 1992. The claim was that Dent and his colleagues got the wrong address and, having broken down the door and scared the shit out of the Phans, thought they could cover their tracks by *finding* a half-pound of heroin in their apartment.

But An Phan turned out to be all but unframable. He was not only a well-known writer, but also a decorated officer in the now-defunct South Vietnamese army, and friendly with a host of unimpeachable American military men. It almost makes you feel sorry for Dent. When it was all over, the SRPD settled the case, shelled out a few hundred grand to the Phans, and shunted Dent off to a patrol job.

Ly continues, "Now they own this building."

"A happy ending," I say.

Terry doesn't even bother to give me a dismissive look. He leans back in his chair, enjoying Ly's gaze. They might as well get a room. Finally, he comes back to earth.

"Would your grandfather be willing to come to court?" Terry

addresses the question to An. "I know it must be tough for you, to think about it all again, but it would mean a lot to us."

Ly translates. An nods repeatedly. His ash reaches its breaking point again, and on his fifth or sixth smiling nod, it tumbles off the butt. His hand shoots out to grab it. Terry passes Ly a business card upon which, I note, he has scribbled his cell number.

# 41

I'T'S MONDAY, MAY 31, Memorial Day. It also happens to be my birthday. Terry and I stand at the top of the bleachers at Hills High School's football field. From here there's a view of Santa Rita, north to south. And to the west, the bay, San Francisco, the Pacific. The sky is blue. The trees are green. We are above the smog, so the air is breathable. I remember my name and most of my history. For that, I'm grateful.

But the temperature, at eleven-thirty A.M., is ninety-something degrees. And I'm wearing a suit. So, I'm not predominantly grateful. I'm predominantly sweating.

We sit while Marcus Manners and two teammates run passing patterns. Marcus's arm is like a grenade launcher. The ball spins so perfectly in the air that it looks still. There's no arc. Manners fires it at shoulder height. It remains there. Over thirty yards perhaps it drops two inches. And he's insanely fast. He covers the width of the field in less time than it takes me to consume a potato chip.

Later we move down to the seats closest to the field. Marcus and his teammates stretch out after the workout. Manners finally sees us and jogs over.

On this date in 1969, shortly past seven A.M., my mother drove herself to Santa Rita General Hospital, parked the car, waddled into the emergency room, and collapsed on the floor. A dispatcher tracked down my father, on the job somewhere, and, if you believe him, which

I do not, S. headed to the hospital. Which is where the history gets muddled. Over the years I have heard—from S., from my mom, from Ferdy—car trouble, wrong hospital, sidelined by crime in progress, and so forth. Truth is, S. knew I was on my way, and, aware that I would mostly likely spend the next twenty years getting in his face, he no doubt stopped to have a few hundred martinis.

Thirty-five years later, I hope simply to make it through the day without anyone making a fuss. When, if, I turn forty, I suppose a small gathering of friends and family might be nice. A speech or two, maybe, acknowledging my contributions in both the legal and musical arenas.

But thirty-five feels like a birthday to be had, quietly, alone. Vegas is in doubt. Circumstances seem to have finally, though not completely, smothered my romantic fantasies. I'm busy trying to figure out how not to get steamrolled in the Manners case. I may or may not end up at the bottom of the San Francisco Bay, strapped to a concrete-filled oil drum, because of my association with Manners. I don't feel like pretending to enjoy myself.

I spend several minutes filling in Marcus on developments in the misdemeanor case. We're forty-eight hours from picking a jury.

"It's your decision. All I can do is lay out the options. If you plead, you'll do forty-five days, but you'll know what's what. If you go to trial, maybe you beat it, but maybe not. If not, you could do a year."

Marcus turns to Terry. "What do you think?"

"Unless there's something we don't know, I'd say take the deal."

"All right," Manners says.

"You sure?"

"I'm sure I don't want to go to jail for a year."

"I'm sorry there's not more I can do."

I ought to feel elated. Nothing stands between me and Barry now. But I feel like crap. Gutless. Cowardly. I'm not a trial lawyer. I'm a mouse.

I hold up a subpoena that arrived in my office this morning. Marcus is required to appear before the grand jury tomorrow morning.

"You know what this is?" He nods. "The good news is they can't actually make you testify. I can't be in the room with you, but if anything you don't understand happens, all you have to do is say you want to talk to me, and they'll let you out. I also wanted to let you know we think we've got the document Ella Swell meant you to have."

"Where'd you get it?"

"Why don't you just take a look. We'll wait."

No way we can leave him alone to deal with its implications. God knows, the kid will run out and take a swipe at Pluck. Or flip out and ram his car into a wall.

But the narrative does not ruffle him. He reads slowly, without visible reaction. We sit in silence for ten minutes. He does not ask questions or look up.

"She didn't tell me she was sick."

"Sometimes it's hard for people to admit it to themselves. Actually she was sicker than she says. Her doctor thought she'd be gone in a month or two." Silence. "You okay?"

"Yeah. Where'd this come from?"

"It was sort of hidden in Total High. We assume Brice Bulley helped her store it. She obviously meant you to have it."

"Anything here change your story about what happened at the house?" Terry says.

"No."

"You didn't see Pluck at the house?" I say.

He doesn't respond for a few moments and then says, "Are they going to charge me with killing Ella?"

"They're going to try. I think we have to sit tight and see what happens. They have to convince sixteen grand jurors that you pulled the trigger. That may be harder than they imagine."

That, of course, is complete nonsense. Grand juries do what prosecutors tell them to do. Marcus Manners *is* going to be indicted for shooting Ella Swell. Realistically, my role in the mess is almost over. Even if I wanted to stay involved, no one's going to let me try a high-profile murder case. I'll settle the misdos, shake Manners's hand, and try to make it to the plane for Vegas before Manners is charged and Santa Rita goes the way of L.A. after the King verdict.

Terry pulls his car out of the Hills High parking lot.

"Three-five," he says.

"Unbelievable, huh."

"You thought I forgot?"

"I didn't think. I hoped. You ever think it would come to this? Middle age?"

"I never did. What does it feel like?"

"It feels like being sixteen, but really old."

"Dinner?"

"I gotta do some prep for the grand jury tomorrow."

"You're going to spend your birthday at work?"

"It's not a big deal, Terry. We'll celebrate in Vegas. That's all I want to think about right now, getting on that plane. By the way, it's going to be fine with Silvie."

"Seriously?"

"Yeah. It's my problem. You're right. I just gotta let it go."

"And how do you do that?"

"I have no idea. Turns out she's boffing her boss—"

"Fischer—" Even more horrifying than Bateman.

"No. Sid Bateman."

"Wow. Bateman. That's disgusting."

"She can sing, though. Can't take that from her."

"That's *seriously* disgusting."

"Is it possible to keep this between us? Like maybe spare Maeve and

Preet the gruesome details? Seems like we're walking the razor's edge to Manilow right now."

"Eyes on the ball."

"Exactly," I say. "Think of it as a birthday present."

"Done. Happy birthday."

Who are the three most pathetic men in the Santa Rita criminal justice system? Which three professionals have such wretched lives that they spend a national holiday, the beginning of the summer, of barbecue season, working, alone?

Me, of course. I'm at the office, reading up on grand jury procedure.

And Milo. I see him on my way out of the Hall. I tell him Marcus caved, that we shouldn't have a problem settling the misdos. To celebrate, I buy him lunch.

And Judge Garnett Reasoner, whom we find reading the paper in a nearby café.

"Good morning, Judge," Milo says.

Reasoner looks up at a clock on the wall.

"You're twenty minutes behind."

We all stare at the clock for a few moments. I sneak a look back at Reasoner. It must suck to be that old.

"We have an agreement on the Manners case, Your Honor," I say. "My client has agreed to plead to the drug charge."

"Open?" Reasoner responds. In other words, Marcus pleads and accepts whatever sentence the judge arrives at, with no jail term agreed upon beforehand.

"I thought you said forty-five days?" I say, slightly stunned. I wonder if I should tell him it's my birthday.

"That was a month ago, Seegerman. Things change."

"What's changed?"

"Watch your tone, Counsel."

Wait, we're not in chambers. We're in a deli.

"I'm sorry, Judge. But you did say forty-five days. We based our discussions on that."

"I *said* forty-five days. Now I say *open*." He smiles. His teeth are gray. "That's the beauty of being the judge."

I can't possibly let Marcus Manners plead open. Reasoner will almost certainly give him six months in the county jail. For a first offense, even if Dent didn't plant the pot in Marcus's car, it's far too much time. I have no idea whether I can beat either the dope or the dog counts, but now it seems clear I'm going to have to try. Nice birthday.

Home at six-thirty. I check the mail. No cards. No gifts.

In keeping with his attitude toward my arrival in the world, my father does not acknowledge my thirty-fifth. Although it's a bit hard to fault him, now that he can't remember to scrub his teeth with the fuzzy end of the toothbrush.

I decline Ferdy and King's invitation to dinner. Courting disaster, I call Silvie from my car. She's not there.

"Dear Silvie. Just calling to wish myself a happy birthday. I hope you're good. I'm sorry about my immaturity. I'm hoping thirty-five will cure me. We'd all like you to come to Vegas. Me especially. We need you. Please."

Cindi calls for an update. She does not know it's my birthday. Perfect, I think. I'd actually like to go out for a decent meal, maybe have a few drinks. It's not that I want to be alone. I'd just like to be able to be miserable, and those who love me will be hell-bent on talking me out of it.

"I'm starving," I say. "You want to talk over food?"

"Sure," she says slowly. "We're still clear on, you know, I can't—"

"Abundantly clear, believe me."

Fifteen minutes later, halfway up the forty concrete steps to Cindi's house, I stop for a minute to watch the sunset. I wonder where Silvie is right now. I wonder whether the remainder of my thirties will be happy and rewarding, or whether my memory will start to fade. I wonder what I'd be doing right now if my mom were still around. A large, older woman, badly out of breath, hustles to the bottom of the stairs. She's wearing fuzzy zebra slippers and a housecoat.

"Excuse me," she yells up at me. "Are you going to see Cynthia?"

Cynthia. "I think so."

"Would you mind taking this up to her? The mailwoman got these mixed in with ours."

I descend, grab the mail, and watch Ms. Zebra Feet trudge back to her house. I glance at a label on a clothing catalog. It's addressed to Brenda Howe.

# 42

I DROP THE MAIL, back down a couple of steps, and then skip four at a time, until I hit the street. I jump in my car, drive a couple of blocks, pull over, and grab my phone.

"Run an address for me," I say. Preet's on the line. "Also, I need identifying information on the cop that died in the J-Posse shooting in '88, somebody Howe. It ought to be in one of the articles or an obit or something." We hang up. I turn the name over and over on my lips. Brenda Howe. In ten minutes the phone rings.

"Mitchell and Brenda Howe are at that address, since 1995. They're the parents of the cop. Happy birthday, by the way."

"Thanks. Siblings?"

"Sarah and Cynthia." I stare at a No Parking sign that has been half-digested by the maple tree to which it is bolted. "Should I ask?"

"What?"

"Should I ask what's going on? Are you thirty-five?"

"What?" My brain is full.

"Where are you?"

"I'll talk to you later."

I drive to Department 13. But it's closed for the holiday. I think about ramming my car into the front of the building. No one can stop me.

Instead, I make my way across town and park in front of McCoun's, my dad's regular gin trough. When I arrive, there are a dozen dimly lit faces in the place, none of them together. A city ordinance bans cigarettes, even in bars, but smoke chokes off the light fighting its way out of two bare bulbs. I straddle a stool at the bar, order a pint, a shot, a steak, and cry.

Not for long, though. I cry when the circumstances call for it. But I'm not a blubberer. I fall apart and come back together quickly. I get it over with and move on. The liquor helps. I have another beer before the food comes. And another shot.

"Are you coming?"

It's Cindi, on my cell phone. I'm not drunk, but I'm not sober.

"Cindi, how are you?"

"I'm fine. Where are you?"

"At a bar."

"I thought we were having dinner."

"And *I* thought your name was Cindi Paris." Silence. I say it again, with a bad French accent: "*Cindi Paris.*"

Silence. More silence.

"What's going on with you?" she says.

"An excellent question."

I stick with the accent. I like it. It makes me sound as ridiculous as I feel. I cannot possibly continue this conversation. It's bound to have something to do with her dead brother. It requires sensitivity, and I don't feel at all sensitive. I'm mad, but I don't know at what or whom. Something weird is going on, but I have the distinct sense that if I pursue the issue with Cindi, I could end up feeling even worse than I already do. So I tell her I'm sorry and hang up. The phone rings a moment later. A couple of heads at the bar twist my way. I smile and indicate that I'm turning it off. I look at the bartender.

"It's my birthday, you know."

"You want me to sing?"

I'm alone on my birthday. Getting old is terrifying. And the worst of it isn't the chance of losing my memory. It's the hair that worries me most. Ferdy's got it coming out his ears, on the top of his nose, poking out of the collar of his T-shirt. I spend hours each week plucking and shaving. I don't wax yet, but who knows? And Silvie. The thought of her in bed with Bateman is nearly unendurable. It's nauseating, although my queasiness may have something to do with the moccasin-smothered-in-ketchup I'm shoveling into my mouth. But still.

Suddenly, unexpectedly, I'm resolved, euphoric. I decide to have another beer and then go find her. I'll tell her it's okay. It's time to let go. I love her that much. Or I'll beg her to come back. I'll refuse to move until she promises to give it another try. Anyway, I have to see her. It's my birthday for fuck's sake. Before I can attract the attention of the barman for my bill, my brother walks in.

"Preet called the house."

"And said?"

He orders a whiskey, downs it, and parks on a stool. Then he orders another, and so do I, and we hold them aloft.

"Happy birthday," he says.

"What did he say?"

"He said you sounded weird. You really shouldn't drink."

"*I* shouldn't drink. Do you have the *slightest* recollection of me saving your ass a couple of weeks ago, at Department 13?"

"He said you sounded upset. Are you upset?"

"No."

He smiles and puts on his four-year-old voice. "You wook a whiddle upset."

"I'm fine."

"Why are you alone in a bar on your birthday?" He gives me the most irritating of his raft of irritating looks—the big-brother-has-advice-for-little-brother look.

249

"What's your problem?"

"*I'm* not the one getting shit-faced at McCoun's on my birthday."

"Fine."

"It's *time*, little man."

That's what my mom used to call me. And the bit about it being *time* has nothing to do with my birthday or my lack of sobriety. It's *time*, in King's view, for me to get tested, to face the music, to get on with my life. My brother's theory is that not knowing whether I will someday lose my mind to early-onset familial Alzheimer's disease is the source of my myriad problems.

A small crowd has gathered at one end of the saloon, which is about as wide and long as a submarine. I hear familiar strains, Manilow, piping out of a large amp hung from the ceiling. I look at the bartender.

He shrugs. "Barry-oke."

"You must be kidding me."

"It's been a big night for us. Barry's back, you know."

"Really? I had no idea."

"Oh yeah, he's everywhere these days—he was even a judge on *American Idol*. You don't get much bigger than that."

"Really? *American Idol*. That's amazing."

One of the reasons Manilow has been so badly and unfairly underappreciated is that his songs appear, deceptively, to be simple, undemanding. Any Joe or Jane who can carry a tune figures he or she can handle "Mandy" or "I Write the Songs." If that were the case, though, Preet and Terry and Maeve and I would be wasting our time. Barry isn't easy. Barry is hard. His charts don't look like folk songs or pop tunes; they look like standards. Barry grew up on jazz, so it's not surprising that his music is filled with flat minor sevens and diminished fifths, that it's suffused with mood and key changes. The phrasing is nearly impossible in some places. The tunes

250

only *sound* simple on the records because Barry Manilow is a freaking genius.

I wobble to the back of the bar and watch a young man in a business suit massacre "Weekend in New England." There's a line of wannabe crooners, but the small crowd can see I'm not to be tangled with. I smile and tip precariously forward, and then back, telling everyone it's my birthday. With some help I climb onto the small platform and ask for "Somewhere in the Night." I clutch the microphone, and when the brief intro concludes, I do my best to ruin the tune. I belch and screech out the words, until someone in a position of authority removes me from the stage. He jams his shoulder into my armpit and hoists me off the floor. I may hurl. He whisks me to the front door. King joins me on the curb.

"You're a moron," he says.

"Agreed. I'm going," I say. I managed to drink four beers and three shots in just short of two hours. I'm not in top form.

"I'll drive."

"I'm fine."

"I'll still drive."

He muscles me over to his car and starts for home.

"Take me to Silvie's place."

"Yeah, right."

"I won't even get out of the car. I just want to go by."

"What for?"

"Come on," I whine. "It's my damn birthday."

We arrive ten minutes later. It's a stubby duplex in a quiet residential neighborhood. Formerly quiet, anyway. I leap from the car before King comes to a stop. I run onto the front lawn and start squealing her name. The sound echoes up the street. In a minute a few lights go on up the block. A few faces appear in a few windows. I yell and yell and finally a window in Silvie's upstairs unit slides open. My heart thumps. There is little light, so I cannot see her face. But I can hear her voice.

"Who's that?" I stare up at her for a moment. An unpleasant wave of sobriety washes over me. "Gordy?"

I race back to the car and order King to take off.

# 43

THE CROWD MILLING outside the Hall is already a few hundred strong and it isn't nine A.M. They are chanting, "Free Marcus, free Marcus." Each syllable is like a knife into the middle of my eyeball.

Not chanting are police officers gathered in groups of four or five, eyeing the crowd, fingering their batons. Also not chanting are people holding cameras and notepads, trying to think of what they can possibly say on television or write in the newspaper about a secret proceeding; the Swell grand jury. Everyone—chanters, cops, reporters—is frying her or his butt off.

Cindi Paris pops out of a van. I walk over to her.

"I'm sorry about last night," I say.

"I don't appreciate being hung up on." I don't appreciate being hungover. The protesters aren't helping. "I was worried."

"I was on your steps. Your neighbor came over with some mail—"

"I gathered."

"Cynthia."

"I always hated that name."

"It's a nice name. But I have no idea who you are now."

"I should have told you. I'm sorry." Her colleagues mill around near us. She lowers her voice. "No one knows, Gordy. I swear I had no way of knowing the Manners case would lead to this. It's an important story and I didn't want to lose it."

"It's all about the work?"

"Ella Swell didn't know who I was either. I started using that name when I interviewed her in jail. Yes, it's about the work."

"And you talked to me because—"

"I was curious about Marcus, because Ella was so taken with him. When he got arrested, I figured you'd be a good source. The rest I had no way to predict."

"She said that."

"What?"

"That she was taken with him."

"She had very strong feelings for him."

"She *said* that?"

"Yes, she *said* that. If you're asking me whether they were sleeping together, I really don't know. I never asked her. Given the way she looked, I doubt she had romance on her mind."

"The cops confirmed she was dying. She only had a couple of months left."

"Jesus. I knew it."

"Totally and completely off the record."

"Yeah."

"Seriously, Cindi, my job's at stake over this."

"I'm sorry I didn't tell you. I should have told you."

"Swell wrote the whole thing down. It was just as you thought. She planned to out Pluck as the informant on the bookstore bust. She went to see him. Just a few hours before she died."

"That's incredible."

"Incredible, but off the record." She smiles. "Swell also said she was having an affair with Pluck before the '88 raid. You didn't know that either."

"No."

"Did Swell give you any reason to believe she was a lesbian?"

Cindi chuckles. "She never made a pass at me."

"That's not what I'm asking."

"I didn't know her that well, Gordy. Really."

"Please forget I mentioned it."

"*That'll* be easy. Are they still going after Marcus?"

"That's my sense. The cops know about the journal, but I don't think there's any evidence against Pluck. I'm sorry about your brother."

"Thank you." She tilts her head and smiles.

I smile back.

She says, "Have you been having any more problems?"

"Many, but nothing life-threatening," I lie.

Marcus was supposed to appear before the grand jury at eleven A.M. It's nearly one. We sit in an empty hallway, waiting. I tell him about my conference with Judge Reasoner. I explain the judge's new position—take the plea and the six months. Reject it, and maybe get a year.

"Unless the jurors go our way," I say.

Or unless the grand jury indicts him posthaste. I can't imagine Reasoner would push the misdos out to trial with a pending murder charge.

"What do you think I should do?" he says.

"Well, in my opinion it's, I mean, it seems clear that—"

It's strange, this moment. It feels like something's about to happen. To me, in the world. Something.

"I suppose I think it's a shitty offer and I'm not the worst trial lawyer in the county. So let's give it a shot."

We shake.

A few minutes later Silvie pokes her head out the door of a courtroom that is being used for the grand jury proceedings.

"Mr. Manners," she says. Her long hair falls into her face and she swoops it away with her hand while she holds the door with the other. The things I used to do with that hair. "Lovely seeing you last night, Gordy."

"I was channeling my dad."

"Convincingly. Happy birthday, by the way."

"A little late."

"That's not my job anymore." She doesn't look happy saying it. But she doesn't look unresolved either.

"I know. I'm sorry. Thirty-five kicked my ass. You get my message?"

"Yes."

"And?"

"And I told you I want to do it. Assuming we can avoid the stalking episodes and so on."

I bow and then try to follow Marcus into the courtroom. "You won't mind if I sit in."

"That's hilarious," she says.

She holds the door for Marcus, bracing it with her succulent butt, and then closes it while I try, weakly, to push my way into the room. Then I stop, put my mouth up to a crack in the door, and say, "I love you." She is long gone, though.

I sit on a bench in the hallway, ready to assist if Marcus should need me. Terry joins me.

"I heard about Cynthia."

"You heard what?" I had not, after all, given Preet any idea what significance attached to the information about the Howes. Terry raises his eyebrows. "You guys truly scare me."

"*She* could have been the shooter," Terry says.

"She knew Swell for years. She had plenty of opportunity before now."

"She *did* forget to tell you Robert Howe was her brother."

"She also correctly pointed out that we met before Swell's body was discovered. She had no way to know the dog-napping case would turn into this mess."

"Unless she was the shooter," he says, holding up a long index finger I have the urge to break in two, except that he's the guitar wizard and Vegas approaches.

"She wasn't the shooter, Terry."

"How do you know they've known each other for years?"

"Cindi told me."

"Aha."

"It's not a theory. It's hardly even a guess."

"It's at least a guess. How long has he been in there?"

"Too long."

The DA can ask as many questions as he likes. He can keep Marcus in the box for hours, while the kid refuses to answer question after question. But usually the grand jurors get fed up fairly quickly, so a person who declines to testify rarely lasts more than fifteen or twenty minutes. Manners is inside for an hour. And then another hour. When he finally emerges, it is nearly four. He has not left the room to ask a question.

He volunteers nothing.

"How'd it go?" I say.

"Fine. They said I'm not supposed to talk about it."

"You're allowed to talk about it with me. I thought we agreed you were going to refuse to testify."

"I changed my mind."

"I guess so," I say, laughing, although why exactly I don't know. It may be the distinct sense I have, now, that the kid knows, has known from the beginning, exactly where he's going, that I'm just along for the ride.

"You told them what happened up at the house."

"Yeah."

"That took three hours."

"I told them everything."

"Like what 'everything'?"

Lucy Pluck struts around a corner, calls out, "M," and jogs over to us. They kiss quite passionately. I avert my eyes. I don't think he was sleeping with Ella Swell. Maybe Swell was in love with him. Maybe he reminded her of her life before prison. But Marcus loves Lucy. That much seems clear.

The young lovers stroll off. I wait outside the grand jury room. Marcus was the last witness, but the proceedings do not break up for another forty-five minutes. Finally, Silvie emerges, along with Bateman and detectives Baptiste and Bacon, and others who presumably are the grand jurors.

Mick walks up, looking ebullient. "Hey guys."

"What'd you do to my client?"

"He's an amazing kid, Gordy. He really delivered."

"Would someone like to fill me in?"

"No," he says, and walks away. He looks over his shoulder quickly, winks, and turns away. I wink back at him, though he cannot see me, and thus the wink is purposeless.

# 44

I SPEND THE NEXT several hours going crazy trying to figure out what the hell's going on. But I have no luck. My client's nowhere to be found. I can't locate Pluck or Speed. Mick Bacon is stuck in meetings with the Swell investigation team. And neither Silvie, nor anyone else in the DA's Office, will pick up the phone. The frustration is overwhelming. I'm the lawyer. I'm in the circle.

Cindi drops by the office at six. She wants to know what's happening. She can't get anyone to take her calls either. In a sane world, I would know. But I don't. She suggests we eat, after her six-fifteen live spot in front of the Hall. I have no idea whether to trust her, or believe anything she says. But she seems to need the company.

We walk out front together. She asks whether I'd like to be interviewed. I decline. She makes her appearance, flawlessly, although she says nothing of particular interest: *Crowds continue to gather in front of the Hall in support of Marcus Manners; the grand jury proceedings are ongoing; the misdemeanor case begins in the morning. Next report at eleven.*

Milo is at the bar when we walk into Department 13. He notices Cindi. And then me. I'm pleased to see he's half drunk. In a couple of hours he'll be all drunk, and therefore particularly ineffective in the A.M. When Cindi goes off to use the facilities, I ask him if he's heard anything about developments in the Swell case. I tell him Manners was behind closed doors for three hours. He has no clue. I stand around while he whispers to a few of his DA colleagues. They shake their heads.

"No one has heard anything, Gordon," Milo says, with as grave an air as I've seen on him.

By seven-fifteen we're squished into a booth. Terry and Preet have joined us. Preet takes a bashful interest in Cindi, who doesn't seem the least troubled by the attention.

In the middle of dinner my cell rings.

"I'm outside. Don't bring the whole family."

Mick and I walk around the block to an alley.

"I don't know why you didn't bring him in before. You would have saved everyone a lot of headache."

"You know, this whole business is rather frustrating." My gathering sense that I have no idea what is going on and I have no control over anything makes me mad. "I gave you his story, Mick. What the hell else do you want?" He stares at me for a few moments.

"He has a new story. Swell told him the stuff in the diary, about Pluck being the snitch in the '88 case. She told him she'd been involved with Pluck. She told him *before* she got hit."

All of the following is according to Mick, whom I generally believe to be a reliable source, but given the chaotic and murky circumstances, I won't vouch for at the moment:

Marcus testified before the grand jury that Swell called him on the 27th of April. She picked him up. She asked him to stay with her, to protect her. They drove to the guesthouse on the Swell estate. She told Manners she was having a problem with her foot, so he helped her walk inside. He carried a box from her car into an upstairs office. He heard her scream. He heard shots. He ran to the top of the stairs. And he saw Councilman Jeremiah Pluck, gun in hand, fire a third time. Then he saw Pluck walk out a sliding glass door at the back of the house.

"He never told me he was a witness," I say. "He only said he heard the shots."

"He's telling the truth, Gordy. The kid knows stuff we didn't release. I told *you* the shots hit her in the hand and the arm and then the chest. That was bullshit. She was turning, trying to get away probably. The third shot went back to front, came *out* her chest. Manners got it all right."

"All that is perfectly consistent with Manners as the shooter."

"Nah. What's his motive?"

"I thought you said Swell killed his mother. Remember?"

"I said that?"

"Yeah."

"Well, Pluck had a better motive. No way he gets elected if he cheated on his wife with a white lady, let alone the fact that he was working for us."

"Which you still claim you didn't know."

"He was your dad's boy, Gordy. For all the shit Pluck's given the SRPD over the years, I'm shocked. He tried to cover his ass too, told us a while ago that Swell came to see him the same day."

"He said the same thing to me."

"He knew witnesses would have her at the office a few hours before the shooting. So he tried to deal with it up front, make like it was no big deal."

"Manners have anything else?"

"He said he got the shit kicked out of him a couple of weeks ago."

"Over the dog. SI guys."

"According to Manners, three older black dudes with a message from Pluck."

"Did Marcus happen to mention another time, before that? Some SI guys, *white* guys, pissed about the dog, knocked him around? I was there for that one, Mick."

"I don't see how it matters."

"Did you ask Marcus if he was sleeping with Swell?"

"He says no."

"What about if he knew she was sick?"

"No. But I'm saving the best for last. He IDed the gun. Swell figured Pluck would come after her, so a few weeks before she sprang the bad news on him, she asked Marcus to do her a favor. He hit the streets and found her a revolver, which is consistent with no casings at the scene. You never told Marcus that, did you? About the casings?"

"No."

"There you go. Manners says he saw the gun in the house when he first went in, on a table, but after Pluck took off, it was gone."

"Why wouldn't Swell get the gun herself?"

"She's got a record. She couldn't get the papers. She wouldn't know where to get one on the street."

"Of course."

"How come you look so miserable?" Mick says. "This is a good thing."

It is. Good that Marcus doesn't go away for life. Good that Swell's real killer is exposed.

But not so good that I have to try the loser misdos on television tomorrow, in front of a judge who would very much like to sentence me on behalf of my client, in the presence of a gallery perhaps badly disconcerted by Pluck's rapid collapse.

And not so good that the pieces of this puzzle are falling into place too quickly, a little too easily, like a hastily assembled structure bound to collapse under its own weight. Right now I feel certain not only that the other shoe is going to drop, I feel certain the other shoe is a steel-toed shit-kicker, and that it is going to land on my head.

# 45

I T'S WEDNESDAY, JUNE 2. I sit at counsel table with Marcus and Terry, while fifty prospective jurors file into the gallery. A television camera is parked next to the jury box. It looks fixed on me. I paste a half-smile on my face while I think, *do not under any circumstances pick your ears or nose.* Manners shows up just in time for court, in the company of an SRPD officer.

You have to feel sorry for jurors. A letter arrives in the mail, ordering you to come to the Hall of Justice. It doesn't say come whenever you can. It doesn't offer to give you a lift. It says come next week, Thursday, at two. You have to hire a babysitter, find parking, and sit in an overheated room, for several hours, until we're ready for you. Then we haul you into court, insist that you answer a lot of personal questions in front of a crowd, and either we reject you, which makes you feel like coming in was a waste of time, or we put you on a jury, which is worse.

In the latter case we drag you though a trial in which we bore you, confuse you, and ignore you. After which, without the slightest training, we put you in a small room with eleven people you may or may not like and who may or may not have socially accepted standards of hygiene and ask you to decide if someone committed a crime. And for this extraordinary effort, in Santa Rita, we pay you nine dollars a day. Nine bucks. You'd be better off wandering the streets collecting cans. At least that way you'd get some exercise and a tan.

Judge Reasoner introduces the court staff and counsel and Manners. I put my hand on my client's back when the judge says his name. I hope the gesture makes clear this young man is no dog-napper or drug addict. The judge continues. He reads the charges and a list of witnesses. He excuses a few people who absolutely, positively cannot be here for the rest of the week. He releases a few others who say they are acquainted with the defendant or one of the witnesses. Then he reads the standard instructions on the trial process and reasonable doubt. None of it makes much sense, and the jurors' faces do not reflect comprehension. They look as if they are in the waiting room of a dentist's office, about to go in for root canal. There ought to be a question-and-answer period. There should be milk and cookies.

The clerk seats fourteen prospective jurors and Reasoner turns the questioning over to the lawyers. This is voir dire, where we get to ask the jurors about their jobs and families and favorite television shows, to try to unearth biases for or against the defense or the prosecution, and then to dismiss a few we can't abide.

"Counsel for the People, whenever you're ready."

Milo is in worse shape this morning than I could reasonably have hoped for. He's slouched down in his chair. His shoes are untied. If he slept last night, it wasn't for more than a couple of hours, and it may well have been on the floor of the restroom at Department 13.

After a moment, he shifts up in his chair and then rises. "No questions, Your Honor. I will pass any challenges to the defense."

This happens sometimes. Normally, it's a tactical move, designed to send a message to the jurors. *I won't play the game of trying to decide who'll be more for me than against me. He's guilty, and I'm confident our evidence is strong enough that you'll agree, whoever you are.* But I wouldn't have expected the gambit from Milo, and this morning I assume it has little to do with strategy. Milo looks ready to keel over.

But whatever his motivation, the move boxes me in. Normally I'd spend a while getting to know the potential jury pool, educating the entire venire—both those in the jury box and those remaining in the gallery—with my questions and comments. But if Milo pretends to trust them, it will look bad if I don't. I explain the situation to Manners. The jurors stare at us. They do not look particularly friendly.

"Mr. Seegerman?"

"That's fine, Your Honor. We'll pass."

"Very well."

Reasoner sends the rest of the potential jurors home. Six courtroom deputies—three times the usual number—exit into the hallway outside. A minute later a wave of humanity crowds through the door and fights for seats in the room. Press. Public. Many of the faces by now are familiar. Speed, Lucy, Bea. Marcus's friends and supporters. Cindi and her media pals. One person is missing. Pluck.

Now there is another contingent too, one I noticed outside the Hall earlier but hoped would not make its way into the trial. It's the SI crowd—white guys in golf attire and with a couple of cigars stuffed into their shirt pockets who look very much like the men who assaulted Manners, and later my feeble vehicle; women with bowl-cut hair and white slacks and pastel-colored knit sweaters—come to support Jackson Bulley, to exact their pound of flesh from the dognapper.

When the gallery finally settles, the clerk swears in the twelve jurors. Judge Reasoner reads from a book of pretrial instructions. He explains the structure of the trial. He makes clear what is evidence (testimony, documents, stipulations between the parties) and what is not (opening statements, closing arguments, objections by the parties).

I figure Reasoner would sweeten at least a little when dealing with jurors. Most judges do. But he's as sour and cold while instructing the jury as he is when sentencing a defendant to life. He warns them not to discuss the case with anyone until it's time for deliberations. He tells them not to be late. He treats them like teenagers stuck in detention.

When he's through, I expect the judge to release us until the next morning. Voir dire was supposed to consume the afternoon. We set opening arguments and the first witnesses for Thursday A.M. But I suppose Reasoner knows he's living on borrowed time.

"Mr. Valucovoik, would you care to present an opening statement?"

All three hundred pounds of Milo are stunned. And it's not the judge's contorting his name that does it.

"May we approach, Your Honor?" Milo says. I wince. In a chambers meeting Reasoner read a list of trial dos and don'ts. Number three, after *No Speaking Objections* and *Rise When You Address the Court or a Witness*, was *Don't Ask to Approach*. Number four is *Don't Pace*, which is going to be hard for me. "I would like to discuss a scheduling matter."

"There is nothing to discuss."

"Judge, I thought we were going to begin in the morning."

Titters from the gallery. Reasoner slams his gavel against the bench. He scans the crowd for troublemakers.

"Mr. Vowlachuvuk, if you have an opening statement, give it."

"I thought we were—"

"I heard you the first time," Reasoner snaps. "Mr. Seegerman, do you have something to say?"

I look over at Milo.

"I will make a statement, Your Honor," he says, wandering a few steps toward the jurors, looking utterly forlorn. "Good afternoon, ladies and gentlemen. My name is Milo Velikovic and by my English you can tell I was not born in Santa Rita. I am from Serbia, which used to be part of Yugoslavia."

I could object. But before I can think through whether the speech helps or hurts, Reasoner is out of his chair and on top of Milo.

"Do other judges sit through this nonsense? Move on, Counsel."

"Sorry. I will move on."

Now I wonder. The guy is so bad he's almost good. I start to notice little things about Milo, the way he twists his hands around one another when he speaks, the way he leans precariously forward, the discombobulated hair. Can anyone be this pathetic without it being partly orchestrated? All that, plus the fact that he passed on the first jury panel, makes me think I better stay awake.

"Sometime on the night of April twenty-sixth, this guy"—he sticks his clenched fist at Marcus, as if he were punching him in the face— "drove his car onto private property in the hills. We know he was there because someone saw him and saw his car."

"Objection, Your Honor."

"Counsel," Reasoner glares at Milo. "We have yet to hear from a single witness. Refrain from arguing the case."

"Sorry." He smiles at the jurors, and continues. "The next day the man who lives in the house—his name is Professor Jackson Bulley— went outside to feed his dog and the dog was gone. The dog was in the kennel the night before. Professor Bulley put the dog there himself. But in the morning, no dog.

"A day later a police officer found Professor Bulley's dog tied up behind this guy's apartment building." Again, he points at Marcus. "A couple of other important things you will hear about at this trial. Probably you already know that Mr. Manners is a famous football player in Santa Rita. I've seen him play, and let me tell you, he's great. You should see him—"

The judge cuts him off. "I hope you brought your checkbook, Counsel."

Milo looks at the judge, but does not respond for several tense seconds. Finally he says, "Anyway, he plays for Hills High School. And everyone knows about the competition between Hills and SI. The dog that disappeared from Professor Bulley's house is the SI dog. His name is Red."

Milo raises his eyebrows, smiles into the TV camera, and then turns back to the jurors.

"Finally, when an officer went to Mr. Manners's house to talk to him about the dog, the officer looked inside the same car that was up at Professor Bulley's house and he found a bag of marijuana in the car. That's the two counts against him. The theft of a dog and possession of marijuana. Thank you very much."

Now I'm sure Milo planned the whole thing. The speech is not extemporaneous. No way. He passed the jury, and claimed not to be ready to address the jurors, knowing Reasoner would insist. He looks like he's about to flub, and then pulls a perfectly reasonable opening statement out of his butt. The jury first feels sorry for him, and then proud of him for working so well off the cuff. He figures, correctly, that I'm not ready to go.

It occurs to me, now, that Milo may have a reputation for being a bad trial lawyer because Milo has cultivated that reputation. The snake.

# 46

"**M**R. SEEGERMAN. Would you care to make an opening statement?"

Actually, no.

"Thank you, Your Honor. As Judge Reasoner mentioned, my name is Gordon Seegerman and I work for the Santa Rita Public Defender." I turn to Terry, who stands. "Before I begin, I'd like to introduce Terrence Fretwater. He's an investigator in our office who has worked on this case. He'll be sitting here throughout the trial assisting me."

As in, *Listen, jurors, folks watching from home. I realize I'm a little funny looking and a lot awkward. I offer Mr. Fretwater for your viewing pleasure.*

"I'm sure we're all charmed, Mr. Seegerman."

The crowd chuckles. But Reasoner did not mean it as a joke. He meant it as an insult. He registers his displeasure by thumping the gavel on his bench.

"You'll hear a lot in this case about the person sitting with me. He's captain of the football team at Hills, where he'll finish up in a few weeks. He's among the best high school athletes, not simply in the state, but in the country. He's also an honor student. He's had a hard road—he lost his mother when he was a young child—"

"Blah, blah, blah. Sounds like argument to me, Mr. Seegerman," Reasoner grumbles. "I'm beginning to doubt that either of you has ever been in trial before."

"And you'll hear a lot about the dog named Red who disappeared from an estate in the hills and ended up behind the four-unit apartment building in West Santa Rita where Marcus lives with his dad. As Mr. Velikovic suggested, the dog is the mascot for SI. It's a dog that a lot of people in this town would recognize. It's not the kind of dog that's easy to disguise or sell or do anything with other than go to SI football games.

"And finally you'll hear about some marijuana found in a car sometimes driven by my client and sometimes driven by his father.

"But I want you to listen very, very carefully when Mr. Velikovic puts on his witnesses. What you will not hear from the prosecution is any evidence my client took the dog or possessed marijuana. None."

I plunk down in my seat. The crowd shuffles in theirs. No doubt they would like to stand and cheer. They would like to breach the bar and throw their arms around me. Reasoner lifts his gavel off the bench and the room quiets.

When court adjourns, I hold Marcus at counsel table. I'd like to have a few minutes with him. His SRPD handler walks up and says Marcus is needed at the DA's Office.

"Do you mind?" I say. "I'm having a meeting with my client."

The cop does not move. Marcus stands.

"I'll see you in the morning," he says. He is not apologetic.


I sit with King and Ferdy and S. in our living room watching the late news. I'm a Channel 2 loyalist now. The anchor straightens his papers and addresses the camera with a stern face.

"Stunning developments today in the Swell homicide investigation. For more on that we go, live, to Cindi Paris at the Santa Rita Hall of Justice. Cindi."

"Thanks, Richard. Today, focus was on a courtroom inside the Hall where the district attorney and Marcus Manners's lawyer"—the unbelievably attractive silky-voiced Manilow tribute singer Gordon Seegerman—"presented opening arguments—"

"Not 'arguments,' Cindi," I say. " 'Statements.' Opening *state*—" Ferdy shushes me.

"—in the misdemeanor case against Manners for the theft of a dog taken from the Swell estate several weeks ago."

Over Cindi's description of events I see clips of courtroom action. It's hard sometimes to believe how funny looking I am, especially parked next to Manners and Terry. It's really quite unfair.

The camera returns to Cindi. "But elsewhere in the Hall the investigation into the shooting death of Ella Swell abruptly changed directions. It has been widely rumored that the grand jury, convened just yesterday, was focused on Manners as the key suspect. Sources have informed Channel 2 that after only one day of testimony, the grand jury has gone on a break, and that the prime suspect in the Swell homicide case is now city councilman and mayoral candidate Jeremiah Pluck. Police searched Pluck's residence today and have been questioning additional witnesses."

"Pluck. Figures." Ferdy shakes his head.

I shush him back.

"Cindi, can you tell us what led the police to Pluck?"

"The SRPD and the DA are being very tight-lipped, Richard. Obviously with a suspect as well respected in this community as Pluck, they are being very careful not to make any mistakes. I can only speculate, really. But one possibility is that Manners himself gave evidence in the grand jury that shifted the investigation. My understanding is his appearance before the grand jury marks the first time Manners has made any statement about the case. Unfortunately that statement is not available to us, so we really don't know."

"Is anyone speculating about a motive?"

"The police may have a motive, but officials aren't saying. The only connection we know of between Swell and Councilman Pluck is that they were both involved in a West Santa Rita bookstore in the late 1980s. And we know Swell ended up in prison after police raided the store looking for drugs, and a police officer was killed. Other than that, no one's commenting. We'll simply have to wait to learn more."

As I lay in bed, I can hear sirens—fire trucks and police cars and ambulances—racing across the flatlands. I can hear helicopters chopping through the night sky, their spotlights bearing down on West Santa Rita. I think, *Rodney*.

# 47

I T'S NOT AS BAD as that, but it's pretty damn bad. The cops spend a long night chasing down looters and blocking access to the Santa Rita port where a crowd of rock-throwing kids tries to force its way onto a container ship. Rioters break windows at stores in West Santa Rita and downtown. The fire department has to deal with a series of small conflagrations; nothing enormous, but enough to keep the sirens blaring and me up most of the night. In the worst incident, reminiscent of the King riots, men block the path of a cab, drag the Chinese driver from the car, and beat him senseless.

By the morning calm is essentially restored, but the heat hasn't let up, and from calls I receive before eight in the morning—from Terry and Aineen—the scene outside the Hall looks a lot less peaceable than it has during the weeks of daily demonstrations. The SI folks are hiding inside their SUVs until court. The West Santa Rita crew seems on the verge of storming the building. I have no idea what's become of Pluck, but given how badly and quickly things have deteriorated, I wish he'd make some kind of appearance.

If S. had even a few remaining marbles, he'd have saddled up before sunrise and ridden into the west side to restore order. As it is, he sits at the kitchen table, humming, while I prepare his cereal. He continues to hum while I attempt to feed him, which makes for quite a mess. I tell him to stop. He continues. I tell him I'm going to sew his mouth and nose shut with dental floss. He ignores me. I say, "Fine," and start to eat his breakfast. That shuts him up.

Ferdy arrives, takes a gander at the television, and begins a rant that does not let up, even when I collect my things and run out the door. I can hear him from the driveway. The essence is simple: *It's about time. The revolution has finally come to Santa Rita.* I don't bother to point out that the rioters, so far, have mostly wilded in their own neighborhood. The vast homes that surround our decrepit dwelling remain very much intact. The white DA will become mayor. We'll have some extra work in the PD's Office, a few black guys will go off to prison, one Chinese cab driver will be in physical therapy for a year, and a bunch of insurance companies will raise their rates. As for fundamental political change, I have my doubts.

Mick and Marcus Manners are in my office when I arrive at slightly before eight A.M. A uniformed police officer is posted at the door. Mick has his feet up on my desk.

"Make yourself at home, Detective," I say. "So, now that my client is your star witness, maybe you could do me a favor and make this ridiculous misdemeanor case disappear."

"I'd like to, Gordy—"

"But—"

"Bulley and his SIF friends are pushing Fischer pretty hard. Even if he was inclined, we'd have problems doing the kid any favors right now. Pluck already has Dennis Rosenthal on board." In other words, Pluck has hired the best private defense lawyer in northern California. The cops don't want to weaken Marcus's value as a witness against the councilman by dumping the misdos and looking like they're rewarding the kid for his testimony. "Anyway, I got you the goods on Dent. You shouldn't have a problem."

"I have myriad problems. Are we meeting or can I have a few minutes to get coffee and talk to my client before we have to go to court?"

"We've moved Marcus and Lucy to a safe house. We'll deliver them here in the A.M. If you want them otherwise, you call me. Also, I'm posting an officer on Marcus."

"A bodyguard. Very impressive." Marcus smiles. But not smugly. He sits quietly, listening to the banter, taking it in.

"It'd be better if he was out of uniform," I continue. "I don't want the jurors to get the idea he's dangerous. Also, if you could get me some sushi for lunch. But no mackerel."

Mick gets up. "I'll see what I can do."

"Are you guys going to make an arrest, or do we have more grand jury proceedings to look forward to?"

Mick walks to the door. "Patience, little man. Patience."

The door closes. Manners says nothing. I follow after Mick.

"You really think the security is necessary?" I ask.

"You got a problem with it?"

"Just curious. Seems a bit excessive."

"Trust me. It's not excessive."

"That's it? That's all I get?"

"What else do you want?" he says. His tone is professional, less chummy than usual.

"I want to know what's going on?" He turns and takes several steps down the hallway. "Wait." He stops. "Let's just say you're on the verge of taking Pluck down. Any reason to believe I'd be a target?"

He turns and chuckles. "You?"

I reveal the calls and notes, the incident several days ago in the hills.

"You should have said something."

"I felt stupid. I figured it was SIF loonies."

He stares at me, his police brain churning. "You want me to post someone on you?"

"Seems like Pluck's incentive to go after me has evaporated, now that you have Marcus."

"Maybe. Let me know if something else happens. I'll do a little digging on the pinky guy."

I feel better, protected. This must be what it feels like to be eight and have a real father. I return to my office.

"How's Lucy?" I say.

"She's all right."

"It has to be pretty hard on her, though?"

"We'll be all right."

"I feel a little silly about this whole thing. Normally when one of my clients becomes a witness for the state, I have a little more involvement, you know?"

Marcus nods.

"Mick's a good guy, but he's a cop," I continue. "You understand? I'm trying to make sure you come out of this whole thing okay."

"Yeah."

"Mick worries about getting the bad guy," I add. "We worry about you."

"Thanks."

"You're welcome. You were very convincing when we showed you the journal."

"I didn't really know what was going to happen. I wanted to deal with it myself."

He's not sorry. He's not confused or reticent or anxious. He's the quarterback. He's in charge.

# 48

JACKSON BULLEY IS on the stand. Milo is pacing. Reasoner is steaming, but so far hasn't cut in. The testimony is beyond riveting. I have to slap myself several times to stay awake. For a moment I think Reasoner has actually died, right there on the bench, leaning back in his big black leather chair, his eyes rolled into his head.

Bulley says the dog is named Red. He is five, a mutt, a mastiff mix of some sort. The dog has a dyed red stripe on his back. The dye is reapplied every two months by a professional hairstylist. Red and Bulley attend many SI sporting events. Bulley deposited the dog in his kennel at around ten P.M. on Monday, April 26. Bulley carefully latched the pen. The next morning he found the gate closed, but the dog gone. He searched the property with his son, Brice, who, Bulley makes sure to tell the gallery, will be attending Yale in the fall. Then he called the police. Later, after Red turned up, Bulley identified the dog.

"Cross-examination, Mr. Seegerman."

The gallery wakes up.

"Just a couple of questions, Professor."

There are many reasons not to be a criminal defense lawyer. People are forever asking me how I live with myself, working to help criminals. Most of us are overworked, underpaid, looked down upon. Playing the underdog is exciting, at first. But the thrill wears off quickly, when you realize underdogs are underdogs for good reason. We are outgunned, ill equipped, destined to fail.

So what makes it worth it? Among other things—an endless supply of dinner-party stories, constant reminders of the limitlessness of human folly—there is cross-examination. Imagine it. Someone you don't like, an arrogant asshole like Jackson Bulley, for example, in the box, under penalty of perjury. And you have the constitutional power to compel him to answer your questions, to squeeze him, to make him look like a liar. It's among life's most heady experiences, even if nothing much comes of it.

I continue, "You're an SI fan, right?"

"Sure."

"That's why you have the dog and go to all the games and so on."

"I don't go to *all* the games."

"But you're especially a fan of SI's football team."

"I'm a fan. I went to SI and I continue to be involved in alumni activity."

"You're a member of Saint Illuminatus Forever."

"Yes."

"What's that?"

"It's a fund-raising body, primarily. We have social gatherings. We sponsor various charities."

"Who are the members of Saint Illuminatus Forever?"

"SI alumni."

"All SI alumni?"

"No."

"Mostly men, mostly sports fans."

"That's probably true."

"You were at the game this year where Hills beat SI by a large margin."

He smiles. "Yes. Not a pleasant experience."

"And you saw Marcus Manners on the field that day."

"Oh yes."

"You saw what a tremendous player he is."

"Hard to disagree with you there."

"You saw him run for a couple of touchdowns himself."

"Yes."

"You saw him do the Hills victory dance in the end zone."

"Yes." He chuckles.

"You saw him taunt the SI team throughout the game."

"I saw the Hills players acting like adolescents. Had we won the game, our players would have behaved the same way, I'm sure."

"But watching Manners score those touchdowns and do his dance and taunt your players, that must have angered you."

"Please, Mr. Seegerman. That's ridiculous. It's a game."

"Okay. I accept that. But when you heard your dog had been found behind a building where my client lives with his father, you didn't think it was the father who took your dog."

"No."

"You assumed it was Marcus Manners."

"Well, I think I fairly concluded that it was more likely the conduct of an eighteen-year-old than a mature adult."

"But you didn't *see* Marcus Manners take your dog."

"No."

"And you can't say who did."

"No."

"Nothing else, Your Honor."

It's what does not come out in Bulley's testimony that is most interesting. A retracting iron gate blocks the entrance to the estate. Bulley might have testified on direct that the gate was closed on the evening of the 26th. If Bulley were willing to announce in public his belief that his wife was having a relationship with Marcus Manners, Milo would have powerful circumstantial evidence that Marcus, either alone or with his buddies, was part of the dog-napping crew. Manners probably knew the code for the gate, because Swell probably gave it to him. And, without a way to get onto the property, how could the dog have been removed?

But Bulley can't bring himself to testify he was cuckolded by a future Heisman trophy winner. And God knows it's not a subject I intend to raise. Whether or not he was doing Swell, the kid had been on the property many times, and it's logical to think he would have been able to get through the gate. It's not in our interest for the jurors to learn any of it.

Velikovic puts on a few other scintillating witnesses: the woman who waved down the patrol car on the morning of April 28, the officer who subdued the dog by giving him half of his bologna sandwich, and then paraded the mutt around the apartment building until, finally, he reached Marcus's door.

Every third question Milo asks is leading or objectionable on some other ground. But I'm more interested in moving things along than making his life miserable. And what's to be gained? The story is the story. The dog disappeared, he ended up in Marcus's backyard. There's nothing I can do with it.

When Terry came back from interviewing Layne Maddox a few days ago he described him as the love child of Ernest Hemingway and Liberace. The description is dead on. He's a hirsute, thickset man, five and a half feet, deeply tanned, like someone who spends a lot of time tuna fishing or hunting big game. He also has an unfortunate hairpiece, which seems guaranteed to melt under the midday sun, mammoth turquoise rings on seven of his ten fingers, including his thumbs, and an outfit so floral that when he takes the stand, my allergies immediately kick in.

He speaks slowly, carefully, like someone who may have been on the stand before.

"What time was that?"

"I always leave my house in the neighborhood of ten P.M. It was around that time."

Milo has a blowup of a map on an easel. He moves it close to the

280

witness box and asks Maddox to point out the route of his evening dog walk. Up Francis Lewis Lane, past the entrance to the Swell estate, then up the hill several blocks. He returns the same way. The whole walk takes about a half hour.

"You saw a car on the side of the road?"

"Yes. There is an area of gravel about thirty yards before the gate to the Swell place. I noticed the car when I reached the end of my driveway."

"And what did you see?

"First I saw the car. When I got a bit closer, my dogs started to pull toward the car. A moment after that I saw the man."

"Can you describe the car?"

"Small. I'm not exactly sure about the color because there wasn't very much light. It was green or blue, I think, a dark color. When I got closer, I noticed it was a Honda. I saw the little, what do you call it, the thing with the 'H' on the trunk."

"Then you saw the man?"

"I assumed there was someone there, or an animal, because my dogs were pulling toward the car. Then they started to bark. At that point I noticed a tall black man leaning against the passenger-side door."

"The man had his back to you?"

"Yes."

"Then how could you tell he was black?"

"Well, my dogs often bark at black people. I can't understand it. They never bark at anyone else, even the postman. But black people, they are guaranteed to bark like mad."

Maddox seems legitimately embarrassed for his mutts.

He continues, "When we got halfway across the road, the man turned his head slightly. At that point I could see enough of his face to see that he was a black man."

"Did you see enough of the man's face to be able to identify him?"

"No, I'm sorry. He was tall. His hair was short. I didn't see his clothes because he was blocked by the car."

"Did you see the license plate of the car?"

"Yes. But I only remember that it began with '2K.' It was a California plate beginning with '2K.' That's the best I can do."

"After your walk, when you came back, did you see the car?"

"No. It was gone."

"Thank you, Your Honor. I don't have anything more."

Cross.

"You don't know whether the man you saw on June 26 was Marcus Manners."

"No. And I ought to add I'm a Hills fan."

Reasoner leans in. "Mr. Maddox. Your sports allegiances are entirely beside the point. Please answer the question put to you."

Maddox twists his body around to face the judge and stares him down for a moment. Then he returns to me.

"You described the person you saw as black, tall, and short hair. You think that would describe a fair number of people in this county?"

"Objection."

"What? That's common knowledge."

"Mr. Seegerman, if I want argument, I'll ask for it. Sustained."

"The license plate began with '2K.'"

"Yes."

"Have you ever seen another car with—"

"You're trying my patience, Counsel. Move on."

"The car was a Honda."

"Yes."

"Are you familiar with the various models of Hondas?"

"Not really."

"What kind of car do you drive, Mr. Maddox?"

"A Toyota Landcruiser."

"Pretty big car, the Landcruiser."

"Yes. It's a good-sized vehicle."

"So even a midsize car would look pretty small to you."

"No, I think I can tell a small car from a midsize one."

"You don't know if it was a Honda Civic or, say, a Honda Accord."

"That may be."

"All you know is it was small."

"It looked pretty small to me."

"And it was a Honda."

"From that doohickey on the back of the car, with the 'H.'"

"Have you ever seen the doohickey on the back of a Hyundai, Mr. Maddox."

"I'm not sure. Probably."

"Would you say it looks very much like the doohickey on a Honda?"

"That I don't know."

"Do you remember anything else about the car?" It's a total throwaway. I have nothing in mind. I'm just trying to convince the Manners crew in the gallery and at home that I've done this before.

"Yes. It had only two seats. There was no room behind the seats."

Milo is not paying attention. I repeat the question for his benefit.

"It was a two-seater? You're absolutely sure."

"Yes. I'm sure. I remember thinking to myself a person with that kind of car couldn't have a dog and a wife. There'd be no place to put them both. Which got me to thinking about dogs and wives and choosing between them." The gallery titters.

Unbelievable. Figures Dent would get a brief description of the car, but wouldn't ask even one follow-up question. And while Terry talked to Maddox, I can hardly fault *him*. He had Dent's report, and he assumed what I assumed until ten seconds ago—that Maddox had described a Honda Civic.

There's an explanation for the discrepancy, although it's as damning to Manners as if Maddox *had* indeed seen a Honda Civic with a "2K" plate by the Swell estate, which it is now clear he did not.

"Thank you, sir. That's all I have."

# 49

I SIT DOWN AND whisper to Terry.

"Have Preet get the license plate number on Lucy Pluck's car."

His eyebrows shoot up. He gets it and takes off.

"Your next witness, Mr. Vulacuvak."

"Officer Karl Dent."

Dent is the investigating officer in the case, so he's been sitting with Milo at counsel table. Between them they must be responsible for half of the doughnut consumption in this county. Dent plods across the courtroom, belly first. He looks grave, on the verge of a soliloquy, while the clerk offers the customary swearing-in—*do you swear to tell the truth, the whole truth, and nothing but the truth.* Dent wouldn't recognize the truth if it clubbed him over the head.

The officer climbs slowly into the witness box. He pours a glass of water, adjusts the microphone, and is finally ready.

Milo's direct is fine. He could skip most of it. It makes no difference that Dent got a call about the missing dog. It makes no difference that he interviewed Bulley or his son or Maddox. He is a percipient witness to only one thing, and that's the pot he found in the Civic.

Cross.

"Officer Dent, you remember the car you found the marijuana in, right?"

"I remember it quite well, sir."

"When you went to the Mannerses' building, you had the license plate number for that car."

"Indeed."

"And you knew what kind of car it was."

"Correct."

"It was a Honda Civic, right?"

"Correct."

"How many seats in the car."

"Four seats, sir."

"You searched this *four-seat* car and you found an old paper bag with marijuana in it."

"Correct."

"The marijuana was sitting there on the floor of the car."

"I located the bag containing marijuana directly in front of the front passenger's seat, sir."

"No attempt to conceal it, right?"

"Certainly there was an attempt to conceal it. The drugs were in a bag. The bag itself was not concealed."

"In your years of experience in law enforcement, do people tend to put their drugs where someone walking by can easily see them?"

"I wasn't walking by. I was—"

I cut him off. "Move to strike as nonresponsive."

"Please listen to the question, Officer Dent."

Be still my beating heart. A ruling in my favor.

"Would you like me to repeat it?"

"Please do."

"You've been a Santa Rita officer for many years, right?"

"Yes, sir."

"So you must have seen a lot of drugs in a lot of different places."

"I've seen more than my fair share of narcotics, sir."

"So, in your experience, people tend to put their drugs where other people *can't* see them, right?"

"As to marijuana, I'd have to disagree with you, Counselor. Many people no longer think of it as illegal, which of course it remains. They may tend to be less than vigilant. Remarkably, I've seen young people walking down the street smoking marijuana. In this case, as I've noted, I think, the drugs *were* concealed. They were hidden inside a paper bag."

I could move to strike most of the response, but Dent's lecture, his professorial tone, is bound to irritate the jurors. Cross-examination 101: give the witness the rope and let him hang himself.

"You found my client's fingerprints on the marijuana, right?"

"It is next to impossible to lift prints from paper, sir, so the answer to your question is no. We did not locate Mr. Manners's fingerprints or anyone else's fingerprints on the paper bag."

"But someone saw Marcus Manners with the marijuana, in the car, right?"

"We have no such witness, sir."

"Then Marcus must have admitted that it was his, when you arrested him for stealing the dog."

"He did not."

"He told you the marijuana was *not* his, correct?"

"That's right."

"He told you he has never, ever, in his entire life smoked marijuana or used any other sort of illegal drugs, right?"

"Those were not his words, but that was the gist of his statement to me."

I walk back to counsel table, letting that bit sink in. Then I turn back to him.

"You like high school football, Officer Dent?"

"Objection." Milo is supposed to stand to make his objection, but he simply cannot get out of his chair fast enough.

"Stand still and state your grounds, Mr. Vulichuvac."

"How is this relevant?"

"Sustained."

"May I, Your Honor?"

"No."

The gallery stirs and Reasoner pounds the bench feebly with his small fist. "Quiet."

"I would like to make my record." He says nothing. "Is Your Honor going to rule?"

Finally, aware that I intend to make a speech, Reasoner removes the jury from the courtroom.

"This is our defense, Judge. Officer Dent knew the dog-stealing charge wouldn't go very far alone. He's a loyal SI fan. He's been to every game in ten years." I have no idea whether this is true. It sounds pretty good, though. "He's a member of Saint Illuminatus Forever."

Reasoner leans over the bench, glaring. "As you well know, Seeger-man, I am a member of SIF."

"It's my position that Officer Dent planted the drugs in the car. Marcus Manners is an A student with no history of drug use whatsoever. You walk down the halls of Hills High and every person will tell you the same thing. Marcus Manners does not use drugs. Period. This was a setup and we have a right under the Fourteenth Amendment to present that defense."

"If you proposed that space aliens put the marijuana in the car, I'd be no more inclined to permit you to pursue it. It is a defense, undoubtedly. But it is a defense as to which you have no evidence. All you have is the fact that Officer Dent attended SI, that he likes football, and that he is a member of SIF. You have a woefully inadequate quantum of proof to impugn this man's integrity. The objection is sustained. Bring in the jury."

"With due respect, Your Honor, that's not so. Our witness list includes a man named An Phan. Mr. Phan will tell this jury that having mistakenly broken down the door to his house, and scared the wits out of his family, Officer Dent planted drugs in his house to cover up for his shoddy police work. Mr. Phan prevailed in a civil rights action against Officer Dent. This officer has a history of misconduct, and I'm entitled to examine him on it."

"But so far no such evidence is before me or this jury. So, you're showing is inadequate. The jury, please."

I suspected this would happen. My hope is that the jurors will read about the court's ruling in the paper, or hear about it from friends in the gallery. I give it another try, just to give the jurors something else to think about. The more questions I ask, and the more objections Reasoner sustains, the more they'll wonder what's being kept from them.

"You were aware, Officer Dent, when you heard where the dog had been found, and later, when you pursued the information provided to you by Mr. Maddox, that Marcus Manners was the star quarterback for Hills High, right?"

"Objection. Relevance."

"Sustained."

I turn to the gallery, head down, and affect a frustrated scowl. Then I turn back.

"You attended Saint Illuminatus—"

"Objection."

"Three strikes, Mr. Seegerman. I'm sure the sheriff would be pleased to have you as his guest this evening." In other words, in the county jail.

"Nothing else, Your Honor."

Milo puts on a cop chemist who testifies that the green stuff in the bag Dent *says* he found in Marcus Manners's car is marijuana, 32 grams' worth. I have no cross. It's three-thirty. We're done for the day.

# 50

**A**FTER WORK, Terry and Preet pick me up for a pre-Vegas dinner at Maeve's.

Before I have my butt on the back seat of the Benz, Terry mugs me with questions about the Swell case. I swear them both to silence and fill them in. Manners knew Pluck was the snitch in the '88 case. He knew Swell and Pluck were involved, that she planned to out the councilman. Manners is the state's witness. Pluck's mayoral run is terminal.

"I knew something was up with that kid," Terry says. "Maybe Fischer engineered the whole thing."

"The mind boggles," Preet says. I chuckle. Terry does not.

"Pluck's murder trial should be fun," Preet says. "How long until the National Guard gets called in?"

"Assuming we even get to a trial," I say.

"Why wouldn't we?" Terry says.

"I don't know. They still have to get it by a grand jury. Seems like everything they have points to the kid as much as it does to Pluck. From what I understand, all they really have is Manners's say-so, and the fact that he has information that puts him at the scene when she gets hit. There's still the blood on his shoes and his skin under her nails. Mick's ignoring a million holes in the case, probably because he and Fischer are drinking buddies. Plus, Pluck and the SRPD have been going at each other for years."

Terry says, "You see? Bacon and Fischer, Fischer and Bacon."

"Terry, believe me. Mick Bacon is incapable of corruption. All I'm saying is he has it in for Pluck, so he's not seeing the problems."

"What's Manners's motive?"

"I don't know. How about a mercy killing?" I say. Preet cracks up. Terry does not. I turn to Preet. "At least *we* think we're funny." Terry is silent, elsewhere. "The one thing I know is I saw the look on Pluck's face when he heard Swell was dead. I'm not saying I know what happened. And I have no idea if Manners is the bad guy. He seems harmless to me. But one thing I'm totally confident of is that Pluck didn't know Swell was dead."

Several moments later Terry says, "1997 Honda del Sol. License plate 2KHL263." The two-seater.

"Registered to Lucy Pluck?"

"Lucille, actually."

"It's pretty unbelievable. You'd think Dent or Milo or someone would have figured this out," I say.

"So the girlfriend took the dog?" Preet says.

"More likely Manners borrowed the car," I say. "He parks, opens the gate for his buddies. Then he walked back to the car to play lookout. That's when Maddox saw him."

"So what happens to the dog?"

"I suppose one of Marcus's friends had it for a day and then dumped it at his house. Wouldn't surprise me if one of them is responsible for the dope too."

"What about that?" Terry says. "You promised to put Peretz on."

"What's the use? Even if he didn't assert the Fifth and decides to tell the truth, what do I get? *We* took the dog."

We tick through the Vegas plan. Preet will fly in midday with the equipment. Terry, Silvie and I will make the earliest flight we can. Then we'll troll the Mandalay for Barry fans, handing out invites to our ten P.M. show at the House of Blues. Twelve thousand or so should be in town, many of them at the hotel for a Manilow fan club convention. If Manilow makes it to our gig, the place better be packed.

"How's your future grandfather-in-law?" I ask Terry. It's his job to prep An Phan for his testimony in our case.

"He's ready."

Dinner at Maeve's is awkward and depressing. The woman is a freaking mess. Her usual truculence has dissolved into pure dejection. She's enormous, bedridden, pasty-faced, greasy-haired. There is nothing about the present circumstances—missing Vegas, missing Barry, Silvie, the imminent arrival of a child with a penis—to feel good about, and she's wallowing. She plows through bags of guacamole-flavored Dorito chips with hostile abandon. Empties litter the floor.

We reassure her that she'll be back in no time, that Barry probably won't show at the gig anyway, that Silvie's voice lacks character, that we miss her. None of it makes the slightest difference.

On our way out she says, "If the kid shows up tonight, I'll be on that plane," and smiles weakly.

"How'd it go?" Ferdy asks when I walk in, past eleven. King is out for the evening. Ferdy's been sitting S.

"Could go either way."

"I tangled with Reasoner a few times myself, you know."

"Oh yeah?"

I escape into the kitchen and stand there, hoping he gives up. He does not.

"The problem with Reasoner isn't that he has the wrong politics," Ferdy calls out. "The problem is he has the wrong politics *and* he's clean. Doesn't drink, doesn't smoke. He doesn't go in for girls."

"How about boys?" I mumble.

"In the old days a couple of Jimmy Milano's boys tried to bribe him. He turned them in. Could you believe it? A judge who doesn't take a bribe? It's just not right."

"I'm going upstairs."

"Come here. I want to talk to you." I back down and into the living room.

"Uh oh."

"Uh oh, nothing. Sit. King said he found you down at McCoun's on your birthday."

"I was under the impression you don't countenance snitches."

"It's different if they're working for me. What is it? Silvie?"

"Silvie. Being thirty-five. Missing my mom. Starting to think I'm really a lawyer, that who I am is filing motions and dealing misdemeanors and that's it."

"Not such a disaster."

"No?"

"It's an honest living. Plus, you got Manilow."

"Even still, I feel stuck. Watching Dad and wondering if that's all there is to look forward to."

"Maybe it's time to get unstuck."

"Maybe."

I sit in S.'s room for a while, watching his chest slowly rise and then quickly collapse, listening to the air wheeze through his ample nostrils. My father has always been an epic sleeper. My mother used to send King and me to wake him on weekend mornings. We'd jump on his bed for several minutes before he stirred. And even after he said, "I'm up, I'm up," we'd have to keep at him for several minutes or he'd fall out again.

I know I have to let them go, Silvie, my mother, these phantoms I cling to. Even Barry. It's one thing to play the music, to take it to the Barry bashers. It's another to wait for his approval, or to expect that even if he does show in Vegas, even if he does give us the nod, that I'll feel less stuck. Thirty-five years old. I suppose it may be time to stop waiting.

\*      \*      \*

Late, in my room, laptop aglow. I try to study my notes for closing, but I find it almost impossible to concentrate. I stare at the screen, hearing Mick describe Manners's grand jury testimony, and then replay the scene outside Marcus's building when Pluck learned that Swell had been shot. Either I'm a supremely lousy judge of human conduct, or the councilman really didn't know. I have the very uncomfortable feeling that I'm being used, maybe by my own client, to help avoid responsibility for the killing, to frame an innocent man.

So what if Pluck snitched off A. C. Colder in '88. It was the right thing to do. No doubt he would have preferred to keep the matter under wraps, in light of the election. I just don't believe he killed Swell to silence her.

I call Cindi's cell.

When she answers I say, "Are you sleeping?"

"Wait a second." She's at an airport. I can hear the squawking of gate announcements and the roar of landing jets.

"Hello," she says.

"I guess this means you're not sleeping."

"Gordy. Hi."

"You're leaving town before my closing?"

"No. Just picking up a friend."

"Your complication."

"Something like that. What's up?"

That's an excellent question. I'm not altogether sure what I expect her to tell me. She seems closer to it than me, somehow. Because she knew Swell. Because of her brother.

"What do you make of the Swell thing?"

"Pretty weird. But it makes sense, I guess."

"You really think Pluck killed her."

"Ella predicted it. She knew him."

I tell her about my experience informing Pluck about Swell's death.

"So you think Manners did it?" she says.

"Not really, no. I guess I'm worried that I'm missing something and that it's going to end up biting me in the ass."

"Hey, I gotta go. You want my advice? Worry about your case. The other stuff will work itself out."

# 51

**F**RIDAY, JUNE 4, A.M. Judge Reasoner emerges into the courtroom through the door from his chambers and beckons us. He's not yet wearing his robes and his suit stinks of mothballs.

"Are you through, Mr. Velikovic?" He finally gets the name close to right. I feel like shaking his bony little hand.

"Yes, Judge. That's it for me."

"Anything else before we begin the defense case?"

"Your ruling on my witness, An Phan."

"I'm going to exclude Mr. Phan. It's collateral. You had your chance to examine Officer Dent. I won't have you turning this into his trial."

"Your Honor, my client is facing a charge on drugs he swears up and down were not his. I believe him. And with all due respect, this officer has a history of misconduct."

"I understand the argument. If you lose, feel free to appeal."

"It's the whole defense. You said—"

"What did I say?" It is not really a question.

"Then I'll call Dent in my case." Half threat, half request.

I'd only had the chance to cross-examine the officer, which means I could question him only on topics raised by Milo. If I put him on in my case, I ought to be able to go much further, perhaps educate the jury that this is a cop who wouldn't think twice about planting evidence.

"Denied." He disappears through the door into his office.

"This is bullshit," I say. "There's no authority for keeping Phan *or* Dent off the stand in my case."

The door creaks open. "You were looking for authority, Mr. Seegerman?"

"Your Honor—"

He slips out.

My case has been severely truncated. I put on Speed, who says he had the Honda the night of the dog-napping. He testifies that the lock on the door of the Honda Civic is broken, so the car is always open. Anyone could have tossed the bag of pot in the car, including Dent.

The next obvious witness is, of course, Marcus Manners. The jurors have been fondling him with their eyes for two days. They're waiting for the future Heisman winner to delight them, and relieve them of the burden foisted upon them by the substantial, although not overwhelming, evidence of his guilt.

Although the Constitution gives a criminal defendant the right not to testify in his own trial, this is the sort of rule jurors can't stand. They want to see the alleged bad guy in the box. They want to hear his side of the story. And they tend to punish a defendant who doesn't take the stand in the obvious way—that is, by convicting him. All of which makes the decision whether or not to have a defendant testify among a defense lawyer's most difficult strategic calls.

I choose not to call Marcus. The law doesn't require me to snitch off my client, to tell the cops or the court or the jurors that he's admitted taking the dog. In fact, the attorney-client privilege requires me to keep quiet about what I know. But the law draws the line at me putting Marcus on the stand and helping him commit perjury. Anyway, from what I know of Marcus, he might well *not* lie. And truth, at least as to the dog-napping, is the last thing I need.

My job is to raise doubts, and I've done enough of that during Milo's case to have a shot, at least at the dog charge. In another case I'd be worried the jurors would conclude Marcus is guilty by his decision not to testify. But they know about his accomplishments.

They've seen his pretty face. The next time they see him he'll be on national television. Even if he did take the dog. Even if he did smoke some pot. What difference does it make? Just look at him. He's going to be a star. Perhaps they won't want to be the ones to sully his record.

At the lunch break, Reasoner clears the room. He orders counsel to remain. When the jury is gone and the last stragglers exit, the courtroom is silent. Reasoner is on the bench, staring at some papers.

"Your Honor. I want to apologize for what I said before. I was frustrated because of the court's ruling. Without Mr. Phan I have no defense to what I strongly believe are totally bogus drug charges against my client."

"Are you through?"

"Yes. I'm sorry, Judge. I really am."

"You do not deny that you insulted the court."

"I made a mistake in anger. I'm very sorry."

"I fine you one thousand dollars and order you to spend the next hour in custody. Remove him from the courtroom."

An embarrassed-looking female deputy takes my arm and walks me through a side door into the lockup. It's not so bad, really. Just a room where the in-custody defendants wait before their court appearances. It's quiet. I'll prepare my closing.

"I'll let you out a little early so you can get some lunch," she says. The door slams behind her.

Like all good defense lawyers, I've been held in contempt a handful of times over the years. It's a decent source of revenue for the city, and with the bench populated almost exclusively by former prosecutors, it's no surprise we find ourselves in the doghouse on occasion. But few judges resort to lockup.

So, for the first time in thirty-five years I'm in a room I'm neither entitled to nor able to leave. Even if for just an hour, it's unnerving. I have the smallest inkling, now, of what it must feel like to go to jail, to hear the gate close behind you and know that nothing you do or say or need or want will alter your circumstance. I've been sentenced to an hour. How can anyone endure a year or ten years? The death penalty is not the ultimate sanction. A long and healthy life in a cage is worse.

The deputy releases me at ten minutes to one. I race down to the cafeteria and motor through half of a tuna sandwich. Then I violently chew three pieces of mint gum to mask the smell. Then I run upstairs.

A group of deputies stand in front of the courtroom door. Although we're supposed to resume at one, it's one fifteen and the room is closed. I push through the crowd gathered in the corridor and arrive at the line of officers. I can see, over them, that the small window into the courtroom has been covered with paper. The deputies decline to tell me what is going on. It's a closed session. They have no idea when Reasoner will admit us.

I sit with Marcus and Lucy and their police escort on a bench around the corner. Forty-five minutes later I watch a line of people emerge from a door down the hall, a rear escape route from Reasoner's courtroom—Mick Bacon, Nick Baptiste, deputy district attorneys Sid Batemen and Silvie Hernandez, the defense lawyer Dennis Rosenthal, and several others.

I catch up with the group. Mick seems less than thrilled to be acquainted with me at the moment. Silvie literally runs away. I stand by Mick with an expectant look on my face. He grabs my arm and propels me—perp-walk style—down an empty hallway.

"What's going on?" I say.

"Pluck pleaded out."

Pluck pleaded out.

"Are you serious?"

"Pleaded, sentenced, and on his way to reception at San Quentin."

"That's unbelievable. Did you have anything other than Manners?"

"Bits and pieces. He knew we'd get there eventually. And Rosenthal"—Pluck's lawyer—"figured he'd do better if he didn't make a fuss. We had him on the murder, but we settled for manslaughter and a gun enhancement."

"What makes you so sure? Twenty seconds ago you guys were about to indict Manners."

"Not me. Anyway, Pluck gave up the gun."

"Holy shit. You guys don't screw around, huh?"

"Believe me, Gordy. This one's been coming for a long time."

# 52

I DIDN'T THINK THE courtroom could be any fuller than it has been for the past two days. But it is. The deputies let a group stand behind the last row of the gallery. Some press people sit in the seats in front of the bar, which normally serves as a sort of on-deck circle for lawyers waiting for their cases to be called. No Cindi, though.

Milo holds a fist up in the air. Through his unbuttoned suit jacket I can see an enormous sweat stain under his arm.

"Ladies and gentlemen. If I make a line between this point here"—he takes four steps and makes another fist above his head—"and this point here, the best way to go from here to here is a straight line. Everybody knows that.

"To convict the defendant of stealing the dog and the marijuana charge, all you have to do is take the fastest road from here"—he sticks a hand in the air—"to here"—and then the other.

"Mr. Maddox saw a tall black man with short hair standing by a small car, probably a Honda, around ten o'clock on April 26. At around the same time Jackson Bulley was putting the dog into his house for the night. The next morning the dog was gone. A day later they found the dog at Marcus Manners's house.

"Remember the points, here"—again with the fists—"and here. If you want to take the long road, you can say it was someone else with the car that night, it was someone else who took the dog, and it was someone else who put the dog at Manners's house. But that way you have to take the long road. The best way, the fast road, as I told you, is the straight line. This guy"—he stabs a finger at Marcus—"parked his car where Mr. Maddox said he did and he took the dog. If he didn't, what's the dog doing at his house a day later? And as you know, he has a good reason to take the dog, because he's the quarterback at Hills High and probably his friends on the team would be very happy about this.

"Same thing to say about the marijuana. Please don't believe the defendant's father when he says he drove the car the night the dog disappeared. It's his son. Who has better reason to lie? He doesn't want to see his son in trouble. You can't blame him. I don't blame him. But you should not believe it. No one else testified Mr. Manners had the Honda that night.

"But even if he did, Mr. Manners didn't testify he had it on the 27th or 28th, and that's when Officer Dent found the drugs. Come on. They were Marcus's drugs. Could someone else have put it there? Anything is possible, if you want to take the long road. But has Mr. Seegerman given you any reason to waste your time? Manners drove the car. He took the dog. It was his marijuana. For these reasons you should convict the defendant of all charges."

Milo's argument seems less than effective to me. It seems bad, actually. But the jurors do not look dismissive. They look interested.

"Mr. Seegerman, your turn."

I'm not the worst courtroom lawyer in the world. I know that. If it weren't for my dad and Barry, I suppose I could be trying felonies, homicides even. I'm comfortable with most parts of the process. I can argue motions and cross-examine witnesses without my stomach churning or my leg muscles twitching or a cold sweat secreting from my back.

But for some reason I can't get past the jitters associated with the moments between the end of the DA's argument and my own. When I get going, I'm fine. But one day I would like a judge to say, "Mr.

Seegerman, your turn," and not have the sudden urge to move my bowels. Once, just once, I would like to stand, thank the judge, pat my client on the back, and then not immediately have the overwhelming desire to strip off my wing tips, lob them into the jury box, and flee.

"Good afternoon, ladies and gentlemen. This is my last opportunity to address you and I want to begin by thanking you for your service. It's no easy task, listening to the evidence, to Judge Reasoner's instruction, and trying to make sense of it all. And while in this case we're only talking about the brief detention of a dog, and a little marijuana, still, this is one of the most important things you'll do in your lives." I walk behind Manners and put my hands on his shoulders. "That's because what's at stake here is this young man's liberty."

This is blatantly improper argument. I'm not supposed to refer to potential punishment. But I always make this argument and there's always an objection. I wait for it. I even glance over at Milo. He's on the edge of his seat, apparently so riveted by my presentation that he's forgotten to object. Reasoner isn't listening.

"As you heard during the trial, my client has had an unusual—"

An alarm sounds outside the courtroom, and then inside. It's deafening. I look at the judge. I look at the deputies. No one has any idea what to do. Reasoner yells something at the clerk. She makes a call. I put my fingers in my ears. The clerk yells something back to the judge. He leans into his microphone.

"We have to evacuate the building. I hope it won't be too long. Jurors, please remember the admonition about discussing the case. I don't have time to repeat it. Members of the public and press: do not approach the jurors or Mr. Manners or any of the lawyers. Let them alone. We will resume shortly."

At that the judge flies off the bench and into the hallway behind the courtroom. The rest of us file out the main door, into the corridor, down the stairs, and out a side door of the Hall. Lucy and Marcus huddle together, apart from the crowd, with their police escort.

I stand with Terry, looking at the young couple.

"It really bothers me. I'm a mediocre lawyer, but I've always been able to get through to my guys. Marcus really never trusted us."

"I don't know. Seems like he tried to tell us, you know," Terry says.

"What?" I say.

"Maybe he didn't come in and lay it all out. But he gave us Total High, right. He basically gave us the password. He must have figured we'd eventually get to the journal."

"Maybe."

And there we stand. And stand. And stand. A deputy informs me that there's been some kind of threat, a bomb perhaps. Given the anxiety that has gripped the city in the past few days, and the looting and arson in West Santa Rita, the cops aren't taking any chances. No one seems to have any clear sense of when we might resume. It's nearly three, and then three-thirty. I'm supposed to be on a plane in a few hours.

By four we're settled back in the courtroom. Cindi's still inexplicably absent.

"Mr. Seegerman."

Everyone, including me, wants to go home. Time to cut to the heart of the matter.

"Mr. Velikovic and I will agree on one thing: The shortest distance between two points is a straight line. What the district attorney failed to tell you, however, is that sometimes on the road between two points there are speed bumps. In a criminal case we call those speed bumps 'reasonable doubt.' And if there are enough of them, let me tell you, it can take you a very, very long time to get from here"—my fists are in the air—"to there.

"It ought to be obvious to you by now that the car Mr. Maddox saw on April 26 was not the Honda Civic owned by my client's father. In fact, I don't even think we're sure it's a Honda. But Mr. Maddox had no doubt at all: it was a two-seater. The car Marcus drives has four seats. And Speed Manners told you he had the car the night the dog disappeared. Speed bump one. No pun intended."

The jurors don't get it. They stare at me blankly. Whatever.

"Speed bump two: Can we really say Mr. Maddox saw Marcus up in the hills that night? I mean, a tall black man with short hair. Can you imagine how many people in this city fit that description? There's really no reason to believe Marcus was even in the area.

"What the DA really has in this case is one fact. The dog was found at Marcus's house. But if you really think about it for a moment, that's the biggest speed bump of all, ladies and gentlemen, because as the judge instructed you, it's not *our* burden to explain what happened. That's the prosecution's job. They have to offer evidence *beyond a reasonable doubt* that Marcus took the dog. The fact that the dog ends up behind his house isn't enough, especially when there's really no evidence Marcus was up near the estate two days earlier and no evidence of how the dog got from the Swell estate to the west side. It just isn't enough. The dog isn't in his apartment. It's not in his bedroom. The dog is tied up behind a four-unit apartment building that is easily accessed from the street. Anyone could have put Red back there and there's no proof *who* did, let alone proof beyond a reasonable doubt that Marcus Manners did.

"Same thing for the marijuana. You're on that road Mr. Velikovic was talking about. This time, the speed bumps are twice as big. First of all, some kids don't use drugs. Marcus Manners is one of those kids. You heard about his accomplishments. You heard his father explain how stupid he would have to have been to use marijuana a few weeks before he's supposed to go off to Colorado for summer training camp, how he'd have been jeopardizing his scholarship. Why would he threaten such a promising future by using drugs? The logical answer is, he wouldn't.

305

"Here's another one: Marcus isn't the only one who drives the car. The car is shared. Which means there's just as much chance the drugs were possessed by Marcus's father or someone else, a friend, a passenger, anyone. There's simply no way to say based on the evidence you heard from the district attorney.

"And another: Speed Manners told you the lock on the Honda's passenger side is broken. Anyone could have opened that door and tossed the drugs in the car. There isn't one bit of evidence Marcus knew the marijuana was in the car, or that he ever possessed it.

"Also, let me tell you something. Police officers are just as capable of lying as the rest of us. They are human beings, and in the right circumstances, human beings lie. I can't say why I think Officer Dent lied in this case about where the marijuana came from. There's no evidence before you on that subject. But I do believe he's lying. It just makes no sense. I don't really believe Marcus's father possessed the marijuana. And I don't really believe Marcus possessed it. I think it showed up in the car when Officer Dent searched it."

Another blatantly impermissible argument, as I've just admitted there's not the slightest evidence in the record to support it. But as Milo seems not to care, and Reasoner is either asleep or expired, I figure, what the hell.

"Ladies and gentlemen. There is woefully inadequate evidence in this case of any of the crimes charged. The shortest distance between you and the end of your service here, which also happens to be the just result, is a quick acquittal on all charges. Thank you."

Milo offers a perfunctory rebuttal, and Reasoner gives the jurors their final instructions. He asks the jurors, first, to meet briefly to decide whether they wish to begin deliberations or wait until Monday. I will them to consider my circumstances: I have a plane to catch, the rare opportunity to play for Manilow. They disappear for two minutes and return. They want to get it over with.

So, hoping the jurors will move quickly, and with Terry in tow, I snack and pace and sit and pace, and smoke. We stand outside, behind the Hall, taking long, lung-clenching drags.

"Couldn't get much weirder, huh?" I say.

He smiles. "You worried?"

"Nah. We'll get there. I'm not counting on him showing, anyway."

"Where's your faith?"

"Hibernating. I'm just looking forward to his show. It's been way too long."

An hour after Reasoner sent the jurors off to deliberate, the call comes in on my cell phone. They're back.

"**L**ADIES AND GENTLEMEN, I understand you have verdicts as to all counts."

The foreman is an older Asian man, slightly hunched. I thought he might be a problem. He's had a stern look on his face throughout the proceedings.

I glance around the hushed gallery. Still no Cindi. I'd hoped she'd be here for my closings, for the verdicts.

I notice, too, the gallery now is dotted with familiar faces—a couple of the men I watched assault Manners, and who beat up my car, including four-finger Fred. They blend into the pro-Red, anti-Manners side of the room almost perfectly. But Fred, in particular, catches my eye when I'm scanning the room and smiles. So that's what it's been about the whole time. The team. The dog. Truly ridiculous. I can hear Bea's voice in my head: *This city has gone crazy.*

I watch a deputy deliver the verdict form to the judge. Reasoner reads it. His face gives away nothing.

"As to count one, Penal Code section 487(f), theft of a dog valued at less than four hundred dollars, we find the defendant, Marcus Manners, not guilty."

The Manners side of the room whoops it up momentarily. The SI fans grumble. And Reasoner risks a coronary by repeatedly slapping the bench with his bare hands.

"Quiet. Quiet. I'll have you all arrested, I swear it," he snarls into the microphone. "Continue, Mr. Foreman."

"As to count two, Health and Safety Code section 11357(c), possession of more than one ounce of marijuana, we find the defendant, Marcus Manners, not guilty."

The crowd erupts. The Manners folks literally start dancing in the aisle, and in their rows, and in some cases on their seats. There is no music, but they seem to share the same beat in their heads, arms pumping in the air, heads bopping, hands clapping and slapping backs.

The SI loyalists do not endure their enemies' jubilation sitting down, or quietly. They take up a chant, "Bullshit, bullshit, bullshit," and start spilling out into the aisle where the revelers are busy reveling.

Two sheriff's deputies plant themselves between the factions but are unable to stem the flow out of the rows and before long I see a small, red-faced white woman poking her hand into the stomach of a tall, skinny black man. Others, standing on their seats, shout across the room. The good news is I'll be able to tell my grandkids I was here, at the inception of the great Santa Rita race riot.

Reasoner lacks even a modicum of control. Disgusted, he descends from his throne and flees.

I turn to congratulate Marcus. His body is twisted around, his eyes scanning the frenzied gallery. He's hunting among the sea of faces, for Lucy. Because of the din in the room, I can only faintly hear his words.

But I can see it clearly, on his lips, the same thing, over and over again, like a lost child walking up a crowded block, against traffic, searching amid the hundreds of feet for his mother's shoes: "L, L, L."

She isn't in the courtroom. She's outside with her SRPD minder. She couldn't take it, I suppose—the crowd, waiting for the verdict. Finally she enters. Marcus locates her and jumps out of his chair. The mob ignores Marcus as he fights his way toward the door. Finally he reaches her. Each holds the face of the other like a precious and fragile glass bowl. Then they embrace and push into the hallway.

All I can think is *Rogelio*.

I point Terry toward the exit. Deputies spill into the courtroom, trying to separate the now fully engaged SI and Manners combatants. Some slap my back as I thread through the mass. A few of the slaps are rather aggressive, which I assume come from the unhappy losers. A flood of lights greets Terry and I as we exit into the hallway. Cameras. Questions. Still no Cindi. *Sorry. Sorry. Gotta go.*

Ten steps down the hall, around a corner. Relative peace.

"What do you remember about the report of the Rogelio Contreras interview?" I say.

"Congratulations, by the way."

"Thanks. I have to see that report."

"Now?"

I glance at my watch. "We're fine. I'll meet you in the parking lot."

I jog over to my office and shuffle through a box of materials relating to the Manners case. Rogelio Contreras. Born April 2, 1964, Mexico City. When I reach the parking lot, I hold the report aloft like it's the Olympic torch.

"You remember who did the Contreras interview?" I say.

"Baptiste?"

"Careful guy, meticulous, right?"

"Probably."

"Took down exactly what Contreras told him, right? Used quotes when he put down anything verbatim."

"I guess so." He's lost.

"Marcus's story, his grand jury testimony about what happened at Swell's, matches Rogelio's, right? Manners walks into the house with Swell. A few minutes later he hears shots. Except for one thing."

"Only one thing?"

"One thing: Contreras say he hears Marcus, or someone, yell right before the shooting, remember?"

"Now we believe Rogelio?"

"Focus, Terry. What does he hear?"

"Who?"

"Contreras. Look at the report." He takes it from me and scans it. "What exactly does he tell Baptiste he hears?"

"'No, Ella, no.'"

"Wrong. That's what Baptiste wrote down, and put in quotes, right?"

Looking at the report Terry says, "Right."

"But that, my friend, is not what Contreras said." I suppose I'm a bit amped. Terry looks worried for me. "What do Marcus and Lucy call each other?"

"'Marcus' and 'Lucy.'"

"Wrong again. *M* is for Marcus, *L* is for Lucy. *M* and *L*."

"Okay."

"So Marcus is in the house with Swell. He sees someone about to shoot her. And what does he yell?"

He gets it. Slowly, he says, "No, *L*, no."

"You can hardly blame Baptiste for missing it. The victim's name is Ella. Maybe Contreras says it with an accent, or even uses the Spanish word for the letter, *ele*. Either way he hears 'No, Ella, no' and he's off to the races.

"Layne Maddox didn't see Marcus at the Swell estate the night before the shooting. He saw Lucy. She's tall. She has short hair. From behind she looks like a man. And she drives a Honda two-seater with a 2K license plate. She was stalking Ella Swell because she figured, like Bulley, like everyone, that Manners and Swell were involved. And the next night she's back at the guesthouse. She sees the gun. 'No, L, no.' Boom. Boom. Boom."

We sit on the curb and share another cigarette. The unruly crowd and, now, enough cops to keep them in line start to spill out of the building.

"In the end, it's always about love, isn't it?" Terry says.

"That's what Barry would say."

We stand.

"And Pluck just falls over for her?" Terry says.

"I don't know. He loves his kid. He figures he can do the time and she can't."

"Maybe he feels bad for snitching off the bookstore thing, for putting Grace in harm's way. Maybe he's trying to make it up to Marcus."

We stare at one another for a few moments and drift over to the car. We both know it's time to let it go. The end of one thing, the beginning of another.

Terry walks me over to my car. We shake.

"Manilow?" I say.

He nods, and says, "Manilow."

# 54

TWO DAYS LATER. Sunday night, June 6.

The Santa Rita Airport is a mess. The flight from Vegas was delayed for two hours because of dense fog in the Bay Area. The terminal is jammed with people who've missed flights. They're stretched out on the floor, surrounded by piles of luggage. They look miserable. I should be, too. I have ample reason, including the fact that Sid Bateman is here to retrieve Silvie. She tries to spare me an impassioned reunion, but Bateman smothers her when she's within arms' reach.

But I'm not miserable at all. I'm fine. I feel oddly resolved, calm. Life, for no good reason at all, is okay.

Traffic is not. It takes us forty minutes to get to Preet's house to unload. The boys chat incessantly about the show, about Manilow, the fans, and Vegas.

I say nothing. I hear very little of the recap. I watch the couple in the car ahead of me arguing, gesticulating angrily. As we pass Santa Rita stadium, I catch a glimpse of the bleachers, green and empty, but still lit. I feel distinctly as if I am watching a slideshow of someone else's vacation. I see it, but I am elsewhere, in my head, arguing the Manners case, sitting on the curb outside Department 13 with Mick, meeting with Pluck. The preceding forty-eight hours have hardly allowed for reflection on the events of the past few weeks. But now it seeps back in. Marcus and Swell and Bulley and Speed. And Cynthia Howe.

\*　　\*　　\*

It's ten when I finally get home.

I call her cell. She answers, but sounds like she's been sleeping. She covers the mouthpiece of her phone, but I can hear her talking to someone, just a few words. Thirty seconds later she sounds more awake, but still hoarse.

"I'm so sorry. I didn't think you'd be sleeping."

"Don't worry about it. I wasn't really sleeping."

Oh God. Maybe I caught her—"Let's talk tomorrow."

"Gordy."

"Sorry. I was just thinking." I pitch her my theory on the Swell case.

"What difference does it make now?" The conversation seems to trouble her. Probably she's just groggy. Who goes to sleep at ten o'clock?

"I don't know," I say. "None, I guess."

Several moments of uneasy silence.

"Pluck pleaded guilty," she says. "That seems like pretty good evidence that he killed her."

Her tone is a bit hostile. I think this person is my friend, but I'm not altogether sure. I would like to ask her if she is okay. She doesn't seem okay. She seems sort of depressed, actually.

"Has anyone said anything about *why* Pluck would have killed Swell?"

"I think everyone's just relieved it's over."

"But the motive stuff, no one's reporting that. Swell's story? Manners's grand jury testimony?" I feel like I'm cross-examining her. She says nothing. "All they really had was Manners's say-so. It just seems incredibly thin." I tell her my memory of Pluck's reaction when I told him Swell had been killed.

"I don't know, Gordy," she says. "He gave the police her gun."

"It could just as easily have come from Lucy. She could have shot Swell and then given it to her father. Then he delivers it, and himself, to the cops."

"Somehow I don't see Pluck being so noble."

"It's his only daughter. How'd you know about the gun anyway?"

"It was in the paper."

"There's a great story here," I say, fishing for the reporter in her.

"For someone else."

I suppose the story dredges up nasty memories of her brother.

"Did you ever blame Swell for what happened?"

"Can we talk about something else?"

It is not a question.

# 55

**M**ONDAY AFTERNOON, in my office, reading reports in the *Journal* and *San Francisco Chronicle* of my stellar performance in the Manners trial, the Pluck plea, and the tail end of the unrest in West Santa Rita.

Preet and a short, stringy-haired, unkempt, undernourished-looking kid, seventeen, maybe, walk into my office.

"Say hello to Brice Bulley."

Brice wanders around the office, picking books off the shelves. "Please don't touch those," I say.

His hands shoot into his pockets, futz around in there for a moment, and then pop out again. He has no idea what to do with them. I urgently require a bottle of Ritalin or a stun gun.

I give Preet a nasty look.

He smiles. "Don't blame me. Terry seemed anxious to find him before. I only heard back from him this morning. I thought you might like to meet him."

"I was at my grandmother's in Maine. I couldn't get near a computer."

"That's fascinating," I say. "Maybe you two should go get some ice cream now."

"So you're the dude who got Manners off," Brice says.

"I am indeed the dude," I say.

"You're just lucky I hate that dog," the kid says.

I look at Preet. He chuckles and says, "I suspected you two would get along."

"Excuse me?"

"I saw them take Red." The kid can't stand still for a second. He's covered every square foot of my office, wandering behind my chair more than once, which I find particularly grating.

"Brice. Sit."

"That's funny, man."

"It wasn't a joke."

He sits, but my extra two decades, my suit, my position of authority, and my stern tone do not affect his mood. Either the kid is simply overjoyed to be hanging out with us or stoned out of his mind or both.

"Don't move," I order.

I call Terry, who arrives shortly. During the interim, Brice has attempted to speak on several occasions. And I have prevented him from doing so, or at least doing so meaningfully, by sticking my fingers in my ear and singing loudly.

"You saw *what*, now?" Terry says.

"I saw Manners and his boys take Red."

"That's not what you told the police," I say.

"No way, man." He is outraged at the suggestion. "I told them I was inside. I didn't care. I was hoping they'd keep the dog. My dad drives me crazy—walk Red, feed Red, watch Red. He's like, way more into that dog than me."

"Then I guess we owe you," I say.

"Plus, I didn't want to do anything to get Manners busted. He was one of our biggest buyers."

By now Terry's laughing his head off. Brice has an enormous mouth-open, tongue-flapping smile on his face.

"Marcus Manners was your customer," I say.

"Totally. All the Hills jocks are potheads. Manners was the biggest stoner in the school."

317

We sit in bewildered silence for a moment.

"Before we arrived, Brice and I were discussing how he embedded Ms. Swell's journal in the game," Preet says.

"She asked you to do that?" Terry asks.

"She wanted me to put it someplace safe, where Manners could get to it."

"And what did you think about what she said?"

"Said when?"

My patience is ebbing. "In the file, Brice."

"I've never read it. I told the detective the same thing. I didn't even know it was a diary or anything like that until Preet told me." The young man does not inspire overwhelming confidence. "She said it was private. I was cool with that. Once she got killed, though, and they found out about our little business, I was like—"

"Wait, wait," I cut him off. "You told the cops about the document in the computer?"

"Yeah. Some detective."

"Mick Bacon. Looked like Popeye."

He nods. "There was another guy too, younger."

"Baptiste?"

"I don't remember. I was mostly alone with the Popeye guy. He said I was going to prison unless I cooperated. I was like, yo, I watch *Oz*—"

"When was this?"

"A few days after my dad found Ella."

"You gave them the file?"

"First Popeye was having some trouble understanding what I was talking about."

Hard to imagine.

"What else did you tell him?"

"I didn't have much else to say. He asked me lots of stuff about Ella, but I really couldn't help. She moved out of the main house a while

318

ago. I saw Marcus and Ella drive in a few times. I told him about the dog and all that."

"I thought you told him you were inside the house," Terry says.

"Only right after the dog disappeared. After they arrested me, I told him what happened. What was I supposed to do, man?"

The kid flitters around in his chair.

"Brice, pay attention," I say. "You told Mick Bacon you saw Marcus Manners take the dog?" He nods, not once, but what seems like a hundred times. "And," I say, not at all certain I should go on, "you told Mick Bacon you dealt Marcus Manners drugs?"

Again with the nodding.

"Was the other detective there?"

"I don't know. He was in and out."

"What did Bacon say?" Terry adds.

"He told me not to tell anyone. He said if he heard I opened my mouth, he'd chop me up and feed me to Red."

That's exactly what he said, too. Sounds just like Mick, homicidal, but humorously so.

Preet, guiding the kid toward the door, says, "Brice has a sizable fine to pay as the result of his recent legal problems. He's going to help me out on a few projects, so we'll be seeing a lot of him this summer."

Oh good.


Mick ignores my calls. Terry and I stop by headquarters, but he's out.

We stand in the Hall parking lot before going home.

"He wanted Manners," Terry says. "He made that clear from the beginning, right?"

"I suppose," I say, my eyes looking, I suspect, entirely glazed over.

I am, I admit, bewildered by the turn of events. Something ought to be made of it, of the new information. But I may well have reached the limits of my brainpower. I spend much of the day staring at the

Manilow poster on my wall, cogitating, seeking guidance, hoping for a breakthrough. But I can't see how it all fits together.

Terry, ever patient, though hardly enlightening, attempts to enlighten me.

"Bacon has the journal. He knows Swell planned to out Pluck."

"So far, I'm with you."

"So he has motive."

"Pluck. Motive. Check."

"Okay. So Mick figures Pluck for the shooter."

"Makes sense."

"But—"

"But—"

"But he doesn't have anything concrete to put him down."

"He?

"Sorry. Bacon, the cops, don't have enough evidence to make an arrest."

"Of Pluck."

"Exactly. It looks like Pluck's the bad guy because he has a strong motive—he wants to be mayor, he doesn't want to be revealed as a snitch and a cheater—but Bacon doesn't have a gun or prints or whatever. And he can't just bring Pluck down and kick the shit out of him or search his house—"

"Because he's Pluck."

"Exactly. What Bacon does have is Manners—the kid was in the house, there's blood on his shoe, his skin's under Swell's nails. He's even got Rogelio, for better or worse, who puts Manners in the house. But—and this is the most important part—unlike Pluck, *Manners* has no motive. *And* Mick likes the way he throws a football, so he decides he's not the shooter and Pluck is. Conclusion? Manners is their witness. So, Mick does everything he can to get Marcus in to talk, and he does what he can to protect him on the misdos. In the end it worked out just as Mick planned. You walk Manners, and the kid gives them enough to push Pluck into a manslaughter plea. It all makes perfect sense if you really think about it."

Think about it or not, it makes no sense at all. Detective Mick Bacon does not cover up evidence of a crime, no matter how small.

"I want to hear it out of his mouth," I say. "Unless Mick tells me he hid evidence from the DA, I refuse to believe it. Anyway, there's at least one enormous problem with this theory."

"Which is?"

"Pluck didn't kill Ella Swell. Lucy did."

That evening, eleven. I finally have an uninterrupted hour to finish reading the last few days' newspapers. There's very little of substance in the articles about the Swell case. The reports note that Pluck pleaded guilty in a closed session and that the grand jury testimony remains sealed. They suggest this is to protect the identities of confidential sources—Marcus Manners, I suppose.

There's speculation about a motive, but nothing concrete. There are quotes from Jackson Bulley ("relieved"), city officials ("shocked and deeply saddened"), Baptiste ("hopes that the city will quickly move beyond the case"), and the DA ("rioters will be prosecuted").

The only reference to concrete evidence that Pluck killed Ella Swell is a statement, attributed to an SRPD spokesperson, that the councilman delivered the murder weapon to police.

The murder weapon. I read the sentence again. *The* murder weapon. *The* gun.

I close my eyes and imagine her, sitting in an enormous, armless, black leather chair pushed up against the plate glass window in her living room. And I see the lights of Santa Rita behind her.

That's not what Cindi said. Cindi didn't say "*the* gun." Cindi said "*her* gun."

I look at the clock. It's too late to call. And I think of the sound of her voice, drawn, weary, done. *Can we talk about something else?*

Maybe it's the Alzheimer's kicking in. But right now, I can hear her say it: *her* gun. *Her, her, her.*

I hop in my car, climb up to the top of the hills, and sail a mile south along the ridge road to Cindi's place. The house is dark. There's a light over the front porch. I knock. No answer. Again. Nothing. I call her home phone, and her cell. No luck. The landing is scattered with several days' *Santa Rita Journal*s. I check the dates by the scant light of the moon. I can't quite make out the print, but I can see from the headlines that the earliest is from before Pluck pleaded out. She's been gone for days.

# 56

I HEAD TO DEPARTMENT 13. I need a drink and a smoke and to be in the company of human beings.

Mick Bacon is at the bar, eating a very late dinner. I approach him stealthily, and try to grab a french fry. He sees me in the mirror behind the bar and nearly scrapes the flesh off my fingers with his fork before I can withdraw my hand.

"This seat taken?" I say, sitting down on the next stool.

"Actually, yes."

I move over a spot and order a beer.

"A date?"

"An old friend. Stick around, you guys might like each other."

"I had an interesting conversation with Brice Bulley this morning," I say.

"Kid got off light. His father back-doored him into probation and some community service. Cash is king, I always say."

"Brice had some fascinating things to say. Remarkable really. Detectives hiding evidence, covering up—"

Speed Manners walks up to the bar and parks on the stool between Mick and me.

"You guys know each other, I guess," Mick says, gnawing at a pork chop bone. "We were just playing twenty questions. You want to play, Speed?"

"Long as you keep buying."

"The kid, Brice, he was a witness for the DA on the dog-napping?" I say.

"You're using up one of your questions." I stare. "All right. My answer is—" He pauses for effect. "*Sí.*"

"He told you he saw Marcus take the dog?" I say. "About the drugs?"

"Yes and yes. That counts as two, right, Judge?" he asks Speed, who nods.

"You had Swell's journal?"

"Yeah. That's four."

"You had it the whole time?"

"I told you, yes. I'm a softy so I won't count that one."

"I'm sure you must have had some compelling reason to lie your ass off about the computer thing, but I got to tell you, I'm hurt."

He looks at Speed. "Was that a question?"

"I don't know," Speed says, downing a whiskey. "I lost track halfway through."

"Okay, fine," I say. "Did Pluck kill Ella Swell?"

Speed chokes on his beer.

"Uh, no," Mick says. "Then again, yes."

I get it. "Scratch that. How about, did *Jerry* Pluck kill Swell?"

"No. That's five and six."

"The first one didn't count," I say.

"What are you talking about?" Mick says. "It should count as two, but I'm giving you a break. Number seven."

"Did Lucy Pluck kill Ella Swell?"

"Yes. Eight."

"Can we quit this?"

"No. Nine."

"Jesus, you're a fascist. All right. Nine. A reporter named Cindi Paris, who happens to be the sister of Robert Howe, your partner in the '88 shooting, somehow knows that Swell was killed with her own gun. Does she know that because she's known all along who killed Swell, and under what circumstances?"

"That's the longest question I ever heard. Yes and yes. Nine and ten."

"Was Pluck the snitch in—" Speed, looking at me in the mirror across the bar, smiles and takes a long drag on his Bud. The fog is still mostly impenetrable, but for a moment I see a flash of light. "Was *Speed* the snitch in the '88 J-Posse case?"

"Yes. Eleven."

"You're serious?" I glance back and forth between them.

"Yes. Twelve."

"Then why the fuck did Swell think Pluck was the informant?"

"That's not a yes or no question."

Big sigh. "Okay, did Ella Swell *believe* Pluck was the informant in the '88 case."

"No. That's thirteen." Mick wipes his face, chugs the rest of his beer, and orders a black coffee.

"But she wrote that in her journal." Pause. "That wasn't a question. That was mulling."

"Judge?" Mick turns to Speed.

"Mulling," Speed says, smiling, enjoying the festivities.

"Ervin Nichols gave us the impression Grace had a relationship with A. C. Colder back in '88. True?"

"Ervin Nichols." Speed says the whole name, giving himself time to remember the face, and then chuckles. "His mother used to come down to Zora Neal's looking for him. She was always crying. How is Ervin Nichols?"

"In prison," I say.

"Let me take this one," Speed checks with Mick, who nods while picking his teeth with the corner of a matchbook. "No. Grace wouldn't have touched A. C. Colder if he'd been the last man on earth. She played him. She made him think he had a chance. She let him brag about how he was getting with her. She even helped him with the drugs. And in return she got his money

325

for the store, for the kids who came there because they had no place else to go.

"I wish you'd met my wife. She was something else. She had a way of making people believe—everyone, men, women, children. You get around Grace Manners and you get the feeling you're the only one in the room. She makes you feel like she sees only you. Every man who ever met her fell for her on the spot."

Mick looks at Speed, annoyed, and says, "'No' would have been enough. That's fourteen, by the way."

"Did A. C. Colder kill Grace Manners?" I say.

"Don't know," Mick says. "We won't count that one."

"Very big of you."

"He was doing a federal bit at the time," Mick adds. "I think it's safe to say either he ordered the killing or his partner did."

"Who was that?" I say.

"Excuse me? I'm not sure I heard you right?"

It's past midnight. I've had a couple of beers. I'm sure he's trying to tell me something, but for the life of me I have no idea what it is.

"Speed," I say. "What's the question you'd ask in this situation?"

"Humm. I guess I'd ask whether Jerry Pluck was Colder's partner in the drug dealing."

Pluck. Jesus.

"Yes," Mick says, displaying zero emotion. "What's that?"

"Fifteen," Speed says.

"Did Marcus know that?" I say.

"When?" Mick says.

"Scratch that. Did Ella know Pluck was Colder's partner?"

"Yes. Four more."

"Did Ella tell Marcus that Pluck was partnered with Colder?"

"Yes. Three."

"They set him up."

"Was that a question or more mulling?" Mick asks Speed.

326

"I don't believe it. They set him up? Marcus and Swell?"

"Yes. Last two." Mick throws down sixty bucks and slides off his chair.

"And Cindi too?" I say.

"Yes."

"She really knew?"

"You wanna withdraw that, Counselor?"

I say, "No," though it isn't an answer to his question at all.

"Okay," Mick says. "Then, yes." He shakes Speed's hand and slaps me on the back. "That was fun. Let's do it again *real* soon."

He walks out.


I'm now only slightly less confused than before. Fortunately, Speed is a thoughtful and talkative drunk, the sort who spends his days poring over volumes of Shaw, drinking shamefully inexpensive vodka, wondering what another life might have looked like. And his nights in fourth-rate bars, making half-intelligent conversation. He slurs his sentences together, but not incomprehensibly so. And he's not going anywhere. Not until I stop feeding the bartender twenties.

"After Colder went to prison, Pluck took over the operation. That boy was twice as in love with Grace as poor Colder. And he got about as far with her. I was getting high all the time back then. I saw them chasing Grace, but I didn't care. Then one day I woke up. I figured the only way I could save my family was to get rid of all of them. I knew about the delivery to the bookstore. I contacted your father and Mick.

"The police raided the store. I didn't mean for Grace or Ella to be there. But at that time I really didn't know how deep they were into the drug dealing. After the officer, Ms. Paris's brother, was killed, your father and Bacon stopped caring what I had to say. They charged them all with murder. Grace and Ella were a problem for Colder and Pluck and the rest of them because of how much they knew about the operation."

"You're saying Pluck had something to do with Grace Manners getting killed?"

Speed shakes his head. "He's never been the cold-blooded type. He was crushed when Grace died. He was a different man after that, I think."

"So who? Colder?"

"I assume so. Part of me thinks Colder had Grace killed just so no one else could have her."

I remember one of the first times I saw Pluck. We were in Marcus's apartment shortly after Swell was killed. Pluck had the phone to his ear, but he was staring longingly at a portrait of the young Manners family. Remembering Grace, I suppose.

"Why didn't Colder get to Swell?"

"Her daddy had them put her in a high-security unit the whole time. Stanton Swell must have paid off every cop in this city to keep her safe. Unfortunately I didn't have that kind of money. By the time she got out of prison, Colder and his gang were long gone."

"Was Ella involved with Pluck?"

"No. She was more in love with Grace than Colder and Pluck put together. She always blamed Pluck for losing Grace." *Lez-bean, lez-bean.* "When Ella found out she was dying, she went to Marcus. She told him what happened in '88. She told him about Pluck."

"But in her journal she said—" I'm an idiot. The whole thing was a setup, the journal too. "What about the gun? Marcus told the grand jury he bought it."

"That was Cindi." *Her* gun. "Ella wanted to make sure no one could trace it to Marcus. So she had Cindi buy it. She waited until she began to feel very bad. She went to see Pluck. If things had worked out, she would have shot herself. Marcus would have planted the gun at Pluck's house and gone to the police. Cindi would have taken Ella's story about Pluck to the public."

I remember the first time I saw her, standing on a corner by the Hall.

"When did Cindi find out about what happened?"

"Same night Marcus got arrested. That's when I found out. I called her."

Speed tells Cindi that Swell is dead, that the plan went awry. So she tosses her cell phone at the sidewalk and falls to her knees.

"And Pluck? He just rolls over."

"It took him a while to figure out what was going on," Speed says. "Eventually Cindi laid it out for him and he knew it was the only way. In the end Lucy did us a favor. He might have fought it otherwise, but with his daughter's future on the line, he crumpled."

I remember. Cindi must have seen Pluck the day I was up at City Hall. He looked like he'd been run over by a garbage truck.

"So you told Cindi that Swell was dead. Who told you?" He smiles and shifts his eyes in the direction of the bar's entrance. "You're kidding me?"

Mick Bacon figures Swell's death might be history playing catch up. He calls Speed and then sits on him until he spills. He lets Baptiste push toward a murder charge against Marcus. But unlike his junior partner, he sees that Rogelio Contreras's story proves Lucy was the shooter.

But there's an old debt to collect, for his partner's death. He knew Pluck and Colder were partners, but Pluck got out of the business after Grace Manners died, and the cops could never make him on the drug stuff. So instead of busting Lucy, Mick lets the story tell itself, doesn't get in the way. He even pushes me to give him Manners because he knows the kid will claim to have witnessed the killing, and that he'll say Jeremiah Pluck was the shooter. Popeye played me, up and down, beginning to end. Just like the chief said.

"You let the man raise your son?"

"I never had a choice, really. I was on the pipe. Grace was in jail. Then she got killed. It was that or foster care. He loved Grace. I felt he would take care of the boy. I was right, too. I admire the man. He couldn't stop Colder from killing her, and he's spent the last fifteen years trying to make up for it. He's been more of a father to my son than I could ever have been."

I watch him sink the dregs of his bourbon.

"It's almost funny," I say. "The night before Marcus and Lucy get wrapped up in this elaborate scheme, he's acting like a totally normal kid, stealing people's dogs, smoking dope."

Speed chuckles. "The *jury* didn't think he did it."

"Which either proves I'm a brilliant lawyer or jurors are idiots. Or both, I suppose."

# 57

THREE DAYS EARLIER. Friday, June 4, in the Hall parking lot. The end of one thing, the beginning of another.

Terry walks me over to my car. We shake.

"Manilow?" I say.

He nods, and says, "Manilow."

He'll be at my house, with Silvie, in forty-five minutes. We should be able to catch the six-thirty P.M. flight and be at the Mandalay by nine.

On my way past the front steps of the Hall I see a group of about thirty pro-Red, pro-SI, anti-Manners demonstrators. In the twenty minutes since the verdict they seem not to have come up with anything more intelligent than "bullshit, bullshit."

Once home, I walk into the kitchen. S. and Ferdy are eating. King, I assume, is drinking, though elsewhere. Ferdy congratulates me on the big win. I stand there, watching my grandfather feed my father small spoonfuls of rice. Chunks of broccoli litter the table around S.'s plate.

"You know what I realized recently?" I say.

"Hmm."

"He never liked me."

"He never liked himself. That got in the way of him liking anyone else."

"That's not true. He liked King. He liked mom, on occasion."

"He liked to have King and your mom to boss around. I hate to tell you, but he saw himself in you. He knew he could never wind you up like the others."

"Ah, but he never bit King."

He laughs. "It's your dad's way of saying thanks. Consider yourself lucky."

My bag is packed and I'm ready to go, but I have twenty minutes to kill, so I jump in the shower. The plane could be late. We might have to go directly to the show. Might as well smell pretty, in case Barry makes it.

My hair is limp with suds when the phone rings. It's on the toilet where I cannot reach it from the tub. I kill the shower and grab the phone, soaking it.

"Yeah."

"Hi, Gordy." It's Aineen O'Connell.

"How's the prisoner?"

"Actually—"

Maeve, not due for another four weeks, is in labor. Aineen has the flu and therefore cannot attend to her mother in delivery.

"Wow."

"And she was wondering—"

Which is to say, *Gordy, it's me Maeve, and while I know you're five minutes from getting on a plane, and while I'm terribly sorry about the timing, I need you. Now.*

"You must be kidding," Terry says.

"I have the very strong sense my choices here are limited."

"Oh God." Long pause. "It's pretty suspicious if you ask me."

"As far as I know you can't fake labor, even Maeve. Is Silvie in the car with you?"

"I'm on my way to her house."

"Tell her I said she should go," I say. "Who knows when he'll be in concert again? We'll get another shot."

"You want me to stay?" Terry says.

"I'll be fine. How hard can it be? I'm not the one squeezing out the kid. Anyway, you guys have to be there if he shows. Send him my love."

Very freaking hard. That's how hard it can be. Hard, nauseating, headache-inducing, nerve-racking. And that's long before we reach the delivery room. By the time I arrive at Maeve's bungalow, her water, and all hell, has broken loose. Aineen screams at her mother. Maeve just screams. I start screaming when I arrive so I don't stand out too much.

After a few moments Maeve and Aineen shriek at me, together, "You're the father. You're the father."

"Okay, okay," I say, understanding them to mean that I have to *pretend* to be the child's creator in order to gain admittance to the main event.

Halfway between the house and the car, Maeve, sandwiched between me and Aineen, stops.

"I'm sorry, Gordy."

"It's all right. Keep walking." She does not.

"I'm *really* sorry."

"Mom, please."

"Don't have the kid on the sidewalk," I say. "He'll be in therapy for decades."

"Silvie's fine," Maeve whines. "I was just jeal—"

The kid kicks her or she has a contraction or something, but in any case she's driven from the point, and toward the car, by pain.

On the way to Santa Rita General, Aineen attempts to give me a crash course in what she keeps calling Lemans, but which I'm sure is actually Lamaze and, instead of simply correcting her and getting on with the lesson, I turn it over and over in my head, thinking, Lemond, which reminds me of bicycles, and Le Mans, which I think has something to do with car racing. And Maeve continues to scream. So basically what I take away from the ride is that Maeve is supposed

333

to breathe, and I'm supposed to help her breathe, though by what means and to precisely what end, I cannot say.

Shortly we are at the hospital. I do not like hospitals whatsoever. I spent too much time as a kid waiting, with Ferdy, for my mom to emerge from them, terrified that she would not. Hospitals are for sick people. Maeve is not sick. What are we doing here?

I have no chance to ponder the question. A nurse offers Maeve a wheelchair. Maeve says she would rather be—no, I can't repeat it. It's just too vile. The nurse seems to find the remark amusing, endearing even, and gently takes my friend by the arm and leads her through a set of double doors. I'm stuck in place, sad to see her go, relieved to be through the crisis, when Aineen pushes me after them, calling me "dad." I jog beside Maeve, who now shakes uncontrollably.

"She's shaking," I inform the nurse.

"That's normal, dear," she answers.

"Gordon."

"Yeah, Maeve."

"Shut the fuck up." She turns to the nurse and mumbles, "Drugs. Now."

But by all appearances the drugs don't seem to do diddly-squat, which, another nurse informs me, isn't exactly normal but does sometimes happen.

With each contraction Maeve curses—God, me, the boys, her daughter, the anesthesiologist, the president of the United States. Not Barry, though. I notice Manilow goes uncursed.

I think, fine, this is a little out of control, and Maeve isn't acting or looking her best. But, I mean, how long can it go on?

Seven hours later, my left hand is fractured in several spots from Maeve's crushing grip. I've had no dinner. I'm soaked through with sweat. I'm wobbly, nauseated, and generally feeling less charitable toward Maeve, now, because, frankly, she seems to be delaying things on purpose. Or the kid is.

In any case I feel like, *Hey, I've already had a pretty long day, with the trial and everything, and it seems like I've done my part here and, to be honest, I'd kind of like to get on with my life.* But I cannot. Because, I soon learn, once you sign up to be the person who holds the hand of the person giving birth, you're actually a prisoner. And no matter how much you've already done, and how generous your decision to be there in the first place is, none of it makes any difference until the kid has safely arrived and the mother is resting peacefully, which in Maeve's case seems, quite simply, not possible.

The contractions start to speed up and, finally, the main event begins. The doctor enters. She insists that Maeve breathe, and then push, and push some more. I parrot her words precisely, which seems safe. And then my cell phone goes off. I meant to turn it off. I really did.

"What the mother fuck is *that?*" Maeve shrieks.

The question, I assume, is rhetorical, so I ignore it. As I do the phone, which eventually rings itself out.

The delivery, which comes as a dizzying and sickening surprise to me, is enormously violent and bloody and terrifying. Maeve appears, throughout, to be possessed, expelling a demon of almost unfathomable nastiness.

More pushing and more breathing, but suddenly we reverse gears and, following the doctor's lead, I demand that Maeve cease pushing and breathing entirely. Maeve lowers her voice a bit and tells me that when this is over she is going to kill me. She does not appear to be kidding. This, despite the fact that—and I swear this to be true upon the life of Barry Manilow himself—I am not the father of this child, and therefore cannot logically be held responsible for Maeve's disagreeable situation.

The head is out. This, apparently, is good news, though for some reason I have always imagined the feet coming out first. Incredible, that a reasonably intelligent person can have been born himself, lived thirty-five years, passed high school health class, had various adult relationships, and seen lots of movies and TV shows in which people give birth, and really have no idea which end is supposed to come out first.

The demon, once exorcised, is blue. No kidding—the kid looks like a Smurf that's been dunked in a bucket of bloody snot. My phone rings again. Maeve looks deceased. The others seem busy. So I figure I'll take the call. I back up to a corner of the room and remove the phone from my pocket. I look at the number. It's Terry.

"What's happening?" He yells over bar noise.

"The beast is among us," I say, yelling over Maeve, who is now weeping loudly. "Where are you?"

"At the bar."

"Silvie came?" I ask.

"Yeah, she's here. She says hello."

Thrilling. "Tell her hi."

"Guess who just bought us drinks?"

"I have no idea who bought you drinks."

"Manilow."

"Barry Manilow bought you drinks."

The minute it comes out of my mouth I know two things, which may appear to be unrelated, and may well be unrelated, but somehow *seem* closely related in the moment. First, I know that I've changed my mind about getting tested. I'm ready. I've waited long enough. Now I want to know. The why of it may never be perfectly clear, but the *it* of it is very clear. It's time to find out.

And second, I should not have said such a thing within hearing distance of Maeve O'Connell, and certainly not so close in time to the birth of her son.

"What the hell does that mean?" She yelps from her splayed and horizontal position across the room.

"She wants to know what the hell that means," I say.

"We've been at the bar since like nine, explaining what happened to the fans. Everyone's drinking to Maeve." I relay the details to the splayed one, who is now clutching the slightly less blue boy child to her chest. "Then about midnight he walks up to the bar and buys everyone a round. We talked to him for a while, then he took off. He's totally cool. He said we should send him a CD."

I call out to Maeve, "They had drinks with Manilow. He says we should send him a CD."

She begins to wail, and then so does the kid, and then so do I.

I walk over and lean down and wipe the sweat off her forehead. And then, through the shaky prism of my tears, I look that kid in the face, and thank him for ruining my life.

# Acknowledgments

Publishing books is a tough business. If I were you, I wouldn't quit my day job. If you insist on pursuing the whole writing thing, here's some important advice.

In case you were contemplating writing a book that has something to do with Barry Manilow, as I did, and you're thinking about suggesting that Mr. Manilow is the most underrated musician of the past fifty years, as I did, let me tell you what you have to look forward to.

First, you are likely to make a lot of new friends among the thousands of Manilow fans around the world, and these friends are likely to become valuable helpmates, critics, and cheerleaders. Which is a good thing. In my case, Scooter in Texas, CJ in Arizona, Ann in Ohio, and Brenda in Chicago deserve my very special thanks. You'll have to find your own helpmates; mine are taken.

The other thing that's bound to happen if you write such a book is that a few miserable souls will disagree with your critical assessment of Manilow, and some of them, who happen to be book reviewers, will take it out on your work. My advice is to turn the other cheek. Or, like me, you can spend the hours in which you ought to be asleep inventing intricate plans for rebuttal and/or revenge. In retrospect, I wish I'd been able to be more mature about the whole thing.

There are a whole variety of other people you no doubt wish were available to assist you in your writing career. Tragically, they are on my team, not yours. For their reading, editing, publishing, promoting, teaching, advice, inspiration, companionship, and general goodwill, thanks to Julianne Balmain, Yvette Banek, Marian Brown, Lara Carrigan, Dave Cronin, Colin Dickerman, Elena Dorfman, Sabrina Farber, Fisch, Laurie Fox, Alona Fryman, Lisa Grinfeld, Jake, Jennifer Jameson, Jonathon Keats, Pam Klein, Lizzy Klein, Melissa Koff, Maureen Lasher, Hilary Liftin, John Manciewicz, Barry Manilow, Al Menaster, Marisa Pagano, Cullen Schaffer, Lisa Schiffman, Sheva, Sheldon Siegel, Megan Underwood, Greg Villepique, Ethan Watters, and last, but God knows not least, the über-agent, Ms. Lydia Wills.

Finally, you are not married to Dr. Jennifer Dykes. As it turns out, I am. Aren't I a lucky dog?

## A NOTE ON THE AUTHOR

Dylan Schaffer has been practicing criminal appellate law for fifteen years. He has represented defendants in matters ranging from drunk driving to multiple murders. He lives in Oakland, California, with his wife, two dogs, and a cat named Fisch. Visit his Web site at www.dylanschaffer.com.

## A NOTE ON THE TYPE

The text of this book is set in Linotype Sabon, named after the type founder Jacques Sabon. It was designed by Jan Tschichold and jointly developed by Linotype, Monotype, and Stempel, in response to a need for a typeface to be available in identical form for mechanical hot metal composition and hand composition using foundry type.

Tschichold based his design for Sabon roman on a font engraved by Garamond, and Sabon italic on a font by Granjon. It was first used in 1966 and has proved an enduring modern classic.